Advance Praise for *The Sunflower House*

"*The Sunflower House* is an unforgettable story of love and sacrifice. Written with heartfelt compassion for people facing choices no one should be made to make, this novel draws you in and leaves you a better person for knowing this story. Allegri is an author to watch, and this is an exceptional debut."
—Heather Morris, #1 *New York Times* and international bestselling author of *The Tattooist of Auschwitz*

"Adriana Allegri's impressive debut is a riveting, heartrending story of love, sacrifice, and redemption set amid the horrors of the notorious Nazi *Lebensborn* program. Immersive and full of compelling characters, *The Sunflower House* is a moving tribute to the power of ordinary people to resist and to overcome."
—Jennifer Chiaverini, *New York Times* bestselling author of *Resistance Women*

"A remarkable debut inspired by unimaginable events during WWII. Heart-wrenching and yet full of tenderness and hope, *The Sunflower House* is emotionally propulsive from first page to last, transporting the reader to the 1930s and into the heart and mind of a young woman whose bravery and selflessness carries the story to its heartrending conclusion. It was meticulously researched and written with a keen sensitivity to the difficult subject matter. I was captivated by the characters and by a piece of history I knew nothing about. Adriana Allegri is an exciting new talent in historical fiction."
—Hazel Gaynor, *New York Times* bestselling author of *The Last Lifeboat*

"*The Sunflower House* is an emotional and captivating read that peels away the secrets surrounding the *Lebensborn* program in Germany. Adriana Allegri has written a spectacular debut that will make a splash in the world of WWII historical fiction."
—Madeline Martin, *New York Times* bestselling author of *The Last Bookshop in London*

"*The Sunflower House* is a gripping tale about the horrors of the *Lebensborn* program, told through the eyes of Allina, a half-Jewish woman who must hide her heritage as she confronts the terrible reality behind the Nazis' twisted drive to become the so-called 'master race.' With rich prose and complex characters, *The Sunflower House* is one you won't be able to put down."
                              —Bryn Turnbull, international bestselling
                                 author of *The Woman Before Wallis*

"This chilling novel sheds light on a little-known WWII atrocity through the eyes of its reluctant heroine. Heartbreaking and beautifully written, *The Sunflower House* is a story about a woman upended by trauma and secrets, who must ignore her conscience and become part of the lie she loathes most in order to survive, go forward, and love again. An inspirational read that will linger long after you've finished the last page."
                              —Shelly Sanders, bestselling author of
                                 Daughters of the Occupation

"In her debut historical novel, Adriana Allegri transports readers into the heart of a story that is both poignant and evocative. . . . The novel is a brilliant debut."   —Mary Calvi, fourteen-time Emmy Award–winning
                                 journalist and author of *If a Poem
                                 Could Live and Breathe*

THE SUNFLOWER HOUSE

A NOVEL

Adriana Allegri

ST. MARTIN'S PRESS
NEW YORK

First published in the United States by St. Martin's Press, an imprint of St. Martin's Publishing Group

THE SUNFLOWER HOUSE. Copyright © 2024 by Adriana Allegri. All rights reserved. Printed in the United States of America. For information, address St. Martin's Publishing Group, 120 Broadway, New York, NY 10271.

Designed by Jen Edwards

www.stmartins.com

The Library of Congress Cataloging-in-Publication Data is available upon request.

ISBN 978-1-250-32652-2 (hardcover)
ISBN 978-1-250-32653-9 (ebook)

Our books may be purchased in bulk for promotional, educational, or business use. Please contact your local bookseller or the Macmillan Corporate and Premium Sales Department at 1-800-221-7945, extension 5442, or by email at MacmillanSpecialMarkets@macmillan.com.

First Edition: 2024

10 9 8 7 6 5 4 3 2 1

For my mother, Germana Pretto Allegri, who
taught me I could do anything I set my mind to,
and who was a woman of enormous strength,
compassion, and grace

THE SUNFLOWER HOUSE

PROLOGUE

Summer 2006
Ramsey, New Jersey

KATRINE

The call from Englewood Hospital comes at two o'clock in the morning.

My husband and I jolt awake to the telephone's sharp *brrring*, but I'm first to reach the phone. The nurse's calm, measured voice is somehow more terrifying than his words. It's only George's arm around my shoulders that keeps the shaft of panic in my throat from erupting in a scream.

My eighty-six-year-old mother is in the ER—with a sprained wrist, contusions, and a bump to the head. "Your mom was lucky. Given her age, the injuries are minor," the nurse says. "Can you come pick Allina up and drive her home?"

My mother didn't want to bother us in the middle of the night, according to the nurse. She showed up to the hospital alone, in a damn taxi. Unbelievable.

I thank him and hang up before giving in to tears. George tugs me close and rubs my back until the ache in my chest eases.

"We dodged another bullet," he murmurs against my ear. "She's fine, Kat. Your mom's a strong woman. Like you."

"I know," I whisper.

"Let me come with you."

There's no sense in having us both at the hospital, so I tell George to stay here. I'll need his quiet strength and humor later on today, and he can call the girls once I get Mother home, run interference if need be. Maggie and Brynn may be grown with families of their own, but they're fiercely protective of their gran.

My sweet husband brews me a cup of tea while I dress. He hands me the mug with my morning blood pressure meds.

"It's early, but take 'em now," George says. "Pressure's probably going through the roof." He sighs hard as I pace the kitchen, then gives me a look I've seen many times—a loving, hazel-eyed stare-down that's half order, half plea. One that says: *Take a breath, Kat. For me. Please.*

After forty years, George knows every dark corner of my control-freak heart. I find comfort in his gravelly baritone and the warmth of his fingers as they cover mine. The man doesn't let me leave the house until my hands are steady.

I make the half-hour drive to Englewood in twenty-three minutes, with a swarm of worries buzzing around in my head. *How did she fall? Will she need more help, or in-home care?* There's also the tired argument we've fought for months, the one that always ends in guilt: *Should I have convinced her to come live with us last year when she gave up her car?*

Like other women with elderly parents, I'm learning how to mother my own mother. Most days are a clumsy dance of love and fear and angst, filled with missteps that make me heartsick. And weary.

When I finally lay eyes on her in the emergency room, relief has me light-headed. My mother has a small bandage above her left eyebrow and a wrap around her right wrist. Purple bruises are beginning to bloom on her arms. And yet, she's sitting up on the edge of the hospital bed, holding court over the medical staff while they check her vitals. Her back is straight, the slender legs are swinging, and that regal chin is high in the air. After she orders an aide to fetch a glass of water, the nurse laughs.

She's a force of nature. An eighty-six-year-old hurricane of a woman.

Laughing through tears, I push past the gap in the curtain around her hospital bed. Her eyebrows lift in mild surprise, as if I've turned up late for our weekly lunch date.

"Ah. There you are, *Katchen*," she says in her commanding German accent, using a pet name I haven't heard in decades.

More tears, but I blink them back and take her hand. "Mama, look at you. What happened?"

She gives me a peck on the cheek, then rolls her eyes before dismissing my question. "I'm fine. You're overreacting, as usual. It was a small mishap."

The nurse coughs out a laugh. "Your mom dodged a bullet, but she's a pistol herself." He wags a finger. "Behave, sunshine. No more mountain climbing."

Mother harrumphs, clearly offended at being teased like an old lady. But then he winks at her, and the woman is transformed. Coloring, she pats his arm and thanks him for his expert care. That's when I know my mother will be fine. Even injured, she's well enough to notice a handsome young man with deep blue eyes.

When those eyes shift to mine, they're filled with amused sympathy. "Good luck," the nurse murmurs, before escaping down the hall.

Once more, I ask my mother how she hurt herself.

That stubborn chin pops up another notch. "I was cleaning out my bedroom closet and lost my balance. It could have happened to anyone."

Somehow, I don't think so.

"You used the step stool, didn't you?" I ask in my most patient voice. The stool she'd promised never to use by herself. The one I should have taken out of there years ago.

Mother snorts and looks down, suddenly fascinated by her swinging feet.

God help me. I want to strangle her. "You could have broken a hip. Or worse."

The look she slants out the corner of her eye promises rebellion.

We speak carefully during the drive back to her house, but the air is thick with guilt, frustration, and too many words left unsaid. Halfway home, though, she reaches for my hand. Hers is colder than it should be, and trembling. Despite all the bluster, she's shaken.

"I'm tougher than you think," she says, perhaps to convince herself as much as me. "Getting old isn't for the weak."

As if I didn't know this. I'm only twenty years behind her. But I let the irritation go for now. We hold hands the rest of the way back to her house.

The charcoal sky has paled to lavender by the time we pull in to the driveway of my childhood home. After sixty years, much remains the same. The red brick is a bit darker, but the paint around the windows and shutters is crisp evergreen. And the oak tree and patch of lawn in her front yard are immaculate, thanks to the service we bring in twice a month. Money was always dear, but my mother knows how to take care of what she has.

She makes it into the house, limping but unassisted, and informs me that *no*, she will not go to bed. The sun is rising, for pity's sake. And she's starving. It's early for a full breakfast, but a nice cup of chamomile and some butter cookies will hit the spot.

Yet another strategic surrender is in order. I get an icepack and some ibuprofen and settle her on the living room sofa. She plumps up the rust and mustard pillows with her good hand, settles back onto them with a heavy sigh. The furniture—which was at the height of style in the 1970s—has seen better days. Like her, it's still hanging on, in remarkable shape for its age.

I head into the kitchen to fetch the requested tea and cookies.

"Leave the dishes alone," she warns. "And stay out of my bedroom. I'll straighten that mess up later."

There are two dishes, a fork, a spoon, and a mug in the sink, which makes the kitchen a disaster area by her neat-freak standards. Disobeying her direct order, I load the dishwasher while the chamomile steeps, then wipe down every inch of the faded avocado countertop.

When I return to the living room, she's out like a light. Thank you, God.

I drop into a chair, grateful for the chance to take stock, get a good look at her. Open-mouthed and snoring, my mother's cheeks are hollow. Her angular jaw is softer. These changes are small, but they make her appear much older. And there's something different about her breathing, a slight hitch at the end of each exhalation that wasn't there even a year ago. As her chest rises and falls, I'm suddenly terrified it will stop.

Fear hits like a blow to the solar plexus. My mother is the only person in the world who knows all of me, who remembers me from my beginning. I'm not ready to lose her.

That fucking step stool is getting hacked to pieces and dumped in the trash. Today.

I hurry to her bedroom, leaving the door open a crack so I'll know if she stirs. The state of the room shows exactly what happened. Her closet door is wide open with the step stool just inside it, although the thing is on its side under a pile of blouses on hangers. A flash of how she fell—the loss of balance in reaching for the top shelf, an attempt to steady herself by grabbing her clothes, then the slow-motion crumple to the hardwood floor—makes me want to smash everything in the room to bits. Instead, I hang each fallen article of clothing with care, breathing in the sharp, lemony scent of Jean Naté that clings to them.

When I go to right the stool the damn thing is jammed, stuck in the doorframe. It comes free on the third yank, but the struggle uproots a segment of floorboard. This flooring is falling to pieces, an obvious hazard.

I ease onto my knees to press the scuffed plank back into place, but the gap below the flooring is large. It's actually more than a gap. The slat is clever camouflage for a hiding place, one that's a perfect fit for the item wedged inside. The thing is the size and shape of a home safe box, and wrapped in an old silk scarf—a navy-and-white-polka-dotted one I remember from grade school. It was Mama's fancy scarf. She used to wear it all the time.

The hairs rise on the back of my neck. A better daughter would respect her privacy, slip the plank back into place, and walk away.

But I don't.

The box is so heavy it takes both hands to lift. I set it on the floor, then unwind the silk scarf and the thicker red velvet one underneath it.

Too late, I realize the enormity of my mistake. I'll never be able to unsee the monstrous thing.

It's a large wood box made of honey oak in an elegant chevron pattern. A tiny brass key taped to the side is a design of curlicue perfection. The lid is lacquered to a satin gloss.

And marked with a swastika.

That word, *swastika*, brings hot prickles of panic to my cheeks. It sucks all the oxygen out of the room. The swastika is a symbol of bigotry and hatred, and the death of millions of innocents. Of annihilation. For a generation of Germans, it's also an icon of disgrace, a shared guilt many would rather forget.

Our heritage shames us. My mother has never said those words aloud to me, but I know that's what she feels. I have always known this.

I was three when we arrived in America and have no memories of the country of my birth or how we came to live in the United States. I can't even speak the language. Mother never permitted German in the house. *We have left the Fatherland behind us,* she'd insist when I begged for stories about my father or our homeland. *We're Americans now. You're an American.* After years of arguments and pleading, I stopped asking about the past. I lived in the shadow of her secrets by pretending they didn't exist.

Have I been naïve, or unwilling to see? The single mother who loved me so fiercely, the woman who worked two jobs to keep a roof over our heads was, what? A goddamned Nazi.

No. I can't believe it.

I slide the box into my lap, pick at the brittle bit of tape to get at the key. My hand quakes so much the key drops to the floor with a clatter. The coppery tang of fear coats the back of my throat.

No sound from the living room. She's still asleep. I have to know.

The box unlocks with a soft snick, and I lift the lid, inhaling the sweet vanilla of old paper and ink. Inside is an odd jumble of items. German newspaper articles. A heavy gold locket, engraved with an *A* in ornate script. An opera program from a 1939 production of Richard Wagner's *Siegfried* at the Bayreuth Festival. A pile of letters, the envelopes stiff and speckled with age. Faded postcards. There's also a photo of Mama in a ruffled nurse's apron—my mother was a *nurse?*—and surrounded by a group of children seated cross-legged on the floor. The children look sick, their expressions are listless, and her smile is too tight to be genuine. I flip the photo over, but the note scribbled on the back gives only her name and the date: Allina, 1940.

There are other snapshots of children, too, ones that make me queasy. Long, pristine rows of babies in cradles, wrapped with military precision in identical blankets. Toddlers at meals, seated on low benches. Others standing at attention with heads held high, chubby arms throwing Nazi salutes.

So many children. And no mothers in the photos. Or fathers. Only nurses.

One last photograph, a headshot, peeks out from the bottom of the box, and I pull it free.

The man in the photo is handsome even though he's not smiling. His slicked-back hair is severe, as are the planes of his face, but his eyes are kind. Our eyes meet, this man's and mine, and my breath catches. Squeezing my eyes shut, little lights explode behind my eyelids. I can almost remember his face.

When the memories finally come, they flash across my brain with stunning clarity, like snapshots from a photo album.

He's smiling down at me, face haloed in sunlight, as we walk through a field of sunflowers toward a whitewashed house. His hands, rough and calloused, lift me onto his shoulders before we gallop down a hallway into a room filled with books and a huge, curved fireplace. He slides an arm around Mother's waist as they lean in to kiss me good night. I remember the spice of his aftershave and the rasp of whiskers against my neck.

We have left the Fatherland behind us.

Examining the photo again, I try to view the man's face objectively, to avoid inventing similarities if there are none to see. Yet there's a likeness to the lines of our jaws and noses, and the shape of our eyes is similar. Closing mine, I try to remember more, try to force new images from my brain. But nothing else will come.

"*Katchen.* What are you doing?"

I turn at the sound of my mother's sharp, accusing voice. She's standing in the bedroom doorway, lips pursed.

When her gaze drops to my lap, she turns away with a cry.

I lift the box, offering it without a word. Every question is stuck in my throat along with hundreds of others asked over the years, all gone unanswered. Silent and fighting through waves of panic, I watch my mother attempt to gather herself. She will not look at me. Head bowed low, she presses a hand to her throat, then her stomach. Her breathing is labored, ragged.

Finally, Mama takes a deep breath, straightens her shoulders, and looks me in the eye. Her cheeks are wet. Her green eyes are dark with pain and fear.

"It's not what you think." Her good hand trembles as it reaches out, entreating. "Come back to the living room. Please. I can explain everything."

PART 1

———†———

Badensburg

CHAPTER 1

Summer 1938
Badensburg, Germany

ALLINA

"You'd have those filthy Jews here? *Why?*"

Fritz's voice was high and sharp, like the crack of a horsewhip. Sitting up in the grass, he made a show of brushing bits of leaves off his brown trousers and smoothing back the untidy strands of his blond, razored hair.

Allina's cheeks prickled with alarm. Fritz had never been so cruel. The gentle boy she'd grown up with, the one who could coax a saddle onto the most skittish colt, had disappeared. He'd become impossible. Unrecognizable.

Her eyes darted across the picnic cloth, but her best friend Karin sat as quiet and still as a statue with her gaze fixed to the ground. Only the shrill cries of the cicadas filled the silence.

How had it come to this?

They called themselves the Fabulous Four: Allina and Albert, Karin and Fritz. Two couples and the best of friends, they'd each pitched in for today's picnic. Albert was in charge of bread and chocolate, Fritz came with grapes and a bowl of sweet quark cheese. Karin had snuck her mother's rose-patterned china out of the house, and Allina brought strudel and the latest draft of a short story to read over dessert. She loved how they'd laughed over the zany plot twists in "Tristan's Treachery."

Even the weather had cooperated. It was gorgeous out, warm and a little muggy, and the breeze stirring Allina's bangs was sweet with lavender. Five minutes ago, she'd been sprawled on the ground with her head in the crook of Albert's arm. The sun had lulled her, and she'd needed nothing more than the crush of warm grass against the backs of her legs, the cooked-cotton scent of Albert's shirt, and the drowsy caress of his fingers in her hair.

Albert's hand was tight around her arm now, like a vise, warning her to keep quiet.

His amber eyes had narrowed, his nostrils flared, and his generous mouth was set in a thin, grim line. For a moment, Allina wished she could disappear.

"Answer the question," Fritz demanded. He pointed a stubby finger into Karin's face. "Give me one damn reason you'd want that Jew-shit here."

More nervous silence.

Karin's rosy cheeks turned to chalk. She swallowed hard before looking up. "Mina and Oskar were my friends. I miss them," she said in a small voice. Karin bowed her head, and her platinum hair fell like a curtain over her face.

Fritz propped himself back on his elbows and snickered. "You'd probably invite those two pigs to our wedding if you had the chance."

He was unbearable. Karin didn't deserve this. No one did, but especially not Karin, her best friend and the kindest of them all. Karin never had a harsh word for anyone. As for the Neumanns—Allina shivered—the family had packed up and vanished six months ago, in the middle of the night and without a word. No one had heard from them since.

Allina tugged her skirt down over her shins and wrapped her arms around her knees. "I miss them, too," she said, working to keep the temper out of her voice. "Karin's right. We've been friends with Oskar and Mina forever." She'd never cared that the Neumanns were Jewish. For pity's sake, no one in the village had, not really, beyond a thoughtless comment or occasional joke.

Oskar and Mina had never discussed their religion, or asked about Allina's Lutheran faith, for that matter. It wasn't something her friends talked about. Allina didn't see the Neumanns at church, of course, as they worshipped on Saturdays, but aside from that, Oskar and Mina were no

different from the rest of her friends. They'd been playmates and class-
mates, swarming like bees at each other's houses after school and enjoying
long, lazy days at the lake every summer.

Fritz's lips curled back like he'd been forced to take a dose of cod-
liver oil. Then he began his lecture. It was a pathetic, contradictory mix of
lies—the same foul garbage forced down their throats at the mandatory
race education classes they attended on Saturdays.

*Oskar and Mina are spoiled brats. Their father is a communist, like every
other Jew. Jews are sneaky. Selfish. They steal from honest, hardworking Germans, then count their money while the rest of us starve in the street . . .*

She tried to bear it in silence. Sometimes that tactic worked and Fritz
would run out of hot air. But when he called Frau Neumann a lazy cow—
Frau Neumann, who'd cooked for Allina's family last winter when Aunt
Claudia was down with pneumonia—something in her broke.

"You're like a damn parrot, repeating whatever nonsense you hear,"
Allina said, seething. Anger had her ears ringing. "For God's sake, Fritz.
Think for yourself."

Karin gasped.

Albert pulled her closer. "Hush," he whispered. The tension in his
arms, the way his hands gripped her middle, made Allina's heart pound
in her throat.

Fritz smiled—smiled and shook his head, then proceeded to examine
every inch of her face. It was a cold, dispassionate assessment, as if he were
observing an insect crawling up the wall. His pale green stare raised the hairs
on the back of her neck. Allina took a deep breath, but the sweet mix of lavender and grass was cloying. It choked her.

"If you love your Jewish friends so much, perhaps you should spend
more time with them," Fritz finally said. "I'm sure that can be arranged."

Albert sprang to his feet with a growl. "That's enough. Apologize.
Now."

Fritz didn't reply. He stood up instead and advanced slowly until he
and Albert stood nose to nose. The air seemed to shimmer around the
two as they stared each other down. Albert's hands were fisted so tightly
his arms shook.

For a few moments, Allina was sure it would come to blows.

Karin rose to her feet slowly, then crept toward the pair. "Please, Fritzi.

It's our last outing before the wedding. We shouldn't be fighting." Her voice trembled and she touched two fingers to Fritz's arm. "Please."

Fritz swept Karin's hand away.

Then he laughed. It was a high, fake, ugly sound. He gave Allina a swooping parody of a bow before dropping down onto the grass.

"Excuse us," Albert said through gritted teeth as he pulled Allina to her feet. Taking her by the wrist, he dragged her away from their friends, down the hill through the tall grasses leading to the lake.

"Let go of me," she hissed, but Albert ignored her and marched faster, his hand a shackle around her arm. "Let go," she repeated. "I can take care of myself." She jerked away and stumbled, tripping over her own feet. While the thick reeds cushioned her fall, they didn't stop her from landing on her knees with an embarrassing squeak.

Albert hauled her upright. A dark flush had traveled up his neck and into his cheeks, and his sandy hair stuck up from his skull at wild angles. "You think you proved yourself back there?" he scolded, even as he leaned in to help brush the grass off her skirt and shins.

Allina was too furious to reply. She answered his question with a sour look and scrubbed at the yellow gingham in a sad attempt to defeat the grass stains.

"Fine," he said, and ran a hand through his hair, settling it. "No talking. Walk with me. We both need to calm down." His mouth tipped up in a crooked grin, one she knew well. One that usually worked.

Albert reached for her hand again, and this time she didn't pull away. Allina tamped down her irritation and let him lead, through thick clumps of rushes that tickled her calves as they made their way along the shoreline. Their silent trek eased the tightness between her shoulder blades, and she relaxed into the familiar sounds and scents of the lake: the deep honks of geese as they flew overhead; the soft rustle of the breeze through the reeds; and the pungent mix of water lilies, trout, and algae floating up from the water. By the time they'd hiked a mile, exertion had her hair clinging to her cheeks, but Allina was grateful for the distraction. She didn't realize the hugeness of her anger, or her panic, until she stopped shaking.

Brushing the hair back from her face, she stopped to gaze across the lake at their tiny village—150 souls who lived and toiled and, for the most part, prospered together. The water mirrored the cloudless blue sky and reflected the crumbling turrets of Gottestränen Castle and the high, thatched roofs of the Baum House Inn. A dozen restaurants, alehouses, and tourist shops, including her uncle's bookstore, dotted the coast. Plots of farmland fanned out from the water, and the summer wheat gleamed in the sun.

Albert scooped up a stone and pitched it at the lake with a deft flick. It skimmed the surface in four quick, light splashes, sending dozens of ripples across the water. After a half minute, the ripples melted away and the mirrored reflection was perfect again.

"It looks so peaceful," Allina said.

Albert pointed their linked hands toward Karin and Fritz, now lounging in the sun. "Everything does from a distance. They seem peaceful, too, from here. It's an illusion."

Albert was right about that. She'd looked forward to the picnic all week, but only half believed they could get through the day without a fight. "I should have been more patient," she said. "Tried harder to reason with him."

Albert let out a heavy sigh. His eyes were sad, and deadly serious. "No, Allina. You must stop arguing with Fritz about the Jews."

The words were like scalding water against her skin. "The Jews? You mean the Neumanns." Allina pulled away to search his face, but the hard set of his jaw proved he wasn't in the mood to listen. "Oskar and Mina, our friends," she said, louder. "Or have you forgotten them, too?"

Albert let out an ugly curse that made her wince. "I haven't forgotten them," he said. "But arguing with Fritz is pointless. Dangerous. You need to learn when to keep your mouth shut."

Allina stumbled back, cheeks burning. Albert's bluntness didn't shock her. He'd begun doling out advice the minute he turned eighteen. But Albert had no business telling her how to behave, not after playing coward in front of their friends.

"You want me to tiptoe around, terrified to speak the truth," she said as panic bloomed in her chest. "Are you really so afraid?"

Albert laughed, but it was a harsh, strangled sound. Allina realized she'd brought him to the brink of tears. "Of course, I'm afraid! The Neumanns are safe for now, damn it. It's you I have to worry about."

Before Allina could ask how he knew the Neumanns were safe, Albert yanked her into his arms and kissed her.

She stiffened while the heat rushed through her body. Albert's mouth was sweet with chocolate, but his lips were hard as they moved over hers, and desperate. Wrapping both arms around his neck, Allina poured every ounce of anger into kissing him back. Thoughts of their argument, of anything else, melted away. Nothing mattered but the need to be closer.

Albert pulled away too soon and with a grunt of frustration that made her quiver.

"Promise me you'll be more careful," he whispered.

Allina shook her head to clear it. No. This wasn't an argument they could kiss away. She tried to wriggle out of his arms, but Albert wouldn't have it.

"I love you," he said. "Your safety is all that matters. I leave for Berlin the week after next. I won't be here to protect you. Please," he said, and kissed her again. "Promise me."

Allina rested her head on his chest, breathing in the familiar scents that clung to his shirt—clean cotton and grass, and a sharpness that came from his skin. She'd never doubted Albert's feelings or her own. She'd loved him all her life. Every happy memory was tied to Albert in some way. There could never be anyone else.

"I love you, too," she murmured, before she began to weep. Because Allina was also sure, with every part of her heart, that if they didn't start speaking up, the truth would be lost forever. It was already happening. With every passing day, all that was good and right in the world seemed to be slipping away.

When Allina came down to breakfast the next morning, Uncle Dieter was waiting at the kitchen table. Instead of calling out his usual, boisterous greeting, he sat quietly, fingers drumming slowly on the wood tabletop. Uncle's long, thin face was pale, his blue eyes were bloodshot, and the furrows bracketing his mouth were deeper than usual.

"Sit down," he said, in a voice so sharp she obeyed immediately.

"Fritz's father paid me a visit while you were at your morning chores,"

Uncle said. "Herr Meier told me you argued with Fritz yesterday. About the Neumanns."

Allina stared out the window to avoid his accusing gaze. The two long, narrow cords running from the porch posts to the oak tree at the backyard's edge were crammed with the blouses, skirts, and trousers she'd hung at dawn. They billowed like flags against the azure sky.

Uncle Dieter struck his hand against the tabletop, hard enough to rattle the silverware. "At the mighty age of seventeen, you pick a fight with a member of the Hitler Youth Patrol," he bit out, in a voice so low it made goose bumps raise on her skin. "Are you trying to get yourself arrested?" He rose from his chair and began pacing the length of the kitchen.

The back of Allina's throat began to ache. Uncle's fear was contagious. She took a slice of bacon off the serving platter and ripped it in two before dropping the crumbly pieces onto her plate. Her appetite had vanished.

"We argued yesterday," she answered carefully, "but it wasn't as bad as that." She hadn't mentioned Fritz's precious Führer, not once. And arrests might happen in Munich or Berlin but not in sleepy little villages like Badensburg, where families depended on each other to survive.

"Herr Meier intervened with his son for the sake of our friendship. He said he would not do so again." Uncle's voice raised, and he ran a hand through his salt-and-pepper hair until it stood on end. "He begged me to talk sense into you, child. Fritz and Karin plan to move to Munich next year. Don't you know what that means?"

Overcome with anger, Uncle Dieter began to wheeze. He let out a series of harsh, barking coughs that left him breathless, then leaned back against the wall, ruddy cheeks in stark contrast against the whitewashed plaster.

Panicking, Allina held her tongue. Uncle would make himself sick if he wasn't careful.

Aunt Claudia bustled into the dining room just in time. It was clear she'd been listening, because her cheeks were flushed as red as crab apples and her gray eyes were the color of her iron cookstove.

Scowling, Auntie slammed the coffeepot on the table. Liquid sloshed on the embroidered tablecloth, like a spatter of brown blood.

Uncle slunk over to the table with a sigh and took his seat.

Auntie kissed him on the forehead. "Drink your coffee and read the newspaper, Dieter," she said, and straightened the collar of his chambray shirt. "Allina and I will make your favorite strudel."

Allina shook her head. Her aunt couldn't be serious.

"You heard me, young lady," Aunt Claudia said, pulling Allina out of her chair. Allina stifled a shriek as Auntie steered her into the kitchen.

Auntie had mixed a batch of strudel dough before sunrise and let it continue to rest while they washed up and prepared the filling. The two worked in silence, which was fine with Allina; she didn't want to make things worse.

Still, she couldn't settle as flashes of Fritz's cold gaze and veiled threats replayed in her mind. His cruelty toward Karin and the Neumanns— such ugliness would have been unthinkable even a year ago. How could Karin marry him?

Allina took her frustration out on a juicy apple, sending bits of fruit flying across the counter when she cored it with a vicious twist.

"Good. Let your anger out," Aunt Claudia said with a dry laugh. She pointed to the mangled fruit in Allina's hands. "When you're done torturing that apple, we'll speak, calmly, woman to woman."

Oh, she was in for it now. Claudia Strauss never yelled to make a point. No, the calmer Auntie got, the more serious the offense.

Auntie turned the ball of dough onto the floured tabletop to roll it out. "Your uncle and I sympathize with our Jewish friends. You know that," Auntie said in her no-nonsense voice. She worked the pin over the dough with brisk movements. "We've told you to keep our sympathies private. That makes you angry."

Allina pushed the damp bangs off her forehead. "And ashamed." *And sad. And nauseous. We're hypocrites, all of us.* She didn't want to argue anymore, so she hurried to the sink to scrub the sugar from her sticky fingers.

This kitchen, more than any other part of the house, always made Allina feel loved and safe. She'd learned to cook her aunt's special sauerbraten roast on the ancient iron cookstove and washed the oak floorboards hundreds of times to Auntie's exacting standards of cleanliness. The two pine shelves over the sink were bowed with age and the weight of homey blue-and-cream plates, floral teapots and vases, and dozens of empty canning jars they'd soon fill with pickled vegetables and preserves to get them through the long winter. Allina's friends were always welcome in Auntie's kitchen, and no visitor left without some soup, or bread and butter, or a glass of milk and warm strudel.

Now everything was falling apart.

When Allina returned to the table to help stretch the dough, her aunt's lips were pinched with worry. "Your uncle is right. We're lucky Herr Meier intervened with Fritz. Things are changing, even in our tiny village, and not for the better." Auntie slid her arms beneath the sheet of pastry and lifted her chin. "Come. Help me with the dough."

Allina walked to the opposite side of the table and slid her arms under the sheet of pastry, mirroring her aunt's movements. They worked silently, circling the table slowly while pulling the dough outward.

"Perhaps you're right," Allina finally said.

"Perhaps?" Auntie's eyes raised heavenward. She stopped and brushed the dough with oil before they made another pass around the table. "Do you truly believe arguing with Fritz was smart? Think, please, before you speak."

Fritz's icy stare flashed through Allina's mind again, and her stomach tumbled. "It was the right thing to do, but I'm not sure how smart it was."

"Better," Auntie said with a sigh. "At least you've thrown me a crumb of hope."

Silence descended while they continued their work. They circled two more times until the pastry was paper thin and reached the edges of the table.

Allina grabbed the bowl of filling and began spreading a thick line of apple mixture along one edge of the pastry. The stupid spoon wouldn't stop shaking, so she worked faster, but the mixture fell onto the dough in an uneven clump.

Auntie plucked the bowl and spoon out of Allina's hands and set them on the counter. "I know you're frightened," she said, lifting Allina's chin with a finger. The sympathy in Auntie's eyes made her want to run out of the kitchen. "Even as a little girl, you always lashed out in anger when you were scared. But your anger will have grave consequences if you let it control you."

Allina tried to turn away, but Aunt Claudia was relentless. She wrested Allina's hands in her strong, calloused ones and held on tight. "Talk to me. Tell me why you're afraid."

"Fritz was a monster. He tortured Karin yesterday, over the Neumanns. Our friends." The words rushed out of her like water after a dam's
release. "You, Uncle, Albert—you want me to pretend everything's fine,
but I can't do it anymore, I can't—"

Auntie pulled her close with a soft cry, enveloping her in the warmth
of her plump body and the comforting scents of coffee and strudel dough.

"I'm scared of getting used to living like this," Allina murmured against
her aunt's damp neck. *I'm afraid I'll go crazy, like everyone else.*

"I'm frightened, too," Auntie whispered into her hair. "It's a sickness,
this hatred the Führer has for the Jews, and hate infects everyone it
touches."

Allina pulled away. "That's why I stood up to Fritz."

Her stubborn declaration earned an owlish look from her aunt. "Can
you help anyone if you're in prison?"

"No," Allina choked out.

"This cannot be your fight," Auntie said, "or any woman's, for that matter." She gave Allina's nose a tweak. "My brave little mouse, who's not so
little anymore. You must learn discernment. When to speak, and when to
keep quiet."

When to speak? That women should remain silent while the men did
nothing . . . it made no sense. But Allina didn't want to start another fight,
so she held her tongue, managed a nod.

"Your Uncle Dieter still sees you as a child, not the young woman
you've become. He thinks you'll follow orders. God knows, he's always
been wrong about that." Auntie leaned closer. "But we understand each
other. Don't we?"

Closing her eyes, Allina nodded again. It didn't matter that her aunt
and uncle had taught her to always do the honorable thing. All they
wanted from her—all anyone seemed to want from her—was silence.

Auntie gave each of her cheeks a loud, smacking kiss. "Your uncle
needs a distraction. We'll improve his mood by finishing our strudel."

Aunt Claudia thought a good strudel was the cure to every evil in the
world.

"I'm not joking," Auntie said, when Allina rolled her eyes. "Strudel is
serious business. Go fetch the sesame seeds while I roll it." She nudged
Allina out of the kitchen. "Go."

Sighing, Allina trudged down the hallway to the cellar steps. At the entrance to the staircase hung two photographs, and she stopped to look at them.

The first was a photo taken on her eighth birthday. Gap-toothed and smiling and with her hair coming loose from pigtail braids, Allina sat astride Zigi, her dapple-gray riding pony. Her aunt and uncle stood on either side of the animal, with Aunt Claudia's hand on Zigi's rump, and Uncle Dieter's arm around Allina's shoulders.

The second photo was the only one Allina had of her parents. Her mother, Irene, looked exotic in a stylish suit, and she held a swaddled Allina in a tight embrace. Tomas, her father, grinned proudly into the camera with an arm wrapped around mother and baby. Uncle always said Allina had her mother's high cheekbones and sharp chin, although her light hair and eyes came from her father's side of the family.

For years, Allina had begged her aunt and uncle for more information about her real parents. *Your mother and father loved you very much,* they'd always reply, *but it's best to keep the past in the past.* Any further pleas were met with silence and long, sad looks that made her stomach sink. Beyond the spare truth that Tomas was Auntie's younger brother, Allina was sure of only two facts about Tomas and Irene Schenck: First, they were Berliners. And second, they'd died when she was three months old.

Allina rested her head against the cool, rough plaster of the wall. *There are too many secrets in this house. And too many things we never talk about.*

CHAPTER 2

ALLINA

Everything in Allina's life unraveled after Karin and Fritz's wedding.

Albert left for Berlin the week following the ceremony, and while he wrote every day, his letters never erased the hollow ache in her chest. He'd always been the steady ballast that offset her stormy temper, but Allina missed Albert for a hundred different reasons—his teasing humor, the feel of his hands at her waist as they danced, even his pigheaded need to protect her. He returned to Badensburg in July for her eighteenth birthday, and Allina accepted his marriage proposal, to everyone's delight. But Albert's letters since had been odd. Incomplete. Instead of giving Allina the details she craved about Berlin, they were filled with memories from their childhood, or his plans for their life together after they married next summer.

As the weeks passed, Allina saw less of her old school friends. Karin was the only exception—she invited Allina to lunch once a week—but Allina felt a growing chasm there, too. Karin was a married woman now, done with childhood. It was like she'd crossed a bridge Allina could glimpse but not yet travel.

Their luncheons never extended to dinner, by unspoken agreement. Allina didn't trust her temper around Fritz and always left before he got home in the evenings. When Karin spoke of him it was only in the context of what she'd prepare for dinner or the work he'd done around the house. They never mentioned Chancellor Hitler or the couple's plans to move to Munich.

All these shifts left Allina in fidgety limbo. She did her best to stay busy and helped her uncle run the bookshop every day. When business was slow, they buried themselves in Goethe, Dostoevsky, and Dickens, debating the nature of good and evil within the safe confines of a book's pages. Sadly, one of Uncle Dieter's favorite novels, Kesten's *Running Riot*, was no longer part of their conversations. Uncle refused to discuss politics with her anymore, and Kesten had fled Germany years ago after the book burnings that took his works, and those of Einstein, Freud, and other Jewish authors, off bookshelves across the country.

In the evenings, Allina continued to write, although many of her stories seemed pointless and childish. She forced herself to persist, and to bide her time. In a year she'd be married, living with Albert in Berlin.

At the end of July, Uncle developed a persistent cough that wracked his body at all hours. Allina lost count of the number of times she came awake in the middle of the night to his hacking, and his voice became hoarse after the first week. Auntie blamed it on a summer cold at first, then allergies. They tried every home remedy—mustard plasters, castor-oil packs, even eucalyptus-oil inhalations to help his breathing—but nothing worked for long.

When his pants grew baggy, Auntie suggested a visit to Dr. Weiss. Uncle laughed at her fussing and kept on working. He'd said he needed to lose a little weight and, besides, it was tourist season. They couldn't afford to close for even a day during the most profitable part of the year. Allina insisted she could run the bookstore alone, but Uncle wouldn't consent. No doctors. Everything was fine.

One night near the end of August, he coughed up blood.

"You've worked yourself into a case of pneumonia," Auntie scolded. "We'll go see the doctor in the morning."

The diagnosis came back a week later.

"Cancer?"

Allina gaped at her aunt and uncle across the dinner table, aware of the slow ticking of the grandfather clock as the hateful word hung in the air.

Auntie and Uncle nodded in unison. They'd told her the truth using blunt language but, despite their bloodshot eyes, seemed calm.

Uncle shifted his chair closer and reached for Allina's hand. His was strong and warm, reassuring as always.

"I don't want you worrying about me, child," he said. "Everything will be fine."

"Don't lie to her, Dieter. Not about this." Aunt Claudia's voice was sharp, but Allina couldn't tell if it was from anger or fear. Terrified, she turned away. Her gaze roamed the dining room in search of an anchor—something, *anything* to keep panic at bay—and finally settled on the antique oak hutch, filled with cherished treasures: delicate Schwarzenhammer summer rose china, special enough to be saved for holidays and guests; the heavy silver candlesticks and cut crystal vases Uncle had inherited from his parents; and an antique tea service placed just so on the hand-stitched doilies her grandmother had made, a woman who'd died years before Allina was born and whom she knew only through the stories Auntie told. Allina examined these items with a desperate, focused attention until Uncle squeezed her hand again.

His blue eyes watered and he smiled at her with trembling lips. "Doctor Weiss sent my X-ray to a specialist in Cologne. There's nothing to be done. What time I have left, I'll spend here, at home with the two women I love most in the world."

Allina jumped up with a cry and hugged him tight, pressing her face into his shirt and inhaling her uncle's cool, spicy scent. Peppermint and tobacco.

What were they going to do?

"We're going to cook for him," Auntie said later that evening, as she ticked off Uncle Dieter's favorite foods on her fingers. "Apple strudel. Meatballs and spaetzle. Wiener schnitzel." Handing Allina a knife, she gestured toward the table. "Start peeling potatoes."

"You think food will cure him?" Allina shook her head in disbelief, but she carried a sack of potatoes to the table anyway.

"The food will show your uncle how much we love him." Her aunt opened a cupboard, pulled out a stockpot, and slammed it on the stove. "Love can work miracles."

"How much time does he have?" When her aunt didn't answer, Allina's stomach sank. "What did Doctor Weiss say?"

CHAPTER 3

Fall 1938

ALLINA

Carefully keeping her mind blank, Allina scrubbed down the kitchen table. Her fingers were red and chafed to the point of bleeding and the muscles in her arms ached, but cleaning calmed her like nothing else. Wiping the sweat from her forehead, she paused long enough to watch Karin dice vegetables for Auntie's famous chicken soup.

"Stop flicking soap on my onions," Karin said. She looked up from the one she was peeling long enough to send Allina a squinty look. "You're going to drop if you don't rest. Please stop. I'll help clean in a minute."

Allina dragged a chair over to Karin's and sat down. "You're doing too much as it is, especially in your condition," she said, although Karin had never looked healthier. Pregnancy had made her more beautiful. Her oval face was fuller, her peach complexion glowed, and platinum hair fell in thick waves down her back.

"Making chicken soup isn't hard labor," Karin answered with a roll of her eyes. "Besides, I mean to steal all your aunt's recipes. I love Claudia's food better than my mother's." She rubbed her belly. "This baby gives me an appetite for cooking."

Allina laughed. Karin reminded her of a puppy in the kitchen—full

Auntie walked to the sink to fill the pot with water. "Doctors are all well and good, but they have no understanding of God's time. Promise me you'll try to live with hope. We must fill this house with hope and our love for him."

"How long?" Allina demanded.

Auntie bit her lip and kept her eyes on the filling pot. "Two months. Perhaps less."

In the days that followed, they settled quickly into a new routine. Allina ran the bookstore in the mornings and closed the shop at three o'clock so she could spend her afternoons and evenings tackling an endless list of chores. When Uncle grew restless, she read to him—from Homer's *The Odyssey* and Goethe's *Faust*—and they laughed and debated in the same way they'd done her entire life, with one exception: This time, Allina took the lead. It was a tender role reversal of some of her happiest memories, and Allina was grateful each time she could make him laugh, because color would come back into his cheeks. And if a hot, helpless panic sometimes seeped into her chest, she pushed back her tears until he drifted off to sleep.

of energy and always making messes. She'd come to their house every day for the past two weeks.

"Thank God for your help. We couldn't manage otherwise," Allina said, letting her head fall into her hands. The bookstore, the garden, the house, the ever-present ache in the center of her chest . . . exhaustion had her light-headed. "I don't know what day it is anymore."

"You know I'll do anything for you." Karin grimaced as she peeled another onion. "It's just bad luck Albert's stuck in Berlin."

Allina traced the veins in the wood tabletop as her eyes began to burn. She'd written him with the details of Uncle's condition weeks ago and all but begged him to come back.

"I can't understand him," she whispered. Albert knew how sick Uncle was. Why couldn't he come home?

"Dieter looked fit at church last Sunday," Karin said in a cheery voice, obviously meaning to change the subject. "His cough seemed a bit better."

"You think so?" Allina couldn't tell if Karin was being truthful or kind. "He didn't come down to dinner last night." She dragged herself out of the chair, grabbed a broom, and attacked the onion peels around Karin's feet.

Karin kicked the broom. "Go get your journal. The leaves are turning, but it's warm enough in the sun. Take an hour outside—"

A loud, ominous thump shook the ceiling, followed by Aunt Claudia's panicked cry.

"Girls, come quickly!"

Allina and Karin pounded up the stairs. Uncle was lying in a heap on the second-floor landing with his head in Auntie's lap. Yet he was smiling—smiling sweetly and patting Auntie's face, as if to calm her.

Allina dropped to her knees.

"We were coming down to lunch," Auntie murmured, her eyes wide and frightened like a child's. "He said he felt strong enough."

Uncle tried to get up but collapsed again with a groan.

Allina waited on the floor with her aunt and uncle while Karin ran into town to fetch Dr. Weiss. There was a grim set to the doctor's mouth when he arrived, but he took charge immediately, calling out instructions with calm efficiency and portioning out enough work to keep everyone's hands busy. There was water to boil for tea, then towels to fetch, and a basin of warm, soapy water to prepare. Uncle had sweated through his clothes and needed to be changed.

Once there were no more errands to perform, panic bloomed again in Allina's chest. All she could do was stand in silence while Dr. Weiss conducted his examination.

When the doctor pushed up Uncle's shirt, the sight of ribs in sharp relief against pale skin made Allina gasp. He'd worn warm, layered clothing for weeks, and the sweaters had masked the weight he'd lost. Or perhaps she hadn't wanted to see the truth.

Dr. Weiss moved the stethoscope to different spots on Uncle's back, listening to his labored breathing. "How's the pain?"

"Worse," Uncle Dieter grumbled with a shake of his head. "It's getting harder to—"

"To lie?" Auntie's shout was shrill enough to make Dr. Weiss jump back. "When were you going to tell me? After you fell into a coma?" She let out a keening cry before hugging him close. Planting soft kisses on his forehead, she murmured endearments until he broke down.

Allina covered her eyes, but there was nothing she could do to muffle the sound of her uncle's sobs.

Dr. Weiss took her by the arm. "Let's speak in private," he said, easing her into the hall. "We'll bring a bed downstairs into the parlor. Dieter will be easier to tend to during the day that way. At night, you and Claudia can take turns." His eyes were stark with pity. "We need to make your uncle as comfortable as possible. Do you understand what's happening?"

Closing her eyes, Allina nodded. It was the end.

Hours later, Karin found her on the second-floor landing, scrubbing down the wall.

"Allina. What are you doing?"

The urgency in Karin's voice made her stop long enough to look up. "It's ruined," she said, pointing to three ugly gray scratches in the plaster. The marks made her want to bash the wall in. "We damaged the wall when we moved the damn bed frame downstairs."

Karin tried pulling Allina to her feet. "Come to lunch. Your aunt has soup ready."

Allina shook her head and kept cleaning. "I have to fix the wall." Her

knees were aching and her fingers raw, but it didn't matter. Nothing mattered except getting the wall clean.

Karin sank down next to her. "Allina, please. Come downstairs."

"Don't you understand?" Allina threw her brush against the plaster,
adding another mark. "It'll never be the same."

Dr. Weiss told them Uncle would have good days and bad days. *Plow
through the bad ones*, he'd said, *and enjoy Dieter when he rallies*. Allina was
elated when Uncle stopped in the middle of breakfast and stretched his
arms overhead. Letting out a loud yawn, his bushy eyebrows lifted in surprise.

"Not too much pain today?" Auntie murmured. She straightened
the red-and-white-patterned wedding quilt over his stomach and leaned
down to kiss his cheek.

Uncle took the kiss and another bite of pumpernickel. "I haven't felt so
good in weeks." He turned to Allina with eyes that shone bright. "Nothing
on earth is as wonderful as your aunt's cooking. I don't know what it is,
child, but everything tastes delicious this morning."

"You ate every bit on your plate." Allina ran a hand down his arm, heart
skittering at the feel of his bones beneath the thick navy robe. Even Uncle's
smiles looked painful. His teeth seemed too big for his face.

Aunt Claudia topped off his coffee. "There are more eggs on the stove.
Would you like them?"

Uncle grabbed her hand and kissed it, earning two loud pecks on the
cheek before Auntie hurried back into the kitchen.

Allina plucked the worn copy of *Crime and Punishment* from the
bookshelf and tapped it against her palm. "Shall I read to you?"

"Not this morning," he said, patting the side of the bed. He winked
at Auntie when she came back with a plate of scrambled eggs. "We have
something more important to discuss."

Aunt Claudia hurried out of the room.

A warning circled in Allina's mind, but she perched on the edge of the
bed. Uncle probably wanted to talk about Albert, and she'd endure that
conversation if necessary, but she was furious. Allina hadn't received a
letter from him in more than a week.

Uncle took a long, measured breath, as if preparing for an argument. "Let me finish my breakfast first," he said, handing Allina a slice of pumpernickel. "Here. You're skinnier than I am." She spread on a thick layer of gooseberry jam to please him before taking a huge bite. They ate in companionable silence until Uncle spoke again.

"It's time for us to talk about your parents."

Allina sputtered, spraying crumbs across the quilt, and dropped the last bit of bread onto her lap. "Now?"

"Yes, now." Uncle Dieter chuckled and shook his head. "Unless you want to go to battle about that, too?"

But of course. It had to be now. The urgency was there, in her uncle's pained smiles and in the way his hand shook as he scooped her uneaten bread onto the plate and set it aside. Allina had wished for this her entire life. Yet, now that the moment was here, a part of her wanted to delay.

"I have letters from your father and . . . other items." Uncle pointed to the oak hutch. "There, in the bottom drawer. The old cigar box. Your aunt brought it up from the cellar this morning."

Allina found the worn H. Upmann box and brought it back to her uncle. It was filled with newspaper clippings, a manila envelope, and a thin packet of letters bound in red ribbon.

Clearing his throat, Uncle shuffled through the pile of correspondence before handing her an envelope. "Read this one first. Aloud, please." He closed his eyes and eased back against the pillow with a sigh. "It's been too long since I heard your father's words."

Allina's fingers shook as she pulled a single sheet of paper from the envelope. The page was brittle and crammed with bold, even handwriting. She lifted the paper to her nose. It smelled like old books, grassy and musty with hints of almond and vanilla.

With her heart drumming in her ears, she began to read.

7 May 1919

To my favorite sister and her husband,

I write with miraculous news. At last, I have found gainful employment.

Last week, I was on an omnibus when a great ape of a man took the seat next to mine. He had a look of one used to giving orders, like Father, Claudia.

I was eating grapes and offered them up. The man thanked me and took three. "I've had a horrible day," he said. "One of my best men quit without notice."

"I've had my share of bad days," I replied, "but aren't we lucky to live in the most exciting city in Germany?"

The man laughed, said he liked my attitude, and asked what I did for a living. I told him I had a job as a busboy, but I'd moved to Berlin to find work as a writer.

The man gave me a shrewd look, then reached into his coat pocket and handed over a calling card. He told me his name was Wolff, and that he was chief editor of the Tageblatt. Herr Wolff said he had a special position in mind, one that would teach me about the newspaper business. He invited me to call on him for an interview, which I did the next day.

My new boss is often rude and forever in motion. He barks orders and demands everything. I work long hours running errands, fetching coffee and meals, and checking facts for articles. I even clean the toilets!

Each morning, I beg Wolff to give me a chance, any small piece to write for the paper. His answer has been "No!" seven days in a row. But today I heard him laugh after I shut the door to his office. One day, he'll say yes.

Herr Schultz celebrated with me when I gave him the news and asked me to stay on at the café on the weekends. So I maintain my room above the restaurant and eat like a king when I come home.

Although I miss seeing your faces (and your strudel, Claudia) I was always meant to be a Berliner. My only regret is Father. He hasn't acknowledged my letters. I forgive him and hope he'll do the same for me, in time. I pray for you all.

Yours, Tomas

Allina pressed the letter over her heart as a sweet warmth filled her chest. "My father was a writer."

"Yes. Tomas had a special talent for writing, like you." He nodded toward the box. "Those articles are all his, published in the *Tageblatt*. You should read them later."

Uncle shifted over in bed, inviting her to sit closer. She curled up next to him and pressed her cheek to his. It was cool and damp and smelled faintly of shaving soap. "I want to know everything about him," she said.

"You're like your father in many ways," Uncle said. He ran fingers through her hair, working gently from crown to nape in the same way he'd done since she was a child. "Always full of questions, and with too much energy for your own good. Tomas had an enormous *wanderlust*." Uncle pronounced the last word with gusto. "He left us the week after his eighteenth birthday."

Uncle cleared his throat and paused, as if the next words were painful to speak. "When the riots broke out in Berlin, we were terrified. The country was starving, and Berlin had been ravaged by the Great War. We begged Tomas to come home, but he refused. Your grandfather never quite forgave him for that."

Uncle began coughing, hard enough to shake the bed. He accepted the water Allina poured and downed half a glass before settling back against the pillow with a sigh. "Give me a minute, child," he said, patting her hand.

Allina couldn't understand why her aunt and uncle had kept such precious details from her. Desperate to hear more, she waited until his wheezing calmed and the color returned to his cheeks.

"What about my mother?" she asked. "How did they meet?"

Uncle's lips turned down in regret. "Your parents found each other that summer, but we never knew her. There was no money to spare for a visit." He went through the packet of letters and withdrew another. "This will tell you more about Irene. Read it next."

The fear in his eyes raised the hairs on the backs of her arms, but Allina shook off her unease and began.

15 July 1920

To my Allina's beloved aunt and uncle,

A proud papa writes you today, with so much joy my pen shakes on the page. Irene and I have made a wondrous thing, a perfect baby girl. Allina is such a tiny bit. I can hold her whole body in my hands.

When I gaze into my daughter's face, I'm filled with equal amounts of love and terror. Love because I've never seen anything more beautiful. Terror because Germany is going mad. You warned me before my marriage, and perhaps the consequences are inevitable. But I had no choice. Irene is my heart.

If we followed my wife's custom, we'd raise Allina in the Jewish faith.

Allina's mouth went dry. "My mother was Jewish?" she whispered. Uncle nodded. "Keep reading."

Irene insists we raise her as a Lutheran. She makes her choice out of fear, but I can't fault her feelings any more than I can deny what is happening to our country. Last week, two men followed Irene's brother home and kicked his cane out from under his feet. David, who earned the Iron Cross and served with the men who left him sprawled in the street.

These men are thugs. They glorify violence and call it strength. Yet, the Berliners are sympathetic. Too many men are without work and unable to feed their children. I have seen their despair. They make the Jews their scapegoat. Now Adolf Hitler with his 25-Point Plan claims my family are aliens in their own country.

Although Irene will miss her family, we are in agreement. It's time to come home. I hope reading this will bring a smile to your lips, even if our reason does not.

My new family will return to Badensburg by Christmas. I need you to see this miracle we've made. I want you to know my wife.

Yours, Tomas

Allina struggled to breathe through the ache in her chest. As a child, she'd fantasized about her parents, giving them glamorous jobs and exciting lives. But in all her wild imaginings, she'd never conjured this.

"Tomas and Irene died three months later in an omnibus crash." Uncle's voice sounded like it was coming from far away, and she was barely aware of the hand he placed on her arm. "My greatest regret is not meeting your mother. My greatest joy came when Irene's parents brought you to live with us. We agreed it would be safer."

Heat bloomed in her cheeks. For years, Allina's aunt and uncle had avoided all questions about her parents, even when she'd begged. Now here was the reason. They'd hidden the truth about her birth mother to protect her, and with her Jewish grandparents' blessing—grandparents she'd never know now. Aunt Claudia and Uncle Dieter had kept Allina safe but at a hideous cost, and even as her friends had disappeared.

Her tongue was thick and heavy in her mouth. "So my papers—"

He took her hand, squeezed it when she tried to pull away. "Your papers are based on a forged birth certificate, but your real one is still filed in Berlin. You cannot move to the city, child. Not while Hitler is Führer. Irene was Jewish. That makes you *Mischling*." Uncle's voice cracked. "You know what this means. Hitler has already pushed *Mischling* out of polite society. He's taken away jobs, deprived them of schooling. We don't know what more he will do."

The panic hit, high in her belly, and it nearly bent her over.

Uncle tried to wipe the tears from Allina's cheeks, but she sprang up to pace the room. It wasn't the truth about her mother that devastated her. It was the lie. Her aunt and uncle loved her, she'd always believed that. They'd raised Allina as their own. But they hadn't trusted her with the truth—a truth so dangerous it could destroy them all.

The need to run was strong—out of the room, out of this house, anywhere as long as it was away from him. But there was nowhere for Allina to go now, nowhere safe, not in all of Germany.

Uncle withdrew the manila envelope from the box and slapped it against the side of the bed. "Come here. Please, Allina. There's more you must know."

More. How much more could there be? She marched back to his bedside, took the envelope from his hand, and emptied the contents onto the mattress—a birth certificate and papers, all in the name of Allina Gottlieb.

"These offer you a new identity." Uncle pushed the papers into her hands. "If you're compelled to flee, you must destroy your papers and use these."

Allina traced the edges of the documents, which were dog-eared and distressed. "They look real." It was strange how calm her voice was, despite the wild drumming in her throat, the high-pitched ringing in her ears.

Uncle held her gaze, watching her closely. "They're excellent forgeries, good enough to buy you time. One of Albert's contacts created them last year."

For a moment the room seemed to spin. "Albert?"

He nodded again and watched her with glistening eyes.

The truth hit again, like a physical blow. Albert had known—and he, too, had kept the truth from her. The thought was unbearable.

"Albert doesn't work as a bank clerk, does he?" she asked, sinking down onto the bed.

"Actually, he does," Uncle said. "But the important work is done after hours."

Allina balled her fists to keep from crying out. "Why hasn't Albert come home?"

Uncle extracted the documents from her fists and laid them down on his lap, smoothing out the wrinkles with care. "Hitler will expel thousands of Polish Jews from Germany by the end of this month. These men and women have lost their Polish citizenship. They have nowhere to go. Albert is helping who he can."

Allina bent over at the waist to fend off a growing dizziness, the need to throw up. It was too much, too fast to make sense of.

"In your heart, you know he's a good man," Uncle said. "Good men do what they must."

"Do good men lie to the people they love?"

Her barb struck home. Dieter winced. "Sometimes, yes, if they're afraid the truth will hurt those they love."

When she shook her head, he sighed. "We've saved dozens of families these past two years. I know you'll be happy about that, even if you're angry with me."

Allina swayed a little as another realization hit.

"The Neumanns," she whispered. *I have been such a fool.*

Uncle's smile was beatific. "They're in Dragør, safe for the moment."

Allina stared at her uncle. *I would have helped them—helped you, and Albert. But you didn't want my help. All you wanted was my silence.* Perhaps he was finally happy, now that he'd gotten it. She had nothing more to say.

Uncle coughed again, gasped for a breath. He sipped from the glass of water, then took her hands in his. Allina didn't have it in her to pull away.

"You're the child of my heart," Uncle said. "We kept our secrets to keep you safe. Albert loves you. He'll protect you." He pointed at the forged documents. "Those papers offer you a way out of Badensburg if things fall apart." Uncle's voice grew faint as his eyes fluttered closed. "I'm too tired to continue. We'll finish later. Tomorrow." He roused enough to push the box into her hands. "Read the letters and your father's articles. They're your inheritance." He gripped her arm again. "I love you, child."

Allina kissed him on the cheek before she ran out of the room, holding all that was left of her parents in an old cigar box clutched to her chest.

CHAPTER 4

ALLINA

Allina yanked open her aunt and uncle's wardrobe, searching for Uncle's burial suit. Picking through the crammed row of clothing, she ran fingers over the cotton dress shirts and smart twill slacks, the coarser wool trousers and mended chambray work shirts, and his battered gray overcoat. Allina pressed her face to his worsted sweaters, all redolent with the sharp bite of tobacco leaves and mint.

It wasn't here.

Allina's body ached with bone-deep tiredness. She sank down onto the bed, closed her eyes, and willed her mind blank, focusing on the beat of her heart.

The sound of Aunt Claudia's footsteps stomping up the stairs roused her. "I'm sorry," Allina said, rushing to the doorway. "I couldn't find his clothes. Then I sat down for a moment and lost myself."

Aunt Claudia's face was chalky against her black mourning dress, but her gray eyes were soft, concerned. "We have hours," she said, cradling Allina's hot cheeks between cool, rough palms. "Most of the neighbors won't arrive until noon."

Auntie reached into the back of the cupboard and found his suit. She pressed the jacket to her face before handing it to Allina. "Here it is, darling," she said, eyes bright with tears. She hurried to the bathroom and returned with a stiff bristle brush and a bowl of water. "Just clean and press the suit," she added. "He always looked so handsome in it. And the work will settle you."

Settle me? Everything had changed yesterday. Everything. Allina couldn't get past this anger, or her bitterness. Grief and guilt choked her.

She hung the wool jacket on a peg on the wardrobe and brushed it with sharp, angry strokes. Sure enough, the brush slipped from her hands and clattered to the floor. "I didn't get to say good-bye," Allina whispered, wrapping her arms around her middle. "He told me he loved me, but I didn't say it back."

Auntie hugged her close. "Hush," she murmured into Allina's hair. "Your uncle knew how much you loved him."

Allina wiggled out of her aunt's grip. She didn't want to be held. It only made things worse. Her aunt was brokenhearted, but it took everything in her to keep from running out of the room. "I'm still angry. My life is a lie."

Auntie gripped Allina's shoulders. "Our love for you is not a lie. We did what was necessary, to protect you. You were a stubborn, hotheaded child, always reacting without thinking about consequences."

Allina shook her head, even as the truth hit home.

"Listen to me," Auntie said. "Your uncle's last thoughts were of you. Dieter made me swear to keep you safe."

Allina plopped down onto the mattress. The anger seeped slowly out of her body, allowing the emptiness of exhaustion to take its place. "But he never woke up," she said.

Auntie's face crumpled. "No . . . no, he didn't," she said. Auntie took a handkerchief out of her pocket and blew into it. "Have your anger if you need it, but remember how much he loved you."

Scrubbing the last tears from her cheeks, Allina got up to retrieve the brush. She dipped it into the bowl of water and swept the brush down the garment, removing stray flecks of lint with every swipe.

Auntie turned back to the wardrobe. Fishing inside, she pulled out a white collared shirt and examined it for wrinkles. "What will you do about Albert?" she asked softly.

Mention of him only engendered despair. "I knew something was

wrong from his letters," Allina said. "They were strange. Distant. I thought there might be another girl. In Berlin."

"Oh, darling, no. No." Auntie let out a tired gust of air. "It was difficult for him to keep the truth from you. He and Dieter argued about it for two long years. Albert wanted to tell you everything."

But he didn't.

"Will you marry him? You need his protection, now more than ever," she said. "He loves you."

Allina looked away.

"Give yourself time to sort your feelings out." Auntie's fingers were gentle as they brushed Allina's hair back from her face. "When he comes home for Christmas, speak to him. Share what's in your heart."

Loud pounding at the front door interrupted her aunt's advice.

"That will be Karin and Fritz," Auntie said. "I'll get the door. Dieter's pants and shirt need ironing. I'll send Karin up to help you with his shoes."

Allina went back to work, soaking a cotton rag with water and placing it over the fabric of his pants. She was eager to see her friends—even Fritz, who'd brought dinner over last night and sat with them in silence. Today there would be shared grief, and no arguments.

She listened for the welcome sounds of their voices, pressing the iron to the cloth until wisps of steam curled in the air, erasing the wrinkles and leaving neat creases in their wake. For a few moments Allina relaxed into the mindless task of making her uncle's suit look its best.

When Aunt Claudia returned, her face was as white as the walls. "We have a problem," she said, holding up a small piece of paper. "A stranger delivered this note for your uncle. When I told him Dieter was dead, the man ran off."

Allina plucked the paper from her aunt's hand and scanned the short message.

Expulsion plans to be accelerated. Concerned about security. Have you heard from Mannheim?

"Mannheim," Allina murmured. She turned the paper over, but the other side was blank. "They ask if he's been in contact with Albert." Her cheeks began to burn. She'd been so angry she hadn't worried about his safety.

Auntie turned away, hands steepled over her nose and mouth, and began to pace. "Your uncle never shared the details of his activities with me. He told me to rely on Albert." Her voice grew shriller. "What plans? What security?"

The panic in her aunt's voice made Allina's stomach turn over. "We must burn this note," Allina whispered, handing back the piece of paper.

Auntie took a shaky breath. "Yes. I'll go downstairs and do that right now."

"Are there other papers to worry about?" The sour tang of fear hit the back of Allina's throat. "Should we go through his desk?"

Aunt Claudia's nod was immediate. "I'll take care of it." She hugged Allina close. "Finish pressing his suit, then try to rest until Karin and Fritz arrive. It's going to be a long day."

Auntie squared her shoulders and walked to the door. When she turned back, Allina glimpsed once again the steady, confident woman who'd raised her.

"We'll cope with whatever comes, and we'll handle it together, child. Today, and in all the days to come."

CHAPTER 5

Two Days Later

ALLINA

.

She woke from a dead sleep to a staccato burst of gunshots. Allina clutched the quilt close, heart stuttering in the inky darkness.

A panicked chorus of screams pierced the air, jolting her into motion. She jumped out of bed and ran to her aunt and uncle's bedroom. It was empty.

Barefoot and in her nightgown, Allina rushed downstairs and onto the front porch. She tripped and stumbled, landing on something soft. Looking down, she realized Aunt Claudia's body was beneath hers. She inched her face closer, only to spring back with a shriek. Auntie's eyes were open wide, a small black hole marked her forehead, and a dark puddle of liquid pooled beneath her skull.

Nooooooo! Her fingers twitched as she dragged them through the warm liquid, and the cloying, coppery scent made her gag. Pulling Aunt Claudia's head into her lap, Allina rocked, whimpering as she clutched it against her belly. She needed to keep Aunt Claudia warm.

Auntie's face began to flicker with an eerie, orange light. A blast of heat and the crash of splintering wood and shattering glass made Allina shield her eyes as the barn across the road exploded in flames, illuminating the porch with reflected fire. Thick clouds of charcoal smoke billowed from the barn's windows, and the fumes stung her lungs. It was all but impossible to breathe. The animals inside the barn bellowed in terror and began bashing their bodies against the walls in loud, crunching thumps.

Get up! Allina scrambled on hands and knees to the edge of the porch. When she tried to stand, her legs buckled and she careened down the steps, scraping her arms and legs before landing in the dirt. She stayed down, dizzy and shivering, coughing through grit and smoke as she tried to fill her aching lungs.

The animals in the barn were louder now, shrieking in pain, and Allina moaned with them, watching helplessly, hypnotized by the licks of fire traveling up the barn's walls to the roof before the shingles exploded in a violent shower of sparks and ash. The ash fell on two bodies, lying prone in the street, their arms and legs bent at impossible angles.

The sky lit up. It wasn't just the barn. Three other buildings on this street and the next were on fire.

Two officers rushed down the road, boot heels sounding on the pavement. They pounded on the neighbor's door until the Beckers answered, wielding hand-fashioned weapons.

"You have no business here," Herr Becker shouted. He pushed one officer back with a wood plank.

Frau Becker stepped in front of her husband as if to shield him. When her eyes met Allina's, they widened in panic.

"Save yourself," she called out. "Run!"

Get up, get up, get up! Gripping the porch steps, she slid her arms under her body and, with a brutal push, rose to standing.

The officers' heads whipped around. Seeing her, they shouted to each other.

Adrenaline kicked in, and she rushed into the house and out the back door, sprinting for the forest. Allina dove into the underbrush and buried herself beneath a pile of leaves, shredding her fingers as she dug herself into the ground. She whimpered in the cool dampness, the scent of decaying leaves filling her nose. Her lungs rebelled, urging her to cough, so she shoved her face into the loam to muffle the sound. Minutes may have passed, or an hour. Were they gone? There was no way to be sure.

Then rough hands wrapped around her ankles and dragged her, screaming, out of the pile of leaves.

"Who do we have here?" The hands turned Allina over, hauled her to her feet, and smacked her cheeks until they stung.

"Come, girlie, don't you want to play?" The soldier reeked of blood and smoke and sweat. When she tried to pull away, he slapped her hard across the face, stealing her breath.

"No!" She sobbed, head swimming, as two, then three, then four soldiers formed a tight ring around her. "Let me go," she begged.

The soldiers laughed, taunting Allina as they moved in, dark figures advancing in the shadowy night. She couldn't make out their faces, or see their eyes, but she pleaded for mercy. They grabbed her, nails biting into her flesh as they ripped the nightgown off her body. The frigid air raised goose bumps on her skin and she struggled to cover herself.

"No. Please. *No!*" When she stumbled and fell, they turned her over, shoved her face into the ground. Arching her neck back, she spat out dirt and gave a shrill cry.

No! Allina writhed in the muck, straining to get free. She managed a kick that drove one of the men to his knees screaming, clutching between his legs.

"Bitch!"

They flipped her onto her back, and one of the soldiers slammed the butt of his rifle into her skull. Her head filled with a bright, searing pain.

Then nothing, blessed blankness.

When Allina came to, they were still cursing her, pawing at her breasts, yanking her hair. One unbuttoned his pants and lowered himself onto her with a crude grunt. He clawed at her underwear, but she kept her legs clamped together and twisted away from the groping hands and rank mix of sour breath and sweat.

A shrill whistle pierced the night. "Report to the village square. *Now.*"

The soldier let out a vicious curse and jumped to his feet, buttoned his pants. He pulled her up roughly, slung her over his shoulder—and cursed again as Allina emptied the contents of her stomach down his back.

She slipped back into the fog.

The return to consciousness was slow. There was a sense of warmth at first, of the sun's rays on her cheeks, and then a gentle breeze that produced uncontrollable shivers. Allina moaned with each minuscule, reflexive movement. Every centimeter of her skin was alive with pain. *So thirsty.* It was hard to unstick her tongue from the roof of her mouth.

The agony in her head was the worst. Even the slightest motion made her stomach lurch. She tried to lift her eyelids, but the pain drove into her skull so she squeezed them shut again, fighting to control the sick dizziness. The ground underneath her felt uneven, and something large and round dug into the small of her back.

And the acrid stench of metal and woodsmoke—it was overwhelming.

How long had she been asleep? Whimpering, Allina probed her head cautiously. Her fingers came away sticky and warm. Venturing upward, they found a small wound and traced the slow trickle of bleeding down the right side of her face. She cracked her eyes open. The sight of her arms and legs, bruised and streaked with mud, brought back flashes of memory in a horrifying rush.

No! Allina rolled over.

Her eyes met Frau Becker's. She touched her neighbor's cheek, but the woman's eyes were dull. Sightless. Her skin was gray and cold.

Choking back a moan, Allina craned her neck and saw a sea of lifeless forms. She was lying on them, all the dead bodies. The lumps pressing into her back were the skulls of her neighbors.

She heard an animal's tortured, high-pitched howl . . .

"Noooooooooooooo—"

. . . and scrabbled off the hill of corpses, tumbling to the ground as bodies shifted and slid off the pile.

Realizing *her* voice was the source of the screams, she stuffed a fist in her mouth to muffle the sound.

Fighting back panic, Allina took her bearings. She was in the town square.

Nowhere to hide.

When two officers ran toward her, laughing and calling out for her to stay and play, she rose up, attempting to flee. The constricted muscles in her legs gave out, and she collapsed to the ground.

The sharp crack of three gunshots filled the air.

An officer in a *Schutzstaffel* uniform walked toward her, his boot heels echoing on the cobblestones. The man was short and slight. His hair was gray, his gait energetic. As the officer approached, Allina lowered her gaze to the ground, until all she could see were the tips of his black polished boots.

"Stand up," he ordered.

The muscles in her thighs screamed, but she hauled herself upright, shivering as she tried to cover her breasts. Allina risked a peek upward, and they locked gazes. His eyes were a ruthless ice blue, so pale they appeared silver.

He took off his coat and threw it at her. She clutched it against her body.

"What is your name?" the officer asked.

She swayed before righting herself. If she told him the truth, he'd kill her.

"What is your name?" he demanded, his face turning a mottled red.

"A-Allina," she said, remembering the fake papers Uncle had given her only two days ago. "Allina Gottlieb."

"You're indecent," he bit out, lips curling back as he looked her over.

Allina lowered her head and shook, stared at his boots again. Another wave of dizziness hit, but she managed to keep from dropping to the ground. The officer took a step closer. He chuckled when she cowered and began walking around her in a slow circle. She squeezed her eyes shut.

The officer grabbed her chin and jerked it up. "Open your eyes," he commanded. When she did, he brushed the soot from her cheeks and tilted her head back and forth, examining her as if she were a vase or a piece of jewelry. Allina bore his scrutiny without flinching, but she couldn't stop trembling.

"Voss!" the officer shouted.

A soldier trotted up. "Yes, *Gruppenführer* Gud." He was young, with a round face spotted with pimples. The soldier's eyes slid down her body before darting away. His cheeks flushed a dull red.

"Take this one to her house," Gud commanded. "Allow her to dress and bathe."

"Yes, *Gruppenführer*." Voss straightened his spine.

He shifted his attention back to Allina. "Pack a suitcase. Take sturdy clothing. Nothing of value." The general's voice was as hard as his gaze. "Do you understand?"

Allina nodded and clutched the jacket to her body.

Gud scribbled on a piece of paper, signed it with a flourish, and gave it to Voss. "Show these orders to anyone who questions you."

The soldier saluted. "Yes, *Gruppenführer*."

"You will not touch her. You will allow no one to touch her."

The boy swallowed, throat muscles working hard. "Of course, *Gruppenführer*."

"Be back in an hour."

The soldier saluted again. "*Heil* Hitler."

"*Heil* Hitler." Gud turned back to Allina. "Cover yourself," he ordered, gesturing at the coat she was holding against her body, "and make sure to wash. You're filthy." He walked off without another glance.

Allina wound the coat around her body, struggling to belt it with fingers that twitched. She kept her distance from the soldier as they walked to her house. Although she gave the directions, Voss stayed a half step ahead. He nodded to the officers who passed, but blocked her from their view. Allina heard the jokes as the soldiers walked by, the rough comments, the snickers. She kept her eyes to the ground.

When they got to the house, Auntie's body was no longer on the porch, although a smear of blood remained. Allina stepped around it and walked inside.

The sturdy oak furniture and her aunt's pretty rose-patterned china and linens were smashed, shredded, ruined. She trailed her finger along the length of a bookcase, and a low mewling rose in her throat. The oiled wood was still silky and beautiful, but the shelves were splintered apart. There was nothing left.

The young officer motioned up the stairs. "Be back down in half an hour," he said, as she limped up the staircase. "Hurry."

The soldiers must have been called away before they could destroy the second floor, because her room was untouched. She hurried to the closet and selected her gray wool coat, five plain dresses, and sturdy shoes. When she tugged her suitcase from the top shelf, her uncle's cigar box fell to the floor. The contents spilled in a pile at her feet.

Her father's letters, his newspaper articles. There'd been no time to read them. If the *Schutzstaffel* found these, they'll kill her for sure, but these bits of paper were all she had left of her family. Leaving the documents behind was risky, and the thought of destroying them, unbearable, so she wedged them under the dresses in her suitcase.

She had to get clean. Allina limped into the bathroom and jerked the cabinet door open, searching for a washcloth. A small sewing kit fell to the floor. She picked up the kit and froze.

My God, my God, I will wear my secrets.

Allina hobbled back into her bedroom and worked with frantic speed, detaching the coat's lining in three places, then sewing the letters and clippings into the lining and inside pockets before sealing them shut. She examined her handiwork, checking the needlework and patting down the coat. Her stitches were neat enough. The papers made a soft, crinkly sound, but not so much that most would notice. Rushing, she threw her clothes and the sewing kit into the suitcase, along with her new papers—the forged ones for Allina Gottlieb.

She hurried back into the bathroom and turned on the bath. One glance in the mirror made her stumble back in shock. The girl in the glass had ashen skin, a swollen, split lip, and stark cheekbones beneath a layer of grime and soot. The right side of her head was caked with blood.

Allina soaked the washcloth and held it to her hairline before rubbing off the crusty mess of blood and grime. The wound began seeping again, but at least it wasn't covered in dirt.

Shivering, she climbed into the tub, scrubbing furiously at her body with soap and a brush. Her throat ached but no tears would come—in some far corner of her mind, she wondered why—but her stomach quaked and her limbs jerked, uncontrollably at times, as she washed. The blood and filth melted into the water, swirling in sanguine curls before disappearing down the drain.

Her skin was raw by the time she stepped out of the tub. But she was clean, and she'd stopped trembling.

Allina tackled her old papers next, shredding and soaking them in hot water before tossing the pulpy mass in the trash. *Allina Strauss is dead.* She dressed quickly without looking in the mirror, yanking on her coat over a navy dress and slipping shoes over wool hose.

Suitcase in hand, she limped down the stairs to find Voss in the kitchen, stuffing his face with food he'd raided from Auntie's larder. He blinked when he saw her before pushing hunks of bread and cheese into her hands. "We have to hurry," he said, gesturing to the door. "Eat while you walk." She managed a few bites of yesterday's bread before tossing the rest away.

When they arrived at the square, the *Gruppenführer* was at luncheon, seated outdoors in front of the ApfelHaus Café at a table set with white linen and fine china. The table was covered with a cooked chicken, roasted potatoes, vegetables, bread, fruit, and wine. The sky was blue. The sun was out. Silverware and crystal glinted in the sunlight. And the *Gruppenführer* sat there with his back turned to the piles of bodies, although their images were reflected clearly in the café's windows. How could he not see them?

She began to shake again.

Gud dismissed Voss with a wave of his hand. "Sensible clothes, sturdy shoes." He didn't smile, but his eyes lifted at the corners as he examined her. "Are you hungry?"

Allina shook her head.

"You won't mind if I eat." He motioned for her to sit and tucked into his food. Allina perched on the edge of the chair, careful to angle her head so the corpses weren't directly in front of her.

Only last Saturday, the square had been filled with the aroma of warm strudel and boisterous greetings from her neighbors as farmers, food vendors, and shop owners offered their wares. It was here where children shrieked with joy on pony rides each spring, got their fingers sticky with fresh blackberries in summer, and dunked for apples every autumn.

Now the town square was silent, save for Gud, who ate with gusto as he called out orders to his men. Several walked around with clipboards, making notes. Some went through clothing, scavenging jewelry and personal items, while others hauled trash and the dead from one location to another. A small group of officers at the center of the town square operated moviemaking equipment.

"They're documenting today for the Reich and our Führer," Gud said before shoveling in another enormous mouthful of food.

The *Gruppenführer* offered neither an additional explanation nor the reason for the massacre of what looked to be dozens of innocent people. Allina swallowed hard, tasting bile as her stomach threatened to rebel. Perhaps a third of the townspeople, murdered. She didn't dare ask why.

She scanned the piles of bodies but couldn't glimpse Karin's face among the corpses. There was no way to know if her best friend was dead or alive. *Please let her be safe.* Karin and the precious, unborn child she carried. Every structure facing the square had its shutters closed, curtains drawn. Any villagers within, if alive, were out of sight, in hiding.

Allina shuddered and closed her eyes. There was nowhere safe, now. Nowhere to run.

"Our country is better for the events of this day," Gud added. "I'd accept that reality sooner, rather than later. Your life . . . it's different now." He gestured at the piles of bodies with his fork before taking another huge bite of food. "You must choose a new life today, one not tied to this town."

The man was insane. They'd killed dozens of men and women in her village. Hysterical laughter bubbled up, but she choked it down.

"Why are you helping me?" she managed.

"You remind me of my granddaughter," the *Gruppenführer* answered. "Your features and coloring, the way you hold your head are all very much like my Giselle. You have the spirit of the Reich." When Allina shook her head, he gave her a warning look. "I'd claim that spirit, if I were you. It's your choice now. To live or to die." He took a healthy gulp of wine, smacked his lips. "Why am I helping you? Because I can. Trust me, you don't want to throw this chance away."

Allina's gaze darted between the mountains of corpses and the bountiful feast on the table. He took another bite of food. A bit of meat, shiny with fat, was stuck in the corner of his mouth as he chewed. Her stomach rebelled and she hobbled to the side of the building, retching up the bread she'd eaten. Allina stayed there, bent nearly in half and gasping from the pain.

She was trapped. Out of options.

Wiping her mouth, she walked back to the table.

Gud stood up and nodded. "You're a strong one. Good girl. Follow me."

"Hold still," the doctor ordered, as he tended Allina's head wound. "One last stitch." They were standing by the *Gruppenführer*'s automobile, and the doctor was clearly put out, working in haste while two officers packed the vehicle.

Allina couldn't silence her gasps. Her body was a single, massive bruise. The stitches burned and the side of her face throbbed with hot, dense pain. Shivering, she gritted her teeth, did her best to remain motionless. The sun was high in the sky, but she couldn't get warm.

Clipboard in hand, Gud glanced up from the papers he was signing. "Be quick about it, Baehr. We need to get on the road while there's daylight left."

"Yes, *Gruppenführer*." The doctor snipped the last suture and placed a sticking plaster on the wound with a surprisingly gentle touch.

Exhaustion overtook her, and Allina sagged against the side of the vehicle. Her eyes fluttered closed.

"You must change the dressing once a day," the doctor instructed, "and wash around the wound. Don't get the sutures wet." He tapped her cheeks until she opened her eyes. "Do you understand me?" His gray gaze was sharp, but not unkind.

Allina nodded.

"In three days, take the bandage off." He pressed on the edges of the sticking plaster again, and she let out an involuntary cry, eyes watering from the pain.

"Enough," Gud said. "We're late as it is."

The doctor backed off. "*Heil* Hitler!" he said, and saluted.

"*Heil* Hitler!" Gud saluted before turning to Allina. "Get in the car."

She climbed into the back, hissing as she slid onto the glossy leather seat. The cushions were plush, but they pressed against every bruise. When Gud hopped in beside her, she moved into the far corner and turned to the window, trying to make herself as small as possible. She pressed her cheek to the cool glass and let out a sigh.

"Be quiet," Gud ordered. "I have work to do."

She fell into a deep sleep before the car made it to the main road.

She woke to hands forcing her thighs apart. Gud pulled her skirt up, shoved her hose and panties down, and pushed her onto her back.

"No! Stop!" She pummeled his shoulders and clawed at his hair.

He reared back and slapped her so hard her ears rang.

"You told me I reminded you of your granddaughter," she begged.

There was desperation and madness in his silver gaze. For a moment, Albert's warm amber eyes flashed in her mind, and she choked on a sob.

Gud shoved her knees up again, and spread her legs. He cursed as he fumbled with the buttons of his trousers.

Allina tried to resist, to shove him off, but her arms and legs would no longer obey. Closing her eyes, she angled her head and pressed her nose into the leather seat cushion, away from the stench and sight of the monster above her. When he entered her the pain was excruciating and stole her breath.

Make it stop. Please make it stop.

Her mind turned inward, and random sounds and smells and images flitted through her consciousness. Gottestränen Lake at sunset. The soft, rhythmic clicking of Auntie's knitting needles. Sweet, yeasty bread dough. Uncle reading from the *Tageblatt* at breakfast. Warm candle wax and incense. Eventually, the memories ceased and Allina was enveloped in quiet. The pain was gone.

When Allina opened her eyes, she was gazing down at their bodies. Gud was thrusting in a crude, urgent rhythm while her own limp form lay across the back seat, unresisting.

She tried to call out but couldn't make a sound.

Am I dead?

A bright light flashed and she slid into nothingness.

She roused to rough hands shaking her.

"Make yourself presentable," Gud barked. "We've arrived."

CHAPTER 6

June 2006
Englewood, New Jersey

KATRINE

"He was responsible for the death of my aunt Claudia and dozens of our neighbors," Mama murmurs. Her eyes are bright with tears.

My mother has shared the details of her suffering for nearly an hour in a halting voice that made me weep. At times, she spoke in little more than a whisper. At others, she couldn't look me in the eye. As I listened, and as my horror grew, it took all my strength to keep from interrupting—to just let her get the words out and hold her trembling hand.

Why was Badensburg targeted? I'm afraid to press my mother with this question. The space between us is still too heavy with grief. And my heart aches, both for the girl who lost everything at the hands of monsters, and the woman who has borne that pain alone for nearly seventy years. She's kept these secrets, her deepest pain, from me my entire life. How lonely she must have been.

"I'm sorry, Mama. I'm so sorry." She closes her eyes when I cup her cheek, then leans into my palm. "Do you need to rest? Should we stop now?"

She shakes her head immediately. "No. No, I want to continue. I only need a minute."

This openness, her willingness to talk about her history, is something I've longed for all my life. It terrifies me now.

Wrapping an arm around her shoulders, I ease us back against the sofa cushions and run my fingers through her hair. She relaxes with a sigh, lays her head against mine.

My mother has never let me hold her like this. In all my life, I can't remember a single time when she allowed me to offer comfort. There have been so many walls between us. Perhaps I've never really known her at all.

The realization breaks me all over again.

"You were brave," I whisper, letting the tears fall. "Braver than anyone I know."

She snorts, a small, welcome sign of feistiness. "I was too stubborn to let Gud win. The man is long dead and buried by now."

And burning in hell, if there's any justice. Rage hits, and I hold her tighter, every muscle in my body taut, readying for a fight against an invisible opponent. But anger won't help. I concentrate on breathing instead, and on her hair, which smells of lavender shampoo.

Taking my hand, she threads our fingers together. "Once I tell you everything, you'll understand. You'll know why I could never speak about the past."

"But I do understand. You were brutalized. You lost your family—"

"No, *Katchen*. There's more to it than that. Much more." She takes a deep breath. "When we came to America, I knew if I worked hard, if I was patient, we could make a life here. But I had to let go of Germany first. There was no other way to survive." She pins me with the intensity of her gaze. "And it wasn't easy being German in this country after the war."

Kraut. Filthy Nazi. Murderer. How often had I run home crying after being called those names? Too many. Children are cruel, but they learn from their parents. Plenty of adults hurled the same slurs at us in the market. My mother's thick German accent had drawn out every bigot in Englewood, like pastry crumbs lure cockroaches out of the dark.

"I remember."

"I wanted you to grow up with every opportunity. That meant speaking and living, even thinking like an American. I forced us to turn our backs on Germany. There was nothing, *nothing,* good left in that country."

There's more to be said, much more. It's in her eyes, her hesitation and careful wording.

Heaving another sigh, she points our joined hands at the box, lying in wait on the coffee table. "I'm sure you have many questions."

Everything she's shared, and every item in that box, raises questions. *Why did she keep our Jewish heritage from me? What happened to Albert? Who the hell is my father?*

I want to ask them all. But the pain in her eyes, the trembling compression of lips, reminds me to slow down. My mother has kept these secrets for more than sixty years. She needs to tell her truth her way, and in her own time.

"Just tell me what happened next, Mama. Where did Gud take you?"

Mother grabs the box, takes out a postcard, and hands it to me. On the front is a photo of a building that looks like a school or a hospital. The back reads *Die Mutter-häuser des Lebensborn.*

"Gud took me to Hochland Home in Steinhöring, not far from Munich. It was a *Lebensborn* home. One of the Reich's most heinous secrets."

My stomach clenches at the thought of what that could mean, but I'm too afraid to ask. So once again, I wait.

"It was a baby factory."

PART 2

Steinhöring

SS ORDER FOR THE ENTIRE SS AND POLICE

Every war is a letting of the best blood. For the people, many a military victory has, at the same time, been a shattering defeat of their blood and vital power. The death of the best men—which, deplorable though it may be, is an unfortunate necessity—is not the worst consequence. Much worse is the lack of children.

A man can die peacefully if he knows his family and everything he and his ancestors have worked for will continue through his children. The best gift for a widow is the children of the man she loved.

Beyond the boundaries of civil laws and customs, there is also the high task, outside marriage, for German women and girls of good blood to become, not through frivolity but from a deep moral sense, mothers of children by soldiers going to war. Only fate can tell if those soldiers will come home or fall for Germany.

Also, the holy duty for men and women, whose place is at home by State command, is to continue to reproduce themselves. We cannot forget that victory and the shed blood of our soldiers would be meaningless if not followed by colonization of the new soil.

In the last war, many a soldier decided to produce no more children during military conflict because of concern for his wife's welfare in the event of his death.

This factor need not be considered by you SS men, for any such anxieties are obviated by the following provisions:

(i) For all legitimate and illegitimate children of good blood whose fathers have been killed in the war, special trustees personally chosen in the name of the Reichsführer SS will assume guardianship. We will stand by the mothers of these children and will make ourselves materially responsible for the education and upbringing of the children themselves.

(ii) In cases of affliction or distress, the SS will care for all children, legitimate or not, and for all pregnant mothers. After the war, if the fathers return, the SS will give generous economical help if an individually proved application is made.

SS men and mothers of these children, prove that in your readiness to fight and die for Germany you are also prepared to pass on life for it!

[Signed] H. Himmler
The Reichsführer SS

CHAPTER 7

Hochland Home
Steinhöring

MARGUERITE ZIEGLER

Marguerite Ziegler rolled over in bed and flicked on the lamp to check the clock on her night table. It was 1:17 a.m. The bright headlights and loud roar of an engine were impossible to ignore, even if she wanted to. Visitors at this late hour usually meant an emergency of some sort—or that a high-ranking official was here on a matter of great urgency.

Either way, as head nurse, it was her responsibility to greet them.

"*Schwester* Ziegler, reporting for duty," she murmured. She struggled out of bed and into her standard brown uniform, ran a brush through her brown, frizzy nest.

A barrage of pounding sent her scurrying down the stairs. When she opened the front door and saw *Gruppenführer* Reinhardt Gud tapping his foot with impatience, Marguerite snapped to attention.

"*Heil* Hitler, *Gruppenführer!*" Marguerite straightened her collar and glanced at his companion, a pale young woman in a shabby gray coat.

"*Heil* Hitler, *Schwester* Ziegler. I believe you were expecting us?" Gud brushed past Marguerite and strode into the intake office, dragging the young woman behind him.

"Of course, *Gruppenführer*," Marguerite said, hurrying after them. "Dr. Baehr called to tell me you'd be here today." Though not at this hour.

Thank goodness she'd had Ida-Lynne oil the furniture and shake out the carpets yesterday. Any visit from a high-ranking officer demanded perfection. "I apologize for making you wait. Medical Chief Engel is aiding *Oberführer* Ebner with new testing programs this week, and we're short-staffed—"

"Fine," Gud said, waving away her apology. "The two girls I referred to you last week have settled in?"

"They have, *Gruppenführer*." She took a closer look at the young woman at his side. Although the girl was neat and clean, her bottom lip was swollen, there was bruising on her neck, and a large bandage covered a considerable portion of skin above her right eye. She was also trembling and too pale. Shock, perhaps. The young lady reminded Marguerite of some of the women she'd nursed toward the end of the Great War, not her Hochland Home girls.

"Is this our new resident?"

"She is." Gud's hand supported the girl's elbow, and he urged her forward. "Allina may already be carrying my child, *Schwester*, in service to the Reich."

The young woman's gaze drifted to the wall. While she seemed not to have heard their conversation, the bruises on her neck, which were in the shape of four fingers and a thumb, darkened. Marguerite suppressed a shudder, retrieved a pen and intake form from her assistant's desk, and forced all opinions out of her head. "Very well, Fräulein . . . ?" Her voice trailed off as the girl's blank expression remained unchanged.

"Gottlieb." Gud tossed his cap on the counter. "Allina Gottlieb."

"Welcome to Hochland Home, Fräulein Gottlieb," Marguerite said, enunciating each word slowly to make sure the girl heard her. "Please have a seat. I'll begin with our standard questionnaire."

"There's no need to conduct the intake test and medical examination."

"But *Gruppenführer*," Marguerite protested, "*Reichsführer* Himmler expects a member of my staff to complete intake paperwork for every girl when she arrives—"

"I'll speak to Himmler, *Schwester*," he interrupted. "You need not concern yourself. As I said, this woman may already be carrying my child."

Gud might be a high-ranking officer, but he didn't outrank Heinrich Himmler.

"Please, *Gruppenführer*, I must insist—"

"I trust you've made good use of the Biedermeier pieces I sent?" he asked in a low, silky voice, reminding her of the truckload of antique furniture delivered last week.

Marguerite's mouth went to sand. "Th-they're lovely, *Gruppenführer*. I've never seen finer workmanship."

"Need I remind you," Gud said, eerie pale eyes sparkling with anger, "that I took great pains to divert some of what we collected in Munich to Hochland Home?"

"I'm very grateful for your support, *Gruppenführer*. We all are." Marguerite took a calming breath. The telltale numbness in her scalp meant her blood pressure was spiking.

"You're a smart woman," he said with a low chuckle. "There's no need to fill out your little forms, *Schwester*. My personal physician examined her. Allina is in remarkable health."

Marguerite laid the pen and intake form down. She'd have to be very careful with this girl. "Of course, *Gruppenführer*."

"Until we're certain she's bearing my child, you may put Allina to work here in service to our Führer. I expect you to treat her as you would any member of your staff."

The young woman swayed, then collapsed against the wall with a moan. Gud managed to catch her before she crumpled to the floor, and Marguerite ran over to help support her weight. Allina flinched as she slipped into unconsciousness. Her hair smelled like a child's, unperfumed save for the clean scent of soap.

"The ride here was . . . taxing." Gud grabbed Allina's suitcase and tried unsuccessfully to angle one of her arms around his neck.

Marguerite swallowed her frustration and tapped the girl's cheek until she roused. "Wrap your arms around our shoulders, Fräulein Gottlieb, and we'll help you to your room."

Allina nodded, but shrank from Gud before she slipped back into unconsciousness. They propped her up between their bodies and managed to drag her up the stairs, although progress was painstaking. Allina Gottlieb didn't stir even when her feet thumped on the steps. Her body was dead weight. Marguerite was breathless by the time they reached the second floor.

As they staggered down the hall, she noticed six bedroom doors were cracked open. *Nosy eyes, nosy ears.* "Get back into bed, all of you!" she hissed.

Six doors shut immediately.

Gud stumbled and dropped the suitcase, letting out a vicious curse. He managed to swing Allina's body around before she dropped to the ground. She remained unconscious, half-balanced on his body, half-propped on the floor.

"Where's the room?" he asked, then picked her up in his arms.

Marguerite cocked her chin toward the end of the hall. "Down there," she said, wiping the perspiration from her cheeks. "At the end, on the right. It's small, but private." Hopefully Gud wouldn't be insulted by the accommodations. The room was next to hers and one she kept free for girls approaching the end of their pregnancies, and held only a bed, small dresser, nightstand, and chair in unfinished pine. Most of the women shared more luxurious lodgings, but a roommate was out of the question, given the girl's condition.

He carried Allina the rest of the way with Marguerite following, suitcase in hand. When they got to the room, Gud helped strip off the young woman's coat and shoes and ease her under the thick navy quilt. Marguerite didn't want to disturb her, and there'd be time to change clothes in the morning.

She took a moment to straighten Allina's items, meager as they were, by hanging her coat on a hook by the door and placing her suitcase and shoes below it. Turning back to the bed, she saw that Gud was smoothing back the girl's honey-colored hair with a faint smile on his lips.

When their eyes met, Gud cleared his throat and followed her out of the room. "I had my physician tend her head wound before we left," he said, adjusting the button beneath his collar as they hurried down the hall. "Have a doctor see to it in the next few days."

"Of course, *Gruppenführer*," she said, leading him down to the front room. "We'll take good care of her."

"You're a credit to Hochland Home, *Schwester*." He brushed his fingers over the front of his jacket, avoiding her gaze. "I shall tell *Reichsführer* Himmler how well you served the Reich this evening."

Marguerite folded her hands at her waist. "It's both a sacred duty and my pleasure to serve you, *Gruppenführer* Gud."

He picked his cap off the counter, placed it under his arm, and walked to the door. "I require written reports twice a month with details on her physical progress and temperament, as well as her work here."

"It will be my honor to report her progress to you, *Gruppenführer*," Marguerite said, bowing her head.

"I shall check on her personally each month. I expect you to relieve her of her duties on those days." He quirked his eyebrow. "Do you understand me?"

Marguerite nodded. "Yes, *Gruppenführer*."

He smirked at her. "*Heil* Hitler."

"*Heil* Hitler."

Gud walked out into the night.

Blowing out a sigh of relief, Marguerite trudged upstairs to her room and undressed. She stretched out on the mattress and took several deep breaths, attempting to will herself asleep.

Unfortunately, her mind wouldn't stop churning.

Gud's demands were unprecedented. The lack of proper intake paperwork, his insistence that the medical exam was unnecessary—Director Ebner would go into a rage when he found out, and Marguerite would be the one to experience the full force of that anger. Hochland Home's exacting intake procedure was key to the program's success. Every file had to be complete. Any errors or missing information were unacceptable.

Then there was the condition of the girl. Despite Gud's assurances, it would be obvious to anyone with a brain that Allina Gottlieb was not in good health. She'd been brutalized, but by whom? Gud showed uncharacteristic softness toward her, and she was young enough to be his granddaughter.

Too much thinking will get you in trouble. Marguerite would have to arrange for the exam and intake paperwork as soon as the girl was in acceptable shape. As for what position she might find Allina at Hochland Home—well, she'd have to think about that. Carefully.

Marguerite slipped under the covers, determined to get another three hours of rest. There'd be time to deal with this fine mess in the morning.

An hour later, she roused to loud crashes, tortured screaming, and pounding on her bedroom door.

"*Schwester* Ziegler, *Schwester* Ziegler," a girl cried from the hallway.

Marguerite bolted out of bed and swung the door open. "What's going on?"

"It's coming from that room." Rilla Weber, a sweet girl with dove-gray eyes late in her sixth month, pointed toward Allina's door, which stood ajar. "I went in to check, but I didn't recognize her, *Schwester*."

"She'll wake up the entire floor," complained Berta Schneider, a statuesque blonde who was due any day. "Make her stop." Berta yawned and shuffled back to her room.

Marguerite hurried to Allina's room and found the young woman writhing in bed, still dressed, but flushed and sweaty with her skirt twisted around her waist. The lamp had fallen on its side on the nightstand, and the heavy blue quilt was lying in a heap on the floor.

The last thing she needed was a girl with a fever. Righting the lamp, Marguerite pressed her hand to the young woman's forehead. It was cool. She tried untwisting Allina's skirt to make her more comfortable, but the poor creature shrieked and jerked away from her touch.

"Her screams raise the hairs on the back of my neck," Rilla said. Approaching the bed, she caressed her rounded belly through her robe. "She was crying for a man named Albert."

"You should be in bed, Rilla." Marguerite placed her hand on Allina's shoulder, but she howled again, shook it off, and began to pant. "This one needs quiet. And rest." Should she risk a sedative? Probably not, given the girl's head wound. She hated to involve one of the doctors at this point— doing so would raise any number of inconvenient questions—but if there was no improvement by morning she'd have no choice.

Rilla came closer and took Allina's hand.

Allina opened her eyes with a strangled gasp, focusing for a few seconds on Rilla's calm gray gaze. "Auntie," she whimpered, before falling back asleep.

Rilla sat down on the chair next to the bed. "Let me stay with her for a little while."

"All right. You need your rest, though," Marguerite said, laying a hand on the girl's shoulder. "Try not to overtax, for baby's sake."

Rilla sat with Allina until sunrise.

Marguerite rapped on Allina's door and poked her head into the room. "It's time to get up." She walked in and threw open the thick blue draperies, allowing the morning light to flood the bed. Allina didn't stir. This wouldn't do. The young woman had slept like the dead yesterday, a relief given her nightmares the evening before, but she'd taken nothing more than water in the last thirty-six hours.

She clapped her hands. "Wake up, now."

Moaning, Allina lifted her head. A spark of comprehension lit her gaze, which was meager progress.

"I let you remain in bed yesterday to rest," Marguerite explained. "Today, you must meet everyone."

Allina swung her legs over the side of the mattress and attempted to sit up, only to collapse onto her side with a ragged gasp.

"I know you're sore," Marguerite said, hurrying over to help Allina stay upright, "but your muscles will tighten and atrophy if you don't move." More important, food would speed the healing process. She'd refused the simple beef broth Marguerite had brought up last night.

It took several agonizing minutes before Allina was able to sit up unassisted. "Very good," Marguerite coached. "Let's get you washed before breakfast." She kept a careful grip on Allina's arm as the young woman stood. Allina listed to the side a bit, but righted herself.

"Good. You're doing well." Marguerite placed a light hand on her back. "Walk with me." She picked up the girl's suitcase and escorted her to the bathroom.

Allina stood by the tub, staring at the immaculate white porcelain tiles. She didn't seem to know what to do next.

"Are you able to wash yourself?" Marguerite asked.

Allina nodded.

Marguerite ran a warm bath and rooted around in the cupboard for a washcloth and a bar of rose-scented soap. Allina took the items with another small nod.

She sat on the toilet to wait, averting her gaze to give the young woman a measure of privacy. After a few seconds, it was impossible to ignore how slowly she undressed. Glancing over, Marguerite covered her mouth to muffle a gasp. Allina's body was covered in a kaleidoscope of colors. Virtually every bit of her flesh was marked in some way.

Marguerite hurried to the tub and helped Allina climb in. The girl sank into the water with a plaintive cry. Shivering, she ran the washcloth over her skin with a light touch and stretched her limbs gingerly. After a few minutes, her movements improved.

Marguerite swallowed the grit in her throat. The water in the tub had turned pale pink. "We'll make sure you're able to bathe each day. Hot water eases the pain. Do you need help with your hair?"

"Please," Allina whispered.

She soaked and soaped the young woman's hair, taking care to avoid the bandage. She was surprised when a flicker of pleasure crossed the young woman's features. Allina might be pretty once the bruising faded. "Tilt your head back. Let me rinse." When Allina complied, she poured bowls of clear, warm water over her hair. "It feels good to be clean, doesn't it?"

"Yes, thank you." Allina offered a ghost of a smile, but her dark green eyes were flat.

"Let's dry your hair before you dress." Marguerite wrapped her hair in a towel and gave it a gentle rub before stepping back to give the girl room. Steadier, Allina climbed out of the tub with little assistance. She selected a charcoal-gray dress from the suitcase and dressed with efficiency, even drawing her damp hair into a neat ponytail without help.

"Very good. Now come with me," Marguerite said, and grabbed the girl's elbow. Doing so proved to be a mistake. Allina stumbled back with a yelp and cowered against the wall. "It's all right," Marguerite crooned in a softer voice, one she used with the children when they were frightened. "We must get you ready and go downstairs, or you'll miss breakfast." She backed out of the bathroom slowly and waited, but it took a full minute of encouragement before Allina followed her with slow, cautious steps down the hall to her sleeping room.

"You can unpack later," Marguerite said. Dropping the suitcase off, she pulled a round silver pin from her pocket. "Here's a piece you must wear while you stay at Hochland Home. It's beautiful, isn't it?" she asked, handing it to Allina. "Can you read what it says in the circle?"

"'Every mother of good blood is a sacred asset of our existence,'" Allina whispered.

"We serve the Reich and our Führer here," Marguerite said, as she fastened the pin to the collar of Allina's dress. "We women must stick together." She waited for a sign of agreement but didn't receive one. She'd need to watch this one.

Before they entered the dining hall, she pointed out the sign set on an easel by the door, which read:

The best proof that a German man and woman can show of their con-
viction, the depth of their National Socialist spirit, and their gratitude
to our Führer who awoke in us a national awareness, is to become
happy parents of a large and healthy brood of children!
                              —Heinrich Himmler, SS *Reichsführer*

While Allina's eyes followed the words on the sign, her face remained
impassive. Marguerite tamped down her annoyance. This girl would understand how lucky she was soon enough. Allina could make a good life
here, like so many others had.

"Isn't this room lovely?" Marguerite asked as they entered the dining
hall. Allina didn't reply, but her eyes widened. Thanks in no small part
to *Gruppenführer* Gud's generosity, the main dining hall was every bit as
elegant as a restaurant in the Excelsior, the Kaiserhof, or any fashionable
hotel. The walls, redone just last month in cream damask wallpaper, fea-
tured lush oil landscapes of the German countryside; richly hued Aubus-
son carpets adorned the floor; and the linens, silverware, crystal, and china
were exquisite. "Every item is a recent reallocation from Munich's Jewish
population." Marguerite sniffed when Allina closed her eyes.

They approached the buffet table, and the smoky fragrance of bacon
made Marguerite's stomach growl. The table was loaded with bread, eggs,
meats, and potatoes in silver chafing pans; carafes of coffee and orange
juice; and a huge crock of hearty oatmeal. Allina gaped at the bounty of
food.

Marguerite nudged her toward the buffet. "*Reichsführer* Himmler
wants all our girls and babies to be healthy. A variety of foods, including
fresh fruit and grains, are necessary." She pointed at the serving dish of hot
cereal. "He even developed a special porridge for expecting mothers. Let
me introduce you to the others, and then you may eat whatever you wish."

Nearly a hundred women sat together in their customary groups. The
younger, unmarried girls were full of chatter and giggles, as usual. The older
women, more focused and mature, sat quietly at their own tables. Everyone looked healthy this morning. Pink-skinned and bright-eyed, Hochland
Home mothers were the healthiest in Germany.

Marguerite clapped her hands twice. It took a few seconds for the
women to still their chatter and put their forks down.

"Ladies, this is Allina Gottlieb. She's recovering from an accident and a special guest of *Gruppenführer Gud*." Murmurs rose in the crowd, so she clapped her hands again. "Allina may join in many of your activities and classes. For the time being, she'll work with me in the intake office. Please welcome her."

Curious glances and whispers of welcome filled the room, although Allina seemed unaware of their regard. Rilla Weber rose from her table and approached them. "Good morning, Allina," she said with a friendly grin. "I'm not sure you'll remember me, but we met the night you arrived. You're looking much better today."

Marguerite could have hugged Rilla for that. Sweet child. She'd make a good nurse if she had a mind to.

Allina cleared her throat. "I remember someone held my hand." Her eyes met Rilla's, and for a moment her gaze was less hollow. "Was it you?" she asked.

"Yes," Rilla said, taking her hand, "and I hope we can be friends. Come to my table, and we'll get you some breakfast."

Marguerite took a long, deep breath. Perhaps everything would fall into place for Allina Gottlieb, after all.

25 October 1938

To: Reinhardt Gud, Gruppenführer SS
Re: Status Report, Allina Gottlieb

I am pleased to report that Allina has settled in at Hochland Home.

For the time being, she serves our Führer in the intake office. Allina is of superior intelligence and mental ability, a competent typist, and above average in filing skills and other office duties. I count myself lucky to have this exceptional young lady's assistance.

Her physical state improves. Allina's head wound has healed, her stitches have been removed, and there will be minimal scarring. Most of the bruising has faded, and her remaining injuries should resolve themselves within the month.

In the days following her admittance, she shied away from a full physical examination by Dr. Engel. I took it upon myself to conduct one this morning, and to complete her official intake documentation, per explicit orders from Director Ebner.

Allina's temperament remains melancholy. She has little interest in interacting with the other girls or the officers who visit Hochland Home. Rilla Weber, an expectant mother here in service to the Reich, is a notable exception. I expect their friendship will be a bridge to her relationships with others.

A personal note: Word of your wife's recent illness has reached us. Permit me to give you my condolences and wishes for her speedy recovery. While I realize your wife's condition will, regrettably, delay your next visit to Hochland Home, please be at ease. I will take extraordinary care of Allina during your absence.

It is a privilege to serve you in this matter, and to serve our Führer.

[Signed] Marguerite Ziegler
Head Nurse, Hochland Home

Marguerite leaned back in her chair and reread the memo. Reports like this one were always a matter of striking a delicate balance. Too much sunshine, and Gud would be disappointed when he visited. Too much angst, and he might visit sooner, rather than later—and his visits were something she hoped to curtail. The girl was not fit for male company. Allina visibly panicked when she came in contact with any of the visiting SS officers.

Marguerite rubbed her eyes and sighed. Time would tell.

CHAPTER 8

MARGUERITE ZIEGLER

Plucking a raisin bun from the breakfast buffet, Marguerite glanced around the dining room before making her way to Rilla's breakfast table. Allina was nowhere to be seen, which was strange. The girl had been on time to meals every day in the four weeks since she'd arrived.

"Has anyone seen Allina this morning?"

"I ran into her in the hall earlier, *Schwester*." Rilla took a sip of tea and frowned. "She complained of a stomachache. Shall I check on her?"

"No need. I'll attend to it." Marguerite hurried upstairs, but Allina's sleeping room was empty. After a five-minute search, she found the young woman in the bathroom in an alarming state. Allina was fully dressed but seated on the cold white tiles with her arms wrapped around her legs and her chin resting on her knees. She rocked back and forth, convulsing with laughter. Marguerite crouched and put a hand on Allina's shoulder. "What's wrong?" The girl was quaking. Had she gone mad? "Answer me, Allina. Look at me."

When Allina lifted her face, Marguerite couldn't curb a gasp. Allina's cheeks were wet and her moss-green eyes were *alive*. They glowed. She took Marguerite's hand, although it was another frantic half minute before she calmed down enough to speak. "I need a Camelia pad and belt, *Schwester*. My monthly courses have begun."

Marguerite got up to search the bathroom cupboard for a sanitary napkin. "Change your undergarments, then join me in my office," she said, projecting a steadiness she didn't feel. "*Gruppenführer* Gud needs to know how you'll serve our Führer here. He telephoned yesterday, asking about your progress."

Allina's head snapped back as if Marguerite had struck her, and her cheeks went nearly as white as the floor tiles. "What will he do when he finds out I'm not pregnant?" she whispered.

What indeed. Most likely, Gud would be sorely disappointed to learn Allina wasn't with child. Marguerite was stuck, and with limited options. She needed a plan.

She clasped Allina's shoulder. For once, the girl didn't flinch. "We'll discuss the possibilities later. First things first. Clean up and change your clothes," she repeated, handing Allina a pad and belt, "then join me downstairs."

When Allina reported to her office fifteen minutes later, the transformation in the young woman's appearance was startling. She was clear-eyed and pink-cheeked and had pulled her hair into a simple twist that highlighted her cheekbones and the delicate lines of her heart-shaped face. Marguerite motioned to the chair across from her desk, delighted by Allina's elegant posture as she took her seat. What she'd suspected initially was now easy to see: Allina Gottlieb was in every way a well-bred, beautiful young lady. No wonder Gud had chosen her.

Marguerite nodded at Ida-Lynne when she slipped into the room. Her assistant set the vintage silver tea tray on the edge of her desk with a tiny *oomph*.

"Thank you. I'll pour."

Ida-Lynne tucked the pale gold strands escaping her braid behind her ears. "Yes, *Schwester*." She backed away, but her eyes, which were the color of cement, stayed on Allina until the door creaked shut.

Now to business. Marguerite looked at the girl, who sat with hands clasped tightly in her lap. *Right. Best to pull the bandage off quickly.* "What did Gud tell you about Hochland Home before you arrived?"

Allina's expression smoothed into a tight ivory mask. "He told me nothing, *Schwester*," she said in a tiny voice. Her gaze fell to her lap.

Which left Marguerite to handle the explanations, along with any messy details. "Hochland Home was the first *Lebensborn* facility and serves as the model for all others," she said crisply, pouring the amber liquid into two cups. "We have six homes in Germany at present, with plans for many more."

When Allina gave a jerky nod, she added, "You've worked with me in the office nearly a month now. I'm sure you've some idea of what we are." She handed the girl a cup of tea. "And the services we provide."

The young woman bit her lip and set her cup and saucer down with a clatter.

"Don't be afraid. Tell me what you know." Marguerite waited patiently, inhaling the citrus-infused wisps of steam curling above her cup.

Allina added a sugar cube to her cup and stirred it slowly. "I believe this is a hospital. Or a clinic," she said, "for pregnant women." She took a sip before setting the cup on the saucer. "And also . . . an orphanage?"

Good. Despite Allina's fraught start at Hochland Home, she'd obviously been paying attention. "Our facility is both of those things, but we're also much more," Marguerite said. "Hochland Home carries out a sacred duty. Its mission is to ensure Germany's future. We give unmarried girls a stable home during pregnancy and offer exceptional care for mothers and babies after delivery. Our children go to some of the most privileged families in the Reich." She took a sip of tea and grimaced. Ida-Lynne had let the Ceylon steep too long.

Shifting in her seat, Allina nodded again.

Marguerite dropped two more sugar cubes into her cup, then spoke her next words with care. "We have more than fifty nursing mothers and sixty expectant ones here at the moment, but only a third were pregnant when they arrived. The rest met the fathers of their children here. SS officers are encouraged to visit Hochland Home, and others like it, every month. Some of my girls have been fortunate enough to birth multiple babies here in service to our Führer."

A bright flush crept up Allina's neck and into her cheeks. "Are all the women unmarried?"

"Nearly all," Marguerite said. "A half dozen officers' wives are currently in residence. They'll stay for a few weeks after they give birth. Of course, those women will go home with their children. It's an honor to care for them for the short time they need us." She offered Allina a plate of shortbread on the tray. Sweets might lift the girl's mood.

Allina selected a biscuit but set it down on her saucer. "How do the mothers find out about Hochland Home? I've never heard of it before."

"We're quite exclusive. Only those of pure Aryan blood are accepted." Marguerite bit into the biscuit, sighing a little at its buttery sweetness. "Most girls are endorsed by their doctors," she added, finishing off the biscuit and brushing the crumbs from her fingers. "The *Gruppenführer's* personal physician recommended you."

Allina flushed a deeper pink. "And what will be expected of me, now . . . now that I'm not pregnant? Will he come back for me?" Allina wrapped her arms around her stomach, as if fending off a chill.

"His wife is gravely ill. I wouldn't expect a visit until spring." The girl closed her eyes briefly, then nodded.

Marguerite bit into the second biscuit. It was chalk in her mouth, and she tossed the uneaten half back on the plate. Nothing good could come from allowing this one to tug at her heartstrings, however sympathetic her situation might be. "When he visits, you'll have to receive him," she said in a harder voice. "We women must do our part. No one stays at Hochland Home without purpose."

Allina's chin quivered.

"You could do worse. Understand me, young lady. *Gruppenführer* Gud protected you when he asked me to put you to work as a member of my staff. It means you have a place here." She leaned back and stared, forcing the young woman to meet her gaze. "Do you have anywhere else to go?"

Allina glanced away.

"There's no space in my budget for an additional salary, but I can offer room and board for loyal service. If and when you become pregnant, we'll reassess your position." Marguerite gave Allina a bracing smile. "Who knows? If you bear a child for the *Gruppenführer*, he might . . . set you up in an entirely different situation."

Marguerite took another sip of tea and waited for the truth to sink in.

"I'd be grateful to work here," Allina finally answered, her voice tight.

She had spirit, this one, more than Marguerite had initially thought. "Excellent. I'd like to offer you a position in the nurseries. I need a fill-in nurse for when extra help is needed." The young woman's eyes brightened. "Hundreds of women have applied to be a Hochland Home nurse, you know. It's a highly respected position. *Reichsführer* Himmler himself has deemed our efforts heroic."

"I understand." Allina nodded. "Thank you, *Schwester*."

"Your work in the front office shows you've an eye for detail, so I expect you to keep the children's files in good order. And, you've the right temperament. You're an adaptable sort." She stood and handed Allina a pencil and a pad of paper. "There's been no time to give you a tour before today. Let's do that now before I take you to the nurseries."

CHAPTER 9

<u>ALLINA</u>

Not pregnant. Not pregnant, not pregnant, notpregnantnotpregnantnot pregnant—

Allina kept a polite smile on her face as *Schwester* Ziegler went on about the new, enviable position in the nurseries. She could bear any assignment in this place, anything at all, now that she knew she wasn't pregnant with Gud's child.

During her first few days here, Allina had existed in a gray fog, imprisoned by the pain in her body and a persistent headache that jumbled her thoughts. As the injuries faded, violent flashes of the events that brought Allina to Hochland Home began to surface. The memories came at odd moments, often during her morning shower or at meals when she was unoccupied, and they left her gasping for breath and her heart pounding. Images of Aunt Claudia and Uncle Dieter produced bouts of wild panic.

Allina had disciplined herself, forced those terrifying thoughts and memories out of her mind, and concentrated instead on gaining her bearings. When not typing an endless stream of reports for the head nurse over the past month, she'd been privy to dozens of conversations among the staff and expectant mothers. Allina had kept silent, hiding her understanding and growing revulsion.

She'd need to use all the knowledge gleaned, and more, to survive here. Until she could devise some means of escape, Allina was trapped at Hochland Home—a *Mischling* office worker in service to Aryan mothers and babies for the glory of the Reich.

Allina shuddered. She'd never felt so alone.

"Follow me." *Schwester* Ziegler grabbed a set of keys from her desk drawer and beckoned to her. Allina ran to keep up as the woman hurried out of her office. "We've got less than an hour, and there's much to learn and absorb before you report for duty tomorrow."

The head nurse explained that Hochland Home's ground floor was split into three sections. They began their tour in the administrative area, which was done in serviceable gray linoleum and white paint and smelled strongly of rubbing alcohol. As they walked through the examination rooms, the head nurse went over the extensive intake procedures for new mothers. She stressed the importance of recording each resident's bloodlines and ancestry, their height, weight, and body measurements—as well as an analysis of their facial features and hair, skin, and eye color, as compared to the Aryan ideal. Then they toured the private offices for senior staff. Like *Schwester* Ziegler's office, these spaces were fancier, filled with padded chairs, mahogany desks, and identical portraits of the Führer.

At the end of the corridor was a room Allina had never entered. The head nurse unlocked it with a flourish and gestured inside.

"This is Central Filing. We keep records for the entire program here— files on each mother and child, along with adoption records from every *Lebensborn* home in Germany. The reports you've worked on these last weeks are all filed in this room." Allina stepped inside the cavernous space, which housed dozens of gray metal cabinets laid out in rows. "Only senior *Schwestern* work here, by order of Director Ebner," she added in a clipped tone that made Allina back out in haste.

Next, they toured the North Wing, which housed the kitchen and dining halls and operated as the social center for resident mothers. The kitchen had the latest equipment, and every room boasted antique furniture, artwork, and rugs done in rich fabrics and colors.

"Much of this beauty is courtesy of your patron, Reinhardt Gud," *Schwester* Ziegler said with a pointed smile. "We're very grateful for his continued support."

Allina's cheeks flushed with heat, but she gritted her teeth to approximate a smile as *Schwester* Ziegler pushed on. They toured the instruction rooms for character training classes, a great hall for larger gatherings, and a half dozen well-appointed parlors the head nurse claimed were used by residents to meet privately with suitors.

"We also maintain a large recreation lounge for officers on leave," she added as they traveled to the end of the hall. "We want them to feel at home and ever welcome."

When the head nurse opened the door to the rec room, Allina came face-to-face with a small group of men in uniform. All five looked her up and down and offered broad smiles.

No. She backed away as her vision swam, colliding with *Schwester* Ziegler. Allina's heart stuttered.

"*Schwester* Allina is the newest member of our staff," the head nurse said crisply, and clapped a clawlike grip on her shoulder. "You'll see her from time to time. Come now, Allina."

They ended the tour of the North Wing with a stroll through its back courtyard, which was open to mothers, visitors, and even *Schwestern* during break time. The courtyard was close to freezing but Allina was grateful the head nurse gave her a minute to lift her face to the sun. After a few deep breaths, her racing heart slowed.

Finally, they journeyed to their ultimate destination. The nurseries.

"Each room in this wing has a sign posted on the door with the age of the babies inside, as you can see." *Schwester* Ziegler's eyes brightened as they entered the room for six-month-olds. The walls were a pale yellow, and the cream linoleum floors and white countertops were spotless. On one end of the room was a row of sinks and a high work counter, and two dozen cribs were arranged in the center of the room in precise, straight rows. An equal number of wingback chairs in an array of colors bordered the room's perimeter.

One of Hochland Home's *Schwestern*, dressed in a standard brown uniform and white nurse's apron and cap, stood at the back, making notes in a file.

"Good morning, Marta," the head nurse called out softly. The nurse bobbed her head, pushed an errant strand of wiry gray hair behind her ear, and went back to scribbling in her files. "Marta's been with me since the beginning of our program here. She's an exceptional nurse, and always keeps her files in order."

Every crib was filled, and the nursery was a lovely, sunny space. Obviously no expense had been spared. But the room was quiet as a tomb.

Allina's hackles rose. "*Schwester*, how is it so many babies are quiet in the middle of the morning?"

"An excellent question. We follow a precise regimen to give the children discipline." Ziegler walked down a row of cribs, beckoning Allina to follow. "My staff relies on our schedules, as well as our files. We couldn't run the house without them."

Schedules were fine—but they couldn't account for a room full of silent babies.

"I can tell from your expression you're confounded by our success," the head nurse said with a chuckle. "We follow the latest advances in childcare—schedules Director Ebner and *Reichsführer* Himmler created themselves."

The head nurse stopped in front of a crib. "Marta began her shift at six o'clock in the morning by bathing and changing the children. Then the mothers feed them," she said, gesturing to the wingback chairs bordering the room. "Once they're fed, Marta puts the children down for a nap." She pointed to the clock on the wall. "At ten o'clock, Marta will change their diapers. The children will feed again before she takes them to the courtyard. She'll bundle the little ones tightly before putting them into their prams because it's cold, but they need fresh air."

Allina peered into the crib. The child within was still. Its eyes were open but unfocused.

"Don't the children get hungry at different times? Surely they don't all soil their diapers on the same schedule." She leaned closer, nearly choking on the stench. "I believe this child needs its diaper changed."

The head nurse sighed. "The children begin with different needs," she explained slowly, as if Allina were a child, "but we make sure each little one's behavior aligns with our schedule over time." She glanced down the rows of clean white cradles and chuckled. "Can you imagine what chaos would ensue if hundreds of children maintained their own schedules?"

Allina nodded, although her mind was rioting. Children couldn't thrive in such a cold, sterile environment, yet the head nurse was singing its praises. It was beyond her understanding.

"Our babies get the best nourishment, clean air, and peaceful surroundings. Everything they need to grow into dutiful citizens," she continued. "By eighteen months, they're weaned off mother's milk. Most leave Hochland Home shortly after. There's a high demand for these children." Ziegler walked to the front of the room, forcing Allina to follow.

"I still don't understand how you can teach an *infant* to be quiet."

Schwester Ziegler took hold of Allina's arm and walked her to a cradle at the front of the room. "What would you do if this little one cried out?"

Allina peered into the bassinet. Her heart fluttered as the child's gaze, which was as dull as the other child's, seemed to drift along the ceiling. "I'd pick him up to see if he's hungry or if his diaper is soiled, and feed him or change his diaper if necessary," she answered. "Then I'd walk him around until he dropped off to sleep."

The head nurse shook her head. "Yet that's the very thing you should not do." She pointed into the cradle. "This child is perfectly well. If he were sick you could tell by his complexion and take him to the infirmary. But a good nurse must walk away from a healthy crying baby."

When Allina opened her mouth to interrupt, she held up her hand. "By teaching self-control, we help them grow into respectful children. Respectful children become law-abiding adults." The head nurse gave her a quelling look. "The newborns are a noisy bunch, but most are ready for this room by six months. They learn their needs will be tended to eventually and stop fussing."

"Do the *Schwestern* ever play with the children?" Allina asked.

"Play and touch at this point would overstimulate," *Schwester* Ziegler said crisply, as she steered Allina out of the nursery and down the hall. "They'll have plenty of time for that once they're with their adopted families." She slanted Allina another harsh look as they made their way toward her office. "The Führer requires all of us, nurses and children alike, to follow rules. Do you understand?"

"Yes, *Schwester*." Allina pressed pad and pencil to her stomach and followed the head nurse down the hall.

"Very few mothers go home with their babies," Ziegler added as they entered her office and took their seats again. "Most will tell you it's their

choice to let us tend the children. Developing an attachment serves neither mother nor child. Trust me, it won't serve you either."

Allina swallowed hard. "I understand."

"You were taking notes while we were in the nursery, and there's a
gleam in your eye. Do you think you can serve Hochland Home well as
a nurse?"

"Yes, *Schwester*. I know I can."

CHAPTER 10

ALLINA

During her first weeks in the nursery, Allina's arms and legs twitched with fatigue by the end of the day and creaked with stiffness every morning. The work was mindless, and the hectic pace gave her little time to think. It was better, really, to go from one task to the next, with her mind as sharp as a pin and focused on the present moment: the cradles to be stripped for the following day's wash, or a counter in need of disinfecting, or a wriggling baby to be adjusted in its nursing sling.

Allina liked the early shift because it was the busiest. She'd rise in the dark, wash, and gulp down a raisin bun and enough bitter coffee to chase the sleepiness from her brain before reporting to the nursery at six o'clock.

Each morning passed in a hurricane of activity and always according to Hochland Home's pitiless schedules. Her assigned nursery of eighteen newborns was small; other *Schwestern* were responsible for as many as thirty children. Nevertheless, by noon every child was breastfed twice, bathed, measured, weighed, changed, and wheeled into the garden for fresh air. She maintained files on each of her charges, noting dozens of characteristics—everything from the length of time the baby nursed, to its height and weight and the circumference of its skull, to observations on the shape of its eyes and nose and any changes in hair and skin color.

Afternoons mirrored the mornings, with the added burden of laundry—there were mountains of diapers, towels, and sheets to fold—so her hands smelled perpetually of bleach and Persil.

Meals were quick and on the run because *Schwestern* were forever in motion, like chickens released from a henhouse. Allina learned to snack when she could, and to snag an extra roll or piece of fruit from the buffet at meals. After dinner, she attended mandatory character training classes that offered instruction on everything from hair and skin care (*no cosmetics allowed, ladies, remember, natural beauty is best*) to the art of conversation (*be kind and pleasing with a soft voice and smile, and never enter into political discussions*). The courses were as dull as rocks, but the droning lectures had one benefit. Allina fell asleep quickly each night, usually within minutes. Still, she often came awake in the early hours of the morning, gasping for breath and lurching off the mattress, with the taste of dirt in her mouth.

Her waking mind rarely turned toward Badensburg. She reached for them sometimes, the memories, to test herself, but any images faded like shadows into the corners of her brain before she could grasp them, leaving nothing behind but a spinning weightlessness in the hollow of her stomach.

It was curious how rarely she was able to conjure the faces of those she loved most. When she tried, their faces were like quicksilver, disappearing in a flash. Even the image of Albert—his teasing smile and warm, amber eyes—brought on a crushing weight in her chest.

On the rare occasion thoughts of her former life intruded, they were almost always childhood memories: of balancing carefully on a kitchen stool as she pushed dough through the spaetzle maker into a steaming pot of chicken stock, or of her sticky, red-stained fingers picking gooseberries for pastry. Each flash of memory was oddly flat and emotionless, like a scene from a movie, and she was always alone in them. These random thoughts concerned Allina. She knew she should feel something, but she didn't.

Her coat—and the items she'd sewn into its lining—were the only things that caused a sense of restlessness. As the days passed and her physical wounds continued to heal, Allina's interest in her father's letters bloomed. But there was no way to get to those letters safely. She had virtually no free time and wasn't allowed outside the compound—and since her sleeping room door was unlocked, there was no privacy. Getting caught would be disastrous. To keep from losing her mind, Allina focused on the children and reminded herself to keep the past in the past.

"Good morning, Berta. How are you feeling today?" Allina pasted on a smile as the tall, flaxen-haired blonde entered the nursery. Every mother seemed to be running late this morning, but no one was more obnoxious than Berta Schneider. Berta had the face of a bisque doll. She should have been beautiful, but Allina found her perfectly arched eyebrows, pouted bow lips, and turned-up nose annoying.

Allina noted Berta's lateness in her file, satisfying one of Hochland Home's rules, although the girl would never be chastised for her tardiness. The head nurse might preach about the need to stick to schedule, but she counted on her *Schwestern* to keep things moving smoothly.

Berta ignored Allina and the nursing mothers as she fluffed the embroidered skirt of her sprigged cotton dirndl. Loosening her blouse, she took the nursing sling from the arm of a wingback chair and looped it around her neck before taking her seat. Allina pulled Berta's newborn from his crib and positioned him in the sling so his face was close to Berta's breast. The infant latched on to her nipple and began to suck.

"Ouch!" Berta called out. She tapped her baby's forehead and looked at him with exasperation.

Sabine Hindz, a new resident who'd arrived at Hochland Home just days before her delivery, glanced at Berta and chuckled. "Your son is a healthy eater," she said, adjusting Johann, her newborn, in his feeding sling. Sabine was older than most of the others in the nursery, married, and at twenty-nine had come fully into her beauty. Her glossy chestnut hair was cut in a fashionable bob and styled in soft finger waves. The fine lines around her mouth and eyes did nothing to diminish her porcelain skin or silver-gray gaze.

"I wish my Ingrid would latch," added Lotte Menke, as she looked down into her newborn's face. Lotte's chubby face was wan and her blond hair hung down her back in a lank mess. The smudges under her mint-green eyes spoke of perpetual distress and made her seem much older than her seventeen years.

Allina set a hand on Lotte's shoulder. "Worrying never helps. Little Ingrid's feeding habits will improve, she just needs a bit of encouragement."

"*Schwester* Allina is right," Sabine said, speaking with the confidence of an older, experienced mother. "Klaus, my first child, was a poor eater in the beginning. Now he's an eighteen-month-old terror."

"Do you plan to keep this baby, too, Sabine?" Allina asked.

"Of course," Sabine replied, smiling down at her perfect son. "We'll try for another as soon as we can. My husband is very excited for more sons. Or even a daughter."

"Why didn't you have Johann at home?" Lotte asked. "When my parents found out I was pregnant, they couldn't wait to send me here, but . . ."

"Viktor serves in the Sudetenland," Sabine explained with a quick lift of her shoulders, "and neither of us has family close by. I can't tell you how grateful I am to *Schwester* Ziegler. I don't know what I'd do if she hadn't allowed Klaus and me to stay here." She stroked Johann's cheek tenderly. "A few weeks at Hochland Home is better than any vacation. I'll be fully recovered when I go home."

"*Schwester* Ziegler always says it's a special privilege to serve the families of soldiers," Allina assured her. "You're welcome here for as long as you need us."

"*Schwester* Ziegler knows what a privilege it is to serve us," Berta said, pinning Allina with her chilly blue gaze. "I wish I could say the same for the rest of her staff." Shifting in her chair, Berta snagged last week's issue of *Die Dame*. She didn't look at her baby or touch him again.

Allina straightened her white nurse's cap and walked the room's perimeter, checking on the fifteen other mothers and their babies and adjusting nursing slings as necessary. Soon feeding time was over for everyone but Berta, and the rest of the women handed over their infants and filed out of the room. Allina settled the newborns down for their naps, grateful that full bellies would mean at least twenty minutes of peace. She walked to the work counter and amended her files, adding a few last notes about each child's feeding behavior.

She checked the clock—*10:45*—and sighed. She should weigh them in another fifteen minutes, but the children were sleeping quietly and an overflowing basket of laundry was waiting for her on the back counter.

Rilla Weber rushed into the room carrying a small cloth-covered bowl, but she skidded to a halt as soon as she saw Berta. "Oh. Hello," she said, wrinkling her nose.

Berta waggled her fingers in Rilla's general direction without looking up.

Rilla hurried over to Allina. "You have to taste these," she whispered. "Chef Greiser made the most delectable cinnamon biscuits." Rilla dug under the red-and-white-checked cloth and handed her one. It was still warm from the oven, and the spicy scent of cinnamon and brown sugar made Allina's mouth water. She bit into it with a happy moan.

Rilla laughed. "*Schwester* Ziegler thinks you need fattening up." Her rosy cheeks dimpled as she reached into the basket and took one for herself. "You don't mind, do you? I'm starving."

Shaking her head, Allina couldn't stop the grin from spreading across her face. She tried to keep to herself, but Rilla had made it clear that she wanted to be friends. At fifteen, Rilla was three years younger than Allina—one of the youngest residents at Hochland Home. She reminded Allina very much of a playful kitten. Her gray eyes tilted up at the corners and her pointed chin jutted whenever she was being stubborn or expressing an opinion, which was most of the time. Intrusive but kind, Rilla was different from the others. Softer. And Rilla sparkled. If Allina had ever been this lighthearted, she couldn't remember.

Allina placed her hand on her friend's belly, which strained the fabric of her pink gingham jumper. "Your little one will be fat and healthy for sure."

"Is he done yet?" Berta called out, jabbing a finger at her baby's head.

"Nearly so." Allina checked the wall clock again and hurried over to Berta. "Is Neils your first child?" she asked, attempting to find a neutral topic.

"No." Berta frowned. "It's my second. I want to give five children to my Führer by the time I'm twenty-five."

"I see." Allina took the baby from Berta's feeding sling and transferred him to the cradle. "I'm sure your husband is proud."

"I'm not married," the girl snapped. Her eyes were as beautiful and cold as sapphires. "It's my duty to bear as many children as I can while I'm young and healthy. Why does it matter who the father is, as long as he has the right bloodlines?"

"Of course," Allina murmured. "You're absolutely right."

An image of Karin's merry blue eyes flashed in Allina's mind, and her heart skittered. Her best friend had been radiant when she'd announced her pregnancy this past summer . . .

No. Don't think about this now. Allina backed away and glanced at Rilla, who rolled her eyes at Berta and, bless her, began folding diapers.

Berta buttoned her blouse and flounced out of the room without a backward glance.

"That one is an ice queen," Rilla murmured, grabbing a clean diaper from the laundry basket. She folded it in three quick movements, added it to the pile, and took another.

Allina coughed to mask a chuckle, although Rilla's assessment was accurate enough, and made her uneasy. Berta had a sly intelligence that put everyone on high alert. She watched everything too closely.

Checking the clock, Allina hurried back to the counter and noted the beginning and ending feeding times to amend Neils Schneider's file: *Nursed 16 minutes.*

"Most of the girls here don't want to be mothers, not real ones, anyway." Rilla caressed her belly through her maternity jumper. "They give up their babies. Everyone says it's the right thing to do, but I want to keep mine." She plucked a towel from the basket and snapped it in the air before folding it into a tight square.

"How will you take care of your baby all by yourself?" Allina shook out two cradle sheets and tossed them over her shoulder.

"Steffen and I plan to marry," Rilla answered, taking more towels from the basket. "We fell in love before I came here, and he arranged my stay himself."

Rilla plopped down into a chair. "I love him, and he's going to love our baby."

"And if you don't marry?" Allina asked. "Will you go home?" According to *Schwester* Ziegler, few marriages happened between the girls and officers.

"I won't have to." Rilla dipped her head as her voice grew shrill. "Steffen loves me. We'll marry when he returns from duty."

Allina laid a hand on Rilla's shoulder. The young woman shook it off. "I'm sorry. I didn't mean to upset you, but we both know what this place is." She bit her lip, hesitant to say more.

"Don't pretend to disapprove of me," Rilla said, lifting her chin. "I'm not like the others, and you know it." Shifting in her chair, Rilla crossed her ankles and let out a disgusted snort. "Berta's already searching for her next victim. There were a dozen officers at last night's mixer, and she flirted shamelessly with every single one."

The visions in Allina's mind, involving Berta and any number of officers, made her sick to her stomach. She went back to the pile of laundry and folded in silence for a minute until the lure of the empty chair beside Rilla was too much. "I'm glad I missed the mixer, then," she said, taking a seat.

"They won't let you get out of the mixers forever," Rilla said in a soft voice.

"*Schwester* Ziegler's ordered me to go to one next week," Allina murmured. But the thought of the men . . . all in uniform . . . it filled her with panic.

Rilla took her hand, frowning when Allina snatched it back. "You don't have to flirt. Some of the men just want to dance," she said, pointing to her pregnant belly, "or in my case, talk. Most are young, and nice enough, and we're all a little lonely. Far from home." She folded her arms over her breasts. "Or don't the rules apply to you?"

Allina fixed her gaze to the floor.

"Remember, good National Socialist women are hardworking, pleasant, and always obedient," Rilla added, mocking the lesson they'd discussed in excruciating detail at one of last week's character training classes.

"You should be more careful about voicing your opinions," Allina said, as her pulse thrummed in her throat. "If it's obvious to me you don't agree with what's going on here, then it's obvious to everyone else."

"I don't speak honestly with anyone else," Rilla said. She reached for Allina's hand again and held on tight when she tried to pull away. "You're the one who needs to be careful. Your face always betrays what you're thinking."

"Allina! Over here!" Rilla's voice carried over the din, and she waved from a table in the corner of the meeting hall. *Schwester* Ziegler had put her foot down; Allina was to attend tonight's mixer *or else*. So she was here. But her legs were quaking.

"I'm glad you decided to come," Rilla said as Allina took a seat. "There aren't so many men here tonight, and quite a few girls have already paired off." Rilla's color was high, and her blond ponytail swung to the Polynesian melody of Elena Lauri's "Dreams of the South Seas" as she danced in her chair. "The officers brought piles of new records. Isn't the music wonderful?"

Allina sat very still and risked a peek at the hall. A dozen SS officers in uniform and perhaps twice that number of women were assembled, with half of the group huddled around the glossy wood cocktail tables along the room's perimeter, and the other half busy on the dance floor in the center. The air was thick with cigarette smoke.

Raucous laughter erupted from the edge of the dance floor. Two soldiers were acting out a funny parody, kicking up their heels as they marched with mugs of lager in their fists. The dancers all wore smiles and kept to the center of the room, wrapped up in the music and each other. Most had glasses in hand. There was obvious flirting among the entire group, but the men kept a respectful distance. Everyone seemed to be having fun.

A flash of that horrible night, of the ugly taunts and groping hands, and Auntie's face lying in a pool of blood, spiraled through her brain and had her chest tight with panic. She shook her head, trying to clear the images. *Don't think about it now. Stay calm. Breathe.*

"Relax." Rilla nudged her. "It's not so bad, is it?"

She closed her eyes, unable to speak.

High, drunken laughter made them swivel in their chairs. A young, blond soldier was at the next table. The soldier's hair was mussed, and it was obvious he was too far into his beer. Berta Schneider was in the man's lap as he slouched in his perfectly tailored uniform. She tossed her pale hair in his face and begged for a story.

Allina couldn't bear to look at them anymore.

Rilla rolled her eyes. "That's Berta for you."

"Dreams of the South Seas" ended, and one of the men ran over to the phonograph to select the next record. "Oh, I love this one!" Rilla said as the new song began, "Rudi Schuricke! His voice sends me straight to heaven." She clapped her hands.

Allina let out a ragged laugh. Thank God for Rilla. Her naïve enthusiasm would see Allina through tonight. Leaning back in her chair, she closed her eyes. As the tune filled the room and washed over her, she tried to empty her mind and enjoy the simple melody.

"Well now!" The baritone voice booming behind her made Allina jump. "Here's the sweetest pregnant lady in all of Germany, and pretty, too, in your pink dress."

"Loritz!" Rilla squealed and stood to give the tall, blond soldier behind them an exuberant hug. "I'm so happy to see you." Still leaning against him, she turned to Allina. "This is Loritz Kortig, my Steffen's oldest, dearest friend." She hugged him again. "Loritz is a unit leader now, aren't you?" she asked, smiling up into his face.

"I am," Kortig said, tucking his hat under his arm, "but don't worry, I won't make you salute me." Turning to Allina, Kortig's smile broadened. "I don't believe I've had the pleasure of making your acquaintance, Fräulein."

The young officer was broad shouldered and handsome by anyone's standards, but the frank appreciation in his glance made Allina's stomach twist.

"Loritz, this is my friend Allina Gottlieb." Rilla sat down and took Allina's hand. "She's here under the protection of *Gruppenführer* Gud."

His expression cooled. "I see." He gave Allina a courteous bow. "I know the *Gruppenführer* by reputation." He looked toward the makeshift bar at the back of the room. "You have nothing to drink," he said to Allina, laying his hat on the table. "May I get you a glass of wine?"

"Yes, thank you," Allina murmured, grateful to see him retreat, although wine was the last thing she wanted.

"Loritz is nice," Rilla said, squeezing her hand. "Trust me. He's fun, and a wonderful dancer." The tune changed again, this time to "I Dance into Heaven with You." Rilla swayed in her chair as the waltz began.

Allina wrapped her arms around her middle as the pain hit. Albert had loved this song. It was one of their favorites. He knew the lyrics by heart and crooned to her whenever they danced to its slow, romantic melody. *Stop it. Stop! Think of anything but him . . .*

Kortig returned, glasses of wine and beer in hand, and pulled up a chair between them. "Are you all right, Fräulein?" he asked, his fine brows knotted in concern. "You're pale."

"Of course," Allina murmured. She leaned toward Rilla, hoping for mindless conversation to drown the song out of her head.

"Are you responsible for our new bounty of music?" Rilla asked. "We had nothing but boring instrumental pieces until this week."

"Partly responsible," Kortig said with a wink. "These are mostly Munich acquisitions. Why shouldn't Hochland Home benefit from some of the relocations?" He took a gold case from his pocket and extracted a cigarette.

Rilla's eyes fell to her lap.

"You're too sentimental." Kortig tapped the cigarette against the case before he lit it. "We've moved them to more appropriate lodgings, ones better suited to their situation." He took a deep drag and shrugged, blowing circles of smoke into the air. "The Jews have no need of these items. We're simply putting them to good use."

Allina gulped her wine, but it did nothing to soothe her, burning a trail to her stomach instead.

"Let's talk about something else, please." Rilla grabbed his arm. "Tell me, how is Steffen?"

"I wish I could've sent him here in my place, as that would make you happy," Kortig answered. "*Gruppenführer* von Strassberg needed my help with an urgent matter in Munich." He took a long draught of beer and wiped the foam from his lip. "But you must know how Steffen is doing. He writes you every day, little one."

A flush filled Rilla's round cheeks, but she crossed her arms over her belly and frowned. "His letters are sweet, but short. He shares nothing of his day-to-day activities."

"The details would bore you. Most are tedious." Kortig shrugged and took another drink. "Others are . . . unsuitable to share with women, particularly those in your delicate disposition."

Allina shuddered. She turned back to the dancers, hoping for distraction, but all she could make out was a sea of uniforms. They were everywhere. She squeezed her eyes shut, trying not to think about Albert, or the song, or the dozens of men in the room drinking to excess while they danced and flirted with women they hardly knew, women proud to bear children they'd never love.

Come and let us dream with quiet music, our romantic fairy tale of happiness,
> *And dance with me into heaven . . .*

"Would you give me the honor, Fräulein?"

When Allina opened her eyes, Kortig was smiling courteously and extending his hand with grace, as any gentleman would.

Her throat closed. It was all but impossible to breathe in here.

"I-I'm sorry," she stammered. "I don't feel well."

"Allina, what's wrong?" Rilla said. "Wait—"

She ran for the door.

"Wake up, Allina, wake up!"

She lurched awake to hands shaking her shoulders. Rilla's eyes were fierce and her grip was surprisingly strong as she forced Allina to sit up in bed.

"I'm awake," Allina croaked. Her mouth tasted like dirt and her night-gown was soaked through. She grabbed Rilla's hand. It was cool and dry. *Nightmare. It's just a nightmare.* She fell back against the pillows with her heart pounding in her ears.

"You were screaming and calling out for Albert again," Rilla murmured. She wiped the perspiration from Allina's face with the sleeve of her nightgown. "Do you remember your dream?"

Gunshots. Fire. Auntie. Screaming. All the bodies . . .

Allina shivered and turned her face into the damp pillow. "I don't remember anything." She swallowed hard to keep from heaving. It was the mixer, and Kortig, and all those uniforms. They'd made her remember again, it was all coming back, and, God help her, she wanted to forget. She couldn't live with the images in her brain.

"Who's Albert?" Rilla asked softly. "Is he the man who hurt you?"

Allina turned around in time to see her friend's eyes fill with tears.

"I saw you the night you came in," Rilla murmured. "Someone hurt you very badly, didn't he?"

"Yes," Allina whispered, "but not Albert."

"Who is he, then?"

Allina shook her head. Her eyes and throat ached, but no tears came.

When Rilla pulled her close, she buried her face against her friend's pregnant belly and shook.

"It's all right," Rilla said, stroking her hair with a mother's tender touch. "Things will get better. You'll see."

CHAPTER 11

Winter 1938

ALLINA

Allina checked the clock in the nursery for the tenth time in as many minutes. Time was standing still tonight. It was 9:30 and she wouldn't be relieved until midnight.

She reached back to adjust the pins in her nurse's cap, but her hands shook too much to make a good job of it. She yanked the pins out instead, allowing the cap to fall to the floor. Her hair tumbled around her shoulders, each heavy lock a distinct, tender ache tugging at her skull, and she raked her fingers through the mess to rub out the pain. The perfect rows of cribs cast a crisscross of shadows against the floor in the dim light. Eighteen identical cradles. Eighteen sleeping babies. Every file was in pristine order, and the furniture, floors, and countertops were spotless. No one could fault this room, at least, for uncleanness. She'd made sure of it.

Her heart rate spiked for no apparent reason, as it had done many times since the mixer, and Allina's breath hitched while she paced down the rows of cradles. More memories of Badensburg and that black, violent night had come back this week, but even without those images she often found herself in blind, animal panic. Tonight, the need to flee was overwhelming. *I want to run somewhere, anywhere, but there's no place to run.*

Albert's warm eyes and gentle smile flashed in her mind as the maddening questions circled in her brain: Had Albert heard about Badensburg? Did he think she was dead, or was he trying to find her? Could she sneak a letter to him? Should she try to escape to join him in Berlin?

Stop it! Stop thinking. Covering her eyes, Allina forced Albert's face from her mind. There was no way to contact him without risking his safety. As for escaping this hellish place . . . her papers were fakes and it was too dangerous to live in Berlin, assuming Albert was still there. His efforts might have taken him to other cities by now.

No, Allina was trapped here until she could secure a means of escape. And nearly every minute of her day was planned out at Hochland Home.

Damn the head nurse for switching her to the late shift. Days in the nursery passed quickly enough, but the nights—filled with thundering silence, suffocating darkness, and her tortured, circular thinking—had her running off the rails. Allina went to the window and pressed her forehead to the cold glass. Trees shuddered in the wind, creating shadows that bobbed and weaved like restless ghosts, and the December snow floated in thick, chaotic swirls in the air. Closing her eyes and taking deep, measured breaths, she willed her racing heart to slow. She had to get rid of the tightness binding her chest.

She walked to one of the cradles and peered inside. Neils Schneider. Berta's son. Awake but mute, the baby pumped his legs and blew spit bubbles as his pale blue gaze drifted across the ceiling. He was a beautiful child, golden-haired and pink-faced. Innocent. The head nurse would say her touch wasn't warranted, but Allina reached in and caressed the curve of his cheek. Neils flinched and turned away, but she persisted, running a finger down his forehead and along the length of his button nose. The little one sneezed, scrunched up his face, and let out a whimper.

They get so little love, not from their mothers or us. It was just days before Christmas, but there was no tenderness or joy at Hochland Home.

To hell with house rules. To hell with them all. Defying instructions, she picked him up and walked the length of the room, joggling her arms until he favored her with wet gurgles and a sweet pucker of pink lips. She pressed her nose to his neck, inhaling the milkiness and talcum powder clinging to his skin. "You're such a handsome boy," she whispered, setting her hand on his tummy. Neils's gaze zeroed in on her face, and he wrapped a moist, chubby fist around her thumb.

A warm ache filled Allina's chest. She smiled into his perfect little face and began to sing.

> *Silent night, holy night*
> *All is calm, all is bright . . .*

Neils was asleep before she finished, which was just as well, since her voice was cracked and hoarse by the end. Allina set him down in his cradle and retreated to a chair closer to the nursery's entrance, shuddering as she grabbed a pillow and sat down.

Help me.

But God wasn't listening.

Helpmehelpmehelpme—

Burying her face in the pillow, Allina rocked and stomped her feet until her heels stung, forgetting herself and blind to the needs of the children, their mothers, and everyone else at Hochland Home. At first her tears were silent, but when she let go, the screams began. She wailed into the pillow, choking on the burning, hard ball of ugliness in the pit of her stomach.

When no tears were left, Allina continued to rock with her head cradled in the down. She felt better, weak but oddly light with exhaustion. Her mind was a perfect blank. Her heart was still beating. And she could breathe without feeling the air was out to choke her.

It was then that she felt the man's gaze. A curious sensation that stirred the hairs at her nape made her stop rocking and lift her head.

An officer stood in the doorway. He was tall and slim and his uniform bore the insignia associated with the rank of *Gruppenführer*. Like Gud. This one was younger, however, and broad shouldered. His blond hair glinted with pomade. He had an arrogant face, with a square jaw, a straight, high-bridged nose, and sharp cheekbones. His gaze was dark and penetrating. In the dim light she couldn't tell what color his eyes were, but she couldn't look away.

He hesitated and rocked back slightly on his heels, with hands linked behind his back. "Forgive me for intruding, *Schwester*," he murmured. "I was passing by the room and heard you." He bowed in deference, waiting for her response.

Allina lowered her head long enough to wipe the tears from her face. When she glanced back up, she saw concern in his eyes. A spark of anger ignited in her belly. She suddenly had a desire to slap the gentlemanly manners off his face.

When Allina spoke, her voice was as smooth as ice. "I apologize, *Gruppenführer*, for my weakness. It won't happen again."

The officer's eyebrows lifted in surprise. Strictly speaking, the words were acceptable, but Allina knew her tone was not. He remained silent for a few seconds while she continued to stare at him, too rudely to be misinterpreted, and too angry to be afraid.

He cleared his throat before speaking again. "You were singing to the children before, and your voice . . . it's quite beautiful. 'Silent Night' has always been my favorite at Christmas."

Allina stood, clasping her hands at the waist. "Again, my apologies. Religious songs aren't allowed here, as we both know," she said, fighting to keep the bitterness out of her voice. "*Schwester* Ziegler prefers the Führer to God. Clearly, God is nowhere to be found at Hochland Home."

The officer opened his mouth, then closed it and cocked his head, as if listening to an internal voice. He remained absolutely still as he searched her face.

After a half minute of charged silence, the officer gave a slow nod. "God is here, *Schwester*," he replied gravely. "He may seem very far from both of us right now, but he's here. We can't lose faith."

She had no response to his statement, and that seemed to satisfy him. His mouth relaxed in a grin. The transformation was instant and unsettling. He was handsome when he smiled. She looked down at her shoes.

"I've intruded on your duties long enough. Perhaps we'll be fortunate enough to continue this conversation another day," he said. "I hope you feel better, *Schwester*. Happy Christmas."

She peeked up in time to watch him click his heels, bow, and withdraw from the room.

Allina fell back into her seat, limp with relief, and too dazed to do anything but stare out the window. As the storm howled, she became mesmerized by the patterns of whirling snow floating like puffs of smoke in the inky night.

The officer's intense, probing gaze flashed in Allina's mind and she shivered, regretting her temper. Weeping, singing, and speaking of God to a *Gruppenführer*. What was wrong with her? And what would he do if they met again?

CHAPTER 12

KARL

Karl poured himself another cup of coffee as the young officers banged their fists on the breakfast table. The men were in boisterous moods this morning.

Tedrick Bamm, a newly consigned officer, stood to toast his comrades. "The girls don't call us the stud-bulls for nothing. I saw some tempting new cows to plow in the field last night." He raised his coffee mug, flexing scrawny biceps.

"I'm ready, Bamm. There's plenty of me to go around," said Hans Müller, wagging scraggly blond brows. Recent luck with the ladies had fed Müller's ego to monster proportions. He claimed his blue eyes made every girl at Hochland Home swoon.

Unit leader Loritz Kortig stood and cocked a hip against the table. "Gentlemen, please. We should be more civil when discussing our most sacred responsibility."

Karl eyed the officer over the rim of his cup. Kortig was Karl's youngest unit leader, well connected, and already the father of two *Lebensborn* children. Would he rein his own men in?

"Our duty is clear," Kortig continued, placing a hand over his heart. "We'll make sure our women receive honorary cards and Mother's Cross medals. In return, we can enjoy the pleasure of their company as often as possible."

The men burst into raucous laughter and pounded on the table.

"These young women," Karl said, in a mild voice, "should any of them choose your acquaintance, serve the Führer, just as you do." The men clapped their mouths shut and trained their eyes on him. "They deserve your respect."

Bamm snapped to attention. "Yes, *Gruppenführer!*"

"Of course, *Gruppenführer.*" Müller walked over and refilled Karl's coffee cup.

"I meant no disrespect, *Gruppenführer* von Strassberg." Kortig dipped his head as he took his seat.

For a few minutes, the only sounds in the dining room were the scraping of forks and knives against plates and the thuds of coffee mugs hitting the table.

Karl folded a thick piece of bacon in half and gulped it down before turning his attention to the latest issue of the *National Observer*.

FOR THE FUTURE AND GLORY OF THE REICH

The Nazi philosophy of life, having given the family the role in the State to which it is entitled, must take measures to preserve the sanctity of German blood on German soil. We rely on men and women of good will, who, through high moral purpose, honor the commitment to create new life. Whether married or unmarried, all women of pure blood who bear children for our Führer, with the assistance of racially unobjectionable young men, shall be deemed heroic. The State will do everything in its power to care for these women and the children they bear to preserve this valuable national wealth. . .

Tossing the paper aside, Karl finished his coffee. The grounds were bitter when they hit the back of his throat.

"I apologize again on behalf of my men, sir. Our eagerness gets the best of us." Kortig pointed to the article as the men murmured their agreement. "It will be our honor to attend tonight's mixer, dance with the ladies in attendance, and let nature take its course for the glory of the Reich."

"Don't let their willingness fool you," Karl cautioned. "Most are hus-band hunting." Although why a woman would want Kortig, Bamm, or Müller for a husband was beyond him.

"Rumor has it a few are interested in *you*, sir," Bamm added helpfully.

At thirty, Karl was four years past the recommended marriage age and had fathered no children. His subscription to the *Lebensborn* program was high enough to be uncomfortable, and several senior officers had begun pressuring him last year.

"Berta couldn't stop talking about the mysterious *Gruppenführer* von Strassberg last night." Müller straightened his jacket. "She's a wild one, that Berta."

"I'll leave her to you, Müller," Karl said with a wink.

"Try not to get into too much trouble, gentlemen," Karl added as he stood. "*Heil* Hitler!"

"*Heil* Hitler!" The soldiers saluted. Roughhousing, they pushed at each other as they exited the room. A chorus of whistles and footfalls echoed down the hall.

Karl sank into his chair. The men were right about one thing: Most of the women at Hochland Home were ready and willing. A tipsy pair had approached him last night, suggesting he take them, one after the other. They were shrill and desperate, and only wanted him because of the uniform he wore. Karl turned them down and escaped to wander the halls in peace.

Then he'd stumbled across that young *Schwester* in the nursery. He'd watched her unravel as she crooned to an infant in a lovely, aching voice that went straight to his gut. He probably should have given her privacy, but he'd been unable to turn away.

She'd seemed innocent with her tawny hair loose around her shoulders and was painfully thin beneath her stiff nurse's apron. But her eyes . . . they were like a cat's, a warm moss green and tilted up at the corners. The tears clinging to those thick lashes had made them more beautiful.

The young *Schwester*'s mouth, on the other hand, was as effective a weapon as his Browning. She'd lashed out at him without any attempt to check her temper. It was an unbelievable risk, mocking the Führer so boldly.

She was spirited. Obviously intelligent. An exciting and scary combination, although he was damn sure she wouldn't care about his opinion.

Karl snorted. He'd do well to stay away from her. It was fortunate next week's meetings in Berlin meant he'd be away from Hochland Home. He couldn't afford to be distracted, and an affair was out of the question. As beautiful and compelling as the young lady was, she was bound to get herself into trouble if she couldn't curb her tongue and impulsive nature.

CHAPTER 13

ALLINA

Schwester Marta barreled into the break room just as Allina settled down with her morning mug of tea.

"Rilla's waters just broke," Marta said. "She's asking for you, so I'll cover your duties for the rest of the day. The poor thing is still hours away from delivery. She's scared. Please come."

Allina sprinted down the hall to the birthing rooms. Rilla's eyes were wide and her nightgown was soaked with sweat, but she smiled when Allina perched on the edge of the bed.

"I'm here," she said, and took her friend's hand. Rilla held on for hours, through contractions and stories and silly songs they crooned together, until Allina's fingers went numb.

As the labor progressed, Rilla began calling out for her mother in a broken voice that made Allina's heart ache. "I'm going to die," she sobbed. "Tell my parents I'm sorry."

"Nonsense," Allina said, pressing a cold compress to her forehead. "The pain is normal. Try to relax between contractions. Your body knows what to do."

The labor went on too long, and *Schwester* Ziegler shooed Allina out of the delivery area sometime after midnight. She went to her room but didn't manage a wink of sleep.

Rilla's baby arrived shortly after 5:00 a.m. the next morning. Ziegler herself knocked on Allina's sleeping room door to invite her to see mother and child. She was first, at Rilla's insistence, to see the perfect baby boy.

Cradling the newborn in the crook of her arm, Allina gave her friend's shoulder a gentle shake. "Rilla," she whispered. "Your son is hungry."

Rilla came awake with a frown, but the sight of her child brought a radiant smile to her face. "What time is it?" She reached eagerly for her baby. "How did you manage to sneak Tobias into my room?"

"It's half past two." Burying her nose against the baby's neck, Allina inhaled his sweet fresh scent. "*Schwester* Ziegler had too much wine last night. She's snoring away like an old goat." Allina grinned and laid the baby in his mother's arms. "What she doesn't know won't hurt her. I thought you'd enjoy the extra time with him."

Rilla undid her nightshirt and pulled her son to her breast. The moment Tobias began to suckle, she leaned back with a deep sigh of contentment. "He's two days old, and I'm overwhelmed with love," she murmured, eyes fluttering closed. "I didn't know this kind of love existed." She caressed her baby's scalp and planted a soft kiss on his forehead.

And, just like that, you're a mother, Rilla.

"He's beautiful," Allina whispered as the tears built behind her eyes. "You're going to be the best mama." Pulling a chair over, she wiped her eyes and sat with Rilla while Tobias's hungry suckling filled the silence.

Rilla looked at her curiously. "Don't be sad. You're still young. There's plenty of time to have babies of your own."

"God, no." The thought of having a baby made her want to throw up.

"You don't want children?" Rilla asked softly. "But you're so good with them."

"I don't want to talk about it."

Rilla grabbed Allina's hand and held on, not allowing her to back away. "What happened to you before you came here? I may be younger than you, but I'm not a fool. Your nightmares haven't stopped. You go white as milk when *Schwester* Ziegler mentions Gud's name, and you're skittish around the soldiers. Please tell me."

"I can't." Allina shuddered.

Rilla averted her eyes. "All right."

It was easy to see she'd hurt her friend, but there was no help for it, so Allina changed the topic. "He's nearly done. Will you be able to sleep?" She ran her hand down Tobias's back.

"I hope so." Rilla sighed, then gestured at the short stack of postcards on the bedside table. "Maybe I'll write my parents instead. I've been putting that off."

"How long has it been?"

"Six months," Rilla said in a small voice. "My family are strict Catholics. Very old-fashioned." Rilla's eyes closed as she continued to cuddle her baby. "They wanted to send me to relatives in Berlin. My aunt promised to raise the baby as her own."

"I see."

Rilla swallowed hard. "We didn't part well. They were furious when Steffen found a place for me here. I left with my clothes, not much else." Tobias's head listed to the side, and Rilla kissed her son's head. "But we'll be fine, won't we," she whispered before handing him back.

Rilla grabbed Allina's arm before she could go. "You won't tell anyone about my parents, will you? *Schwester* Ziegler knows we're Catholic, but you don't need to remind her."

"I won't tell a soul, Rilla. Your secret's safe with me."

"I'd keep your secrets safe, too, you know."

But Allina's secrets were too heavy a burden, ones that might put Rilla and her baby in danger. And if Rilla betrayed her . . . No, she couldn't bear it. She was safer alone.

"Allina, wake up. Please. I need your help!"

She roused to the anxious, cobalt gaze of *Schwester* Wendeline, who stood at the side of her bed.

Allina rubbed her eyes, trying to clear away the sleep fog. "What time is it?"

"A little after seven." When Allina groaned, she added, "I know your shift ended an hour ago, but Marta and Ida-Lynne are both ill. And *Schwester* Ziegler is . . . indisposed." One of the sweeter nurses on staff,

Wendeline was wringing her hands. "She's going to be so upset with me. I haven't gotten the toddlers out of bed yet."

"Toddlers?" Allina must have misheard. Hochland Home didn't have groups of older children in residence. They were in high demand and adopted as soon as they were weaned.

"Please, Allina." Wendeline looked like she was ready to cry, so Allina threw on her nursing uniform and followed, surprised when the older nurse scurried up the stairs. "This way."

"Where are we going?"

"Third floor," Wendeline huffed as she stopped at the top of the stairs.

"I didn't know there were any children up here."

"These are the special treatment rooms," Wendeline explained. "Senior *Schwestern* care for these children. They take extra effort."

When she opened the door at the end of the hall, the astringent, musty scent of stale urine hung in the air. The room was filled with rows of low, narrow cots, set close together in barrack style, and covered in coarse navy blankets.

Allina covered her nose and tried breathing through a growing sense of alarm. There were two dozen occupied beds here, so the room should have been filled with the sounds of children. Most of the young ones were silent and lying down, tucked tightly under the covers, their blank stares fixed to the walls or ceiling. A few were upright in their cots, chubby hands plucking at their blankets, and babbling like infants.

Two toddlers had managed to wriggle out from under the covers and were crawling around on the floor.

One little boy saw them enter. He giggled and scrambled to his feet.

"Sheh-shuh," he lisped. He teetered over to Allina and buried his face in her skirts.

"Be a good boy, Otto, and follow *Schwester* Allina," Wendeline murmured. She plucked the second child from the floor and handed him over, pointing to a door at the other side of the room. "Through there," she told Allina. "The children must be fed first. We'll take care of their diapers later. There's no time to change them twice this morning."

The next two hours were a frenzied mess. Allina helped Wendeline transport the rest of the children into their dining room and get them fed. The toddlers sat on the floor at low tables, eating scrambled eggs and porridge with their hands. No attempt was made to use spoons, and some had little appetite—a small wonder as so many were sitting in soiled diapers.

After breakfast, it took nearly an hour to change them. The state of the children's bottoms was deplorable.

"We do what we can," Wendeline said. She handed Allina a tin of Penaten ointment. "These little ones aren't ready to adopt yet."

"Why not?" Allina whispered.

"That's for Director Ebner and *Schwester* Ziegler to decide. There's a specific checklist each child must meet before adoption can take place."

"Surely this setup can't benefit any of the children—"

The head nurse entered, cutting off all discussion. *Schwester* Ziegler's face was gray and her eyes were still puffy from last night's overindulgence.

When her gaze met Allina's, the woman skidded to a stop. "Why are you here?"

"I asked her to come, *Schwester* Ziegler," Wendeline explained, wringing her hands again. "Ida-Lynne and Marta didn't report to work this morning. I'm grateful for her help."

The explanation seemed to satisfy the head nurse, who nodded. "Thank you for filling in, but I'm here now. You may go."

The woman's stern tone demanded obeisance, so Allina had no choice. She felt the heat of *Schwester* Ziegler's gaze on the back of her neck long after she'd exited the room.

In the days that followed, Allina couldn't get the sounds and smells and sights of the third floor out of her mind. The lurching gaits, unfocused expressions, and sore, oozing bottoms haunted her, so much that she'd gone to the third floor and worked extra hours on the days when her schedule allowed. She'd also begged *Schwester* Ziegler to reassign her to the third floor, but the head nurse had refused. *You're still new here,* she said. *Too often, you let emotion eclipse your judgment.* Allina had glimpsed compassion, even anguish, in the older woman's gaze before her expression hardened. *These children serve a purpose,* she'd added. *We must trust the Reichsführer's plan.*

In that moment, Allina saw the head nurse with different eyes. Something essential in the woman was shattered. It was like looking at a face in a fractured mirror, with the image broken into pieces that no longer fit together. Any kindness Allina had sensed in *Schwester* Ziegler was nothing more than an echo of the woman she'd once been, a woman who was disappearing. A woman who would follow orders and destroy others, even as she destroyed herself.

CHAPTER 14

ALLINA

Rilla stood with Allina at the front of the main dining hall with her new-born son nestled against her bosom. "I can't go through with it," she whispered, reaching for Allina's hand.

"For your son's sake, you must." Allina squeezed Rilla's clammy palm in support. She was powerless to help her friend. "Think of what you'll deny Tobias if you don't take part in the naming ceremony."

"I know," Rilla said. Her eyes were bloodshot from crying, and if the way she gripped Allina's hand was any indication, Rilla was holding on to her composure by her fingernails. "But it's an abomination."

Allina shifted her attention to the makeshift altar in front of them. It was perfect. And horrible. A red silk skirt embossed with a swastika was draped over the table, and in the center was a large, framed picture of the Führer, flanked by lush green plants, vases of red and white tulips, and lit candles. A pedestal holding a bright red satin pillow stood in front of the altar. The final touch was a banner hanging over the entire display proclaiming GERMANY AWAKE! in oversize letters.

The head nurse's quick, confident stride clipped down the hallway. Entering the room, *Schwester* Ziegler made a beeline for them. "Good morning, ladies." She eyed Rilla's dress with an encouraging smile. "What a lovely shade of green. It's very becoming on you, dear." When her gaze lifted to Rilla's face, she pursed her lips. "Is everything all right?"

"I'm just tired, *Schwester*. All the excitement."

"She's fine." Allina fixed what she hoped was a convincing smile on her face. "We've been looking forward to the celebration all week, haven't we, Rilla?"

Rilla's weak nod was unconvincing. Before Allina could comment further, she felt a prickle at the back of her neck and turned around.

Him.

The SS officer who'd walked in on her in the nursery was here. Allina's pulse quickened. Dressed in a perfectly tailored gray uniform, he paused long enough to give her what anyone else might consider a charming bow. When she didn't return it, he bowed again and turned away to continue a discussion with a group of officers.

"He's attractive, isn't he? And . . . interested." Rilla bit her lip.

Allina shot Rilla a warning look. "I hadn't noticed."

Ziegler's eyes widened. "Has *Gruppenführer* von Strassberg taken an interest in you, Allina?" She cleared her throat. "I'd be careful there. We all know you're under *Gruppenführer* Gud's protection."

The assessment was a slap across the face. "I'm most certainly not interested in him," Allina said. Her stomach clenched. "We've met only once. Until now, I didn't know the man's name."

The head nurse's narrowed gaze remained skeptical. "Von Strassberg is certainly charming enough. And like you, he has a softness for the children."

"Why do you say that, *Schwester?*" Allina asked, trying to keep her voice light. Even now, he could be thinking about how to punish her for what he'd witnessed in the nursery, or find a way to use it to his advantage.

The head nurse shot Allina a sharp look. "He works behind the scenes, so we get the best food and medical supplies. A little extra, here and there." The head nurse pursed her lips, considering, as she stroked the plumpness beneath her chin. "I'd regret doing anything to jeopardize his support."

There was a pregnant pause as all three women considered that statement.

Dropping her eyes, Allina focused on the altar, brushing an imaginary speck of lint off the table's surface. "Does he ever . . . consult with you on the children?"

"No," Ziegler said in a tight voice, "as I've said, his involvement with Hochland Home isn't part of his official duties." She surveyed one of the tulip arrangements with a critical eye and repositioned a few of the blossoms.

"He didn't sound like a typical soldier." Allina shifted the portrait of the Führer so it was positioned dead center between the two vases. "When I met him, I mean. His accent isn't common."

"The von Strassbergs were well connected at one time," the head nurse replied. "His father was a distant cousin of Kaiser Wilhelm." She shifted the Führer's portrait back a centimeter in the other direction. "Although his childhood was filled with tragedy, if memory serves. Both parents fell to the Spanish flu. His grandmother and aunt raised him in Switzerland."

"He was orphaned," Rilla murmured. "Of course he'd have tender concern for the children."

Allina trailed her fingers along the tablecloth and held her tongue.

Unfortunately, the town registrar chose that exact moment to make his entrance. Nikolas Stolt was a short, stubby man with the pushed-in face of a bulldog, but his hazel eyes were friendly.

"Are we ready?" He rubbed his hands together, clearly relishing the ceremony to come.

"I trust you'll find everything in order, Herr Stolt," *Schwester* Ziegler said, clasping her hands tightly at the waist. "I can't attend today's ceremony. One of our new mothers is having complications following her delivery." She checked her watch and turned to Allina. "You're in charge this morning. The ceremony shouldn't last more than half an hour. Please make sure the reception clears by 10:45 so we can set up for lunch. As for my other expectations," she said, with a quick glance in Rilla's direction, "I leave this young mother in your capable hands."

"Yes, *Schwester*. Come, Rilla." Allina guided her friend to the first row and sat Rilla down in front of the altar. All Rilla needed to do was keep quiet during the ceremony.

Taking their cue, five SS officers, including Loritz Kortig and von Strassberg, walked to the head table and formed a semicircle around the pedestal. Kortig took his place in front, since he was officiating.

"Before we begin the ceremony, I'd like to make a few personal statements." Kortig smoothed back his hair before turning to speak to the audience with energetic confidence. "Steffen Hermann and I have been friends since childhood. Today, he represents Germany in the Sudetenland and devotes his life to serve the glory of our Führer."

"It's a privilege to welcome Tobias to our great purpose," Kortig continued. "National Socialism is an ideology which demands the whole man, even our lives, when necessary." He gave Rilla a wide grin. "What you and Steffen have created in your son is Germany's future."

Kortig walked to Rilla and opened his arms to receive the child. When he took Tobias into his arms, the baby began to cry. At first the infant's sobs were weak, but as the seconds passed, he began wailing in distress.

"What good strong lungs this young one has," Kortig joked, flushing a dull red. Walking back to the pedestal, he joggled the baby but was unable to quiet him.

Frantic, Rilla stepped forward. Allina held her friend back while the baby's screams filled the room. After a while Allina couldn't stand the crying herself. Clearly, he had no idea how to handle children. Allina opened her mouth, ready to take the boy, but the *Gruppenführer* raised a finger.

"May I?"

Kortig faltered, but when he handed the squirming bundle over, little Tobias quieted almost immediately.

Von Strassberg grinned and tucked the boy with an efficient motion into the crook of his arm. Chuckles filled the hall. When their gazes met, the intensity in his eyes made Allina glance away.

Kortig straightened his shoulders. "It's a pleasure to welcome this child to the glory of the Reich. We begin with a reading from our Führer's great work, *Mein Kampf*." His voice filled the room as he read:

> *The state must declare the child to be the most precious treasure of the people. What we fight for is to safeguard the existence and reproduction of our race and our people, the sustenance of our children and the purity of our blood, the freedom and independence of the Fatherland, so that our people may mature for the fulfillment of the mission allotted it by the creator of the universe. Every thought and every idea, every doctrine and all knowledge, must serve this purpose.*

Allina closed her eyes and bent her head, pretending to listen. Rilla had warned her often enough how her face betrayed her emotions, and she couldn't afford to let anger show. By focusing on the inhalation and exhalation of each breath, she drowned out Kortig's lecture.

When Allina opened her eyes, the *Gruppenführer* was watching her. His gaze dropped to her hands, which were fisted at the waist. Taking another deep breath, she unclenched them.

Kortig finished the reading, and von Strassberg placed Tobias on the red satin pillow. Two officers drew their swords, crossed them in a giant X, and placed their joined blades on the baby's belly. Kortig continued with a blessing:

We believe in the God of all things, and in the mission of our German blood, which grows ever young from German soil. We believe in the race, in the carrier of the blood, and in the Führer, chosen for us by God.

We take you into our community as a limb of our body. You shall grow up in our protection and bring honor to your name, pride to your brotherhood, and inextinguishable glory to your race.

We name this child, Tobias Weber, as we make him part of our family and welcome him into the glory of the Thousand-Year Reich.

The two soldiers raised their arms, lifting their crossed swords above the infant's head with a metallic zing. Then they uncrossed the blades with a flourish, sheathed them, and clicked their heels in unison.

"*Heil* Hitler!" Kortig said loudly, as he saluted the picture of Adolf Hitler on the altar.

"*Heil* Hitler!" the audience called out in response.

Von Strassberg drew himself to full height and raised Tobias toward the picture, as if to offer him to the Führer. There was no emotion in his face, just a brief tightening of his jaw.

Rilla dug her nails into Allina's palm, but there was nothing to do, no protest to make. She held her friend's hand tighter.

Tobias gave another lusty cry, breaking the silence. As the crowd burst into laughter, von Strassberg hurried over to place the boy into his mother's arms. "He's a beautiful child, Fräulein," he murmured to Rilla, although his penetrating gaze remained on Allina's face. She shivered, and took a half step back.

"Thank you, *Gruppenführer*." Rilla nuzzled her baby's cheek.

Loritz hurried over to join them. "I'm sure he'll make Steffen proud, Rilla," he said with an oily smile.

"Please, won't you both join us for refreshments?" Rilla asked in a faint voice.

Kortig and von Strassberg accompanied them to the buffet table, where a staff member was busy portioning out slices of cake. The *Gruppenführer* wasn't much taller than Kortig, but he seemed to tower over the younger man and filled too much of the space around him. Allina took a hasty step back and bumped into Rilla. While he didn't seem to notice, von Strassberg took a casual step away. "Go find some seats for us," he murmured. "We'll bring the food to you. It's the least we officers can do for a new mother and faithful nurse." He had the gall to wink at her before she walked away.

The two men brought the sweet-laden plates to the table, and silence descended as they dug into the delicacies. The chocolate cake was dense and sugary enough to make her teeth ache, but fresh fruit in midwinter was the real treat. Allina avoided the *Gruppenführer's* curious gaze by concentrating on peeling an orange.

Their few minutes of peace ended the moment Rilla stopped to kiss and cuddle Tobias.

"You pamper your son," Kortig chided over a forkful of cake. "He'll never be a decent soldier if you keep it up."

"He isn't a soldier yet," Rilla said. Shooting Kortig a testy look, she ran a finger down Tobias's nose.

The *Gruppenführer* directed his attention at Allina. "You're quiet today, *Schwester*. Don't you have an opinion?" His lips curved up, teasing. "Is this loving mother ruining her son's chance of becoming a good soldier? Perhaps you'd be willing to share your expert knowledge on child-rearing."

She should have been more afraid, but there was too much humor in his face. Tossing a half-eaten section of orange back onto the plate, Allina rose to the bait. "I see nothing wrong with a mother holding her child, *Gruppenführer*."

Rilla grabbed her arm. "Spoiled or not, it's time for this young one's next meal. If you'll excuse me, I must attend my son. Allina, will you accompany me?" She rose and headed for the door.

Allina gave the *Gruppenführer* a final, searching look and followed her friend out of the room.

"What's going on?" she asked Rilla. "Tobias nursed before the ceremony, as we both know."

"I'm baptizing my son." Lifting her chin, Rilla pulled away and hurried down the hall.

"*What?*" Allina's eyes darted up and down the empty passageway. "I wish that were possible," she whispered, running after Rilla to keep pace, "but you know *Schwester* Ziegler won't permit it." She grabbed Rilla's arm and pulled her to a halt.

"I don't care about her rules," Rilla said. "I'm leaving for St. Gallus now."

"Rilla, your son was born in Hochland Home. The Reich doesn't approve of religious ceremonies."

"I don't care what the Reich approves of or doesn't approve of. I allowed my son to be welcomed into service with that mumbo jumbo." Rilla jerked her shoulder toward the main dining hall and continued down the hallway toward the courtyard entrance, forcing Allina to follow. "We have to hurry. Father Regenauer is waiting."

Allina scrambled after her, wincing as her shoes clopped on the linoleum. "When did you find time to arrange this?"

Rilla stopped and whirled around. "Does it matter? I need a sentry to make sure we're not being followed." She gazed lovingly at Tobias, kissed his golden head. "We need your help."

"It's too dangerous," Allina said, grabbing her friend's arm. When Rilla shook off her grip and started down the hall again, Allina followed. "You need an escort, and no officer here would dare accompany you. Himmler himself has prohibited baptisms. You're putting your safety at risk, Rilla, along with your son's."

"Tobias will be baptized. Are you going to help me or not?"

Rilla's color was high and the tilt of her chin proved there'd be no reasoning with her.

"All right," Allina agreed. Although this was surely a catastrophic idea,

Rilla was her only friend here. And every day, that friendship proved more precious. "All right. I'll help you."

They came up with a plan, a simple one. Allina couldn't accompany Rilla to the church—there was too much risk if they both went missing, and she was in charge of the reception, in any case—but St. Gallus was a ten-minute walk and Rilla thought she could make it there and back in an hour. Allina acted as sentry as Rilla snuck out of the house. She promised to be back in precisely one hour, but Allina propped open the door to the North Wing's courtyard with a loose brick, just in case.

When Allina returned to the reception, most attendees were still too enamored of their food to notice Rilla's absence. A few asked about her toward the end of the festivities, including *Gruppenführer* von Strassberg, who had a mind like a mousetrap, but Allina satisfied their curiosity with the oldest excuse: Tobias had gas. A faithful nurse would tend to him. As for Rilla, she was overly tired after the morning's ceremony and decided to take a nap.

Everything would have gone off perfectly had Rilla not returned ten minutes early and at the precise moment the head nurse walked by the door to the courtyard.

It was a case of disastrous luck all around.

Allina's gut tensed when *Schwester* Ziegler dragged her into the administrative office.

Ziegler took a seat behind her desk and leaned back in her chair. Her face was ashen and her eyes had darkened to charcoal. "Tell me exactly what happened to Rilla this morning."

"I'm not sure what you mean, *Schwester*." Allina sat tall in the hard, unpadded chair and clasped her hands in her lap to keep from fidgeting. She'd been in this office many times, but never under such dire circumstances. Even the towers of files stacked precariously on the head nurse's imposing mahogany desk seemed menacing and ready to topple onto her at any moment.

"I gave you the responsibility of chaperoning Rilla to the ceremony." Ziegler picked up a pencil and drummed it on the desktop, the staccato beat matching the rhythm of her words. "Your job included getting her back to her room safely. Do you remember our conversation about your duties?"

"Yes, ma'am." Allina fixed what she hoped was a respectful smile on her face. At least Rilla was safe. As a Hochland Home mother, she'd never bear the brunt of the head nurse's anger. No, the fault would lie firmly at Allina's feet.

Ziegler leaned in, piercing Allina with the intensity in her gaze. "How did Rilla manage to get her son to St. Gallus for his baptism?"

"I don't know, *Schwester*." Sure she was flushing, Allina managed a tiny shrug. "She just disappeared."

"Disappeared, you say?" Two bright pink splotches appeared on the apples of her cheeks. "Into thin air?"

"Yes, ma'am."

"Rilla comes from a religious family, but those beliefs are not permitted here, as you well know," the head nurse said in a high, brittle voice. "I trusted you to keep her close at all times." Ziegler was grinding her teeth now, which was as satisfying as it was unnerving, but Allina couldn't afford to let either emotion show.

"Let me repeat my question," she said. "How did you allow Rilla out of your sight long enough for her to disappear?"

"I can't say, *Schwester*." Allina gripped the arms of her chair and fought the urge to look away.

The head nurse slammed her hands on the desk, hard enough to send a tall stack of files to the floor in a tumble of paper. "You can't say?"

"No, ma'am." Allina bit her lip.

Let this be over soon, please.

Ziegler took a pen and notepad from the top drawer of her desk before slamming it shut with a sharp jerk. "I'm very disappointed in you." Her face flushed a deep shade of purple as she began scribbling notes onto the pad. "For the most part, you've done well in the nursery," she said, "but this act of flagrant incompetence requires disciplinary measures." Tossing the pen on her desk, she stood, towering over her. "We're lucky neither Rilla nor her baby were injured. You have failed the Führer today, and I cannot accept such failures. I will send a letter to *Gruppenführer* Gud immediately."

A firm knock on the door interrupted the lecture. *Gruppenführer* von Strassberg walked in without waiting for admittance.

"Pardon the intrusion, *Schwestern*." He bowed at the head nurse with deference.

Allina gaped at him. What had the man heard? His dark blue eyes glinted. His smile was a bit too friendly.

Ziegler rocked back on her sturdy heels before taking her seat again, back stiff as a broom. "What can I do for you, *Gruppenführer*?"

"I overheard your, ah ... exchange ... with Allina while I was waiting in the hall, *Schwester* Ziegler." Von Strassberg lifted one shoulder in a casual shrug. "I regret having caused you any distress. The young lady is trying to avoid involving me in this unfortunate oversight."

Allina remained very still in her chair.

"I beg your pardon, *Gruppenführer*." The woman's eyes blinked with owlish confusion. "How are you involved in this matter?"

"Allina and I were involved in a diverting discussion after this morning's ceremony," he said, flicking his indigo gaze down the length of Allina's body to make his meaning clear.

Allina attempted to swallow, but her mouth was too dry and she nearly choked.

"I'm afraid I gave her no choice." The *Gruppenführer* beamed at the head nurse, flashing even, white teeth. "She can't be blamed."

Ziegler's mouth opened in shock. It made her seem like a caught fish gasping for air. "I'm grateful you've taken me into your confidence," she said after a few seconds. "I can appreciate Allina's reticence in the matter. Thank you for enlightening me."

"My pleasure," von Strassberg said with another wide, satisfied grin.

The head nurse turned to her. "Allina, you may go now," she said with a smile that didn't reach her eyes.

"Thank you, *Schwester*." Allina rose slowly, gripping the arms of her chair to keep her knees from knocking. The *Gruppenführer* helped her up. He held her at a respectable distance, but her body reacted violently and she stiffened.

Still gripping her arm, von Strassberg bowed. "Good day, *Schwester*." He steered Allina out of the room.

As soon as the door closed behind them, Allina whirled around to face him. "Are you trying to destroy me?" she hissed, looking up into his calm, even-featured face. "Do you know what *Schwester* Ziegler believes now?"

He raised a finger to his lips to shush her. "You were in trouble. I wanted to help." He grabbed Allina's wrist and propelled her down the hall to the North Wing. His fingers were uncomfortably warm.

Two mothers approached, and they offered Allina identical, knowing smirks. Von Strassberg stopped long enough to favor them with a courteous bow as he tucked Allina's hand into the crook of his arm. She tried to pull away, but it was no use.

He hurried her to the entrance to the North Courtyard. When they reached the entryway, he closed both the interior and exterior doors, which created a small, glass-lined box. It was an ideal spot to conduct a private conversation, as the windows would reveal an intruder's approach from either direction, but the space was claustrophobic. He filled too much of it.

Allina wrapped her arms around her middle and backed away, pressing her shoulder blades against the ice-cold plaster. "*Why?*" The one-word question was all she could muster.

"Lower your voice, please." He held up his hands. "I've just given you an exceptional cover story. *Schwester* Ziegler is caught and she knows it. She can't discipline you without incurring my wrath, and now she's worrying how Gud will react if he finds out. You should be grateful for that, not angry."

"What do you know about my relationship with Gud?" Allina whispered. A flash of memory—of his body moving over hers—made her shudder.

"Your connection to him is common knowledge." Narrowing his eyes, he watched her closely before taking a step back. "Though I doubt you're linked in the way so many assume."

"You have no idea what you're talking about."

The man went still as he continued searching her face. "Perhaps not, but the details are none of my business," von Strassberg murmured, "unless you choose to share them with me at some point. Either way, your world has shifted as a result of my intervention, and for the better. She's less likely to bully you now."

"But what about *him?*" Allina asked, hating how her voice shook. "What will *Gruppenführer* Gud do if he thinks we've formed . . . an alliance?"

"Don't worry about Gud. I can dispense of him within the week."

"You don't understand—"

"I'm better connected than Reinhardt Gud," he interrupted, "and willing to help you. To offer my protection."

Satisfaction was evident in his face. For a moment she wished she had the courage to slap it. "Gud claimed he was helping me, too." She leaned forward, close enough to see his sharp intake of breath. "What, exactly, would you claim in return for your protection? We both know nothing comes free at Hochland Home."

The question made him go still. After a moment, he nodded as if making a decision, then yanked open the door and hurried her back into the hall. "Grab your coat," he said, "and meet me back here in three minutes. We'll speak in private outside." He bowed and walked down the hall without giving her the chance to reply.

KARL

He led Allina to a far corner of the courtyard and gestured to a stone bench. She obliged him by sitting down, but slid to the edge of the seat and as far away from him as possible. Not a good start.

If the flush in her cheeks was any indication, Allina was still furious. But Karl couldn't answer her questions, not until he knew if her knack for insubordination could be useful.

When Markus telephoned last night, he'd pressed again for evidence on the dozens of children who'd gone missing from Hochland Home. It was, potentially, a scandal of massive proportions, one that could topple Heinrich Himmler and affect the balance of power.

The files were the key. Any details on missing children were locked away in Hochland Home's Central Filing Office. Karl needed someone on the inside to access those files.

"I know you have questions. But before I answer them, I have one of my own."

Allina's response was a heavy sigh, but she inclined her head with careful politeness.

"Why do you work here, if you dislike it so much?" The question came out sharper than necessary. Karl tempered his frustration and tried again.

"It's clear you disapproved of the naming ceremony. You put yourself at risk, working here, helping your friend. From what I've heard, *Schwester* Ziegler is as strict as Himmler himself. Aren't there other duties you could perform in less conspicuous surroundings to serve the Reich?"

Pain flashed in that lovely green gaze for a few seconds before she composed herself.

Allina ran her hands down the front of her coat. "You think I chose to work here," she said in a flat voice that made the admission worse. "I have nowhere else to go. My family is gone. Gud is my patron."

"You've lost your entire family?"

She nodded, compressing her trembling lips into a tight line.

"How?"

Allina tipped her nose up, refusing to speak. Stubborn. She was shivering intensely. Karl unwound his muffler and offered it to her, but she leaned farther away.

As he gazed across the winter landscape, the silence settled over them like a blanket. The icicles clinging to the roof's edge melted slowly in tinkling plops, and as the tree branches released their heavy burdens, they showered the ground with shimmering powder.

If she didn't relent soon, he'd need to apply another tactic before they both froze to death. When he opened his mouth to try again, she relented with another sigh.

"I'm from a small village called Badensburg, west of here. In Rur Eifel." Allina looked at him then, really looked at him. Her eyes were shimmering with grief. Fresh grief, barely contained.

Fucking hell. He'd heard the grimmer accounts about the slaughter at Badensburg, had hoped they were boasts made by Gud's coarser men.

"I'm so sorry."

Her chin quivered, and when she spoke again it was in the high, frightened voice of a wounded child. "I saw everything. The houses burning. The bodies. I can still smell them sometimes, when I close my eyes." She balled her fists. "I tried to hide, but—"

His insides lurched, but Karl stuffed the anger down.

"They left me for dead." Allina wrapped her arms around her stomach. "When I woke up, Gud was there. He let me live." Her voice still shook, but it was deeper now. Angrier.

He cleared the grit from his throat. "I see."

She slayed him with her green eyes. "No, *Gruppenführer*. You could not possibly see."

"I do," Karl said, reaching for her arm, "and I'm sorry."

She jerked away. "Don't touch me."

He closed his eyes and waited.

"Why Badensburg?" she whispered.

No. Karl pinched the bridge of his nose to ease the headache growing behind it. "I'm sorry. I can't tell you that."

Allina managed to look down the length of her nose at him, an impressive feat as she was a head shorter. "Badensburg is a tiny farming village. A threat to no one. What reason could there be to kill so many innocent people?"

The truth might be more cruel than kind, but she wanted an answer, and he needed to earn her trust. Best to tell the story quickly. A sharp blade always did the best job.

"The Gestapo caught an operative in Berlin hiding Polish Jews. The man was sloppy. He got caught but killed himself before his interrogation could be completed. When they went to his rooms, they discovered he'd been using an alias. His real papers led to your little farming village. Gud went there to arrest members of a resistance group."

Allina's eyes went wide, but he pushed on. "At least two dozen men from your town were involved, but we had only the leader's name. When Gud got there, he learned the man had just died. Gud's regiment was to round up the townspeople to question them and find the traitors, but many rebelled. Things turned violent, and the soldiers got out of hand. I'm sorry."

She whimpered and covered her mouth with her hands. "What was the leader's name?"

"Dieter Strauss."

Allina leaned over without a sound, folding herself in half. Karl forgot himself and lay a hand on her shoulder. She didn't react. Perhaps she couldn't feel it, she was shuddering so badly. He ran his hand in slow, even strokes over her hair while she shook. It was like silk against his fingers and smelled faintly of roses.

After a long, terrible minute, she pulled herself up. Allina's face had lost every hint of color and her moss-green eyes were flat. Dead.

"Dieter Strauss was my uncle," she whispered. "And my adopted father. We buried him a day before Gud arrived."

Unbelievable. It was a miracle she'd survived. Karl had heard that Gud's mission in Badensburg went sideways, but it must have been even more chaotic than reported. Then again, Gud was a butcher and rarely efficient.

"You didn't know your uncle was the leader?"

"No, I didn't know any of this." She moaned, closed her eyes. "The operative. The one hiding Polish Jews," she said, voice hitching with every breath. "Was he from Badensburg?"

Karl nodded. His hackles raised.

"What was his name?" she whispered.

Certain the world was shifting on its axis, he answered. "Mannheim."

"Albert." Allina covered her face and began to sob.

Worse and worse. "Who was Albert?"

"My fiancé," she choked out. "We were to wed next year."

"I'm sorry," he murmured. But those words were useless, meaningless. There was nothing he could say to make this better for her.

Once more, he waited while her crying tore at his gut. Allina was still trembling so much her limbs twitched. The girl would go into shock if she wasn't careful, but she shook her head when he suggested they go inside.

"You've given me the truth," she said finally, wiping her cheeks. "I've been wondering all this time. Thank you for telling me."

Then her chin tipped up again, defiant. "So what will you do with me?"

"Do with you?"

"Now you know about my uncle, my fiancée, how they conspired against the Reich. What are your plans for me, *Gruppenführer?*"

She was so brave. After everything she'd learned, she still demanded the truth. Yet Allina Gottlieb was alone in the world, more damaged than he'd thought, and at greater risk than he'd imagined. In an even more precarious situation than Karl was in himself.

"I can't answer you right now," he said, as gently as he could. "I think I've been the source of enough pain today. Go inside. You need to get warm."

Her eyes widened in shock, then fear. Before he could try to offer reassurance, Allina scrambled off the bench and ran out of the courtyard.

Fucking hell. All of his carefully laid plans might turn to shit before they began if he wasn't more careful. Karl had no right to ask anything of this girl. Earning her trust would be all but impossible.

If he had a decent bone in his body he'd help her, then leave her alone. God help them both.

CHAPTER 15

Reinhardt Gud, Gruppenführer SS
Ravensbergweg 8, 14478 Potsdam
3 January 1939

Reinhardt,

I've recently become acquainted with Allina Gottlieb, a young lady under your protection at Hochland Home. I write to ask you to relinquish
her to my care.

   Your duties in Berlin are significant, and your devotion to Frau
Gud after her illness is as admirable as it is necessary. I, on the other
hand, live just outside Munich, and as a young, unmarried man, have
adequate time to attend to all her needs.

   If you have concerns about my request, I suggest we broach the issue
with the Reichsführer.

   You should receive this letter by special courier. I ask that you ex-
tend me the same courtesy to ensure prompt reply.

Yours in service to our Führer,
Karl von Strassberg

Karl von Strassberg, Gruppenführer SS
Sonnenbichlweg 4, 82319 Starnberg
5 January 1939

Karl,

As always, you make your case like a politician.

   I see no need to bring the matter to the Reichsführer's attention. No doubt Heinrich would side with your logic. You're Klemperer's Golden Boy, as I'm well aware.

   I wish you all the satisfaction you deserve and look forward to repayment of this considerable favor at some future date.

   Please give Allina my best.

R.G.

ALLINA

Allina couldn't stop her hands from shaking. She shoved the letters back into von Strassberg's hands. "How should I interpret these?" she asked.

It was barely above freezing, but the temperature had little to do with her shivering.

Allina had revealed too much in the courtyard last week, speaking aloud for the first time about all she'd lost in Badensburg. She'd been reckless. A victim of her own shock and grief, she'd misinterpreted his honesty for decency.

Then nothing. No contact for seven days. The *Gruppenführer* hadn't reported her yet, that much Allina was sure of. If he'd done so, the head nurse's punishment would have been swift and catastrophic.

Now she knew why he'd kept her secret. He expected payment. Of course.

Ten minutes ago, he'd bounded into the dining room, interrupting her meal to drag her outside. *Read these*, he'd said, before placing the letters into her hands. He'd grinned, triumphant.

Now the man was frowning, straight brows furrowed. "I thought—I hoped you'd be happier. Unless you'd rather remain under Gud's cloud?"

"I'd be happier if I knew what you expected in exchange for your protection," Allina said. She covered her mouth as the words sank in and tried to breathe through a growing panic. He was too large, too calm, too *close*, and the space between them hummed with energy.

Von Strassberg's face went still before he spoke. "You can't believe—" He let out an ugly curse that made Allina wince, and leaned back, enunciating his next words carefully. "I'm trying to protect you. What do you take me for?"

She shook her head and slid away, to the bench's edge.

"You don't trust me," he muttered in a voice that betrayed resentment. "Of course not. Why should you?" His broad shoulders slumped. "I could swear to ask for only what you'd willingly give." His gaze captured hers again, but the indigo eyes were flat now. Ancient. "Never mind. Actions are more important than words." Von Strassberg hauled himself off the bench, brushing his collar as he turned away. "Time will tell, Allina. Time always proves the truth. In the interim," he added, patting his pocket, "I'll share these with *Schwester* Ziegler so she knows the situation."

"Very well," Allina whispered. She didn't want to believe him. She hated the niggling sense of unease between her shoulder blades that felt more like doubt than anger or fear. Damn the man for expecting her trust.

"I'll leave you in peace." He bowed and turned to go, hesitating at the last minute. "Actually, there is one thing you can do for me. Have tea with me tomorrow." His lips curved in a tentative smile before they gave up, settling into flat regret. "Just tea."

CHAPTER 16

ALLINA

Ignoring the baby at her breast, Berta Schneider lounged in her chair and perused the latest issue of *Die Dame*.

"Tell me, *Schwester*," Berta said, flipping the magazine's pages with bored flicks of her wrist, "will *Gruppenführer* von Strassberg be visiting again today?"

Berta's voice sawed at Allina's frayed nerves, but she bared her teeth to simulate a smile. "I couldn't say," Allina answered, working around the magazine to rearrange Neils in his feeding sling. "I don't keep the man's schedule." Feeding time was almost over, and thank heaven for that. There were a half dozen mothers left in the nursery, and in ten minutes the children would be down for their naps and Allina would be alone and at peace. The break couldn't come soon enough.

Allina was exhausted from all the questions about the *Gruppenführer*. The women were full of sly sneers and teasing remarks this morning, ones that made her so self-conscious she could barely meet their eyes. She'd dropped two folded stacks of diapers in the last hour, thanks to their clucking.

"Come now, Berta, don't tell me you're jealous," Rilla taunted. "After all, you can have nearly any officer you want." She baited Berta with a saccharine smile. "Except for *Gruppenführer* von Strassberg. He doesn't pay attention to anyone but Allina."

"Rilla, please," Allina muttered. She sent her friend a bug-eyed look before turning to Lotte Menke, who was holding up her baby girl. Allina's stomach sank at Lotte's frown. "Little Ingrid grows stronger each day," she assured the young mother before transferring the infant to her cradle. "Try not to worry. Some newborns take longer than others to become good feeders. Right, ladies?" she asked, turning to the group of nursing mothers.

Unfortunately, the women were more interested in catty arguments than lifting Lotte's spirits. And Rilla was full of herself this morning.

"*Gruppenführer* von Strassberg has called on Allina every day for two weeks," Rilla said, wagging her eyebrows. Pulling Tobias from his sling, she gave the baby a loud kiss on the forehead before handing him to Allina. "He's an attentive patron," she added, buttoning her white blouse up to its embroidered collar. "Plus, he's managed to convince *Schwester* Ziegler to give Allina an extended break every day. That's enough to make *me* love the man."

A few mothers giggled in response. Allina turned away and laid Tobias in his cradle, fussing with his bedding in the hope it might hide the hot flush creeping into her cheeks.

Laying her magazine aside, Berta swept her long, blond curls over her shoulder. "He'll grow bored with her soon enough. Doesn't he have an office in Munich? I'm sure he'll get tired of the drive, sooner or later," she said, flicking a bored glance down Allina's body, "along with everything else."

"I doubt very much an hour's drive makes a difference to the man," Sabine Hindz said, then turned her arresting silver eyes on Allina. "He seems quite taken with you, dear. And not just in the gutter sense."

Berta continued to fume.

"I don't know about that," Allina managed. She walked to the back of the room and made a show of consulting one of her files.

"We all see the way he looks at you when you're not watching," Lotte said.

"With respect," Sabine added, caressing her baby's head. "My Viktor looked at me the same way before he proposed."

"Perhaps it's because Allina doesn't throw herself at his feet," Rilla said, slanting Berta a deadly stare through her lashes. "Act like a lady, and you're treated as such. Act like a slut—"

Berta leaped out of her chair. "Get him off me." She huffed while Allina hurried to take Neils out of the feeding sling. Berta flounced out of the room, slamming the door.

Allina shook her head and laid Neils down. "You go too far, Rilla." The other mothers were quiet as she transferred each child from nursing sling to cradle, but they sent Sabine and Rilla grudging looks before filing quietly out of the room.

"I'm to blame, *Schwester*," Sabine said as she caressed Johann's pink cheeks. "My teasing encouraged her. I'm sorry." She turned to Rilla. "You and I are lucky. We've made love matches," she pointed out. "The other girls are here under different circumstances. Still, they serve our Führer all the same. We should be a bit kinder, dear."

Allina turned away to massage the knot of pain between her brows.

"Mark me," Sabine called out to Allina, lifting a finger, "*Gruppenführer* von Strassberg is interested in more than a liaison. You could do worse." With a saucy wink, she turned and sashayed out of the room.

Which left only Rilla. Covering her face, Allina plopped into the chair next to her friend. She'd come unhinged if she had to endure one more question.

"You've been avoiding me for days." Rilla crossed her arms over her chest. "What's going on?"

"Nothing," Allina moaned, eyeing Rilla through her fingers. She hauled herself out of the chair and made her way to the back counter to amend her files. "I'm tired, that's all."

"You're lying," Rilla said with a huff. "You avoid me because you think I'm too nosy."

Allina glanced up long enough from the files to shoot Rilla a withering look.

"All right, we both know I'm nosy. I'm nosy because I'm your friend. He likes you, Allina. Everyone sees that. And the *Gruppenführer* intrigues you. Don't try to deny it."

Allina held on to her patience and added a short note—*feeding has improved, 15 minutes*—to Ingrid Menke's file. "He visits every day for tea, and we talk. That's all."

This wasn't a lie, exactly. They did speak of everyday things, although he always managed to sneak in a few irritating questions about child-rearing and her nursing duties. Von Strassberg also watched her, often with a degree of attention that made her aware of the fit of her nurse's uniform and the way she sat in her chair. His behavior was never crude. Most of the women here would be charmed by his quiet courtesy. But the man made her twitchy.

"If it's innocent, why are you blushing?" Rilla leaned across the counter and pushed Ingrid's file away. "What do you two talk about, anyway?"

Allina tossed down her pencil, frowning as it left a long, jagged mark on her paperwork before rolling off the pile of files. "Everything. Nothing. Books. Music." Her voice rose as she began to pace. "He brought me chocolate caramels yesterday, and we debated Nietzsche's *Beyond Good and Evil.*" She didn't want to think about him, though. Thinking about the *Gruppenführer* would mean admitting that for a while yesterday, she'd forgotten her fear. His gentle teasing and quick mind reminded her of Uncle, and the pattern of their debates had become comfortable. Familiar.

"He's interested in your thoughts and opinions," Rilla said, tilting her head. "That's more than most of us can hope for. He's . . . different." Her eyes narrowed. "You don't want to like him, do you?"

"No," Allina admitted. "I don't." She wanted to hate him, even if she couldn't find fault in his manner. The man had been nothing but chival-rous and kind. He hadn't asked a single question about Badensburg since that afternoon in the garden.

His courtesy was as confusing as it was maddening. There were a hun-dred unspoken questions simmering between them, her awareness of him like tiny electrical currents against her skin. He wanted something from her, but not, as Sabine put it crudely, in the gutter sense. Allina was sure of it.

"You've gone pale now. I'm sorry," Rilla said. "I can't understand why you won't give him a chance. Do you know how many here would love to have *Gruppenführer* von Strassberg as their patron? He's young and handsome. And he makes you laugh." She bit her lip, considering. "Is it because of Albert?"

Allina forgot to breathe until she realized Rilla couldn't possibly know the truth. Even so, her friend had hit the target. Her chest burned. "Albert's barely cold in his grave," she snapped. "Or should I be a dutiful National Socialist and go with the *Gruppenführer* anyway, like every other ice queen at Hochland Home?"

Rilla's face filled with remorse, and she cupped her hand over her mouth. "Oh, I didn't know. You didn't tell me," she said, taking Allina's hand and pulling her down into a chair again. "When did it happen?"

"October," Allina said, her voice a dull whisper. "He was in . . . out of the country. I didn't find out until . . ." She shook her head. "Now it's too late." Too late to hear the truth from his lips. Too late for her to apologize.

"He was an officer, your Albert?" Rilla murmured, clinging to her hand in sympathy.

Leaning back in the chair, Allina closed her eyes to avoid the question. "He was a hero."

"You miss him," Rilla said, placing a warm, solid hand on her shoulder, "Of course you do. You loved him, I can tell."

Yes, she'd loved him, although it was guilt and not sorrow that bubbled up in her chest now, dark and sticky as tar. "We wasted so much time."

But that wasn't the worst of it. Unable to sleep last night, Allina had fought to conjure Albert in her mind for a restless, panicked hour that left her twitching with tension. She'd succeeded, finally, and pictured his golden eyes, the way he moved, and the feel of his hands in her hair. But each memory was fleeting and dissolved within seconds into frustrating shadow.

She was forgetting him, forgetting his face.

"Please don't give up hope," Rilla said. She kissed her cheek. "Things are bound to get better. You'll see."

Allina shook her head, but had no answer for her friend. She was caught here in a life she didn't choose, with a past filled with bitter regret. There was no way out, and her future was in the hands of an SS officer who already knew too much about the events that brought her to Hochland Home. There was no way to know what the man might do if Allina let down her guard again—or if he somehow guessed her greatest secret.

The *Gruppenführer* glanced across the table and gave her another one of his patient, charming grins. "I'm glad you have some extra time this afternoon away from your duties," he said. Opening today's issue of the *Berliner Tageblatt* with a sharp snap of his fingers, he turned his attention to the front page.

Allina tapped the edges of the crisp newspaper until he lowered it. "*Schwester* Ziegler has given me an extended break every day for more than two weeks, as you well know," she said, trying to keep the annoyance from her tone. "Those tins of Van Houten cocoa powder worked their magic on her mood, *Gruppenführer*." The head nurse's sweet tooth was legendary. Thanks to von Strassberg's generous donation and Chef Greiser's baking skills, the woman was in a magnanimous mood. Everyone had indulged in hot cocoa and mounds of buttery, chocolate biscuits for days.

"It's Karl," he reminded her, dryly, for the tenth time this week. He finished perusing the front section and handed it to her with a charming flourish before turning to his reading.

Allina glanced at the front page, but the winter sun streaming through the window was hard to resist. Lifting her face to the light, she closed her eyes and let the warmth sink into her skin, grateful they were the only two people in the room. His visits were now commonplace, but the smirks and curious looks always surfaced when the *Gruppenführer* came to call. Allina took a sip of creamy cocoa and sighed. Chef had added cinnamon to the pot this morning.

"The Führer will give his annual speech to Parliament in a few days," von Strassberg said, shifting his attention back to her. "Have you listened to it before?"

"Always," Allina said. "With my uncle. Why?"

"Be sure to listen to the Reichstag speech this year. You'll find it informative." He snapped the paper after that cryptic comment and turned his gaze to another article, ignoring her.

Allina peeked at him over the newspaper's edge. They were sitting close enough for her to see the crease in his tie. While he didn't seem to notice her regard, the hard line of his jaw softened and the corners of his mouth turned up. She'd grown accustomed to that expression these past two weeks, just as she'd become used to his presence. Even his scent was familiar to her now—not the cloying sharpness of the aftershave favored by so many officers, but a fresh, clean scent, like river water, that came from his skin.

His lips twitched and he slanted her a cool, blue look. "Enough of the news," he said, tossing his reading aside. "I'm more interested in your revolutionary thoughts on child-rearing. Are you ready to educate me?" he asked. While his tone teased, his eyes were serious.

Here we go again. "You ask me that question every time you visit."

"I'm a patient man," he said, focusing the considerable force of his attention on her. "One day, I hope you'll trust me enough to share your thoughts." Swallowing, he glanced down and brushed biscuit crumbs from the front of his jacket. "I can do nothing about your past, but it's obvious your work here brings you little joy. I'd like to help."

The sympathy in his voice made her want to confide in him. It also made her want to run out of the room. "What do you want me to say?" she asked.

"The truth."

Enough. This cat-and-mouse game was too much. Allina rose and turned to the door. "Fine. Follow me."

Allina hurried into the hall, enjoying the way he unfolded his long legs and leapt from his chair to scramble after her. "We have to be quick," she said, leading him farther down the South Wing. "It's easier to show you than tell you, but Wendeline will be off duty in an hour. She won't ask any questions." Allina pushed open the first door, and her ears flooded with the wails of two dozen infants. A harried nurse scurried about the room, peering into each cradle with her hands clasped behind her back.

"This is the newborn room," Allina shouted over the din.

"I'd guessed as much," he yelled back, "by their size and impressive vocal ability."

They walked back out into the hall. "That noise," she said, pointing at the door, "is the sound of healthy children."

She led him across the hall, and they entered a much quieter nursery. Another *Schwester* stood at the back of the room making notes in a file.

"And this room?" Allina whispered. "How old are the children here?"

"The sign on the door says six months," he murmured, lips twitching. "I assume these children are that age?"

"You're a funny man, *Gruppenführer.*" She walked to the door.

"And one with a good memory," he said, holding it open for her. "I believe we met in this room."

She hurried into the hall. "I didn't bring you here to test your memory."

"Why did you, then?" he asked.

"To point out the contrast." She folded her arms across her chest and took a step back so she could gauge his reaction. "Haven't you wondered how we achieve silence in six months? What we do to train the children not to cry?"

"I've heard *Schwester* Ziegler say coddling is discouraged in favor of discipline."

"Of course it is," she whispered. "We can't raise an army without discipline." She held up her hand when he opened his mouth, cutting him off with satisfaction. "Ignoring a baby's cries won't instill discipline. Refusing to touch them, to show affection, is destroying these children."

Frowning, von Strassberg rubbed the back of his neck. "The methods seem harsh, but the *Schwestern* here are a competent lot. Who's to say the children are being damaged?"

"I am," Allina hissed. She yanked the door to the stairwell open, determined to show him everything.

"Where are you taking me?" he asked as he held the door wide for her.

Allina's bitter laugh echoed in the stairwell. "To our specialized treatment suites."

"What?"

"You heard me." She led him up the stairs to the third floor, easing the door open and scanning the empty hall before ushering him ahead. "Prepare yourself."

When she opened the door to the barracks-style bedroom, the cots were vacant—but the stench of urine made her eyes water. Karl covered his nose with the back of his hand.

"Doesn't anyone clean in here?" he asked.

"It's difficult to keep up." Allina watched as he shook his head in disbelief.

Those straight blond eyebrows drew together sharply.

"There aren't enough *Schwestern* to tend the children," Allina whispered. "We've little time to interact with them, never mind toilet train." Anger made her rap her knuckles hard against the wall. It brought a satisfying sting to her fingers. "We treat them like pets. No, that's not true. Hunting dogs get more affection."

The *Gruppenführer*'s face remained a blank mask. He had no idea what was going on, then. That shouldn't surprise her. The officers kept to the North Wing and rarely ventured into the nurseries. Once their sacred seed was planted, the job was done.

She gestured toward the rows of beds. "The children up here are all still in diapers, but many manage to take them off regularly. You'd be amazed by how much urine a two-year-old produces, *Gruppenführer*," she added. "This smell you find distasteful? It's the least of our problems. Follow me."

They went two doors down and entered the children's indoor recreation area, a long, carpeted, well-lit room with walls painted a fresh mint green and tables loaded with colorful toys and picture books. The room's atmosphere, however, was thick and depressing, and Allina watched von Strassberg take in the view. Although more than two dozen children occupied the room, there was no laughter or playing. Many were lying on mats, gazing at the ceiling. Some were humming or babbling like infants. About half sat on the floor, staring into space and rocking back and forth.

Wendeline hurried over. "Allina, *Gruppenführer*, is everything all right?" she asked, eyes wide with concern.

"All is well," Allina said, serenely. "*Gruppenführer* von Strassberg asked if he could see some of the older children. I was sure you wouldn't mind."

"Of course not." Wendeline smoothed her nurse's apron before folding her hands at her waist. "We rarely get visitors to the third floor."

Von Strassberg cleared his throat. He'd gone quite gray. "Most of these children are, what, two? Three?"

"Yes," Wendeline answered. "They're a bit slow, you understand."

Otto got up to investigate. Allina heard the *Gruppenführer*'s quick intake of surprise as the child limped over to her on bowed legs and pressed the side of his face to her stomach.

"Hello, Otto. How are you today?" She threaded her fingers through his silky hair.

The boy didn't speak, but he gazed up into her face and laughed with glee. After a moment, he turned his attention to the *Gruppenführer* and hobbled over for an awkward hug.

Von Strassberg's expression remained blank at first, although Allina noted the nerve ticking in his jaw. When he reached down to cup the boy's cheek, his lips surrendered in a sad smile. A fierce pang of longing filled Allina's stomach. Yes, he saw exactly what was going on here, and he was moved by it. Her pulse quickened.

He cleared his throat again and patted the boy's head. "I appreciate the personal tour, but we must return to our duties." Otto returned to Allina for another hug.

"I'm sure there's no need for *Schwester* Ziegler to know we've visited today, is there?" he asked Wendeline.

Wendeline paled. "Of course not, *Gruppenführer*."

"Thank you for our hugs, Otto." Allina bent down to press a kiss to the top of his head. "This nice man and I must leave. Go back to your mat, please."

As Otto walked across the room, he passed two children seated on the floor and stopped to pat their heads. Both children hooted, cringing from his touch.

Von Strassberg escorted her back to the break room, where they gathered their coats before walking in silence to the North Courtyard. Allina glanced at him as they made their way to their favorite bench at the garden's edge, but his eyes remained glued to the ground.

She couldn't stay quiet for long. "You were unaware of these children?"

"I'd heard rumors, but . . ." He raked his hand through his hair. "They're all backward." Shaking his head, he sat and pinched the bridge of his nose. "Otto must be the victim of a birth defect—"

"No," Allina answered, joining him on the bench. "None of the children were born with any type of defect. I snuck a peek at Wendeline's files. The children were normal in the cradle."

"But the deformities—"

"Children are less trouble when they're lying down," she said, interrupting again, her throat tight with bitterness. "They require time and attention if we let them loose, so they're tucked in their beds for as long as possible." Allina took a deep breath to keep her voice from breaking. "Even the oldest ones still prefer to crawl."

"And the lack of speech?" he asked.

"Lack of practice." Her hands were fisted so tightly that her nails bit into her palms. "Children learn to speak from their parents by mimicking the words they hear. We barely speak when we tend them. We're too busy, so no teaching occurs."

He shook his head. The muscles in his throat were jumping.

"I also believe poor nutrition plays a part," she added.

"That can't be." He turned to her, his mouth a flat, angry line. "The best food is always available at Hochland Home."

"Available, yes," she said, "but how much attention can one nurse pay to thirty children during meals? There's no time to make sure they eat properly."

He let out a disgusted snort, and Allina reached out, touched his arm.

"I know you ensure extra provisions for Hochland Home. I'm not criticizing your efforts."

"Are you trying to comfort me?"

"I'm telling you the truth," she said wearily. "That's what you want, isn't it? What you keep hounding me for?"

"How many children wind up like that?"

"From the records I reviewed, as many as forty percent are slow."

At her answer, von Strassberg turned away. Forearms braced on thighs, he looked across the garden, at the shrubs coated with snow.

Allina gave him time to come to terms with what he'd seen, watched his hands slowly curl and uncurl as he fought some type of internal battle. He had an aristocrat's features, but the hands of a horseman, with broad, square palms and thick fingers that were made for hard work.

As difficult as it was to watch his tortured reaction, witnessing it made Allina feel better. She hadn't realized how much she longed for someone to share her horror. If the other *Schwestern* questioned Hochland Home rules, they never spoke of it. Their acceptance of these broken children only added to her despair.

When their eyes met again, he was gazing at her with the oddest expression. It was grief-stricken, but determined. She began to hope.

"You understand, now, why I hate it here."

Grunting, he nodded. The pain in his eyes was palpable.

She mustered her courage. "*Schwester* Ziegler told me Otto and others like him will be transferred next month to a special orphanage run by the *Lebensborn* program."

He nodded again.

"I think she's lying. Adopting families want perfect children. They'll never accept ones like these." Allina rubbed at the ache blooming beneath her breastbone. "I must know what will happen to them."

He took her cold hand in his warm one. "I'll look into it," he said, in a low, gritty voice that made her want to cry. "You have my word."

"Thank you," she whispered, squeezing his hand before pulling away. They sat in silence, and as the tension drained out of her, relief took its place. "I've made notes of my own, observations about these children," she blurted out before she could stop herself. "Not official files. Personal ones. Would you like to see them?"

"Absolutely." He went silent again and glanced away. Once again, Allina gave him the privacy of his thoughts. After a time, he leaned back and sighed, as if making a decision. "If you have access to Central Filing, I'll need some files from that room, as well. Special files."

Shock made her go still. He was a *Gruppenführer*; surely he knew what he was asking. "Central Filing is always locked," she said slowly. "We store files on the entire *Lebensborn* program there and release records by official request only, after approval by Director Ebner."

He tapped his knuckles lightly several times on the back of the bench. "That's why I need your help," he said, in a voice so carefully flat the appeal had to be important. "The files are the key to a personal project."

She wet her lips. "Only *Schwester* Ziegler and Director Ebner have the keys to Central Filing."

"I realize that," he said.

His eyes were penetrating; she couldn't look away. A gust of wind swept through the garden, ruffling his hair, and she stared, too absorbed to hide her fascination. "You're not who you appear to be, are you?" she asked softly.

"I'm relieved you finally see that." He smiled at her, eyes crinkling in the corners.

Caught off guard, she inhaled sharply, but he pulled back, breaking the moment's intimacy. "Before you ask, no, I won't reveal any details. That knowledge would only put you at greater risk. You're in enough peril as it is. But I need your help."

Did she trust him enough to steal files for him? He'd sworn to help the children and he'd kept his promise to protect her. Perhaps it was a simple trade they were making, tit for tat. He might betray her in the end. But she didn't think so. The pain she'd seen in his eyes said otherwise.

The choice was clear.

"When do we start?" she asked.

"Tomorrow."

CHAPTER 17

ALLINA

Nudging her chair closer to the *Gruppenführer's*, Allina surveyed the break room over the rim of her teacup. It was all she could do to sit still. She'd been on high alert all day, a tetchy mix of excitement and anxiety humming just beneath her skin.

"We should test our plan first," she whispered. "I've been in that office a handful of times to fetch files. I know how it's organized, but a test seems smart."

"Agreed." He placed his hand over hers. The quick spark of heat from his fingers made her unsteady. She let go of the cup too quickly, and half her tea spilled as it dropped with a clatter. "Sorry," he said, and handed his napkin over to wipe up the mess.

The misstep caught the eye of the two pregnant women at the only other occupied table in the break room. They smiled at her and simpered over their biscuits. Gossips. Allina took a sip of the lemony brew, but it did little to calm her stomach.

"Let me give you the information I have on one child," he murmured, flashing a fake, charming smile clearly for the benefit of the ladies at the other table. The *Gruppenführer* took a scrap of paper from his pocket. He slipped it under her hand, kept the tips of his fingers against hers. "Time yourself to see how long it takes to locate her file."

She peeked at the paper. "Anya Geisen," she read, trying to ignore the tingling in her fingers. "Born at Hochland Home, 1936."

Allina stashed the paper in her apron pocket as the busybodies strolled to the door. One had the gall to wag a finger as she exited. "It shouldn't be too difficult to find with this information. *Schwester* Ziegler is ruthless about the files. They're pristine."

"The file may not be where you expect," von Strassberg said, although he shook his head when she tried to ask why. They'd been through all this before. The more Allina knew, the more danger she'd be in.

Allina sighed. "That means it might take longer to find."

"Which worries me, so let's go over the plan," he said. "When is the best time for you to get the files?"

"*Schwester* Ziegler takes her afternoon break at 4:30. It's at the end of the afternoon shift, when most of us are readying for dinner," she said, drumming her fingers on the table. "The administrative offices are emptiest then, so it's the best time to snag the key from her desk. I'll have to be quick, though. Fifteen minutes, at most."

"Good. Will anyone think it strange if you're carrying a file into the hall?"

"No. Files are part of everyone's work here. To be safe, I'll bring others and slip the borrowed one between them."

"Excellent. And the best way to transfer any documents to me?"

"It's winter. Everyone's seen us walk in the garden. I'll secure the file between my dress and coat."

"And we make the transfer outside." He crossed his arms over his chest and winked. "I could find you work as an intelligence officer. Your mind works in interesting ways."

She flushed under his praise, tried to hide it by stuffing down another biscuit. "My biggest concern is where to store the file after I take it from Central Filing."

"Is there a safe spot in your sleeping room?" he asked. "A locked cabinet? Underneath your mattress?"

"The file won't be safe there," she said, shaking her head. "There are no locks on the doors or closet, and the cleaning staff come into our rooms without notice to change the linens."

He grunted. "I'll need a day to figure out storage." He leaned in closer. "Find Anya's file, then, but don't take it. Try to figure out how the files are organized, but only if you have time. I don't want you risking your safety, understand?"

"I understand." He was invading her space again, and his nearness made her stomach flutter. She wasn't afraid anymore, but the awareness was baffling. Alarming.

"Be careful." He moved closer, until they were nose to nose. "I'll come for you before breakfast tomorrow. Be careful," he repeated.

"Yes, *Gruppenführer*," Allina said, and backed away with a mock salute. "Are there any other orders, sir?"

"Only a request," he said with a grin that probably worked its charm on every woman he met. "Do you think you could find it in your heart to call me Karl?"

Allina answered with a smile but didn't honor his request. The thought of calling the man by his first name made her nervous. Still, she caught herself whispering his name as she went about her duties that afternoon. The hours passed, but it was like walking in a river, upstream. Every second seemed to cling to her skin and drag her backward. Each observation she noted in a child's file made her wonder about the location of Anya Geisen's, and even a double basketful of laundry didn't drown out the sluggish ticking of the clock. Exhausted and jittery by the end of her shift, she jumped out of her seat when Wendeline came to relieve her.

Snatching the head nurse's keys turned out to be the easiest part of her plan. The halls were mostly empty and no one gave her a second look, so she slipped into Ziegler's office unnoticed. The woman was, for all her faults, as predictable as a priest come to supper, so the keys to Central Filing were exactly where Allina knew they'd be.

Unfortunately, her plot ran off course after that. Allina hadn't counted on nerves besting her. Her hands shook so much that she'd dropped the keys twice on the way to Central Filing and again while fumbling with the lock. The harsh, bright jangle of metal hitting linoleum sounded like an alarm and made her curse herself for not inventing a reasonable story, and she was sure a staff member would come running down the hall to seize the interloper. By the time she entered the filing office, the back of Allina's uniform was stuck to her body. She wasted precious seconds sagging against the closed door in relief.

It took another quarter hour to locate Anya Geisen's file. Her paperwork wasn't in any of the labeled filing cabinets, but in an old, dented one at the back of Central Filing—one Allina opened on a whim out of sheer stubbornness, after searching all the others. There were dozens of files in that cabinet, alphabetized by facility and last name.

Who was Anya Geisen?

Allina had barely returned the keys to Ziegler's desk when the military clatter of the head nurse's heels came down the hall. She dashed into the narrow supply closet and squeezed herself among cleaning buckets, brooms, and tall stacks of boxes. Allina waited there with her heart hammering in her ears, jumping each time the head nurse slammed a drawer in her desk and praying the woman wouldn't have a sudden need for a box of pencils.

The noisy rummaging went on for minutes, but it seemed like an hour. When the head nurse left, Allina was boneless with relief.

Rilla's eyes lit with mischief as she leaned in to inspect the locket dangling from Allina's neck. "It's gorgeous." She turned to the group of women huddled around the breakfast buffet. "Look, the *Gruppenführer* had it engraved with the initial of her first name."

Berta turned her face away. Lotte cooed with delight. Sabine gave Allina an I-told-you-so wink.

"The locket was his Aunt Adele's," Allina said with a smile. She ran a finger over the intricately engraved letter *A* on the locket's face before slipping it beneath her nurse's apron and blouse. Its heavy, solid weight was cool against her flushed skin.

"A family heirloom sounds promising," Rilla said, eyebrows lifting as she eyed the buffet. "Oh, there's bacon this morning!" Distracted, she plucked a few strips from the chafing dish.

"You're holding up the line," Berta grumbled, elbowing her way through the small crowd. Allina moved aside as Berta took her time piling eggs and bacon onto her plate. "I think it's gaudy." Berta's lips curled into a sneer.

"Gold is never gaudy, Berta." Sabine frowned. "Your sour attitude is showing. It's not attractive, dear."

Rilla shot Berta an evil glare. "Who cares about your taste, anyway? He didn't give *you* the locket, did he?"

Berta tossed her full plate back onto the buffet, sending bits of food tumbling onto the chafing dishes and tablecloth before she flounced out of the room with a dramatic flick of platinum hair. The women at the surrounding tables turned to each other, wide-eyed, before settling down to their breakfasts.

"It's a large piece, but elegant," Sabine said, patting Allina's arm. "Rilla's right. By gifting you a family heirloom, he's made his intentions clear."

The gossip and assumptions didn't need answering, so Allina graced Sabine with another smile and added a roll and some grapefruit to her plate.

When he'd arrived before breakfast this morning, von Strassberg told her the locket was part of The Plan. Before sharing more details, he'd run off to meet with the head nurse. He'd asked her to put the necklace on immediately, though, and show it to the other women.

"It's so exciting." Rilla grabbed Allina's arm as they sat at their table. "I was hoping to tease him about his intentions over breakfast," she said, taking a bite of bacon. "Why did he have to meet with *Schwester* Ziegler this morning?"

"I'm sure we'll find out soon," Allina murmured. She buttered her roll before taking a bite. The man was an enigma, and his timing made no sense. They needed to discuss Anya Geisen's file.

Rilla glanced over Allina's shoulder. "It looks like we're all about to find out."

The sound of the head nurse's brisk stride always preceded her, but there was no mistaking Ziegler's arrival when she cleared her throat. Screwing up her courage, Allina gulped down another bite before turning in her chair.

Von Strassberg winked and inclined his head. In his hands was a glossy wood box.

"Allina, *Gruppenführer* von Strassberg joined me for breakfast." Ziegler's gaze flicked to the locket. "He told me your friendship is . . . moving forward."

Allina's cheeks burned. "Yes, *Schwester*." She pushed her breakfast plate away and hoped the blush hid her surprise. How far would they be taking the ruse?

"Well, then," the head nurse said. She smiled, not unkindly, and hurried away.

Von Strassberg moved closer and gave the ladies at the table a courteous bow. "I have another small gift for you," he said, setting the box on the table. The amber-colored oak was unblemished, and the piece was stunning in its simple, clean lines. A master wood smith had inlaid pieces of dark cherrywood in a swastika pattern. Allina ran her fingers over the wood, which was lacquered and buffed to a silky gloss.

"It glows," Rilla murmured.

"The box was a personal gift from the Führer," he said.

The other women at the table let out soft *oohs* in delight.

Allina lowered her lashes. "Really?"

"I hope you'll use the box for safekeeping of precious items for many years to come."

She started at that comment and slanted him a glance. He nodded, solemn as a magi, but there was a dangerous glitter in his eyes. The box was the perfect size to hold the files he'd asked her to steal. Allina ran her fingertips over the keyhole. Where was the key?

"*Schwester* Ziegler suggested we take time this morning to discuss the future," he added, with a flash of white teeth. Rilla pinched her leg under the table, hard enough to make her hiss.

He leaned closer and offered Allina his arm. "Shall we walk in the garden? Perhaps Fräulein Weber would be kind enough to take the box to your sleeping room," he said.

"I'd be happy to, *Gruppenführer*." Rilla picked up the box and turned to Allina. "Use my coat and hat if yours are upstairs," she told Allina. "Mine are in the entryway."

Allina rose from her chair. "You've thought of everything," she said, baring teeth.

"I do my best." He chuckled, tucked her hand in the crook of his arm, and led her away from the table.

"You realize what everyone thinks now?"

"People think what they think." He steered her out of the room and down the hall toward the courtyard. "Let them gossip, if it helps us."

As soon as they entered the garden, he propelled her to its farthest edge. It was just past dawn, but that suited her fine. Few would venture here until the day warmed, so they could speak freely, and Rilla's thick wool mittens and muffler were a buffer against the cold.

"Have you figured out why I met with *Schwester* Ziegler in private about the box?" He stopped to blow into his gloved hands, puffs of steam rising in the air.

Shivering, Allina nodded. "She'll let me keep it in my sleeping room without question."

"Exactly." He grabbed her hands, rubbing them between his vigorously enough that she could feel the heat through the wool and leather. "I thought you'd take pleasure in storing any files in a box commissioned for the Reich."

"I like the idea of hiding them in plain sight," she admitted, a little nervous at how well he grasped the workings of her mind, "but everyone's curious about the box now. They'll all want a peek inside."

"Ah, the key," he said. They walked to their usual bench, and he unwound his muffler and spread it over the seat. "Take your locket off, please."

Tugging off her mittens, she sat and pulled the necklace over her head.

"See the two little nubs there?" He pointed to the locket's side. "Press the top one."

She tapped the tiny button, and the locket's cover sprang open to reveal a headshot of a child. The little boy was young, not more than six or seven, with a radiant smile and bright, penetrating eyes. "Is that you?" She ran the tip of her fingernail over the photo. "It must be. The eyes are the same," she blurted. When he didn't answer, she glanced up in time to see the flush rise up his neck.

He cleared his throat. "My aunt loved that picture. I couldn't find a suitable replacement on short notice." He pointed to the locket again. "Push the other nub."

When she did, a second compartment behind the photo opened, and nestled in that compartment was a slender brass key. "How clever," she whispered. "I'd never think of it."

"Good, then no one else will either," he said. "Keep the key in the locket and the locket around your neck at all times."

"Of course." She snapped the locket closed and slipped the chain over her neck.

"And now," he said, sitting back and crossing his legs, "I want to hear about your trip to Central Filing."

Finally. "Getting into the room was simple," she said. "The trick is to act with confidence. If you walk with purpose and look like you know what you're doing, no one questions a thing."

"You terrify me." He rubbed his hand over his jaw, eliciting a rasp that raised the hairs on her nape. "How long did it take to find Anya's file?"

"Fifteen minutes." Allina bit her lip, unwilling to tell him how close she'd come to being discovered. "I'll have to be quicker next time."

His brows drew together in a fierce frown. "Did you have problems?"

"No," she lied smoothly, "but you were right. Anya's file wasn't where I expected it would be. Every *Lebensborn* home has several cabinets in Central Filing, and the files in each are alphabetized by last name. Anya's file wasn't in the Hochland Home cabinet. I found it by chance in one at the back of the room."

He folded his arms over his head. "How?"

"I got frustrated, so I kept opening the empty cabinets until I found one partially full. I didn't have time to examine the files too closely, but none of them seemed normal to me. They were too skinny." She shuddered at the memory of what came after and wrapped her arms around her middle to mask it.

After another long, measured look, he nodded. "All right. This afternoon, I'll need you to take Anya's file, along with four others."

"Do you have more names for me?"

"No, but if my hunch is right, the names won't matter. It's what's in each file that's important." He leaned in. "And remember, your safety is more important than any file."

Allina went back to Central Filing that afternoon and took Anya's file and four more. She was in and out in less than three minutes.

Late that evening, with the five files spread out across her bed, Allina couldn't shake off a nagging sense of anxiety. The records she'd fetched were on three boys and two girls, ranging in age from sixteen months to two years. Each folder contained only a single typed sheet of paper, undated, with the most basic information on the child: name and birth date, parent names, gender, height, and weight. At the bottom of each sheet was an identical, cryptic notation. It was one she'd never seen before: *T/H.H.*

Someone had gone through these records and removed as much as two years' worth of documentation. But for what purpose?

T/H.H.

What was she not seeing?

Sharp trills of laughter outside her bedroom door made Allina stuff the files back into the box before returning to bed. There was nothing more to do tonight. She'd have to wrangle the truth out of von Strassberg in the morning. Slipping under the covers, Allina reached for the locket and pressed it to her chest. She closed her eyes and willed herself to sleep.

The *Gruppenführer* was as stubborn as a bag of rocks.

"What do you mean, you don't want to talk about it?" Scowling, Allina tried to yank her arm from his hold as he propelled her to the back of the garden.

"I don't want to talk about it," von Strassberg said mildly, keeping her arm in his iron grip. "And stop yelling unless you want everyone to know our business." His hawkish gaze followed a resident and her suitor as they walked back into the building.

The temperature had warmed today, melting almost all the snow from the shrubbery, and the bright green shoots of daffodils and paper whites peeked up from the dirt. Warmer temperatures meant more people in the courtyard, but the couples were too wrapped up in each other to offer anything more than amused smirks. No, they likely assumed she and the *Gruppenführer* were in the middle of a lovers' tiff, which was a distressing but logical conclusion. The man knew how to ignite her temper.

"I'm not yelling," she hissed, lifting her chin. "Do you want the files or don't you?"

That did the trick. He blinked—once—before propelling her to their usual bench at the garden's edge. Allina sat down with dignity and a stiff spine, realizing too late she'd made a tactical error. The *Gruppenführer* remained standing, and he towered over her. The tip of his nose was red, though she was unsure if that was from cold or temper.

"Are you threatening to hold the files hostage?" Leaning in, he crowded her, close enough to catch the clean scent of soap and shaving cream. His jaw could have been carved from stone.

She refused to fall victim to intimidation tactics. "I'm telling you the files don't make sense. There's only a single sheet of paper in each one. Nothing else," she whispered. "No nurse's notes or adoption records, or even, God forbid, death certificates. That's years of information gone missing on each child. Nothing's as it should be."

The truth hit in a rush. She covered her mouth.

"What?" His eyes locked with hers.

"There's the same note on each file," she whispered through her fingers. Allina bent down and drew the notation in the dirt: *T/H.H.*

When he rushed to rub out the letters, she knew she'd hit on the truth.

They whispered the words in unison: "Transfer, Heinrich Himmler."

Sick with anger, Allina's hands began to shake. "The children on the third floor."

"Who will be transferred to a special *Lebensborn* orphanage." Von Strassberg sat down and braced his arms on his thighs. "It's possible. I'll need more files, more time, to be sure."

No. She wouldn't let him put her off again, or give only a half answer. There were dozens of files in that cabinet—every last one was stripped of medical information about the child. Allina had risked her safety to secure these files, yet he continued to withhold information from her, without any assurance of what would happen once she helped him.

"Tell me everything you know."

For a moment, Allina was afraid he'd refuse. When he spoke, it was in a clipped tone that made her stomach twist. "The number of *Lebensborn* adoptions is low, given the number of births. A few months ago, a child named Anya Geisen was promised to a high-ranking family but not delivered, with no explanation other than the child had some sort of nervous condition. The family contacted a colleague of mine. We decided to conduct an . . . informal investigation. I hoped her file would show why." He pressed the heels of his hands to his eyes. "We can't jump to conclusions. It might be coincidence."

But the grief in his voice told her otherwise, as did the head nurse's words about the children on the third floor: *These children serve a purpose. We must trust the Reichsführer's plan.*

"Somebody stole the contents of the files because they needed them. They're conducting tests on the children to find out what went wrong." Allina hated, *hated*, how her voice wobbled, but she'd be damned if she stayed silent another minute. "I think the same thing will happen to Otto and others like him."

Von Strassberg grabbed her hand and squeezed it. "If that's the case, I'll get to the bottom of it. Either way, we'll figure out a way to help."

The frustrated respect in his eyes gave her hope. He trusted her with the truth. Not all of it—the man probably had more secrets than the Sphinx—but he'd shared enough for now. Allina had little right to complain about his secrets. She had plenty of her own.

The thought of trusting him with the truth about her mother made her chest tight with panic. It was a ridiculous notion. She couldn't share that secret with anyone.

Allina scanned the garden before unbuttoning her coat to pull the files from the makeshift strap she'd constructed from two nursing slings. "I can get you all the files you need," she said, handing them over. "How many more? The box can hold twenty, at least."

"Ten is better. Safer." Karl slid the folders under his jacket. "Speaking of safety, I'd transfer whatever you've sewn into the lining of your coat to that box as soon as possible."

Allina froze. "You can tell?" She ran her hands over the front of her coat, but the rustle was so faint it was barely noticeable. Had she given him any other clue?

"It's an old trick," he said, brushing lint from his sleeve. "One I've used in an emergency. Most won't notice the sound, but the box is a safer hiding place."

Allina rubbed at her tingling cheeks. "I'll take care of it tonight." The opportunity to keep her father's letters somewhere safe, to finally read them, to know his voice through his writing—it was exhilarating.

Von Strassberg stood and tugged her to her feet. "I leave for Berlin tomorrow to attend the Führer's address to the Reichstag. I'll meet with my contacts there, try to see what I can find out." He slipped her hand neatly into the crook of his arm, and they strolled the garden's perimeter.

"How long will you be gone?" A quiver of nervousness hit her stomach.

"A few days. I've a favor to ask, though, while I'm away." The line between his brows deepened into a frown. "It's one that may be difficult for you to fulfill, but I must ask it." He turned and took her hands in his, rubbing her fingers with his thumbs in a way that made her more nervous.

"What is it?"

He took a deep breath, as if readying for an argument. "I need you to attend as many Hochland Home mixers as you can, beginning tonight."

What?

He squeezed her hands again. "Not for the reason most women here attend them, of course."

Allina wet her lips. They were dry as paper. "Then why?"

He looked away for a second, revealing the tense line of his jaw. "You need to become more confident in male company." His eyes searched hers for a moment before he continued. "We haven't spoken of it again, of what happened in Badensburg. I know you've suffered." He looked away again, swallowing hard. "Suffered at the hands of men wearing the uniform. I've seen you shy away from them in the halls. Even my presence startles you if I move too quickly, and I think I've earned your trust."

"I can't talk about this." Allina pulled away, her mind unable to form any thought other than a panicked *No!* She didn't want to think about what had happened, not ever again. He couldn't know how crippling the violent slashes of memory were, or how they filled her brain at the most unexpected moments, making her limbs lock up and her body betray her. Sometimes she wished she could shed her skin like a snake and leave the hollowed-out husk behind her in the dirt, along with her memories.

"I know it will be difficult," he said, tugging at her hands again. "Your panic, I've seen it before in soldiers who've been to war. Who've known violence." She shook her head, but he was relentless. "If we want to help your children, we can't rely on the other *Schwestern*. I'll have to enlist help from my men." When she gasped and pulled away, he added, "I need you to try to get used to them. To officers, Allina. In uniform."

"When I go to the mixers, I'm afraid I'll see one of them," she whispered. "And of what they'd do, if they recognized me." Allina looked down at her shoes because she couldn't bear to see his expression. She was trembling, so much that her words were little more than whimpers.

He pulled her close, slowly, and with such care she wished she could weep. "I'm sorry," he repeated, lips moving against her hair. The embrace demanded nothing and gave only comfort, allowing her to sag against him and surrender to the panic until it passed. "If you see one of those men again, use my name," he added, his voice low with fury, "and demand his."

She risked a glance up and saw the wolf in him then, in the feral way his lips curled back and the narrowing of his eyes. For the first time, Allina witnessed the threat of violence in Karl von Strassberg, although it was expertly controlled.

His rage was gone so quickly she didn't have time to be afraid. "You've got nothing to fear, as long as you're under my protection," he said. "I promise you that."

She took a deep breath, let it out slowly.

"Will you try?" he asked, taking her hands. "Not for my sake, or for your own, but for the children?"

Allina said yes, because there are times when the path forward, however terrifying, is so clear it's impossible to choose another. She attended the mixer that evening and a dozen others in the weeks that followed. Every officer she met behaved like a perfect gentleman, although she expected this, as she invoked von Strassberg's name at every opportunity. She never encountered any of the men from that night in Badensburg.

Allina battled her fears at every mixer and struggled with her body's panicked reaction. Rilla seemed to sense this and rarely left her side, which made it easier. So, too, did Allina's certainty that *Gruppenführer* Karl von Strassberg would likely kill anyone who dared touch her again.

CHAPTER 18

ALLINA

Allina eased against the rigid back of her kitchen work chair and jabbed her fingers into the knot of muscle at the base of her neck. A mountain of vegetables loomed in front of her, one, unfortunately, that appeared to be growing. She'd been working for an hour, but there were still as many unpeeled potatoes as peeled ones.

Her shoulders hunched when Emil, Hochland Home's sous-chef, lumbered over, his wiry gray brows bunched together. "Keep working, girl. Those should be done by now," he said, jabbing a stubby finger at the pile.

There was no pleasing the man. When she'd asked to volunteer her free time in the kitchen today, the head nurse had shaken her head in mute disbelief. Now Allina knew why: Emil was a terror. *Our dainty Schwestern are as useful in the kitchen as a three-legged table*, he'd taunted earlier, although he'd relented enough to supply her with an ancient, hard-backed chair.

Allina bent her head to the task, peeling faster amid the clang of pots and the hiss of onions sizzling in oil. The kitchen's sweet aroma was heaven, but there was little time to appreciate it. Tomorrow, Hochland Home would host a dinner for more than a dozen SS officers to celebrate the sixth anniversary of Adolf Hitler's appointment as chancellor. Today, the kitchen operated at full throttle. A half dozen staff dressed in stiff, white uniforms stood at the prep counters chopping herbs and vegetables and preparing sauces, with an equal number of helpers ghosting their movements, wiping up the countertop messes left behind, sweeping floors, and scouring pots and pans almost as soon as they were used.

Emil flung open the kitchen's back door and planted hands on his rotund hips. "Damn it, where are my hens?" After a tense five seconds, he slammed the door shut and returned to her table, eyeing the potatoes again. "*Merde*. I can't wait all day for you." He tugged at his bushy gray mustache and turned to the back prep counter. "Tilda! Bruna!" he barked.

Two pale, anxious faces bobbed up from their work. "Yes, Emil," they called out in unison. Bruna and Tilda were sisters with wiry frames, dull brown hair, and broad, rough hands reddened by years of kitchen work. Their brown eyes wore the same wide-eyed expressions.

"Come," Emil ordered, jerking his head toward Allina. "*Schwester* Allina needs help." Tilda and Bruna scurried over, dragging stools that produced duplicate, high-pitched squeals against the ceramic floor tiles.

"Oh, it's such luxury to sit for a minute," Tilda whispered. Plopping down onto the stool, she arched her back.

Bruna's lips pursed as she took her seat and pulled a knife from her apron. "Emil and Chef are in evil moods today."

"Rumor has it *Reichsführer* Himmler himself will attend the dinner tomorrow with his wife," Tilda said.

"That's enough to make Chef pee his pants," Bruna whispered. "The *Reichsführer* is a gentleman, but his wife's a terror."

"Tilda! Bruna! Allina!" Emil slammed his hand on the countertop. "Potatoes!"

Allina bobbed her head and redoubled her efforts. Unfortunately, the quicker she worked, the more slippery her fingers became. She lost her grip at one point, and a potato shot out of her hand, bounced off Bruna's arm, and skidded toward the edge of the tabletop. Tilda snatched it up with a deft movement and plopped it back into Allina's palm without a word, though her shoulders were shaking. Soon, all three women were biting their lips to hold back laughter. Knives flashed, sending bits of peel flying across the table.

Emil treated Allina to a furious, black-eyed scowl. "Sometimes an extra hand is more trouble than it's worth," he muttered, pulling the towel from his waistband to mop his red cheeks. He turned up the radio, and the lively strains of Strauss's *Der Rosenkavalier* soared through the air. After another long minute of hawk-eyed observation, Emil moved away to torture the rest of his staff.

"What possessed you to volunteer in the kitchen?" Tilda whispered.

"I wanted to be useful," Allina lied. "Everyone's working extra, even the mothers in residence. They're helping clean the parlors this afternoon." The truth was, she needed to hear the Führer address the Reichtstag. Von Strassberg had reminded her about it again before he left for Berlin, and the radio was perpetually on in the kitchen. Kitchen duty and work to mask her thoughts were an exceptional cover.

Chef mopped his face and checked the clock. "Switch the channel. It's time," he ordered.

Emil turned the dial and the radio squawked, cutting off the opera's beautiful melody. Once the crackling faded, an announcer declared that the Führer would now address the national congress on this, the sixth anniversary of his appointment as Germany's chancellor.

Thunderous applause sounded for a full five minutes before the Führer began.

> On January 30, 1933, I was filled with the deepest anxiety for the future of my people. Today, six years later, I am able to speak before the Reichstag of Great Germany.
>
> The history of the last thirty years has taught us all one lesson, namely, that the importance of nations in the world is proportionate to their strength at home.
>
> Before the war, Germany was a flourishing economic power. For fifteen years, we were prey to the rest of the world, burdened with tremendous debts. But the German people are nevertheless fed and clothed, and, moreover, there are no unemployed among them.
>
> What is the root cause of all our economic difficulties? Overpopulation . . .

"The Führer speaks with such passion." Tilda placed her hand over her heart before picking up another potato.

"And brilliance," Bruna added with zeal, peeling away.

Emil set a mammoth stockpot under the kitchen faucet and turned on the tap. "Is that all you girls have to say?" he asked with a scowl. He added a cup of salt to the pot as it filled.

"They're too young, Emil." Chef dunked his hand in the water, swirling the salt before he tossed a half dozen hens into the brine. "They don't remember what it was like after the Great War, with everyone grieving and starving in the streets."

Emil grunted his assent and reached for another stockpot as the Führer's guttural, impassioned voice filled the kitchen. Allina forced herself to nod along with the others as he cited a long list of transgressions against Germany—crushing debt, occupation, and the seizure of land and arms.

Another round of frenzied applause sounded just as the head nurse burst into the kitchen. She hurried over to Allina's table, but took a tentative step backward when Emil approached.

"What do you want?" Emil shouted.

Schwester Ziegler's eyes narrowed. "I need Allina's help."

"How unfortunate for you," Emil said, folding his arms over his prodigious belly.

"We've got a problem in the nursery." She planted hands on hips and stared him down. "I'd hate to see anything interfere with the perfection of our celebration tomorrow."

Emil let out a nasal harrumph, but he waved gallantly at the kitchen door.

Damn it. She had no choice. Allina gritted her teeth and followed Ziegler out of the kitchen.

An hour later, Allina hurried back, hoping to catch the remainder of the Führer's address. Emil grunted when she appeared and pointed to the table, now covered with carrots, celery, and onions to be chopped.

"What happened?" Bruna whispered as Allina took her seat.

Allina grabbed an onion and sliced it in half. "Three of the older children got into a fight and bumped their heads," she whispered, attempting to chop, explain, and listen to the radio at the same time. "Poor Wendeline was overcome by all the blood." The onions made her eyes water, and she stopped to wipe them with a corner of her apron.

"It's good Wendeline doesn't work in the kitchen," Tilda joked.

"No talking!" Chef smacked his knife on the counter. "Our Führer is speaking."

> *... the assertion that Germany is planning an attack on America is laughable. Germany has no feeling of hatred toward England, America, or France. All it wants is peace and quiet. But Jewish agitators are continually stirring up hatred for the German people. We must know who these Jews are—these men who want to bring about a war by hook or by crook ...*

The knife fell from Allina's hand and skittered on the wood tabletop.

> *We cannot allow other countries to tell Germany how to settle our Jewish problem. It's shameful to see how the entire democratic world is oozing sympathy for the poor tormented Jewish people, but remains hard-hearted when it comes to helping them.*
>
> *These countries say they are in no position to take in the Jews. Yet in these empires there are not even ten people to the square kilometer. While Germany with her one hundred forty inhabitants to the square kilometer is supposed to have room for them ...*

"We should ship the cockroaches off to England," Bruna said, snickering as she pulled apart a head of celery.

The back of Allina's neck grew hot. Did Bruna understand what the Führer was proposing?

> *Jewry must adapt itself to respectable constructive work, or it will sooner or later succumb to a crisis of unimaginable proportions.*
>
> *If the international finance-Jewry in Europe and abroad should succeed in plunging the nations into a world war yet again, then the outcome will not be the victory of Jewry, but rather the annihilation of the Jewish race in Europe.*

The Reichstag went wild, and a rush of applause and loud whoops and cheering filled the kitchen. Allina kept her eyes on her work.

When she risked a glance up, Tilda had stopped chopping. Her eyes were uncertain. "What do you think he means?" she whispered.

Allina gaped at her. Chancellor Hitler couldn't have made himself any clearer.

"The Führer will do what he must." Bruna had also paled, but her voice remained crisp. "He won't fail us."

"Where will they go?" Tilda asked, putting down her knife. "All those Jews?"

"Does it matter?" Bruna asked.

"Yes, Tilda," Allina whispered, "do you think it matters?"

"The Jews are a most unfortunate race," Bruna answered for her sister. "I've nothing against them myself, mind you. Tilda and I had a Jewish friend at school."

Dropping her hands into her lap, Allina kept her voice devoid of emotion. "What happened to your friend?"

"Odette disappeared," Tilda said in a soft voice. She reached for another piece of celery. "I don't know what happened to her."

Bruna shrugged. "We live in unfortunate times." Grabbing a carrot, she lopped off its leaves with an efficient flick of her knife. "Besides, what does it matter if there are a few less Jews in the world?"

Heinrich Himmler's eyes were a piercing cornflower blue behind his wire-rimmed glasses. "It's a pleasure to meet a lovely young woman," he said, bending over Allina's hand to brush warm, dry lips across her knuckles, "and especially on such an auspicious evening." Pulling back, he tweaked his bow tie and grinned.

Shocked mute, Allina managed to extract her hand from his limp grip. Taking a step back, she smoothed nonexistent wrinkles from the skirt of her navy dress.

Ziegler caught the misstep and swooped in. "We're honored to host you and your lovely wife tonight, *Reichsführer* Himmler. My staff has organized a wonderful celebration in honor of the Führer's speech, and your attendance." The head nurse gave the Himmlers a wide smile as they entered, bowing low and beckoning to them with a grand sweep of her arm.

"Our pleasure, *Schwester* Ziegler." Himmler chuckled. He slipped off his black leather gloves and pocketed them before taking his wife's arm.

The *Reichsführer's* wife scanned the foyer with squinty blue eyes that eventually settled on Allina. She gave a haughty sniff, shrugged off her coat, and handed it over with an imperious flourish. "You embarrass yourself, Heinrich," Frau Himmler said in a biting voice. The woman looked a good ten years older than her husband. Her red velvet gown was fashionable but too tight, and the lines around her mouth suggested her frown might be a permanent accessory.

"Is that right, Marga?" the *Reichsführer* asked, though he shot Allina a wink when he handed off his coat. Allina forced a wobbly smile, one neither he nor his wife noticed. Frau Himmler was too busy hurrying her husband away.

"You're overwhelmed," the head nurse said, laying a bracing hand on her shoulder. "I don't blame you. The *Reichsführer* isn't what you expected?"

Allina shook her head. No, she hadn't anticipated this soft-looking man with kind eyes who conveyed himself with unassuming charm.

"He was impressed with you." Ziegler's fingers lingered over the plush mink as she hung it on the coatrack. "I'm sure von Strassberg wouldn't object to a bit of casual flirting this evening. Though I'd like to make a suggestion for the future." She flicked her gaze down Allina's body.

Flirt. With Heinrich Himmler. Allina took a deep breath. "Of course," she said, hanging the *Reichsführer's* coat next to his wife's.

"Your dress," Ziegler said, "is barely serviceable for an elegant event." She plucked the edge of the wool dress's small, puffed sleeve. "This poor thing must be at least three years old. Remember, you're under von Strassberg's protection now."

"I'm sorry, *Schwester*. I don't understand." Her wardrobe might be unfortunately plain, but the *Gruppenführer* had no say in what she wore.

The older woman's eyes went heavenward. "Your wardrobe, dear. It needs"—she waved her fingers in the air—"spiffing up. And he's a generous sort, if that gold locket is any indication."

Allina's hand flew to the locket as hot pinpricks stung her cheeks. "I see."

What a fine mess this night was turning into.

"You needn't be embarrassed," Ziegler said slyly. "Men often need a tiny push in the right direction. Mention the state of your wardrobe in passing." Her strong fingers clamped down on Allina's arm. "Von Strassberg couldn't take his eyes off you when he arrived. Trust me, the man will do what it takes to keep you happy."

As if they weren't already buried up to their eyebrows in intrigue.

"Is there anything else, *Schwester?*"

The head nurse rolled her eyes. "Oh, never mind. I'm sure he'll notice how underdressed you are at dinner." She touched the black collar of her emerald velvet dress. Pulled in at the waist, it swirled softly around the woman's legs and did a neat job of flattering her fuller figure. "Now that the Himmlers have arrived, you're relieved of your greeting duties. Why don't you check on Chef's progress for me? Tell him we'll be ready to dine in ten minutes."

"Right away, *Schwester.*"

Schwester Ziegler grabbed her wrist before she could go. "I expect you to enjoy yourself tonight," she said. "You and von Strassberg make quite the attractive pair. Relax, please. There's much to celebrate."

Lord, she needed to get out of here. Allina escaped to the kitchen, where Chef's staff was putting the finishing touches on tonight's dinner. On the surface, everything seemed to be in perfect order. The hens were crispy-brown, fragrant with rosemary, and lined up like soldiers on silver trays above the chafing dishes that kept them warm; dollops of rich country butter laced the vegetables and potatoes in a half dozen serving dishes; and a long line of wine bottles had already been decanted on the counter.

Still, there was a frantic hum in the kitchen, and as Allina peeked around the corner, several loud, nasal French curses flew like arrows through the air. When Chef Greiser saw her, the man's long, elegant fingers went to his throat.

"What is it?" he called out. He was sweating profusely, and the front of his normally pristine white coat was smeared with an alarming mix of grease, brown gravy, and what appeared to be blood.

"*Schwester* Ziegler would like to know if dinner is ready."

"We'll serve in five." Although Greiser's voice boomed with confidence, his eyes were stark. "Has the *Reichsführer* arrived?"

"Yes, with his wife."

"Emil," he called out, "pull out the dinner rolls!" He hurried off without another word.

Sighing, she made her way to the dining hall. Thanks to Ziegler's exceptional taste, the staff had outdone themselves in preparation. Every candle was lit, and the long mahogany table they'd installed was set in a perfect blend of opulence and military precision—from the white silk tablecloth and the magnificent candelabras, to the crystal and silver and the deep red roses in the floral centerpieces. The head nurse had selected two recent acquisitions to set the tone: delicate, gilt-edged Arzberg china and vintage Bleikristall goblets that shot prisms of light onto the cloth.

She walked to the French doors and cracked them open to peek into the great room. Festivities were well underway. The officers' wives were clustered at one side of the room and separate from their husbands as they chattered with cocktail glasses in hand. Frau Himmler was seated, holding court over the other wives who stood around her in a circle with brittle smiles and tinkling laughter.

The officers—many of whom approached middle age, as their silhouettes proved, even in well-cut evening clothes—stood on the other side of the room, and they appeared to be having much more fun. Hochland Home's most beautiful women were here tonight, and the fresh, unlined faces lit with feline appreciation as they flirted, vying for alliances with potential benefactors.

Berta was in full, seductive form in a blue silk dress that flowed gracefully over her ripe figure. Soft pin curls made her hair glow in the candlelight as she leaned against the *Reichsführer* to refill his glass with champagne. A dozen bottles were already empty. Many more would be opened, and late into the night.

The celebration would, no doubt, be executed flawlessly.

Von Strassberg's eyes lit up when he saw her, and he stood and raised his champagne glass, drawing everyone's attention. "There you are," he called out with an eager smile, teeth very white against his evening jacket. He walked over with a swift military gait that made the cut of the tuxedo even more striking. His shoulders seemed enormous.

"I wondered what was keeping you," the head nurse said, cocking an eyebrow. "Is dinner ready?"

Allina straightened her spine and forced herself into the room on precarious legs. "Dinner will be served in a few minutes, *Schwester*." Her gaze locked with von Strassberg's, and the sympathy and humor there anchored her. She was floundering, but it helped that he knew it.

"You're radiant." He slipped a glass of champagne into her hand and set his palm on the center of her back. "Drink up," he whispered into her ear, his breath warm against her cheek. "It's going to be a long night."

Ziegler threw open the French doors. "Ladies and gentlemen, let's go through."

In the few minutes it took to settle into her seat, Allina understood exactly how the evening would proceed. The married officers were in high, boisterous moods and preening from the attention. Each was flanked by women, with a wife to the right and a potential mistress to the left, although no one tonight would dare comment on the absurd seating arrangements. No, every last one of the ridiculous geese armed themselves with false smiles and inane gossip.

The only thing that made it bearable was the *Gruppenführer*, who managed to convey his thoughts about the ridiculous chatter with subtle quirks of his lips. He also seemed attuned to her near-desperate urge to flee. Von Strassberg kept her clammy hand pinned to her thigh beneath his much warmer one. He squeezed her fingers any time she leaned a fraction forward.

She did her best to nod at the right times as the conversations floated around them.

. . . Berta, your hair looks lovely tonight, just like Lilian Harvey's. Don't tell me you did it yourself? My, what a clever girl you are . . .

. . . Have you seen Willy Fritsch in By a Silken Thread *yet? No? Oh you must, darling, it's the movie of the year . . .*

. . . Richard has promised us a jaunt to Paris later this spring. We've scheduled a trip to Schiaparelli's showroom. Have you been? No? Oh my dear, you really must go. You won't find more exquisite clothing in the world . . .

"I prefer German designers, myself." Marga Himmler's voice cut like a knife on glass, and the room fell silent while she took another long sip of wine. "I'm sure our head nurse agrees. She seems to share my sensibilities. You've refreshed the dining room since I was here last. Is that an original Liss?" she asked, lifting her glass to the oil landscape on the wall.

"You've a canny eye, Frau Himmler." The head nurse's smile was too tight to be sincere, and she squared her shoulders as if preparing for a blow. "Thanks to the generosity of those under your husband's command, we've refurnished nearly every room at Hochland Home."

Six servers hired especially for today's celebration entered carrying silver tureens, and the nutty fragrance of Emil's *soupe à l'oignon* floated around their heads. The head nurse lifted her finger, and the servers halted their approach. Dipping their heads, they stepped back and waited against the wall.

"These place settings are stunning," Marga Himmler said, running a scarlet fingernail over the gold trim of her plate. "Do you know where they're from?"

"A recent boon," Ziegler said, "from Munich, according to *Gruppenführer* Gud."

Allina froze. Gud wasn't here tonight, and thank God for that small mercy. Just the mention of his name made her want to bolt. Von Strassberg squeezed her hand again. His pulse was racing.

A hush settled over the table. Frau Himmler picked up a fork and examined it closely, twisting it in the candlelight. "Since they're all used goods, I'm sure you've had your staff wash them thoroughly." Her lips curled back in a sneer.

The *Reichsführer* grabbed his wife's wrist and pressed her hand against the tablecloth. "Let's enjoy this wonderful meal, my dear, and choose more elevated topics," he said in a voice that didn't allow for disagreement. A low chorus of shocked murmurs rippled around the table. Frau Himmler sniffed and snatched her hand away.

Allina was on her feet before she knew it, and the scraping of her chair drowned out the murmurs.

"Going so soon, Allina? Whatever for?" Berta asked, sending a deadly glare behind batting lashes.

"The children," she stuttered, taking a step back as two dozen wide-eyed faces looked up at her in unison. "They need tending."

"Sit down, Allina. The children are fine." There were spots of color high on the head nurse's cheeks, and her bared teeth didn't resemble a smile in the least.

"Wait a moment," von Strassberg murmured, "and I'll escort you."

"N-no, please don't interrupt your dinner." Pushing back from the table,

Allina fled down a long hallway to one of the parlors, one residents used when they wanted to meet suitors in private. It was empty, of course. Tonight's negotiations would occur in the open. She switched off the light before collapsing onto a silk wingback chair, wanting to be alone, in silence and relative peace.

Allina didn't worry about the head nurse's displeasure or the inevitable lecture she'd receive for her abrupt departure. She couldn't bear another minute of the cloying, desperate women at Hochland Home, or these men who'd cheered their Führer yesterday during his speech to the Reichstag, or their wives, parading themselves in velvet and jewels and insincere smiles, all eating off china stolen from families their husbands had destroyed.

They all heralded the annihilation of the Jewish people. Her mother's people.

And what about the *Gruppenführer*—had he cheered yesterday with the rest of them? Allina had lain awake for hours last night while her limbs twitched beneath the suffocating quilt, torturing herself over that question. Von Strassberg had shown her sympathy and patience in countless ways. The man had feelings for her, she was sure of it, but his tender regard might change if he knew the truth about her mother. And while he'd sworn to protect her, he had no idea how precarious her situation was—or how much danger they'd both face if others discovered her secret.

The romantic strains of Strauss's "The Blue Danube" filtered into the parlor. Music meant the meal was over. The evening's dancing had begun.

When the *Gruppenführer* slipped into the room, she realized she'd been waiting for him.

"You're in no mood to dance," he murmured, his face still cast in shadows.

"I see no reason for it." She gestured toward the door. "The celebration is a travesty."

Holding out his hand, he moved into the light, illuminating the clean, hard line of his jaw and white bow tie. "Beauty should never be wasted."

She shook her head. His smile was a grim acknowledgment of her pain, but she refused to return it.

"Dance in anger then, or in defiance," he coaxed, holding out his hand again. "Come. Dance with me."

His calmness was a magnet, impossible to resist. She went to him, faltering at the awareness that sparked when he pressed his broad, warm palm to hers. "It's all right," he murmured, drawing her into his arms with care. When she refused to meet his gaze, he nudged her a fraction closer, perhaps to allow her the privacy of her thoughts, but the warmth of his tall, lean body didn't silence her questions. She couldn't stand the sense of limbo anymore, of knowing but not knowing, and of all the unspoken words between them. By the end of the waltz, she was crying softly, shuddering in his gentle grip. He continued to hold her after the music stopped, hand clasped around hers and comforting fingers pressed to the center of her back.

She glanced up. His eyes were warm with concern, and his thumbs were whisper soft as they wiped her tears. The heat from his body and the scent of him, cool and clean, made her stomach tighten. As Allina swayed closer, he dipped his head until their lips were just centimeters apart.

Panicking, she shook her head, backed away.

"I'm sorry," he whispered before clearing his throat. "You can't bring yourself to trust me. I don't blame you for that." He slanted her a shrewd look. "We can't move forward without trust, can we?"

Von Strassberg locked the door, then moved the radio closer to it and switched it on. As the triumphant strains of Wagner's "Ride of the Valkyries" filled the parlor, he walked to the far side of the room and arranged two chairs so they were a half meter apart and facing each other. With a flick of tailcoat, he settled into one, crossing his long legs before fixing his dark blue eyes on her once again.

"You have questions for me. I'm at your disposal," he said, inclining his head as he gestured to the other chair. "You may begin your interrogation."

Allina took her seat, unsure how to begin. He was offering exactly what she'd hoped for. Now her courage was failing.

"Please." He tilted his head toward the radio, still blasting away. "The Wagner will do its job nicely for a bit."

She wet her lips and began with the question that had stolen her sleep last night. "Did you cheer the Führer yesterday, at the Reichstag?"

He swallowed, hard. "Of course I cheered," he said. "Do you think I had a choice?"

"But do you agree with him?" she asked. "Do you agree with what he said about the Jews and . . . and what must be done?"

He nailed her with his dark blue eyes. "No. No, I do not."

The need to share the whole truth had her shaking, so much that she couldn't trust her voice to ask another question. As the silence spun out between them she was unable to break away from the intensity of his gaze.

"Why would you ask me this?" he finally whispered. "Of all the questions you could ask, why would that be the first?"

Allina paused, gathering courage. She had to tell him.

"You know my aunt and uncle raised me after my parents died."

He nodded.

"But I didn't tell you about my parents. My birth mother, my real mother, was Jewish."

His lips parted in shock. He didn't respond to Allina's admission but continued gazing at her in that strange way of his, searching inside her. Seeing her. With compassion, and understanding, and an emotion she couldn't quite identify.

She blinked back tears. "I'm *Mischling*. All my papers are forgeries. My position here was built on a lie."

"Does Gud know?" he asked.

She shook her head.

For a moment it seemed like he was observing her from a long distance. Karl opened his mouth again, then closed it, as though searching for words. "I'm so glad you told me," he said finally. "And I promise to keep your secret safe. I hope you know you can trust me to honor that promise."

"I do." But his promise didn't reduce the horror of the other questions she needed answered. "I must know more about the Führer's plans. If you'll tell me."

It was a pitifully vague request, but von Strassberg must have gotten her meaning, because he paused and looked away before giving a careful reply. "You heard the Führer's speech. He wants every Jew out of the country."

"He used the word 'annihilation,'" she insisted.

"Yes," he whispered. He leaned in to tuck an errant strand of hair behind her ear, but it was the grief in his eyes that stilled her.

Panic rose in her chest, a frozen, silent scream. "How can this be happening?" she asked, ignoring Karl when he shook his head and opened his mouth to speak. "The world won't allow—"

"No," he interrupted, cupping her cheek. "Listen to me."

"England, France, America," Allina said, pulling away. "They'll never permit it." Surely, someone would intervene. She paced to the window, pressing her forehead to the cool glass to ease her frantic breathing. Von Strassberg joined her after a few moments, standing close enough that the heat of his body warmed her through their clothes. He didn't speak. He seemed content to offer the calmness of his presence, as their breaths left foggy circles on the windowpane.

"You always insist on the truth," von Strassberg finally murmured. "Can you bear to hear it tonight?"

Allina turned to face him.

"If you think the rest of the world cares about our Jews, you're fooling yourself," he said with a bitterness that made her stomach tumble. "They barely tolerate their own. The world looks away. No one wants war." He blew out a tired breath. "They looked away when we took back Austria. And now, Chamberlain and Daladier capitulate, hoping the Führer will be content with the Sudetenland. He won't be. His hunger for power, like his hatred of the Jews and the Soviets, is bottomless. But no one wants war," he repeated, "and the Führer knows that. He's counting on it. For now, the world is content to remain blind."

Allina tried to rub the goose bumps from her arms. She couldn't tear her gaze away from his face. She'd never witnessed this defeated cynicism in him before.

Von Strassberg straightened his shoulders, plainly making the effort to take hold of himself, but when he spoke again it was with a clipped military precision that betrayed how much the words cost him. "We'll see greater restrictions, more arrests and roundups. The camps, the ghettos aren't the issue. We have the capacity. What we lack is structure, discipline. The Führer has dozens of scientists and engineers eager to do his bidding, but they bicker among themselves. Progress is slow," he added, blowing out another gust of air. "Time is on our side. For now."

Our side. Despite her horror, she managed to hold on to that one phrase, a single candle in a pitch-dark room. "What do you mean, our side?"

His eyes were dark with grief. "I mean I'll work with like-minded individuals to save as many people as we can," he said, "for as long as I can."

There they were—the words she hadn't allowed herself to consider. Allina gripped the window's ledge to steady herself. "There are plans in place? Plans to help?"

"Organized plans, no, but, as you know, papers can be faked," he said with a wry smile. "Safe transport out of the country can be arranged, given time and resources. There's an effort now to transport Jewish children to England. I'll have to turn my attention there soon."

The enormity of his words had her light-headed. "How many others are there, like you, in the *Schutzstaffel*?" Allina walked back to her chair on shaky legs and sank into it.

"Only a handful," he said with a bitter laugh, "and we're a fractured bunch." He raked his fingers through his pomaded hair until thick clumps of it stood on end. "A few disagree with the Führer's politics, others his military strategy. We can't agree on how to stop him."

There was an edge to his voice and a tightening in the lines around his eyes that made her bold. "I don't think he can be stopped while he lives."

He blinked. "Probably not, no."

A sharp clatter of heels—the lively sound of Hochland Home women in search of private parlors—sounded outside the door, followed by a shrill laugh that sounded too much like Berta's. Karl's eyes widened and he raised a finger to his lips. Allina remained frozen with her pulse pounding in her ears, until the footfalls receded.

"How do you bear it?" she whispered.

"I'm a military man, like my father and his father before him," he answered. "It's my duty to serve Germany and all its citizens, though my real work must happen in the shadows."

His words were affirmation and a gorgeous relief—and also treason, plain and simple. "It's a dangerous deception," she whispered. "A treacherous risk."

"You're part of that deception now," he said, "and you know more than you should, thanks to me." Taking her hands in his again, he webbed their fingers together. "I need your help, every bit as much as your children do. We need each other."

"I've given you more to worry about now, though, haven't I?"

Von Strassberg's smile was immediate, and it wiped the bitterness from his face. For a moment she glimpsed a bit of the little boy in her locket. "Don't be ridiculous. You're my partner in crime," he said. "My brilliant recruit. And the most precious."

In your heart you know he's a good man. Good men do what they must. Allina closed her eyes as Uncle's voice filled her mind, repeating words he'd said about the boy she'd loved.

There was only one question left unanswered. "What are your plans for me?" she asked, softly.

He smiled and squeezed her hands. "I'll do everything within my power to protect you. I've become a master at keeping secrets."

She shook her head. "That's not what I meant. I asked you once what you wanted from me. You never gave a full answer."

He stared at her, looking into her in that strange way of his. A shiver ran through her, settling low in her belly.

"I think you know the answer to that. The choice is yours. I won't insult you by saying I know how much you've lost. You've suffered unimaginable loss." He traced her eyebrows with a fingertip, and the intensity in the gentle caress made her shiver. "That doesn't make me want you any less."

His gaze wouldn't let hers go. They were such a beautiful, deep blue.

"Thank you for the truth, Karl," she whispered.

It was the first time she used his given name.

PART 3

Munich

CHAPTER 19

SS Race and Settlement Main Office (RuSHA)
Munich

KARL

Heinrich Himmler looked like hell. The *Reichsführer's* complexion was a sickly shade of green, his droopy nose was a red and shiny blob, and his bloodshot eyes watered behind wire-rimmed glasses.

Masking a grin, Karl raised his arm and voice in greeting. "*Heil* Hitler!"

The pained expression in Himmler's gaze was gratifying, as was the way he tottered to the side when he stood. After last night's debauchery, it was a minor miracle the man remained upright.

Excellent. Today's meeting might be enjoyable after all.

Massaging the bags under his eyes, Himmler stepped out from behind his desk with care and waved Karl into the office. "What a party. My head still aches from all the champagne."

As bad as the man looked, Himmler's uniform was worse, bordering on unacceptable for any officer: His tie was loose, his collar was slightly askew, and he clearly hadn't bothered to shine his boots this morning. Even the *Reichsführer's* massive cherry desk was in disarray. Normally free of paperwork and polished to a high gloss, the desktop was covered with files, an overflowing ashtray, a half-eaten sandwich, and three used coffee cups.

If Karl was lucky, Himmler's untidiness was a reflection of his mental state.

"Yesterday was a spectacular celebration in honor of the Führer." Karl clapped his hands together and rubbed them vigorously.

The *Reichsführer* winced. "Please. A little less volume." He waved toward the round conference table in the corner of the room. "Take a seat. Haschen will bring tea." Himmler's pasty face brightened as a stunning blonde in a form-fitting charcoal number appeared in the doorway. "There you are, my dear." He puffed out his chest, managing to look both gallant and ridiculous. "On the conference table, please."

The young woman favored her boss with a feline smile, and her hips swayed in a seductive figure eight as she carried a tray of tea and biscuits to the table. Himmler's eyes roamed over her exposed cleavage. The *Reichsführer*'s assistant poured the tea with grace and added two lumps of sugar before handing Himmler the cup. Their fingers touched, then lingered.

It was impossible to miss the intimate glances. The man was infatuated. In lust.

She turned to Karl, and while her smile was wide, it was much less friendly. "Sugar?"

Karl shook his head.

"Thank you, Haschen." Himmler sat back and winked at his assistant. "I'll ring if there's anything else."

"Of course. Anything at all," she called out before sashaying out the door.

The gossip was true, then. The *Reichsführer* was planning a move. Rumor had it Himmler was embroiled in a passionate affair with his much younger secretary. The affair shed light on the divorce law Himmler instigated last year that gave a man the right to divorce his wife if she was sterile or refused to bear children.

Karl gulped down his tea, set the cup down in its saucer, and waited.

"You asked for this meeting," Himmler prompted. "What's on your mind?"

So begins the battle. "I'll come straight to the point. I wish to increase my involvement with this office."

"RuSHA?" Himmler's eyebrows shot up. "You're interested in our efforts here. Why?"

Karl chose the boldest possible play, since daring was a perfect mask for stealth. "Forgive my bluntness, Heinrich, but I'm aware of certain problems that have cropped up in the children at Hochland Home." He leaned back and crossed his arms over his chest. "Many are backward. I've seen them myself."

Himmler nodded. "We're aware of the physical defects, the mental slowness. It's troubling, given their excellent bloodlines." Sampling his tea, he grimaced before adding another sugar cube to his cup.

"Do we know how many children are affected?"

Himmler frowned at that question. "Yes. I do. As I said, it's regrettable, but we'll get to the bottom of things. The Führer has given me free rein, and I've tasked some of our best doctors to find a solution. They're working on the problem at a research facility in Berlin."

So Allina's hunch was correct. They were experimenting on *Lebensborn* children, and only God and Himmler's butchers knew what those experiments entailed. That gave Karl little room to maneuver, and only one real option.

He nodded slowly but said no more, allowing the silence to stretch out between them, hoping Himmler would take the bait.

"What's your point, Karl?" he prompted. "I can see the gears turning from here."

"I believe I know why the defects are happening," Karl said, leaning forward, "but I must conduct an experiment of my own to prove it."

"You?" Himmler reared back with a snort. "Karl, you're no scientist."

Karl dipped his head. "You're right, sir. I'm just a soldier." He paused for a long moment for effect, before leaning in with narrowed eyes. "But when I saw those children, I asked myself: How would the *Reichsführer* see the situation?"

Himmler stroked his chin. "And?"

"I believe the children are coddled, sir. The *Schwestern* do their best," Karl said with a shrug, "but they're women. These young ones need discipline. A soldier's discipline." He knew he'd hit the perfect note when the *Reichsführer* reached for pen and paper.

"Your logic is sound." Himmler scribbled a few notes. "Go on."

"Dozens of men, honest soldiers hardened by work, pass through Hochland Home each month. They can't spend all their time with the ladies," he said. "You know what happens when men have excess time on their hands."

"Too much drinking." Himmler massaged his temple. "Gambling. Fighting."

"Exactly. I'll have a few of my men organize activities. We'll invigorate these children while we keep the men in line."

"Brilliant tactics," Himmler murmured, scribbling additional notes. "You suggest we start the boys' military training in the cradle."

"We'll model the physical exercise on the Hitler Youth program. The transition should be seamless once the boys are old enough to join." Convincing Allina of his plan was another problem. She'd need to play the part of loyal, devoted *Schwester* to help her children.

"And the girls?" Himmler asked, tapping his pen on the pad.

Karl grinned. "We need strong women who'll bear strapping sons for the Reich."

Himmler shook his pen at Karl. "Markus was right about you. He always said you were an original thinker."

"Thank you, sir."

"Very well," Himmler said, tossing pad and pen on his desk. "Conduct your experiment with ten children. My scientists will study the rest. We'll see which team triumphs, eh?"

Only ten. That wouldn't sit well with Allina, but he couldn't push it. This was victory.

Karl grinned. "I look forward to the battle."

"You have three months," Himmler said. "Send me your plans in advance. I want weekly reports from whomever you designate as chief administrator."

"You'll get them."

"I'm sure I will." Himmler narrowed his eyes. "Your interest in the *Lebensborn* program is surprising. You're unmarried and haven't fathered any children. Or have you?"

Karl raised his hands in mock surrender. "Not yet."

"Ah, the girl from last night, the one who left dinner early. What's her name again?"

"Allina Gottlieb."

"She's lovely. A bit on the quiet side," Himmler said, "but I sensed a feistiness under that calm."

Karl coughed, earning a chuckle from the *Reichsführer*.

"I'm assuming her bloodline is good?" Himmler asked.

"Impeccable, sir," Karl lied smoothly. "I realize your office must undertake its own investigation, but I'd be happy to supply the office with the necessary documentation."

"You want more than a romantic liaison with this girl?" Himmler leaned back and squinted.

Karl shrugged. "I've got to convince her first, but the background check for a marriage license takes months to approve. We should begin the process now." As soon as he made sure the appropriate forged documents were in place.

"Fine, fine. The sooner you marry, the better. We expect our men to produce no less than six children from their marriages," Himmler said, "and to spread their seed outside of them."

Hypocrite. Everyone knew Gudrun was the *Reichsführer's* only legitimate child. "That won't be a problem, sir."

Leaning forward, Himmler offered a tolerant smile. "Let me give you a piece of advice. It was obvious last night you feel some tenderness for this girl. You may even imagine yourself in love. But believe me, fidelity is a myth perpetrated by women."

"Is that so?"

Himmler chuckled. "Enjoy the lovely Allina as you will. When the feelings fade, you'll be grateful to the *Lebensborn* program. There are many, many women waiting for the chance to serve Germany," he said. "We sow our seed and create the next generation of proud Germans for our Führer in the process." The man slapped his knees, clearly enamored of his own logic.

"This will be your greatest victory, sir," Karl said.

"It will, indeed." Himmler escorted Karl to the door. "Pending our investigation into the girl's bloodlines, you have my full support."

CHAPTER 20

ALLINA

With an anxious tug at her cap, Allina hurried down the row of nursing mothers. She'd woken a half hour late this morning to gray skies and a fine drizzle that made her sinuses feel like they'd been stuffed with tea towels. Washing only the necessary bits, Allina had choked down a hard, unbuttered roll and fruit—a miserable mistake, as everyone at Hochland Home was running late and she could still smell the bacon she'd sacrificed at breakfast. Worse, not one mother had shown up on time to nurse, and the women in the South Wing were in lazy, spiteful moods. She couldn't afford to have the rest of the day go like this. Six mothers still lounged in their chairs, although the first feeding session had been over for twenty minutes.

Allina turned to Lotte and forced a smile. "You see? Little Ingrid is stronger today." She scooped Ingrid up and laid her back in the crib, but the baby fussed and kicked off the blanket. "She's already gained four ounces this week."

Lotte's entire body seemed to sigh with relief. "Thank you, *Schwester*."

"Thank you, *Schwester*," Berta mimicked. She tossed aside the latest fashion magazine and stood to leave. Allina took Neils and transferred him to the cradle, but the second she set him down, he began to howl, startling several other babies who quickly joined in. The room filled with a chorus of fussy crying, which sliced like knives into her skull.

"It's a shame you can't control the children in your charge." Berta clucked her tongue in mock sympathy and adjusted the blue silk scarf at her neck. "But then, control isn't your strong suit, is it, *Schwester?* Frau Himmler wondered why you left the party in a huff the other night. Von Strassberg went looking for you. Did he find you after all?" She chuckled. "I went looking for him myself."

Rilla sent Berta a nasty glare. "Why don't you shut your mouth for once?"

"Go grab another biscuit from the buffet to stuff your face with. Maybe that'll sweeten your mood." Berta flicked her eyes over Rilla's body. Rilla hadn't shed much of her pregnancy weight yet, an embarrassing sore point.

The other mothers muttered in shock and perverse excitement while Allina counted to ten. On any other day, the exchange might have been funny, but this feud had been escalating for weeks and her nerves were shot.

"I said, shut up!" Rilla leaped up, fists balled at her sides, and lunged toward Berta in three aggressive steps.

Berta tipped her chin up. "Make me!"

"Enough!" Allina slammed her hand down on the counter. Every soul in the room—Rilla, Berta, the other mothers, and all the infants—went quiet for a glorious moment. Allina closed her eyes and let out a sigh.

The babies started howling again.

Allina pointed her finger at both women. "Not one more word—"

Three brisk knocks on the nursery door cut her lecture short. "Come," she called out.

Wendeline bustled in to relieve her, with Karl on her heels. Allina's relief was so intense her knees nearly gave out. She leaned against the counter, not bothering to temper her smile.

Karl managed to bow to the mothers without sparing them a glance. No, his blue gaze was all for her as the women handed over their babies and filed meekly out of the room.

Rilla, of course, stayed behind. "I'm glad you've returned, *Gruppenführer.* Your absence put this one in a horrible mood yesterday," she teased, wrapping an arm around Allina's waist.

Allina pinched the inside of her friend's elbow, but Rilla was in a state. She hip-bumped her back.

Karl leaned against the wall, slouching a bit in his perfectly pressed gray uniform. His lips twitched. "Is that right?"

"I caught her looking in her locket several times," Rilla added with a wink.

Karl's attention shifted to Rilla, who fumbled with the collar of her red gingham blouse. "How interesting, Fräulein Weber, that you kept tabs on her," he said softly. Although his voice was pleasant, there was a hint of menace in the tightness of his mouth.

Allina jiggled Rilla's arm. The poor thing jumped. "Don't you have somewhere else to be, Rilla?"

"We're the ones who need to leave," Karl said. "You'll excuse us?"

"Of course." Rilla bowed her head.

Karl tucked Allina's hand in his arm as he escorted her toward the entrance to the garden. "It's a shame I had to be so abrupt," he murmured. "She's a sweet girl."

"And a perceptive one," Allina answered, reaching for her coat. "She sees beyond your uniform. Be careful, there."

Karl slipped the coat up her arms and around Allina's shoulders. When she turned around, the tips of his ears were pink.

"Did you get my note?" he asked. "I sent one by courier last night." He guided them to their favorite bench at the far corner of the garden.

"Your note only said you were in meetings about the children. I need details."

He leaned back and crossed his long legs, looking satisfied with himself. "I went directly to the *Reichsführer*. He approved an experiment here, one we can use to help those children."

Relief was so intense she nearly hugged him. "An experiment?"

"One to rehabilitate them," Karl said, crossing his arms over his chest. "He agreed to let us try with ten children."

Only ten. "And the others?"

He grunted and turned away.

"Tell me, Karl."

"His scientists will continue to work with the rest to determine the reason for their disability." Karl's voice was too calm, and when their eyes met, his face was a careful blank.

It was her turn to look away. She'd known the truth down deep in her bones, but hearing it was a different thing altogether.

A snow finch soared in on a gust of wind, fluffing its dove-gray wings as it settled on the bench beside theirs. It waited, chirping as it cocked its head and examined them with dark, glossy eyes. After a minute, the bird hopped to the edge of the bench and flew free over the hedge.

"They're going to hurt those children," she whispered. "Kill them."

"Perhaps, yes. Eventually." Taking her hand, he pressed his thumb to her wrist. The touch anchored her. "If we can rehabilitate ten, it will make a case for more. You've got tough decisions to make."

"You want me to pick which children to keep." She rubbed her eyes to keep back the tears. "And, by default, which to send away." Of course the decisions were hers. There was no one else to make them.

"Yes. You must pick carefully."

"I will. The decisions won't be difficult." They'd be heartbreaking, but clear enough. "I'll select the ones with the greatest physical coordination, the best manners and speech."

"Good," he said. "I'll need a file on each that lists their strengths and weaknesses to help us measure improvement."

"Of course," she said. "I'll do it tonight." Allina eased over, just enough to rest her head on his shoulder, accepting his strength, his surety, to prepare for what was to come.

Karl went absolutely still. After a few moments, he rested his head against hers.

"We begin tomorrow," he said. "I've recruited three friends to help. Two of my men, and an old friend, a doctor. They can't wait to meet you."

"So soon?" Surprised, she pulled away. "How will I explain that?"

"You don't have to. I've told *Schwester* Ziegler you're on special assignment to the *Reichsführer*. Your duties will shift, beginning tomorrow. That's all she needs to know."

"I wish I could have seen her face when you told her."

He chuckled at that and pulled her to her feet. "She wasn't happy, but she'll fall in line. If she gives you trouble, I'll handle it."

"It sounds like you've handled everything." Allina took the arm Karl offered, leaning on him as they walked slowly back to the house. "Did you convince her to give us a room to work out of tomorrow, as well? Or perhaps arrange for a buffet lunch?"

A flush crept up Karl's neck into his cheeks. "I've done better than that. We'll work out of my Munich office. Less interference that way. I thought you might want a day away from this place."

A day outside of Hochland Home with Karl. The idea had her heart racing for several reasons, one so important that the words rushed out of her mouth before she could stop them.

"I have a favor to ask."

His grin was immediate. "Anything."

"The items sewn into my coat, the ones I transferred to the box. They're letters from my father, and . . . other things of his. I can't risk reading them here. There's no privacy." She'd escaped to her room three times in the past week to try to read her father's letters and been interrupted every time. Last night after dinner, the head nurse had come into her room without knocking, on an emergency errand.

Karl nodded. "Of course. Bring them with you."

"Thank you." Having her father's letters five feet away in a locked box was maddening. "I've never read them. I didn't know they existed until a few days before I . . . left Badensburg."

He took her hand again, squeezed it. "We'll make time."

Rumors about Allina's reassignment spread through Hochland Home by noon. She didn't have to hear the chatter to know everyone was talking. The prickly discomfort on the back of her neck was evidence enough. Then there were the looks—*Schwester* Ziegler's frowns, Lotte's discreet peeks full of envy, and Berta's loathing sneer—and an annoying cluster of questions from Rilla which, of course, she couldn't answer. *A special project? For Reichsführer Himmler? And Gruppenführer von Strassberg is involved? Why would he be interested in a special project at Hochland Home?*

When Berta approached Allina after dinner and asked if the files she'd seen her *hand over in the garden* had to do with this special project, Allina had a moment of panic before she calmed herself down and walked away. Allina would have to share that observation with Karl at some point, but Berta didn't have the details. Still, the woman was too clever, too deliberate in her menace. Allina had to find a way to cut her down.

She retired to her room after dinner. She missed the evening's character training class, but the satisfaction that she couldn't be penalized for her absence did little to dull the evening's pain. She spent an hour agonizing over her choices, and another creating the files he'd asked for. It was a ruthless task, one that forced Allina to concentrate on the children they'd save instead of the ones they couldn't. When she slid into bed after midnight, her stomach hummed with anticipation and her throat ached with unshed tears. But there was no utility in her sadness, so she pushed it aside. She had to trust they were doing the right thing.

CHAPTER 21

ALLINA

The morning air was crisp as she floated down the front steps on Karl's arm. She'd spent plenty of time outdoors in Hochland Home's courtyards— the daily schedule demanded it—but today was Allina's first time in four months outside the compound. The freedom was exhilarating.

She gasped when they stopped in front of an extravagant convertible with an impossibly long hood. It was neither silver nor gold, but a gorgeous alloy somewhere between. Allina peeked through the window, shaking her head in amazement at the red leather interior and an instrument panel that looked to be inlaid with mother-of-pearl. "I've never seen a car so beautiful."

Karl responded with a crooked smile. "I know it's ridiculous, but I love her," he said, running his hand over the hood. "This beautiful lady is a 1937 Mercedes-Benz 540K. Only a few hundred of this model were made. I'm lucky to have her." He opened the passenger door. "We should go. Everyone's watching."

She glanced back at the house to find a dozen noses pressed to the front window. Sabine and Rilla were all grins and enthusiastic waves, but Berta's lips were pursed in a lemony pucker. She gave them all a merry wave before sliding into the car.

Karl took off with a screech of tires that left gravel spitting in their wake. By the faint narrowing of his eyes, Allina wondered if he was showing off, or at least trying to give the ladies at the window a thrill.

"Are you warm enough?" he shouted over the engine's roar. "We can stop and put the top up. I have another scarf if you need one."

Allina tugged the knitted navy cap on loan from Rilla down over her ears. "I'm fine," she yelled, loving the wind against her cheeks. The curve of the seat was bliss against her spine and the air smelled like rain and damp earth. "Where are we going, exactly?"

"Starnberg," he said. "My home's just outside Munich. I've got a private office there."

The hard line of his jaw was outlined against the heather gray of the pre-dawn sky. Allina became conscious of his body and his wide hands, competent and in control, gripping the steering wheel.

Her eyes fell to his shirt collar. "You're not in uniform," she blurted. Dressed in a camel wool overcoat, charcoal trousers, and a plain white shirt—and without a tie—the man seemed different. Less severe. Years younger.

He glanced over and grinned again. "I thought you'd prefer me in civilian clothes."

Allina shoved her hands into her coat pockets and glanced away.

"Your face always betrays your emotions," he said. "My uniform unnerves you, and I'm sorry for it. I hoped to spare you that today."

Allina nodded but didn't reply, and Karl seemed content to leave it at that. The wind didn't allow for much conversation, so she took the hour's drive to settle into the idea of being alone with him. They'd been careful for weeks, always speaking in whispers and meeting outside to keep from being overheard. Now she and Karl would have a whole day together, and at least the morning by themselves. In his home. She leaned back against the leather seat and closed her eyes, determined not to think. As the minutes passed, the engine's hum did its work and lulled her.

When the vehicle slowed, she opened her eyes to a charming sight. A whitewashed house built in chalet style stood at the end of a long, winding path. It was well proportioned, and the oak balconies and evergreen detail along the gently sloping roof looked freshly painted. Two bunches of fir trees flanked the building.

Karl parked in front of the house and leaped out of his seat. "This was my family's summer home," he said, running around to her side to open the door.

Allina didn't know what to say to that, so she followed him in silence as their heels crunched in the gravel. When they got to the front door, she cocked her head at the sign hanging over it. "*Sonnenblumen Haus?*" she asked.

"My grandmother named it," he said, pointing around the side of the house. "We call it the Sunflower House because the side yard explodes with sunflowers in spring and summer." He opened the door. "Come inside."

The front parlor was bright and scrupulously clean. Thick emerald velvet drapes were drawn open, allowing the huge windows to flood the room with light. The honey-colored floors and ceiling beams gleamed with polish. She loved the crisp, whitewashed walls, which were mostly free of adornment, although a bold oil landscape of the German countryside hung above a fireplace on the far side of the room. The lines of the pine furniture were neat and utilitarian, but there were splashes of ruby and marigold in the cushion coverings and pillows.

The room was exactly like him. Strong, unpretentious, intensely masculine, and a far cry from the crammed fussiness of Hochland Home. It was also a comfortable, lived-in space. While the carpets were Persian and most of the furniture antique, everything bore a gently worn patina of use.

He led her through the dining room to the den, which was much more like a conference room than a personal office. Eight brown leather chairs surrounded a massive oak table in the center. Two tall metal shelves stocked with paper and office supplies took up a good portion of one of the walls, and between the shelves was a sideboard with three typewriters on it. Above the sideboard was a huge window. On the left was an antique hunter's cuckoo clock, its engraved leaves painted in deep green and gold. On the right hung a painting of Adolf Hitler—the standard one found in nearly every home of an unsmiling Führer in a light brown suit. The other three walls were covered, floor to ceiling, by oak shelves stuffed with books of every size and color. They filled the den with the sweet scent of old paper and ink, and she blinked back tears. The room smelled like home.

Karl unbuttoned his overcoat and tossed it over a chair. "My house meets with your approval?"

"The simplicity suits you." She tossed her files on the table.

Karl's answering bark of laughter was a surprise. His face softened, and the fine lines around his eyes eased. He was relaxed here, completely disarmed.

"I'll take your coat," he said, hurrying over. When his hands settled on her shoulders, Allina froze. His hands were warm through the thick fabric, and she fumbled like a child with the buttons. When she handed it over, he took the coat without a word.

With her gaze still trained on the carpet, she tugged off her hat.

"Your hair." He spoke those two words in a whisper, and when she risked a glance up, his eyes were locked on her face.

"It's Rilla's doing," she blurted. Self-conscious, her hand went to her nape. Rilla had begged to style her hair this morning and managed to fashion an intricate coronet of golden braids around her head. It was an old-fashioned look, one Sabine had pronounced perfect for her face. From the dark gleam in Karl's eyes, Rilla would claim her handiwork a success. Leaning in, he traced the path of a single braid around her head, sending a tingle of awareness down to the roots of her hair.

Karl stepped back. "Please, make yourself comfortable," he said in a more formal voice. He took her hat and muffler and hung them up with her coat. "Ursula will be in to serve lunch, but I'll put something together for breakfast. I thought you might want to read your father's letters before we get to work. I'll leave you in peace." He nodded, a little awkwardly, then disappeared into the kitchen.

Allina took a seat at the table and pulled out the small packet she'd buried in a file. She'd chosen one of her father's newspaper articles, along with several envelopes. Now she wished she'd brought more items from the box. It took less than ten minutes to read his letters. They were short and clearly dashed off in a hurry, but Allina pored over every word, each detail a tiny bit of buried treasure.

"Coffee's almost ready." Karl walked into the den, platter in hand, but stopped when he saw her face. "What is it?"

Allina realized her face was wet with tears. She wiped her cheeks. "I'm fine. It's just . . . these are so normal . . . about his job, the day he met my mother at a café, nights out at the theater . . ." She held up one letter. "I don't know what I expected."

He set the platter down. "And this?" he asked, picking up the article.

"I haven't gotten to it yet."

"May I?" He nudged the platter of food her way. It was simple fare that made her stomach growl: brown bread, thick slices of apple, and butter cheese.

Nodding, she took a slice of all three and downed them quickly. Allina was hungrier than usual. The cheese was rich, the apple very tart, and the hearty bread a perfect complement for both.

A half minute later, Karl took his seat with a sharp bark of laughter. "Listen to this: 'Herr Hitler is a strutting peacock who knows nothing about public policy, economics, or human decency. Copies of the NSDAP 25-Point Plan would be best put to use by our citizens after visiting the toilet.'" His shoulders shook with mirth as he handed the article over. "Your father was political. Now I know where you get your nerve."

Half laughing, half crying, she read the article twice, from beginning to end. "Uncle was right. He was an amazing writer."

Karl snorted. "Yes. I like him, your father."

"Now I wish I'd brought the rest."

"Bring them next time. You can keep all his letters here if you wish. They'll be safe." Karl took her hand between his two warmer ones before pulling back. "We need to get to work."

"We do."

He quickly laid out the basics. They had ninety days—three short, terrifying months—to demonstrate improvement. That would take hours of painstaking work and make every bit of documentation critical. Every notation in the children's files would have to be beyond reproach.

But there was good news, too. "*Schwester* Ziegler has agreed to give you a classroom of your own," he said. "We'll keep your ten children separate from the others. Her staff will take care of them in the evenings, but you'll have control during the day."

Being responsible for so few children would normally be a treat, but these little ones were a challenge.

"You'll have help from three allies, as promised." Karl grinned. "Hans and Alexander have the energy of ten men, and Josef served as a medic in the Great War. That's why they're coming to lunch today. They'll be with you the first three months."

He popped a bit of cheese into his mouth. "After the first ninety days, assuming we're successful," he said, "you'll have to train volunteers."

"Volunteers?"

"Yes. If we succeed, the program will expand, but I doubt you'll get additional budget. My men can help when they visit Hochland Home, specifically with physical exercise. The *Reichsführer* has already approved this."

Karl's request that Allina attend the Hochland Home mixers made more sense now. She'd end up working with different men, strange men in uniform, each week.

"We'll need a system to train them," she said, trying not to panic.

"We do. Let me grab the coffee." He walked to the kitchen and returned with a tray. "What should we tackle first?" he asked, filling their cups.

She took a sip and sighed. Good coffee always made her thinking clearer. "I see three major areas of concern."

"Physical fitness, manners, speech," he said, rolling up his sleeves. "See? I've been listening."

"Excellent," she teased, practicing her best teacher voice. "For speech, we should use flash cards, like the ones in primary school."

Karl nodded.

"We show them a picture of the item, give them a physical example if we can, and show how the word is written. They're too young to read, but it's never too early to start learning your letters."

Allina wrote a list of common words and slid the paper in front of him:

A = Apple. B = Book. M = Mother.

Karl picked up a pencil and added *F = Führer* to her list. When she wrinkled her nose, he underlined the word. "Hochland Home serves the Führer," he said. "Never forget that."

"Of course."

"If I can tell you're uncomfortable," he warned, "so will others. You must learn to master your facial expressions. Himmler's a stickler for detail, and

Hochland Home's reputation may suffer to the degree we succeed. They'll be watching everything you do."

"What a cheerful thought," Allina said as Karl laughed. "Give me some information about the children's physical training, please."

Karl leaned back in his chair. "It makes sense to model their training on the Hitler Youth. We'll plan contests to motivate them."

Allina frowned. "Some of the children can't stand properly, never mind walk or run." Even Otto, who was more advanced than the rest, struggled with balance.

"They will soon enough. Poor posture and weak muscles can be improved. We'll show Josef your files this afternoon. He knows how to rehabilitate atrophied muscles."

The man was a tower of confidence. "And manners?"

"We focus on basics first. Standing in line, waiting turns, please and thank you," he said, counting off on his fingers.

"Table manners, raising hands, sharing toys," she added. "Any activity can be used to teach manners." It would be a matter of repetition, reward, and consistency.

"Exactly." He folded his arms across his chest and grinned, looking so obviously pleased with himself that she had to laugh.

"Now, all we have to do is figure out each activity." She leaned in close enough to catch his quick inhale of breath. "Do you think you're up to it?"

Karl grinned. "I'm all yours."

The clock chimed twelve. Allina glanced up from her notes. "I can't believe it's noon already."

"We got a lot done," Karl said. "You'll make a good teacher." Interlacing his hands together over his head, he leaned back with a ferocious yawn, twisting in a way that outlined the muscles in his arms and stretched the cloth of his shirt across his broad chest.

Allina looked away. "We make a good team," she murmured. "I like your idea of combining physical activity, like clapping, with their counting exercises."

He nodded and stretched some more. Allina fussed with her notes

and did her best to ignore the low buzz at the base of her spine, the one she'd tried to suppress for hours. It wasn't his nearness, exactly. They'd sat together before, dozens of times, and his behavior this morning had been chivalrous. Perhaps he'd been more charming than usual, but she couldn't read anything other than kindness in Karl's blue eyes.

Still, friendly feelings couldn't account for the impatience that had overtaken her the five times their fingers had brushed this morning—a sharp restlessness that made her shift in her seat. She wanted to lean over and press her bare arm against his, to feel the heat of his skin.

Standing abruptly, Allina pressed her hands to the back of her neck, working out the stiffness as she reviewed their work. A dozen papers forming the basis of a rudimentary curriculum, including a daily agenda for the children and weekly goals for vocabulary and physical fitness, were spread across the table. Allina was grateful to put her writing skills to use again. It was a thoughtful, aggressive plan.

Twisting, she rolled her shoulders and winced.

Karl rose with a frown. "I'm a poor host," he said. "We should have taken a break an hour ago. Here, let me." He set his hands lightly on her shoulders, waiting for her nod before he began kneading the knot of muscle there. He managed to dig in just hard enough to ease the stiffness without hurting her, and the muscles in her shoulders tingled as they loosened up. She sighed and leaned back into the warmth of his palms.

An electric charge, sharper than before, soon filled the space between them. When she turned to him, he didn't move closer. He seemed content to gaze at her in that compelling way of his, looking into her with his deep blue eyes. The pull was strong and his familiar scent, cool and clean like earth and water, was impossible to resist. She swayed forward, lifting her face, unable to look away from his mouth. He brushed a kiss against her forehead and pulled back, waiting. Lifting a hand to his face, she trailed a finger along the hard line of his jaw. His skin was silky despite the rough stubble, and warm to the touch. The muscles in his throat worked hard as he swallowed.

Karl gave in with a groan, and still Allina watched him, her eyes fluttering closed at the last possible moment.

The kiss was tentative, a bare brush of warm lips, the answering need in her body surprising in its intensity. When he pulled back, she touched her fingers to her lips. They were tingling. "Did you feel that?" she whispered.

"*Hallo!*" a woman called out from the vicinity of the kitchen.

Jumping back, Allina pressed her hand to her throat. Her heart was pounding.

Karl closed his eyes. "That would be Ursula, with our luncheon," he announced, and Allina caught the slightest whine in his tone. "Let me introduce you."

He grabbed her hand and walked with her to the kitchen. A plump, middle-aged woman with nut-brown hair and a face as round as the moon was busy unpacking two huge baskets of food on a butcher-block counter in the center of the kitchen. She glanced up with a sunny smile that dimpled her cheeks.

"Ursula, this is Allina Gottlieb, a friend who's working with me on a special program for the children at Hochland Home," Karl said, gesturing between the two. "Allina, I don't know what I'd do without Ursula. She cooks amazing meals and keeps me fit and happy."

"A pleasure to meet you, Fräulein." Ursula's brown eyes danced. She looked pointedly at their joined hands before giving Allina a quick once-over. "I've a tasty feast to fill your stomachs and warm your insides." Ursula wiped her hands on her gray apron. "The soup's already on the stove. When will the rest of your guests arrive?"

The loud roar of an engine and a screech of brakes made Karl peer out the kitchen window. "Impeccable timing, as usual," he said.

Allina peeked outside as three men emerged from a black, battered automobile. Two were tall and golden haired and seemed to be about her age, and the third was much older, with more salt than pepper in his hair.

"Allina, may I introduce Hans and Alexander Schäfer, your new assistants in the classroom," he said, his hands on the younger men's shoulders. Both were nearly as tall as Karl, blond, blue-eyed, and handsome, with strong chins and broad cheekbones. When the pair smiled, dimples appeared in their right cheeks.

"I'm Hans," said the first, and as she stood, he bowed over her knuckles. "We're pleased to meet you, Fräulein Gottlieb."

"Hans is my older brother," added Alexander, taking her other hand. "But I'm much more handsome, don't you agree, Fräulein?"

Allina burst into laughter.

"Hans and Alexander are the sons of teachers," Karl said, stepping to the side. "While their charm is obvious, it's my hope their parents' skills have rubbed off on them as well."

"Coming through, lads, coming through." The older gentleman inserted himself between the two and tried to push between them, but Hans and Alexander wouldn't give in. They laughed and jostled instead, trying to shove back his advance.

A quick shaft of panic had Allina backing up against the wall so swiftly she nearly fell. There was no logical reason for the reaction. These men were strangers, but Karl trusted them. They were eager and friendly. Obvious allies. They weren't in uniform.

It didn't matter. They were too close.

Closing her eyes, Allina pressed her hands to her stomach.

The laughter ceased, and when Allina glanced up, the older gentleman was watching her closely with pursed lips and the kindest expression in his eyes.

She extended a trembling hand, and he gave her knuckles a gentle kiss. "Josef Koch, at your service. Not as young or as handsome as these three," he said with a laugh, "but I'd very much like to be of assistance." He was as tall as the younger men, but slender to the point of gauntness. His long, friendly, near-homely face reminded her of Uncle Dieter's.

"I'm pleased to meet you all, and grateful for your help," Allina said. The intense mix of relief and nervousness had her light-headed.

"Let's enjoy our delicious lunch," Karl said. He cupped her elbow, and together they led the men into the dining room. "After, we'll talk about how to proceed. Allina and I drew up a rough plan this morning. We need to make refinements."

They all gaped at the mountains of food Ursula had prepared for five guests but made quick work of it. No one spoke for the first twenty minutes.

"We should get back to work before we fall asleep," Allina said once she'd eaten her fill of soup, roasted pork, and pickled cabbage. It was already half past one. Hans and Alexander, who were on their second helpings of strudel, ducked their heads and obediently scraped their plates clean.

"Let's adjourn to my office." Karl scooped up his coffee cup and the pan of half-eaten strudel and led them back into the den.

Dr. Koch pulled out her chair with a flourish. "Karl tells me the ailments may be a result of poor nutrition."

"That's one of my worries," Allina said, sitting down.

"Rickets is possible," Dr. Koch said. "I'll need to see them to be certain. When can I examine the children?"

"Whenever our program director says she's ready," Karl replied.

"What do you say, Madame Director?" Alexander asked.

Allina's heart thumped once, hard in her chest, before it picked up speed. Across the table, Karl's eyes were gleaming. The man was full of surprises today.

"I'll need time to set up our classroom," she said with as much calm as she could muster. "The children will be ready for you the day after tomorrow. We'll begin Wednesday."

"In that case," Hans advised, "we'd better get started."

Karl winked at her. "Gentleman, Director Gottlieb, let's get to work."

They worked like demons for another three hours. By the time the sun was a shimmering orange orb hovering over the horizon, Allina's neck was crotchety again and her fingers were covered with ink.

"You've an eye for detail, my dear," Josef said as he consulted the notes she'd given him on each child. "I'd like to keep these files for another day, do some additional research in my medical journals." He'd pored over her paperwork and made dozens of notations on the margins of every page in his bold, spare handwriting.

"Of course." Allina glanced across the room, where Alexander was making duplicate copies of the flash cards and Hans sat typing exercise instructions. They seemed totally at ease, more like teachers than soldiers.

Ursula came into the den, wiping her hands on her apron. "I've cleaned up and put the leftovers into the icebox, Herr von Strassberg," Ursula said, "and made you another pot of soup from those last vegetables in the larder, and some dumplings. But I must be going soon."

"Of course," Karl said, tossing his paper down and rising out of his chair. "Gentlemen, will you excuse us?" Smiling at Allina, he signaled toward the kitchen.

She followed him into the kitchen.

Karl reached for the set of keys that hung from a hook by the door. "Take the Wanderer into the village," he said, handing them to Ursula. "There's no need to be too conspicuous in your journey."

"As if I'd drive that ridiculous gold car of yours," Ursula teased, cheeks dimpling as she buttoned up a long, black coat.

"Hmm, no," he said mildly, "but speaking of gold, you'll remind Rabbi Guttmann about those special items, won't you?"

Allina shot Karl a sharp look, but he only set his hand on the center of her back.

"We've gathered everything we can," Ursula said. She wound a long, red muffler around her throat and knotted it with a swift jerk. "I'll bring the parcels back tonight."

"Excellent. I'll walk you out," Karl said. He escorted Ursula to a battered automobile. The car had seen better years—it must have been black at some point, but was now a faded, dented gray—but Ursula peeled out into the street with an expert turn, like she'd been driving its ancient metal carcass all her life.

"Where is she going?" Allina asked once Karl entered the kitchen.

"To a prayer service," he said. "I'll explain everything once we're alone. I don't want there to be any more secrets between us."

The intensity in his eyes made the flush creep into Allina's cheeks. For a moment she was sure Karl would kiss her again. "I don't either," she whispered.

"Good." He tucked her hand in the crook of his arm. "Let's help your staff finish up."

In the space of two hours, and thanks to more coffee and the remainder of Ursula's strudel, they managed to organize the rest of their lesson plans. Allina worked until her eyes ached and the writing on her flash cards swam out of focus. When Hans and Alexander gazed up at the ceiling and yelled "No more!" in unison, Karl paused.

"I think we've done all we can today," he said.

Only Dr. Koch remained unruffled. "You have no stamina, children," he said, making one last note in the margin of a file. "Most disappointing."

Hans and Alexander stayed long enough to organize the paperwork by week in neat, filed stacks. In the end, Allina had two full boxes of meticulous plans: sixty days' worth of schedules, activities, and flash cards, all ready for use. She'd tackle the last thirty days in a week or so, after working with the children. Tomorrow, she could begin organizing her classroom.

Dr. Koch left the house with Hans and Alexander at a quarter past seven. Ursula returned a few minutes later and dropped off two large boxes, which Karl brought into the den.

By 7:30, the house was quiet again and Karl and Allina were alone in his kitchen.

"What do you think about leftovers for supper?" Karl asked. He pulled platters of pork and pickled cabbage from the icebox and set them on the kitchen table.

"Leftovers are fine." Allina searched his indigo eyes, which were sadder than they'd been an hour ago. "Tell me about those two boxes stacked in your den."

"They're filled with precious items from families who've requested help. Pieces of jewelry. Some silver. It all needs to be sold, and quickly. A friend will courier these boxes to my Aunt Adele in Switzerland."

"Your aunt's in a position to sell these items?"

Karl nodded. "She'll get a better price, and there's less chance of the transactions being traced back to Germany. Or me. Ursula is Jewish, Allina. She and her family need my help."

Sweet, soft heat bloomed in her chest. "You'll use the funds to help them emigrate to safety."

He nodded. "Exactly. The process is expensive and complicated. But the main issue is time. Time is running out for them."

For a moment she longed to slide her fingers through his hair. She settled for a hand on his shoulder instead. "You're too hard on yourself. You do more than many others."

"Not enough. Not nearly enough."

"I don't understand." The grim set of his mouth was baffling.

"Please, sit," he said. "I thought to wait until after dinner, but there's no use in delaying the inevitable."

Allina did her best to ignore the wild flutter in her throat. The anxiety and earnestness in Karl's eyes were impossible to deny.

Karl took a deep breath before he began. "My grandmother was Russian. She and her family left their homeland sixty years ago."

Allina nodded. "Go on."

"They fled for their lives, Allina. They were Jewish."

For a moment the room seemed to spin. Impossible. Karl was SS. A *Gruppenführer*.

Her silence made him laugh. "It's true. I'm one quarter Jewish. *Mischling*, like you."

For the next hour he told Allina everything: How his grandmother, Ekaterina, had fled Russia during the pogroms, and how she'd fallen for a young Lutheran boy after coming to Germany. Ekaterina married Franz and adopted his religion for the sake of love and fear. The need to blend in was essential for survival and she'd done so with the blessing, no, at the urging, of her family. Karl's grandmother had turned her back on her faith, as too many others had at the time, to survive.

While Jewish blood was allowed in SS officers—not common, but permitted if the Führer approved—Karl had taken things a step further. To work covertly against the Reich, he'd had all paperwork on his grandmother's side replaced with forgeries.

No one knew these truths, save for Allina, Karl's Aunt Adele in Switzerland, and Markus, his closest friend, who'd made sure the forged paperwork was perfect.

"I've wanted to tell you for months. Even before you told me about your mother," Karl said.

"But you couldn't bring yourself to do it."

He shook his head. "I've kept the secret my whole life. I hardly knew how to tell it. And the knowledge puts you in even more danger now. We must be careful."

Allina nodded, blinking back tears as she thought of all the secrets her family had kept—how heavily they must have weighed on Auntie and Uncle during the years they kept her safe. It had been only months since she'd learned the truth about her mother, and Allina's anger and despair had begun to eat her up inside.

Karl insisted his past put her at grave risk, but she didn't see it that way. With the truth out in the open, and this common thread between them, Allina felt safe for the first time since she'd come to Hochland Home.

She was no longer alone.

The cuckoo clock in the den chimed nine o'clock, and its cheery tones filtered into the dining room.

"Let's finish our tea in the den," Karl said, grabbing his cup and the pot.

They pushed two chairs in front of the fire. Allina was tongue-tied after the intensity of their discussion, but Karl seemed untroubled by the quiet. This silence wasn't sad or angry, and she had no desire to fill it with conversation, but it made her restless. As they gazed into the crackling flames, the energy between them shifted, quickening in a way that made her pulse beat faster.

Karl stood up abruptly. His cup clattered on the saucer as he set it down. "We should get going. I'll drive you back," he said.

Allina stood and went to him instead, moving closer until she could feel the heat of his body through her dress. He went still, neither moving toward her nor away.

The pull toward him was strong. She didn't want to leave. She cupped his cheek, unable to look away from the heat in his eyes.

In the end, the gentle caress undid him. She witnessed the exact moment it happened, in the tightening of his mouth, the way he shook his head as his control slipped. He took her hand and pressed his face, then his lips into her palm.

When Karl kissed her, Allina wound her arms around his neck and arched against him, loving the heat of his hands and how her body fit against his. As he touched his tongue to hers, the need moved through her, sweet like molasses, settling between her thighs. She whimpered against his lips and shivered, wanting to be closer. He yanked her to him with a low moan, caging her in his arms.

Everything splintered apart.

Allina lurched away, her chest filled with lead, and the urge to escape ripping all sense from her body. She didn't know the arms around her, just the clawing, desperate need to run. The high-pitched screech of a wounded animal filled the room, but she couldn't see.

Seconds could have passed, or minutes, or an hour. She couldn't be sure. But it was his voice, calling her name over and over, that brought her back to sanity.

Allina. It's all right, Allina. I'm here. You're safe. Come back to me now . . .

When the panic eased, Allina found herself on the floor on all fours like a dog, trembling and digging her nails into the rug. Her body was wedged under the conference table and Karl was sitting beside her, watching her but not touching, his face white and drawn, his eyes dark as night.

She scrambled into his arms and shook.

She woke to the light of the full moon streaming through the window and the comforting sense of being in a warm cocoon. Not quite awake, Allina stretched and arched back. Her head thumped against something solid and hard.

Karl came awake with a yelp. She turned, realizing at last where she was—in Karl's arms, in his bed—and he pulled back immediately, holding up his hands. Searching her eyes. Watchful. Wary.

Last night rushed back in a flood of nervousness and shame, and finally . . . relief. Gratitude. He'd held her gently, cradled her, and whispered endearments as she fell asleep on the floor of his den. And while she had no memory of it, Karl must have carried her to his bedroom afterward and wrapped her in blankets to make her feel safe. He'd stayed with her. Held watch while she slept.

"It's all right," she said. Dropping her gaze to his collarbone, she attempted a smile. "I'm better now." Allina inched closer, as much to prove that statement to herself as to him. She set her cheek on his chest and listened to the steady thudding of his heart. "I'm sorry."

"You've nothing to be sorry about," he muttered against her hair. "Do you understand what happened?"

"Yes," Allina whispered. "I've been this way since that night. In Badensburg." His fingers were infinitely gentle as they ran through her hair, and she leaned into them. "I panic all the time now. I've little control over it. I don't know what to do."

"Of course you don't." He pressed warm lips to her forehead. "I've seen the same type of reactions in men who've gone to war. It's called shell shock, and what happened to you tonight is my fault. I shouldn't have let things get so far. It's too soon."

When she looked up, his eyes were soft and glossy in the light of the moon. He ran his hand in slow, even strokes through her hair.

There was nothing else to say. Soothed by the warmth of his body, she pressed closer and let him lull her to sleep.

CHAPTER 22

Starnberg

ALLINA

Allina woke again at dawn, floating up from unconsciousness to the pale blue light that filtered through the bedroom window and the soft rumble of Karl's gentle snoring. All else was quiet in the house; outside the birds were already awake and greeting the day with soft trills and bright chirrups. She shifted in Karl's arms to watch him sleep, his chest rising and falling evenly with every breath. His hair was bent and stuck up at odd angles, and that marble jaw was a bit less so and covered with dark blond stubble. He was beautiful.

Unfortunately, her bladder was calling. Karl had one arm still around her shoulder—guarding her, even in sleep—so it took some minutes to ease out of bed without waking him. Once Allina returned from the bathroom, she slid back under the covers and tried to fit her body against his, pressing back against his long limbs.

Karl came awake with a shout. Wild-eyed, he jolted upright, blinking once.

"Shhhh. It's all right," Allina said, pressing back his unruly hair.

"Mm-hmm. Good." His eyes fluttered closed. "Let's go back to sleep, then." Pulling her head to his chest, he slid his fingers through her hair. He was trying to soothe, but her body responded unexpectedly. A coil of heat unwound slowly inside her, and Allina shifted closer. She set her hand on his stomach, and the muscles under his shirt tensed.

"No," he said, grabbing her hand with a choked laugh, "no, no, no." He pressed his lips to her wrist. "God knows I want you. But it's too much. Too soon."

For a moment, she looked at him. At the acceptance, the tender regret in his expression.

"I'm tired of being afraid," Allina whispered. "I won't be afraid of you." Unable to say more, she leaned in and kissed him.

"Good Christ," he muttered, though he kissed her back, softly. She whimpered and strained closer, until he ran a hand down the bodice of her dress. The touch was light as a butterfly's wings, but her body rose up urgently to meet it. She squeezed her eyes shut and pressed her hand over his, holding it to her belly while the blood thrummed beneath her skin.

"Don't close your eyes," he murmured. "Look at me. Please." So she trained her gaze on his dark eyes and flushed cheeks, the hard set of his mouth. It was maddening, because the more she saw his desire and the more she wanted him, the softer his touch became, until all her senses became focused on the harshness of his breathing, and her pebbled nipples, and how the ache deep inside intensified as she squeezed her thighs together. But he wouldn't give her more. His teasing seemed to go on forever until finally, he urged her onto her back. Even then he was gentle. His hand roamed over her body in a long, sensual caress from her neck to the apex of her thighs.

"You're beautiful," he said. He kissed her again and stroked her tongue with his. He slid his hand underneath her dress and his fingers beneath her underthings to find the sensitive flesh, which he caressed until a sharp jolt of pleasure made Allina cry out. He kept kissing her and kissing her, lips and fingers working in tandem until time ceased and her body came apart in a rush of heat that made her forget everything else.

Afterward, with her body warm and weightless and her breathing returned to normal, Allina opened her eyes. Karl was watching her intently, his mouth tight with something akin to pain. "Are you all right?" he asked.

Allina was suddenly shy. "That wasn't what I expected," she whispered. Surely, he wanted something more from her.

He turned his face into the pillow and let out a groan. "No. No, I suppose it wasn't."

"Are you—do you—?" She touched a finger to his shoulder.

Karl nodded, face still buried in the pillow. I'm fine," he muttered. His shoulders shook with silent laughter. "Don't worry about me."

Allina's cheeks flooded with heat. "You took the pain away," she whispered.

He raised his head and stared at her. "I'm glad," he murmured, before giving her a lingering kiss she felt down to her toes.

They didn't speak much as they got ready that morning. Shy and unsure, Allina was content to wash up and rearrange her clothes and hair. Karl fixed breakfast—coffee and eggs and leftover bread he buttered for her—and held her hand during the hour's drive to Hochland Home. He had meetings in Munich to attend, but he didn't leave Allina until he'd unloaded the boxes of teaching materials and toured her new classroom. When he kissed her good-bye, he did so in full view of more than a dozen women in the North Courtyard.

All the Hochland Home gossips came out after that, like bees to honey, to inquire after her and wag their tongues. The giggles and sly glances were annoying, and Berta made a bitter, ridiculous comment about *the dangers of mixing work and pleasure*—but Allina ignored them all and went back to her classroom. She was too satisfied to worry, and concentrated on unpacking and preparing her room. She cut colorful pictures from magazines to brighten the walls, rearranged the mats and chairs a dozen times, and carted down armfuls of puzzles, blocks, and toys from that dark, depressing room on the third floor.

Even the head nurse couldn't sour her mood. She dropped by once just before lunch, staying briefly. *We'll all just have to work a little harder, now,* Ziegler muttered before she left, although the tightness around the head nurse's mouth revealed her resentment more clearly than her words.

At lunch, Allina realized she hadn't seen Rilla. After searching every guest parlor and both courtyards, she found Rilla in her sleeping room, sprawled on the bed and sobbing as if the world were about to end. Her swollen eyes proved she'd been crying for hours.

"Steffen wrote me," Rilla whispered. She lifted a limp hand, offering the crumpled piece of paper it held. "He says he can't marry me. His parents won't give their blessing. There's another girl, one they approve of." Her pointed chin quivered with misery. "I'm so stupid. How didn't I know?"

Allina hurried to the bed. "It's all right. Everything will be fine," she said, pulling her friend's plump body in for a hug. Rilla was too cold, and shivering.

"I can't go home," Rilla cried into Allina's neck. Her voice hitched like the child she still was in so many ways. "My parents won't have me. They'd never let me bring Tobias. What am I going to do?"

Allina pulled away to cup Rilla's shoulders. "You're going to stay here and work with me," she said without thinking, "and help me with a special group of children."

Rilla's sandy brows drew together. "Special children?"

Of course Rilla hadn't a clue. Like all mothers at Hochland Home, she'd been kept in the dark. It took nearly thirty minutes for Allina to explain the condition of the children on the third floor and their plan to help them.

"So these children . . . the slow ones . . . you're telling me *Schwester* Ziegler sends them away? To be experimented on? And killed?" Stunned, Rilla sat back against the headboard. She'd stopped crying, but horror had drained all color from her cheeks.

"That's right. Hundreds of children in homes across Germany have suffered that fate."

"And this special project will help cure them?"

"That's our hope, yes." Allina nodded. "No one, not even *Schwester* Ziegler, has tried to help these children. We went behind her back and appealed directly to the *Reichsführer*."

"I knew you and *Gruppenführer* von Strassberg were up to something, but I'd never guessed this," Rilla whispered. "It's a bold move."

Allina took her hand. "And a risky one, as we've got only three months to prove it can be done. But none of the other mothers can know about these children, or our rehabilitation program. I'm counting on you to keep my secret."

Rilla's smile spread like a sunrise across her face. "You trust me."

"Yes, Rilla. I do," Allina said, blinking back tears. "And you'll be doing me a great favor if you agree to work with us. These children are counting on you. Please say yes."

Rilla pulled Allina close, hugged her tight. "Of course I'll help you."

Hiring Rilla (if Allina could call it that, as all she could offer as salary was room and board) turned out to be a blind stroke of luck. Rilla threw herself into caring for the children, in much the same way Allina had when she'd accepted *Schwester* duty at Hochland Home. Rilla was visibly horrified when she met them the next day, as were Hans and Alexander, and it took nearly an hour for the three to wipe the shock from their faces. Only Dr. Koch seemed at ease as he examined each child, checking muscles and coordination, sight and hearing.

Fortunately, the doctor's prognosis was good. *With a little luck and consistent work,* he assured them, *your regimen of physical exercise and activities should achieve the desired result.*

It was Rilla who became the key to the program's initial success, because her mind operated in unexpected ways. Hans and Alexander were towers of energy who possessed the patience of Job, but Rilla helped Allina see the rehabilitation program through a child's eyes.

Their first breakthrough came during the second week, in the middle of what should have been a simple counting exercise. Allina was trying, unsuccessfully, to teach the children their numbers. As she clapped and counted to ten, she asked the children to clap along, hoping it would help. When that didn't work, Hans, Alexander, and Rilla joined her at the front of the classroom, modeling the right behavior. Still, the children didn't participate. The little ones watched her as she counted, and Otto laughed now and again, but no one joined in.

Everything changed the minute Rilla began singing the numbers. And dancing. When she sang and clapped and danced at the front of the room, Otto jumped up to join her. Hobbling over on his little wobbly legs, he laughed and began hopping up and down. "Clap with me," Rilla urged, while Allina continued counting. "Clap, Otto!"

Within a minute, he was doing exactly that. Not expertly, nor in rhythm, but he clapped. Then another child joined in. And another. By the end of the exercise, five of the children were clapping. Some were standing while others remained on the floor, and all were mostly out of rhythm, but none of that mattered. They'd made contact. It was progress. Minor, but progress nonetheless. Enough to have Allina dancing on the inside, in victory.

She moved a phonograph into the classroom the next day.

CHAPTER 23

ALLINA

Two days after Rilla's victory, Karl came to their classroom late in the afternoon. The children were with Hans and Alexander for supper, so Allina was free to greet him with a kiss.

"You're early," she said, and wound her arms around his neck. "Not that I'm complaining."

"Good, I'd hate to disappoint you." He cupped her cheek. "I'm afraid I have news you won't be happy to hear."

Allina's stomach plummeted. "What's wrong?"

"I received new orders today, ones that will make things . . . difficult for me. For us." He took a deep breath. "I'm leaving for Prague. It's my next assignment."

"How long will you be gone?"

"Some months, perhaps a year. We need to establish control. The resettlement will take time." He attempted a smile but the cords in his neck, the way his brows drew together, meant the situation was serious.

Resettlement. Allina felt the weight of that word on her chest.

"What will you do?"

His laugh was harsh. "Whatever it takes to make it through the day." His voice lowered to a gravelly whisper. "At night, I'll work with my friends to smuggle as many Jewish children out of the city as we can."

"I see." Allina should have expected this. She'd been naïve, even selfish. Karl couldn't spend the rest of his career in Munich. But his clandestine activities would make his tenure in Prague dangerous.

He pressed a kiss to her trembling lips. "I'll be fine. And we've got a month before I leave. Plenty of time to make sure your children have a decent start and enough to secure paperwork for Ursula and her family."

Karl grinned then, and it made him seem very young. "And we'll make time for us, of course."

Allina sighed when Karl pressed her head to his shoulder. "I'm afraid. I wish you didn't have to go." He pulled her even closer and they swayed together, dancing in silence while she cried.

Allina spent every spare minute with Karl until he reported for duty in Prague. She devoted her days to the children and her evenings to him at the Sunflower House. They made it a point to dine together each night, no matter how late, on the food Ursula prepared or simple meals they cooked together. He had an extensive library, so Allina read to him from Goethe, Homer, and Proust. When she asked, which was often, Karl would read her father's letters out loud, which was even better.

They slept in the same bed, but did little more than kiss the first week. Allina wanted more, but Karl proved to be a mountain of self-control.

"I won't have you afraid of me," he said on the first night, although Allina insisted she wasn't. "Or pressured," he added on the second, which made her laugh, since she was the one doing the asking. His eyes were often watchful, even haunted, when they were close, which told Allina just how much her reaction that first evening had scared him.

He gave her the gift of time, so she could grow comfortable with his body, allowing her to explore the muscles in his shoulders and the strong, graceful curve of his back. The tension in his limbs and the fine sheen of perspiration above his lip often revealed how much that gift cost him, but she learned to relax in Karl's arms—so much that when the nightmares came, she turned to him instinctively. She loved the way his legs wrapped around her body, keeping her warm as they slept. The man was a heat machine. Only his feet were cold. His icy toes always seemed to find her calves in the middle of the night.

When he finally made love to her, it was a tender, tentative coupling. He was so careful not to hurt her. It brought Allina to tears.

She was eager to retire early each evening, because Karl talked more in bed than out of it. Somehow it was easier for him to reveal his secrets there, and he'd share his most intimate thoughts in the early hours of the morning as freely as he gave her his body.

He told her about losing his mother and father to influenza at nine, and of how he'd moved to Switzerland after their deaths to live with his aunt and grandmother, who, like Auntie Claudia, made excellent strudel. Karl hadn't known his grandmother was Jewish until he moved to Basel; she'd never spoken of it. It was his Aunt Adele who'd shared the few precious details he knew after his grandmother's death.

"Ekaterina's family lost everything when they fled Russia, then she denied her faith out of self-preservation, and kept the secret to protect her children," he said. "So much pain and loss, but you'd never know it. She always told me how lucky her life was, how blessed."

Karl had returned to Germany after university, seeking memories of his parents, and made contact with Markus Klemperer, his father's best friend. It was Markus who made sure his records were wiped of his Jewish ancestry when he recruited Karl for the SS in 1934, Markus who'd protected him and hastened a series of promotions, and Markus who joined Karl in turning away from National Socialism a year later. They'd begun their clandestine projects in 1936, working with a small group of comrades in an attempt to soften the Führer's policies. Barring their ability to do that, Karl and Markus were united in their vow to help whom they could.

"The Führer is like a poison pill coated in chocolate," Karl said, late one night when they couldn't sleep. "If you're hungry enough, you'll eat it. But poison always kills in the end."

He tried to turn away from her then, and Allina took his face in her hands. They had to be honest with each other.

"You swallowed that pill," she whispered, "to save yourself."

"Yes. I wanted to serve my country like my father had. The Führer pledged to return Germany to its former greatness. For a while, I believed him. I turned my back on my grandmother, my own family. On myself."

His bark of laughter was as sharp as a slap. "I was a fool. And I'll spend every day of my life trying to make up for it."

A week before he left for Prague, Allina was charmed speechless when Karl walked into the bedroom and set the breakfast tray down over her legs.

He leaned in and gave her a soft kiss. "Good morning."

"What's this?" she asked, although the question was a silly one. The evidence was on the tray. Karl had brought her eggs and bacon and a roll with butter cheese. The spicy scent of chocolate and cinnamon hovering around the teapot meant it was filled with hot cocoa. And nestled into the napkin on her tray was a single dark blue pansy. Allina couldn't stop the smile from spreading across her face. She'd brought him a pot of them last week to brighten up the kitchen. The pansy was a perfect match for his eyes.

She was starving—not a surprise, given last night's activities. The memories of those activities brought the heat to her cheeks. "Are you plying me with flowers and chocolate?"

"I am," he said, snagging a piece of bacon from her plate, "because I have a question to ask you."

"Mmmmm. It must be a big one." She reached for the pot to pour the cocoa, but set it down when the tips of his ears turned pink.

"There's something I'd like you to consider," he said, "before I leave for Prague." He took her hand and ran his fingers over her knuckles. "I've asked Ursula if we could attend a service with her. I thought you might want to learn more about your mother's religion. That you'd feel closer to her." When she didn't answer, he added, "We'll be safe. I promise you that."

"How do you always know?" she whispered. They'd spoken of Irene Schenck as they read her father's letters, and she'd told him about her longing to know more about her mother. But this was beyond anything she'd expected.

Of course she said yes.

They drove to the service the next evening in Karl's ancient Wanderer. The sun was still above the horizon when they parked in front of a two-story cobblestone house. It was modest with a steeply pitched roof, a bright red door, and candles in the window that seemed to welcome them.

Ursula was waiting outside, and she hurried over. "You came. I'm so glad," she said, taking Allina's hand. "Do you have any questions before we go in?"

Allina's stomach fluttered, nerves kicking in. "I've never been to a synagogue," she answered. "I don't know what to ask."

"Let me tell you what to expect then," Ursula said. "Tonight is Shabbat, our sabbath. We pray together inside, and there's teaching or discussion. I believe you may find it similar, in some ways, to your own church services." Reaching into her bag, she withdrew a small book and placed it into Allina's hand. "I brought an extra siddur for you, so you can follow along." She opened it and pointed to the three columns on the page. "Here's the Hebrew prayer, and then the pronunciation in Hebrew, and then in the third column, the prayer in German. Just do as I do," she added, "or not. You may want to watch without participating. That's fine, too. Remember, you're welcome here."

Allina squared her shoulders and nodded. "I'm ready."

The slight, stooped gentleman who greeted them at the door had a salt-and-pepper beard and kind, intelligent eyes. "You must be Allina," he said. "I'm Rabbi Guttmann." His hands were toasty warm as he clasped them around hers.

"I'm pleased to meet you." Allina bobbed her head and took a deep breath to calm her nerves.

The rabbi ushered them inside. His gaze shifted to Karl. "It's good to see you, my friend," he said, as the two shook hands. "This young man," the rabbi said, jerking his head in Karl's direction, "speaks highly of you. He tells me you're a most uncommon female."

Unexpected laughter bubbled out of her. "Is that right?" She relaxed into his merry brown gaze and unwound her muffler. "Thank you for letting me join you tonight."

The rabbi's smile was serene. "It helps, I think, to understand where one comes from, to have a sense of history." He motioned them to the door at the end of the hall. "We pray downstairs, and there are fewer of us now, but I've no doubt the Almighty hears us from my cellar as clearly as he ever did in temple. Keep your coats on," he added when Allina began unbuttoning hers. "It's chilly."

The murmur of voices in quiet conversation filtered up the stairs as they descended. About a dozen adults were already seated in four rows of chairs. The cellar's walls were made of gray and brown bricks and the room was musty and damp, but dozens of candles were lit in wall sconces and on side tables. The candles did little to heat up the space, but they gave the cellar a warm glow and sent flickering shadows across the floor.

They found three empty chairs next to each other toward the back, and sat together, with Allina in the middle. "Relax," Karl murmured as she smoothed down the front of her coat. He took her hand. Allina nodded at the curious glances and warm smiles of the people who turned to greet them.

A hush descended when Rabbi Guttmann moved to a small podium at the front of the room. He took the ivory-and-blue striped shawl from over his shoulder and unfolded it slowly before kissing it and holding it open. The rabbi intoned in Hebrew before wrapping the shawl around his head and upper body. He held it there for a few seconds before unwinding it and adjusting the cloth around his shoulders.

He straightened his spine and addressed the group. "Hear, O Israel: The Lord is our God, the Lord is One."

Allina closed her eyes and bowed her head as the prayers began. The group recited certain parts together, their soft whispers blending in unison. At other times, only the rabbi's rich, melodious tones filled the room.

When Allina opened her eyes again, the cellar was bathed in a golden haze, and she settled even deeper into the comfort of the voices around her. Ursula pressed the prayer book into her hand, pointing out the passage they were reciting. Allina scanned the translation.

> *You shall love Adonai your God with all your heart,*
> *with all your soul, and with all that is yours.*
> *These words that I command you this day shall be taken to heart.*
> *Teach them again and again to your children;*
> *speak of them when you sit in your home,*
> *when you walk on your way,*
> *when you lie down,*
> *and when you rise up . . .*

My mother prayed this way. She could picture Tomas here so clearly, with one arm around Irene's shoulders and the other on her pregnant belly. That image sent a sharp yearning deep inside, both from the sweetness of the connection she felt, here in this dark, damp basement among friendly strangers, and the bitter certainty she'd never know more of her parents. As she let her mind drift into nothingness, time seemed to melt into the voices swirling around her and in the beautiful cadence of each prayer.

> *Behold our suffering and greatly deliver us. And redeem us soon for the sake of Your Name. For You are a redeemer of strength. Blessed are You, Lord, who delights in repentance.*

When the prayers ended, a pregnant silence filled the space. She took three steps back with the rest of the assembly and sat down.

Rabbi Guttmann clasped his hands in front of him. "This prayer, the Amidah, is very important. We recite it three times a day. But we must be mindful of the words we speak so the Lord knows our intention." He cleared his throat. "You're aware it's my custom to pray for our persecutors. Doing so isn't easy. It's a conscious act of will. Some of you disagree with my choice to include the Führer in my prayers. In fact, three of you came to me yesterday with a question. You asked me: Why do we pray for him in defiance of the Amidah?"

A low murmur rose through the crowd and the rough scrape of shoes against the pavement seemed to underscore the rabbi's words. The hot knot in Allina's chest doubled.

The rabbi raised his hands in appeal. "Does the Amidah call for our enemies to be subdued and crushed, or simply the evil they do? This is the question. Looking to the Talmud, we can find an excellent example that illuminates the answer."

He put on his glasses and read from the paper in front of him:

> *There were certain hooligans who resided in the neighborhood of Rabbi Meir, and they caused him much misery and anguish. Once, he prayed for mercy regarding them, so that they would die.*
>
> *Rabbi Meir's wife, Beruriah, was outraged and said to him: "What makes you think such a prayer is permitted? Is it because the verse*

states 'Let sinners cease from the earth?' But the word as it is written here is not chotim, *the Hebrew word for sinners. Rather it is* chataim, *meaning that which causes one to sin."*

His wife continued to scold: "You should pray instead for the sinners, so they will understand their sin and repent. Then there will be no more wicked people." And Rabbi Meir prayed for them, and they repented.

The Rabbi lifted his shoulders and grinned. "A smart man knows the greatest wisdom comes from his wife's lips." The room erupted in chuckles.

"I pray tonight for the cessation of sinning," he added, "not the destruction of the sinner. Men are not evil, though they may perpetrate evil acts. I won't add to that evil with my own hatred."

The rabbi looked at Karl before he turned to Allina. "Remember, also, that in the midst of this evil, we have true friends, some from unexpected places. Friends who have already transported our children to safety."

Murmurs rose in the crowd again, and sobs.

"Every act of courage is an answer to a prayer," Rabbi Guttmann continued. "We can see the Lord's hand in these actions. I ask you to remember each simple act of grace and have faith."

The rabbi lifted his arms and the congregation prayed again. Allina closed her eyes, allowing her mind to settle as the soft murmurs floated around her.

The prayer ended, and a velvety stillness enveloped the room. Allina lifted her hands to her face. Her cheeks were wet with tears. There was a peace and an ease inside of her that hadn't been there since before Uncle died. The knot in her chest was gone.

She turned to Ursula, who gave her a sturdy hug. Allina relaxed into her plump arms and the familiar scents of bread and apples, onions and spice. These were the scents of her childhood, of Badensburg, of Aunt Claudia, and, for the first time since she'd come to Hochland Home, they brought comfort instead of pain.

Karl's arm came around her shoulders and he steered her toward the cellar steps, where the rabbi waited.

"I'm glad you attended tonight," he said. "Karl's told me about the work you've done at Hochland Home and the work that lies ahead. I predict you two will do great things together."

"You're very kind, Rabbi," Allina answered. "I hope you're right."

"Come back whenever you wish. You're always welcome here." He winked at Karl and chucked him on the shoulder. "This one's a most uncommon man, don't you agree?"

CHAPTER 24

Spring 1939
Hochland Home
Steinhöring

ALLINA

Alexander Schäfer nodded to Allina as she entered her classroom. "Stretch your fingers, boys and girls, stretch your toes," he called out. Alex paused to check his stopwatch before continuing his slow amble along the center aisle of the classroom. "Balance your body on your stomachs," he added, punctuating his words with sharp claps of his hands. "Straighten your arms and legs. That's right. Very good. Reach, children . . . fly, fly, fly!"

The children were wriggling bundles of energy this morning. All were performing the *flying stretch*—one Dr. Koch prescribed to strengthen their abdominal and back muscles—with relative ease. Each child was face down on their nap mats, but only their torsos made contact with the floor. Otto was doing particularly well. His arms and legs trembled with strain but were suspended off the ground in perfect form, with fingers and toes outstretched.

"Excellent," Alexander praised. "That was twenty seconds. Now relax for a bit before we start the next exercise."

The children collapsed onto the mats with loud groans. "You're the best students I've ever seen. Don't you agree, Madame Director?" Alexander called out over his shoulder.

Allina fought to blink back tears. "The best in all of Germany," she managed as she notated her file: *Flying stretch: 20 seconds.* The children's progress was remarkable, easy to see and document.

Three months ago, the children hadn't been able to perform this basic exercise by themselves, forcing Alexander and Hans to resort to manual stretching. It had taken nearly four weeks for the children to become coordinated enough to learn the basic movements, with Otto leading the way, as usual. Progress had been steady, but maddeningly slow.

Toward the end of the program's second month, *Schwester* Ziegler began "dropping by" several times a week to review their activities. These visits weren't planned in advance and shouldn't have happened at all, as the head nurse had no jurisdiction over the program. But since she kept a respectful distance, and didn't arrive with clipboard in hand or appear to be taking notes, Allina bore the scrutiny without complaint. In truth she was stuck, and the head nurse knew it—even as the program's director, without Karl, the chance of lodging a successful complaint with the *Reichsführer* was virtually nonexistent. Allina didn't want to go to battle with the woman, in any case, so she held her tongue, kept working, and prayed that their efforts would be enough.

To her mutual relief and disgust, last week she'd received a congratulatory memo from *Reichsführer* Himmler himself. Whether that was due to *Schwester* Ziegler's visits or Allina's meticulous weekly reports, she didn't know.

Even so, Allina's doubts lingered, particularly late at night when she drifted off to sleep. She worried her affection for the children was blinding her objectivity, that despite their best efforts, the children would never be adoptable.

Allina shook off her unease when Rilla's glowing face appeared at the classroom door. "Here's that shipment of sports equipment you were asking about," Rilla said. She hauled in a large box overflowing with jump ropes and balls of different sizes.

Alexander hurried to the door. "Let me help," he said, taking the box from Rilla's hands. "You shouldn't be carrying that."

Rilla thanked Alex and gave him a not-so-shy smile. She flushed to the roots of her hair, and her gaze lingered, watching his every move as he sauntered to the corner and set down the box.

Two months, and Alexander, had been a balm for Rilla's broken heart. Allina was glad of it. Their relationship was an unexpected development—one Allina had worried about in the beginning—but the pair got on well.

Alex stepped to the front of the room again to address the class. "Fräulein Weber will take over now." He raised his hands in the air, and the children cheered. "If we're very lucky," Alex added with a wide grin, "she might sing." More cheers. "Clap your hands for her, children. She'll start you off with your bridges."

He made his way to Allina's side as Rilla assumed control.

"Roll over," she called out in a singsong voice. "Put your hands and feet on the ground and push up! That's right, make your bridges high." The children rolled over, planted their feet on the ground, and raised their hips skyward.

"She's good with them," Alexander murmured. "She has their trust."

"You're an excellent teacher," Allina answered. Since the first day, he'd peppered his instruction with praise and encouragement. Alexander had a gift; he'd built an easy camaraderie with the children.

Alexander and Hans had been all Allina could have hoped for, tireless and a credit to their parents, although their part of the work was about to come to an end. She'd had to give up Hans last week to his new assignment in Czechoslovakia—now the protectorate of Bohemia and Moravia, as the Führer had so declared it—and at the end of April, Alex would also report for duty.

For the hundredth time this month, Allina sent a prayer heavenward for Rilla. Rilla, who would be the only one remaining, the one best versed in their exercise program, and the one who'd help her train the volunteers when they came to Hochland Home. She'd continue the work Hans and Alexander had begun. There was even talk now of traveling to other homes to work with staff so the program could be expanded.

"Make your bridges strong, children," Rilla sang before counting to ten. "That's it. Very good! We want many automobiles driving over your bridges." Rilla pantomimed a steering wheel with her hands and made grumbling motor noises as she mock-drove around the room.

Rilla's instructions produced a fit of giggles that had the little ones hiccupping and straining to keep control of their bodies.

Once again, Allina had to push back her tears as she notated her files. She'd been crying at the drop of a hat all week, due to stress, of course. The program's success was gratifying, but the schedule had worn her down to nothing. It seemed like every tendon in her shoulders and knees creaked when she got out of bed this morning.

She slipped into the hallway and walked to the break room. Her body craved a strong cup of tea, that's all. Tea, ten minutes in a chair to rest her feet, and a chance to reread Karl's latest letter. Although he'd been in the Sudetenland less than a month, it seemed like time had expanded, escaping like a dropped skein of wool that rolled across the floor. It helped that Karl wrote daily, and his letters were full of sweetness and unexpected romance. Allina had never received love letters like these before, and their intimacy surprised and delighted her.

Allina missed Karl so much that her throat ached whenever she thought about him. Their final days together had been bittersweet, the weight of his leaving like lead on her chest, tempering her happiness. On their last night together, Karl had acted in a way that made Allina fear for him. *I don't deserve you*, he'd repeated into her hair during the last few minutes before sunrise. He'd trembled and held her so tightly that she hadn't asked for an explanation. Instead, she'd clutched Karl's head to her breast and taken him into her body with a fierceness that left them both shaken. He'd kissed her with gentleness afterward, as they wiped each other's tears.

She often caught herself reliving that last night and fantasizing about their few weeks together; how his long, warm legs curved to the shape of her body while he slept, and the way the soft indentation at the base of his spine quivered at her touch, or how his hair stood up like a rooster's coxcomb when he woke in the morning. Devoid of pomade, his hair was lighter, and silky against her fingers . . .

Sighing, she entered the break room.

Karl was never far from her mind, but his latest letter filled her with a restlessness she couldn't shake. There was something missing from his writing, a lightness and humor that occasionally lifted the seriousness of his earlier communications.

Taking a bite of biscuit, she pulled the letter from her apron pocket.

8 April 1939

My heart,

Your last letter made me spit coffee out my nose. Tell Otto I am in his debt. Only the bravest of men would defend you against "mean Schwester Zeigwar." It's no surprise she'd begrudge you for giving out extra biscuits.

Our work here is hard, hard but necessary, and always triumphant as it's in service to our Führer. You may have heard about minor clashes with resisters in some parts of the city. Please don't worry. The vast majority in Prague have welcomed the men with open arms. We march on. Yes, we march on, and I'm grateful to have the memory of a month of evenings with you in my arms.

I had my officers plant a small sunflower garden to remind me of home. Six have bloomed already, with more to come. As for when I'll return to you, that may not be until late summer. I'm needed here, my heart . . .

She slumped in her chair. The letter told her nothing about his daily activities, though "in service to our Führer" showed he was plainly miserable. The main item of importance was in a code they'd devised before he left for duty. The "six flowers" meant he'd been able to arrange for the transport of sixty Jewish children to England, and safety.

She'd demanded honesty from him before he left, and he'd given her the gift and burden of truth. Living a double life in Prague was more complicated than in Munich. By day, Karl followed orders. By night, he did the clandestine work that mattered. He had Markus with him in Prague, and that was a plus. But whether he acted alone or as part of a team, Karl was in danger. And his nighttime activities meant he wasn't sleeping much.

"Is anything wrong, Allina?"

Shoving the letter back into her apron pocket, Allina turned to find *Schwester* Ziegler approaching with sharp, knowing eyes.

Allina scrubbed the tears from her face. "I'm fine, thank you. A bit tired, maybe."

"I could have predicted that. Your special rehabilitation project is more than the most seasoned nurse could handle." The head nurse laid a cool palm on Allina's cheek. "You're a bit warm today, and flushed."

Allina was startled at the gentleness of the touch. Ziegler had been unfailingly rude, with occasional spurts of icy politeness, since Allina had taken charge of the rehabilitation program. The head nurse probably felt she was being upstaged.

"Your eyes are clear and your skin is luminous," she added, "but I don't like the circles under your eyes."

"I've had heartburn nearly every day this week," Allina admitted, rubbing at the ache just below her breastbone, "and I'm restless at night."

"You miss him."

"I wish we'd had more time. There was so much more we wanted to do—"

"Having the *Gruppenführer*'s support is a wonderful thing, I'm sure," Ziegler interrupted coolly. "You've done well for yourself. I don't blame you. Really."

And there it was—a rare opening for peace. Allina took it. "I've wanted to speak with you for weeks but haven't known how to broach the subject."

The head nurse nodded, her steady gaze permitting Allina to continue.

"It's never been my intention to undermine your work here. Karl and I . . . we wished to help the children. You've seen our preliminary success, and that gives me hope." She reached out and touched the head nurse's arm. "No child need ever be sent away again. That's important, don't you think?"

Ziegler sighed. "You're being naïve. You've helped ten children, but you had a staff of four to care for them. No facility can hope to match it. I'd need a staff of eighty here, not eighteen."

"I realize that," Allina said, "but we're moving to the next phase of the program soon. Once Alex leaves, Rilla and I will have to train volunteers."

"Volunteers?" The shock in the woman's face was almost comical.

Allina explained how they'd train officers on leave to help with the children's physical activities. When Ziegler didn't dismiss the idea, she offered examples of simple activities the *Schwestern* could use with the toddlers to encourage social skills and speech.

The head nurse remained silent throughout her explanation.

"Once Rilla and I have the program working smoothly," Allina added, "we could train the other *Schwestern* if you like. Or give you the use of some of our volunteers. You've visited enough to know the program is working. Please say you'll think about it."

Ziegler didn't answer immediately. She still seemed unconvinced.

"I have no interest in your position," Allina added bluntly. God knows, she'd shut the entire operation down given half a chance.

Her reward was a sharp bark of laughter. "I believe you. Some days, I'm not sure I want it myself. Let's find an hour tomorrow to discuss how we might work together. I'll make use of any resources you can spare. Now walk with me. I'll join your special group of children for luncheon today."

They climbed to the third floor. As Allina entered the room set up as a dining area, the smell of sauerkraut had her covering her nose. Chef had been using too much garlic lately.

Allina chose a chair next to Otto's, ruffling his hair before taking a seat.

"Milk, please." Otto called out a simple two-word request as he pointed to the crock of milk. His pronunciation was far from perfect, but it was improving.

Again, she felt the tears come, but she blinked them away and poured him a cup of milk.

The head nurse remained standing. She clapped three times, and the children quieted. "Let us give thanks for this wonderful meal," she called out. "Please stand."

Everyone rose from their seats. The children stood with near-perfect posture. It was almost impossible to tell the difference between them and normal toddlers.

Allina led the meal blessing, which the children followed in unison:

> *Führer, my Führer given me by God.*
> *Protect and preserve my life for long.*
> *You rescued Germany from its deepest need.*

As the singsong chant echoed in the hall, Allina grew light-headed. Their pink, shining faces swam in and out of focus. Their voices grew fainter.

> *I thank you for my daily bread.*
> *Stay for a long time with me, leave me not.*
> *Führer, my Führer, my faith, my light.*
> *Hail my Führer!*

They ended the blessing by saluting the large photo of the Führer at the front of the room. As Otto extended his arm in perfect form, a cold trickle of sweat ran down Allina's back and she stumbled, grabbing the table's edge to keep from falling to the floor. The head nurse's face was as white as the walls and she ran to Allina, but it seemed to take forever, as if *Schwester* Ziegler were coming from a great distance. Allina closed her eyes, overwhelmed with dizziness. She could hear the children's panicked cries, but it was too much effort to speak.

Strong hands pushed her down into her seat. "Keep your head between your knees. Take deep breaths," the older woman ordered, rubbing her back in brisk circles.

After a few seconds, the dizziness passed and Allina opened her eyes. "I'm so sorry. I must be more tired than I thought."

"Something like that," the head nurse said. "Are you able to walk? Let's take some fresh air."

A few of the children whimpered. Allina managed a smile. "Not to worry, we'll be back soon."

She let the head nurse steer her downstairs and into the garden. Signs of spring were everywhere. Trees were budding and the daffodils and irises were in full bloom.

"I don't know what's wrong with me," Allina said, taking a seat on a bench.

"You should, given where you're working."

Allina's eyes must have popped out of her head, because Ziegler laughed out loud. "When were your last monthly courses?" she asked, sitting down next to her.

"We've been so busy, I haven't paid attention," Allina whispered. "But I don't have morning sickness—" She dropped her head, cupping her cheek in one hand. The constant heartburn, her moodiness, her reaction to strong smells. It all made sense.

"You must tell him, of course."

"I'll write to him at once," Allina said, taking slow, deep breaths to fend off panic. There was no way she'd raise her child at Hochland Home.

CHAPTER 25

SS Headquarters
Hotel Flora, Schwerinstrasse 121, Prague

KARL

Karl watched with odd detachment as Allina's letter slipped through his fingers and floated to the floor. His eyes shifted to the empty coffee cup and half-eaten plate of breakfast, then to the crumbs scattered across the table's polished mahogany surface.

She's pregnant.

The small group of officers around him began banging their fists on the tabletop. Christ, he'd made the announcement out loud . . .

Karl tried to push up from the table but landed back in his chair with a hard thump. Damn his legs for refusing to obey his brain. Damn his hands, too. They were shaking. And he couldn't breathe. All the air had left his lungs.

"Three cheers for the *Gruppenführer*," Loritz Kortig shouted, with a savage fist pump.

Tedrick Bamm speared a sausage off his plate and bit into it with gusto. "Another healthy son to defend the Fatherland—"

"—or healthy daughter to breed the next generation of sons," finished Richard Goeffels over a mouthful of coffee. Goeffels was newly consigned, but after two weeks in Prague, the eighteen-year-old was no longer innocent.

"*Schwester* Allina will be a model for dozens of women," added Kortig, taking his seat. "How fortunate to have a new mother as Hochland Home's special program director. Soon, she'll be able to demonstrate proper care using her own child."

Fucking hell. Kortig's assumptions couldn't be further from the truth. Allina's letter was filled with angry, clever euphemisms, making it clear she was unwilling to raise her child at Hochland Home. An uncomfortable, unfamiliar tightness gripped his chest. He'd let his dick lead his brains. He was no better than his men.

Karl jumped when Markus clapped a bracing hand on his shoulder, interrupting his internal diatribe. "There's much to celebrate," Markus said. His black eyes shone with enough amusement to be irritating before he turned to the others at the table. "Excuse us, gentlemen. *Gruppenführer* von Strassberg and I have important business to attend to."

The young officers stood and saluted in unison. "*Heil* Hitler!"

He walked with Markus in silence from the plush red-and-gilt dining room through the even more ornately decorated and chandeliered lobby. Only after they traveled outside and across the street into a favorite meeting spot did they speak. It was barely a park—just a few meters of grass, a ragged oak tree, and two ancient stone benches—but they were less likely to be overheard here, and it was small enough to spot intruders quickly.

Markus opened the case he took from his jacket pocket and withdrew a cigarette. "What will you do?" As tightly as his lips clamped around the cigarette, the corners were tipped up. There was too much humor in his friend's gaze.

Damn it to hell, this wasn't funny.

Karl blew out a deep breath. He hadn't been prepared for the intense satisfaction at her announcement, or his fear, nor the fierce protectiveness that overwhelmed him now. "I don't know. I was a fool not to have planned for this."

"You've a gift for understatement, my friend," Markus said before lighting the cigarette and taking a deep draft that deepened the wrinkles in his weathered cheeks.

"You're like a chimney," Karl said, pounding his friend's back. "It's time to cut down."

"Not likely," Markus managed. He raised a silver eyebrow. "And you're changing the subject. It's time to marry the girl, Karl. I've made sure every piece of forged documentation is in place. Himmler won't have a reason to deny your request for a marriage license. Marry her. As soon as possible."

Karl shook his head.

"You love her." Markus's lips curved up again with humor.

His words were another punch to the gut. "It's obvious?"

"You panicked back there." The tip of the cigarette glowed as Markus continued to puff away. "You never panic."

Karl kicked a rock across the grass. There was no doubt Allina desired him, she was responsive in bed and had clung to him the night before he'd left for Prague. She might even love him. But she still grieved. Not a night had passed without her coming awake, eyes wide with terror, her rigid body locked in a nightmare. And in the middle of the night, she sometimes called out her former fiancé's name. *Albert.*

Then there was their child to consider, who would begin its life in danger, thanks to its parents' Jewish heritage, their duplicity. Perhaps Allina and the baby would be better, safer, without him.

"I'm not sure I can protect her, or the baby. Not forever."

Markus dismissed his whining with a pitying look. "No one can protect anyone anymore, not absolutely." He took another long, slow drag that hollowed his cheeks. "But marriage is your best shot."

"You think marrying a *Mischling* SS officer—one with forged papers working to topple the SS—is a safer bet than a peaceful, protected life at Hochland Home?"

"I do," Markus said. "You're still a *Gruppenfuhrer* and my forgeries are perfection. Marriage is the best protection you can offer. Go to her, Karl. But do it quickly. I'm counting on your return. We need to save whom we can." He tossed the spent cigarette to the cement and ground it out with the tip of his boot. "I can slow down the neighborhood tours for a week or so. Heydrich wants new headquarters, so I'll dispatch some men to assist him instead."

"Heydrich?" Karl asked. "When did he start giving orders?" Heydrich meant Gestapo, and if the Gestapo pushed in, there'd be an endless series of complications.

Markus lifted his eyes to the sky. "Heydrich, Frank, von Neurath," he muttered, naming the three currently jockeying for control. "What does it matter? They all report to Himmler in the end. And our *Reichsführer* has asked for a less-plush location," he added, waving over his shoulder in the direction of the hotel.

"The Petschek Palace," Karl muttered. They'd toured that modern monstrosity when they first arrived. The building had plenty of sealed rooms, both aboveground and below.

"Most likely," Markus answered, smoothing back his silver hair. "Heydrich's always preferred to conduct his special interrogations in the dark. The labyrinth of rooms in the basement are a perfect location."

Karl scanned the hotel's opulent carved stonework before turning away. In the end it wouldn't matter which building they chose. The Flora was the finest hotel in Prague, but it had quickly become his prison.

There was no respite, no rest here, ever, and the energy spent hiding their covert activities often exhausted Karl to the point of numb blankness. When he'd arrived in Prague six weeks ago, the new orders had come down: they had eighteen months to plan and relocate 150,000 souls to parts of the city that were, as Himmler put it, "more suitable to the Jews and their situation."

It was a nightmare.

By day, *Gruppenführers* von Strassberg and Klemperer were high-ranking officers, outwardly devoid of compassion, who barked orders and made notes on clipboards during their neighborhood tours. By night, they did the work that mattered.

They'd managed to get sixty children safely to England, but that effort had taken weeks of sleepless nights, secret meetings in back alleys, and the help of a network of local supporters—people who risked their lives without the protection of the uniform Karl wore.

Sixty children in a month, and even that pathetic number wasn't the worst of it. The selection process was brutal. More often than not, they chose children with light hair and eyes, because they'd be easiest to place. If Karl was lucky, he could save a few hundred this way. Hundreds out of tens of thousands, maybe more. They couldn't risk helping larger numbers. If too many children disappeared, word would spread, and if word spread, Karl and Markus would be found out, and that would jeopardize the effort everywhere.

There had to be a better way. Rumors had spread about a Londoner called Winton who'd had success in securing visas to Great Britain. The man operated out of his hotel in Wenceslas Square, though, which put him at risk. Winton was already under Gestapo surveillance.

Karl pinched the bridge of his nose, trying to erase the ache behind his eyes. No matter what he did to atone, it would never be enough.

"Tell me we're doing the right thing, Markus. That we're doing all we can."

Markus gave him a long, measured look. "You're tired. That's my fault. I promised your father I'd protect you. I thought our work would be enough, but perhaps not. You've always had the soul of a poet, not a soldier."

Karl turned away. "Don't be ridiculous."

"We're saving lives," Markus said, clapping a hand on his shoulder. "Every life matters." He turned and headed back to the hotel without another word, forcing Karl to follow with acid burning in his belly.

"Send the letters today," Markus ordered, as they ran up the steps and entered the lobby together. "One to Allina, letting her know you're going on leave. Another to Himmler, asking him to expedite approval for your marriage. Stay with me for another week or two. Help me plan. Then go to her."

Karl remained in Prague for ten days. They were the longest he could remember. Each morning on the neighborhood tours, he gazed coldly into the frightened eyes of men and women as they clutched their children— he'd become a master at faking that expression—and looked away when they bowed their heads and trembled. The rumors had gotten around about the impending relocations. People talked.

He managed on two hours of sleep each night, and when he rose at dawn, his first thought was of how many days were left until he'd see her. Those fleeting seconds were the only moments of lightness in Karl's day. His thoughts didn't go to Allina otherwise. The work was easier to bear if he didn't think about her. But there was a sense of anticipation, a restlessness in his muscles and sinews, that every passing second was one closer to their reunion.

Allina wouldn't look at him.

"Let me make sure I understand," she said, averting her lovely face, now gone to ash. "You're proposing we wed as a . . . practical arrangement?" Folding her hands, Allina placed them very carefully on the conference table in his den. "I should marry you for my protection," she whispered, looking down at her fingers, "and the baby's." She cleared her throat. "Of course. I see why you'd ask."

The sadness and confusion in her face made Karl's gut clench. He was hurting her, pushing her away. It was the last thing he wanted to do.

When he'd arrived at Hochland Home last night, she'd welcomed him with sweet kisses and happy tears and pressed her warm, soft body to his. Karl was sure of her in those first moments, so confident she'd accept him that he whisked her away to the Sunflower House with plans to propose over dinner. Pregnancy had made Allina rosy cheeked and lit up from within, and her body had already begun to round out slightly. The need to be with her, to hold her, had eclipsed reason. He'd carried her up to his bedroom before dessert.

And afterward . . . well, Karl hadn't planned to propose in bed, so he'd waited until this morning, then until after breakfast, but all his careful plans were in ruins. His logical explanations were ridiculous. He'd made a disaster out of a marriage proposal.

"I think—" He stopped to clear the sour grit that sat at the back of his throat and tried again. "I *hope* you agree that your well-being, and the safety of our baby, matters. It matters very much to me. I won't let anything happen to either of you. You're too important to—"

"Of course," Allina interrupted. She rose and walked stiffly to the window, her hands together at the waist, making him wait.

When she spoke again it was to the windowpane, not him, and her voice was soft with memory. "When Albert proposed, my aunt and uncle told me I should marry him for my own good," she said. "Did you know that?"

"No."

Still gazing out the window, Allina gave an unladylike snort. "I hated that reasoning then as much as I do now, the idea that I need anyone's protection. But my aunt and uncle insisted it was the right thing to do. And I loved him," she added sadly.

She loved him. The truth cut deeply. For a moment he found it hard to breathe. "Of course. We both know I'm not Albert, don't we?" he said, the question escaping in a sharp rush of bitterness. He winced, wishing he could take the words back.

Allina whirled around. "Why do you say that?" When he didn't answer, she took a few steps closer, watching Karl with enough bluntness to make him shift in his chair. She was examining him with fascination, as if he were a pinned beetle on display.

It was time, though, time for honesty—so Karl answered her question by saying what he should have in the beginning. "Your Albert was a hero who gave his life for others. Of course you still love him. I've always known it." He closed his eyes.

The air around him seemed to shift, and when he opened his eyes Allina stood before him with hands clenched so tightly they shook. Her face, on the other hand, along with her expression, had relaxed. Her gaze was soft with relief, and something akin to pity.

She sat down, took his hands in hers. They were such tiny hands, strong and calloused for all their outward fragility. "I've never spoken about Albert, have I?" she asked. "I think I need to. For both our sakes."

"All right." He could bear it. He'd sit here and listen to her talk about the boy she loved, as long as she agreed to marry him.

Allina took a deep breath. "Albert and I grew up together. We were childhood sweethearts. He asked Uncle for my hand in marriage when I was ten," she added, smiling at the memory.

Karl nodded.

"He was my first love. My first crush, my first kiss, my first everything," she said a little wistfully.

"I understand," he managed.

"No. You don't. I'll always love Albert," she said, blinking back tears. "It's true. But I'm not in love with him . . . not now."

Karl gaped at her, in disbelief at first, but in that moment when time slowed to a near-stop and his vision narrowed to her perfect face, he saw it: the love in her eyes.

Karl pulled her into his lap and buried his mouth in her neck, unable to do anything but inhale the sweetness of her rose-scented hair.

"I fell in love with you that first night, in the nursery."

"You did not."

"I did," he said, lifting her long hair off her shoulders. "I'm an idiot. I should have asked you to marry me sooner."

"But you haven't asked me yet," she teased, "not properly."

His legs were still shaking, so he half fell onto one knee. Taking her hand, he slipped the ring from his pocket onto her finger. It was his grand-mother's ring, a pearl set in gold, and surrounded by a single row of rubies. It suited her perfectly. "Will you have me?"

Her smile was as bright as the sun. "Yes," she said, stroking his cheek again. "I will."

Then she kissed him.

Late that evening, Karl woke her with his laughter.

"What's the matter?" Allina mumbled. Turning in his arms, she pressed her nose to his chest. Her face was soft with sleep. "What time is it?"

"Just after midnight," he whispered into her hair, still faintly scented of roses. "Nothing's wrong. I was reliving my winning marriage proposal. With hours to think about it on the drive home, I'd decided you should give up your Hochland Home duties."

Her eyes popped open. "You can't be serious," she said, now fully awake. "There's no way I'd consent to that."

"I'm glad I didn't ask, then. I was hell-bent on keeping you safe. I still am."

"What does that mean?" Allina's eyes narrowed. She was on high alert.

"Marrying me will give you a degree of protection in the short term. The forged papers and documentation I've used are pristine. But being the wife of an SS officer isn't easy." When she opened her mouth to protest, he hushed her with a kiss. He had to be honest with her, so she'd understand the risk they were taking—two *Mischling* parents with false papers har-boring a *Mischling* child while working to subvert the Reich.

"It will put you in the spotlight. And we can't make a single mistake. If our heritage is discovered—yours or mine—the lies will blow up in our faces. Our baby's safety is at risk."

"Then we'll both be careful." Allina lifted that damn belligerent chin of hers. "I'm not making light of the danger. But these children need us, Karl. There are so many who need us."

"I know that."

"We must fight for what we know is right—and for the world we're bringing this baby into." She grabbed his hand and placed it over her belly. "We're stronger together. Tell me you believe that."

"I do," he said, kissing her forehead. "You're my heart." *And my strength.*

Her eyes glowed at his admission and she settled, pressing her cheek to his collarbone. He stroked her hair, trying to coax her back to sleep. When her body tensed, Karl knew their conversation wasn't finished.

"Things are worse than you let on, aren't they?"

"Yes."

"Tell me." He didn't answer, and she pressed a feathery kiss to his jaw. "Please. I know from your letters how unhappy you've been."

So she wanted the truth from him. Again. There was a mountain of ugly truth to tell.

"There was no resistance on the day we entered Prague," he said. "No confrontations, no outward struggle. You could see the fear in their eyes, though, as they tossed bouquets of flowers at the motorcade. They cheered us. They were petrified."

"Go on," she whispered. She trailed a finger along the length of his arm, working from shoulder to wrist and then back up again. But even Allina's touch couldn't ease his bitterness.

"They sensed what's coming. We go through the neighborhoods, day after day, making our lists, checking papers, documenting, reassigning, then transporting . . ." Karl broke off, because he couldn't tell her the worst of it, about the men he'd seen imprisoned, or the ones he'd known would be tortured. No, he hadn't the right to make her bear that. "Most try to appease, or do their best to blend in, to disappear."

He paused to clear his throat. "Last week, a young mother pleaded with me in the street while we were processing her paperwork. She was young, your age, but she pushed her child into my arms. 'My daughter has blond hair and blue eyes, can't you see that?' she asked. She begged me for food, then offered me her body if I would find a way to save her child."

The finger stopped, hovering like a butterfly over his skin. "You don't think she found out that you're helping . . ."

"No," he said, "she was a desperate woman, pleading with a man in power. But all I could think was: This woman could be a relative, my cousin. Or yours."

Her eyes were dark and liquid in the dim light. "What did you do?"

"I told her no," he said, averting his gaze. He couldn't bear to see disgust in Allina's eyes. "I scribbled down her name and address, put it in a drawer. In a week, we'll get a local contact to her. If she hasn't been moved already."

"You'll save that child," she insisted. "You'll find a way."

"If I do, it'll leave a mother childless. That woman won't see her daughter again, not while she's on this earth." He pulled her into his arms, unwilling to say the words. "Do you understand what I'm saying?"

There were tears in her eyes now. "Yes."

He buried his face in her neck, breathed in the sweetness of her hair.

"I've been close to despair, too," she said, wrapping her arms around him and holding on tight, "about the children here."

"Ridiculous," he muttered against her neck. "The program's a success."

"That's true, but we've helped so few—there are hundreds more at other *Lebensborn* facilities we can't save, even if we manage to train dozens of officers to expand the program." Her voice was thick with pain. "As for our successes . . . at lunchtime, they salute a picture of the Führer. They thank him dutifully at each meal. God knows what they'll become."

"But they'll live." He kissed her, because there was nothing else to say. Life meant hope.

"How long can we continue like this?" she whispered.

"As long as we need to," he said. "There's nothing more we can do about it tonight. Go to sleep." He gathered Allina against his chest and stroked her hair until her breathing slowed and her limbs were soft with sleep again.

He'd tell her more tomorrow if she insisted, and assure her that he could hold on, that they both could. Adolf Hitler wouldn't remain in power for long. He'd make sure of it.

CHAPTER 26

ALLINA

Allina slept in on her wedding day. She came awake with a luxurious stretch, squinting as the morning light streamed through her window. The breeze wafting into the room was scented with rosemary and lavender. It was heaven.

Five quick, crisp knocks dragged her out of her reverie before a pink-cheeked Rilla all but kicked the door open. "Happy wedding day," Rilla sang, carrying in an oak tray, although her eyes went wide when she saw Allina's state. "Why aren't you out of bed? We need to get you ready," she exclaimed, setting the tray down on the nightstand. The tray was laden with a stupendous amount of food—scrambled eggs, crispy bacon, decadent French toast, bowls of fruit and porridge, a basket of soft rolls, and a pitcher of orange juice and pot of coffee.

Allina rubbed the sleep from her eyes. "How did you manage to get up the stairs?" she asked, pointing at the tray. "If I eat all that I won't fit into my dress."

"I'll help you eat it," Rilla said with bug-eyed exasperation, "if you'll just get up." She sat down and began bouncing on the mattress.

Allina sat up with a sharp jerk that made her a little dizzy. "Wait, how can you be here? Have the children not eaten yet?"

"Oh, no, you don't," Rilla said, covering Allina's mouth. "There will be no worrying about children this morning. Alexander's in charge for the next hour, and then *Schwester* Wendeline will take over. But you need to get up. If you don't hurry, you'll be late to your own wedding."

Allina eased back against the pillows. "I took a bath late last night," she said, waving Rilla's cares away. "My hair takes forever to dry. And you promised to do my hair today, so you can repair any damage," she added, lifting a pillow-crimped lock. She reached for the plate of French toast, adding extra syrup before taking a large bite.

It was scrumptious. The morning was gorgeous. Today would be perfect.

"My God," Rilla said, hands on hips. "You're not nervous at all. Not one smidge. Are you?" Her question sounded more like an accusation.

"Not one smidge," Allina said over a mouthful of French toast. "After the week we've had, nothing will bother me today."

It had been a frantic seven days. Marrying an SS officer on a week's notice was a task worthy of Solomon, even with Karl's connections. Allina would have lost her marbles without Rilla and Alexander, who assumed most of her Hochland Home duties last week.

It took the better part of three days to push their marriage application through Munich's Race and Settlement Office. The paperwork was exhausting. Karl had arranged for a forged Aryan certificate for Allina, along with a cornucopia of fake birth certificates and baptismal cards on nonexistent parents, grandparents, and great-grandparents. Unfortunately, the web of lies in the forged paperwork meant she needed to memorize her ancestral story. She had to be able to talk about these people as if she'd known them all her life. Karl spent the entire day after his proposal quizzing her about her fictional family to prepare for their interview. Then they endured nearly eight teeth-grinding hours at the Munich RuSHA office, filling out forms and posing for photographs of themselves in bathing costumes, of all things, to satisfy the Reich's strict guidelines.

By the time they met with the registrar—a wiry, beady-eyed little man who kept a bust of the Führer on the corner of his desk, like a faithful watchdog—Allina's eyelids were twitching. But after all their preparation and the endless hours of quizzing, the registrar examined her paperwork with a bland smile and without a single question. She'd studied for ten hours. They'd waited in lines for four. The registrar stamped and issued their marriage certificate in less than fifteen minutes.

Unfortunately, the registrar hadn't been understanding about Allina's request to skip the Reich Bride School. No, it took another day trip to Munich, and some not-so-subtle persuasion in the form of a memorandum from the *Reichsführer*, to exempt Allina from the six-week program. For once, she'd been grateful to Hochland Home's character training courses, as they satisfied most of the school's curriculum. As for the two special courses on the particular duties SS officers' wives were expected to perform—as Karl explained to the registrar: *I'm capable of teaching my new wife how to care for my uniform and polish my boots and daggers.*

Then there was the matter of her dress. There was no time to design a real wedding gown, and Allina swore she didn't need one as the ceremony would take place at the registrar's office. Yet Karl insisted she get a new dress. She'd spent the better part of two days in Munich, submitting to a self-conscious French modiste—a tall, angular woman with eyes like blueberries and a nose like an eggplant stem. The designer had grated on her nerves, but Karl's stunned expression when she modeled the creation made the hours of pinning and tucking worthwhile.

"Hello? Allina?" Rilla rapped on the breakfast tray, clinking the silverware and bringing Allina out of her reverie. "We've got two hours to get ready," she said. "Let's start with that unruly nest of yours. Then we'll get you into that heavenly dress."

Laughing, Allina jumped out of bed and headed to the bathroom to scrub her face.

It took nearly an hour to do her hair. Rilla brushed her thick locks a full two hundred strokes until they shone, and with the tender care of a mother that made Allina blink away tears. Rilla fashioned a high, tight circle of shining gold braids around her head and nestled tiny white rosebuds between them to form a crown of flowers framing Allina's face.

"Perfect," Rilla breathed as she nestled one last bud into place. Allina looked up and their eyes met in the glass. She was too overcome to speak.

"Now stand up and turn around," Rilla ordered.

Allina obeyed, glancing away from the mirror as Rilla slipped the dress over her head. The silky fabric settled over her skin like a sigh. The dress was the most sumptuous she'd seen in her life, and a more elegant one than she'd ever thought to own. It was fashioned of silk velvet—very dear, although Karl had waved away the cost—and in a shade of lavender so pale the dress shimmered lilac in some angles and heather gray in others. The cut was modest and nearly down to the ankle, with ruched puff sleeves, a shirred bodice, and a gently fitted waist that made her swelling middle look sweet. Its neckline was high, and the oversize Peter Pan collar and cuffs were covered with delicate snow-white lace—an elegant frame for the gold locket she wore every day.

Rilla fastened the last of the tiny buttons up Allina's back. "All right," she said after dabbing Allina's lips with the faintest bit of rosy lipstick, "you can turn around now."

When Allina faced the mirror, she couldn't curb a stunned gasp. The woman in the glass was pretty and pink-cheeked, and her eyes were soft with happiness. The velvet whispered against her skin. *Just for today, I'll be a woman on her wedding day. A girl in a beautiful dress. Nothing more.*

Rilla squeezed her shoulders and stood on tiptoe to kiss her cheek. "Perfect."

A light knock at the door made them both turn around.

The head nurse bustled in with a white cardboard box, but she stopped when she saw Allina. Her gray gaze misted over. "Aren't you lovely. Your eyes look so green in that color." She held up the box. "I'm sure the dress-maker created a hat and gloves to go with your new dress, but I thought you might make use of these." She set the box on Allina's bed and un-packed it. Nestled inside a dozen sheets of tissue were a pair of lace gloves and a wedding veil, which she pressed into Allina's hands.

The lace on both items, done in a simple rose pattern, was silky against Allina's fingers. The veil was modest, just a single waterfall tier, and there was a row of three pearl buttons along the edge of each glove.

"These are exquisite," Allina murmured.

"They were mine," *Schwester* Ziegler said with a tiny smile.

For a moment Allina didn't speak.

"I didn't know you were married," Rilla said.

The older woman lifted a shoulder in a sad shrug. "My Hubertus died two years after we wed. Nearly twenty years ago now."

"Oh, but I can't take them, then," Allina said, lifting her hands in protest.

"Please," the head nurse said, pressing them again into Allina's hands. "I'd love you to have them, unless you think they're too old-fashioned. I've no children, other than the ones here. It would make me happy to see them used."

Allina donned the gloves carefully; the lace was strong, despite its intricacy. Rilla took a minute to pin the veil to her hair before Allina turned around to model them.

"Yes," *Schwester* Ziegler said in a soft voice, "they look exactly as I thought they would on you." Then she took a step back and cleared her throat. "After all, you're entitled to as many pretty things as you desire. In a few hours, you'll be the wife of a *Gruppenführer*."

Allina bowed her head. "Thank you."

"Consider it a wedding gift." The head nurse held up a finger. "Now, then. Wendeline and I will take care of your children for the rest of the day," she said, voice crisp and back to business, "and Rilla and Alexander can make do tomorrow. There's no need to return to work until Saturday." She walked to the door, then turned back. "Enjoy your wedding. You're very lucky, Allina. I wish you every happiness."

She turned quickly and left the room without another word.

"That woman," Rilla said, plopping back down onto the bed with a sigh, "will always be a mystery to me."

Karl arrived at Hochland Home thirty minutes early, but Allina only kept him waiting for ten. When she and Rilla entered the guest parlor, he stood with a stunned smile. He held up a bouquet of white roses, bound in lilac ribbon a shade darker than her dress. His hands were shaking. "You're beautiful," he whispered.

A long, low whistle shot out.

Allina jumped. Alex was lounging in a chair, a meter from Karl. "Oh. I didn't see you there, Alex."

He winked. "Obviously, *Madame*, which makes my superior officer an exceptionally lucky groom."

"I am," Karl muttered as he walked quickly to her. Karl's hair was dark with pomade and his eyes were very blue. His face, however, was chalky.

"You're not nervous, are you, sir?" Alexander asked a little too innocently, earning a giggle from Rilla.

Karl lifted Allina's lace-gloved fingers to his lips. "Not anymore."

The ride to Munich was quiet. They kept the automobile's top up in deference to her hair, but rode in easy, pleasant silence for the most part. Alexander told an occasional joke, and Rilla laughed in response from the back seat.

Karl's silence suited Allina. With the hum of the automobile beneath her body and anticipation tickling her skin, she lost count of the number of times their eyes met. She was content to hold his hand, although his fingers were cold and required warming up. Alex was right. Karl von Strassberg was nervous. Somehow it made her less so.

He asked her only one question on the drive: "It's not the wedding most women dream about, is it?"

Her heart cramped with love. Allina knew exactly what he was asking.

There would be no wedding in a church with family today, nor a larger civil service with friends. That was just as well. A simple wedding at the Munich RuSHA office was preferable to the ritual-laden SS ceremony Himmler normally required of his officers. Since Karl was due back in Prague the day after tomorrow, the *Reichsführer* had made an exception, and thank heaven for that. She couldn't stand the thought of another reading from *Mein Kampf* or more advice on how to be a good Reich wife.

"The wedding ceremony doesn't matter," she said, squeezing his hand. "It's the man I'm marrying that's important."

Even the beady-eyed little registrar, who sniffled during the five-minute ceremony and recited his script with little charm, didn't matter. In the end, all that mattered was that she spoke the words and made her promises to him, and he to her. Time stretched out during those five minutes, and she became aware of the beauty in simple things—of the buoyant warmth that spread from her chest into her arms and fingers, and how Karl's face was haloed in the light streaming through the office window. His indigo eyes held hers throughout their vows, and his fingers trembled when he slipped the plain gold band around her finger.

Karl kissed her knuckles when the ceremony was over, then her cheeks, and finally her mouth.

"W-well, now." The registrar patted his stomach. Could it be that this little unromantic man was moved? "If you'll be so kind as to sign," he said, pointing to the registrar's book.

So they signed, with Rilla and Alexander as witnesses, and there were hugs and kisses all around before they left the registrar to his next task and went home to the Sunflower House for their wedding dinner.

CHAPTER 27

June 2006
Englewood, New Jersey

KATRINE

"It was a simple ceremony, but romantic." Mama's cheeks are flushed with love and the memory of her wedding.

My stomach twists. *My father was an SS officer.* This is a sentence no sane human wants to hear. Eleven million dead because of Adolf Hitler and the Nazi Party. Eleven million. There's no excusing that level of evil.

Everyone knows there's no such thing as a "good" Nazi—even if the one in question had a Jewish grandmother and fought to help other Jews emigrate to safety. Karl von Strassberg denied his heritage. He hid behind his uniform. He was part of the machine.

"Do you have a picture of him?"

She pulls a photo from the box, traces his face tenderly with a finger before handing the photo to me. It's the same one that had me shaking this morning on the floor of her bedroom.

"I look like him."

Her eyes fill with tears. "Yes, darling. You do."

I understand now why she never remarried. There have been a handful of men in my mother's life over the years, but nothing approaching the love I see in her face.

"He sounds . . . extraordinary." My careful wording brings both understanding and pain to her gaze.

"Karl was trapped," she says, "by circumstance and the choices he'd made as a young man. But he tried to atone. He thought he could change things." Her good hand covers her heart and taps it, as if in need of soothing. "He risked his life to save others. You must believe me."

I nod, giving in to the need, the pain, in her voice.

I understand why she'd never spoken of my father, an SS *Gruppenführer*—and perhaps, why she kept our Jewish heritage a secret. My mother spent most of her adult life attempting to forget her past in its entirety, and then trying to forgive herself for doing just that.

How can you share such details with a ten-year-old, or a teenager? How do you try to explain your past in shades of gray to that child, when all a child is capable of understanding is black and white? Even the smallest revelation would have prompted an avalanche of questions from me, ones she wasn't prepared to answer.

As for friends and neighbors . . . I understand, now, why my mother was so fiercely independent. Never accepting help from others, she was always hustling, ever busy, and singularly focused on giving me the best possible life. But always alone.

My heart aches for the enormity of her burden, and for our shared history—our heritage—lost to those secrets for nearly seventy years.

Mama squeezes my hand with a bony ferocity that makes me wince. "There was never a right time to talk about any of these things. When you were small, it was out of the question. Should I have told you in high school? Or before you were married? Or once you'd had children of your own?" She shakes her head. "As the years passed, I found more excuses. I committed the same sin my aunt and uncle did."

Yes. She had. But I accept why she did it.

Now, for the sake of my sanity, I must know the rest. And I owe it to her to listen.

"I need to know more about my father, and how he helped you save those children, the ones at Hochland Home. And what became of him . . . in the end." Maybe that will help me understand.

My question brings another radiant smile to her lips. "Their recovery was remarkable, a miracle. The children taught me to never underestimate the human capacity to heal, even under the most difficult circumstances."

PART 4

Bayreuth

CHAPTER 28

Summer 1939
Hochland Home
Steinhöring

ALLINA

Allina waddled over to the blue velvet settee in the front parlor and heaved her swollen body onto the soft cushions with as much grace as she could muster.

"Come, Otto, let's rest for a moment," she said. God, her back was killing her today. She pressed a hand to the base of her spine.

Otto followed obediently and jumped onto the sofa's edge before taking her hand. His moist fingers wriggled in her grip. Allina's throat tightened. They'd been waiting twenty minutes. When would the Schafs arrive?

"Why are you sad?" Otto asked, glancing up at her with wide eyes. He was adorable in his charcoal cotton short suit and crisp white shirt. With freshly scrubbed cheeks and his blond hair parted to the side and slicked back with water, he was the perfect little gentleman.

Allina slid a finger down the center of his nose, sprinkled with freckles from weeks of playing outdoors. "I'm not sad," she lied, blinking away tears. "I'm happy for you."

The sound of approaching footfalls made her stomach sink. Allina took a deep breath and managed to force a smile onto her face by the time the door opened. *Schwester* Ziegler entered, beckoning to the middle-aged couple who stood in the hall. The pair was clad in impeccable silk clothes—she in a red dress and broad-brimmed hat trimmed with onyx feathers, and he in a navy suit.

"*Schwester* Allina will handle things from here," she said, with a sweep of her arm. "Hugo, Luisa, I wish you every happiness with your new son." Ziegler turned and left without another word.

The woman approached Otto and bent forward, one hand pressed to the collar of her dress, the other outstretched. Although he hopped off the sofa at Allina's urging, Otto turned back and pressed his sturdy body against her legs.

The woman's eyes narrowed.

"Otto, these are the Schafs, your new parents," Allina coaxed. "They picked you especially, out of all the children at Hochland Home, to be their son."

Another lie. It was Marguerite Ziegler who had, in fact, chosen Otto for the Schafs, but only after the couple appealed to the *Reichsführer*.

Earlier this year, the pair were sorely disappointed when they didn't receive the child promised to them—one who, unfortunately, was deemed "slow" and sent away from Hochland Home. A child Allina's program wasn't destined to save.

Frustrated, the Schafs had written more than a dozen letters to the head nurse, and then to the *Reichsführer*, demanding help or compensation. As every other Hochland Home child had already been assigned an adopted family, Himmler suggested one of Allina's special children might do.

Otto was the most advanced—nearly perfect, as Ziegler assured her—and Allina could only pray that he would be enough. That this couple would be gentle and patient and kind.

The Schafs had, after all, demanded a flawless Aryan child.

Otto looked up at Allina with guileless blue eyes. "I'll miss you, *Schwester*."

Allina's laugh was a little shaky. "And I'll miss you," she said, wiping a tear from the corner of her eye. "That's why I'm crying. But I'm happy for you, too." She pressed her lips to his silky hair, still scented faintly of lemon soap.

"We should leave as soon as possible," the man said. "We've a long drive ahead of us. It took over an hour to get here." He clapped his hands before holding them up to mimic the steering wheel of a car. "What do you say?" he asked Otto with a grin. "Are you ready to go for a ride?"

Otto perked up, nodding vigorously enough to unsettle his hair. Chuckling, the couple each took Otto by the hand, leaving Allina to follow.

Otto turned to her at the last minute, pulling away from the couple to press his small body against hers before running to the doorway. He jumped down the steps, counting each with excellent diction and landing with a triumphant "Five!" on the front path. "Good-bye, *Schwester* Allina," the boy called out over his shoulder.

Allina watched from the doorway as they got into their automobile. After the vehicle disappeared down the road in a cloud of dust, she walked back to the parlor. Her mind was a blank, and her pregnant body for once felt light and empty, like a balloon. She sat down with a sigh.

Perhaps a half hour later, a warm hand on her shoulder stirred her out of her reverie. The head nurse offered a cup of tea. "This is why I told you from the beginning that it's never a good idea to get too involved with the children."

She set the saucer on a side table and left without another word.

Late that evening, Karl held her while she cried. "I know it's difficult for you, letting Otto go," he murmured into her hair.

"My heart's breaking," Allina said. "I'm terrified for him."

"I know."

"What sort of person will Otto become, with parents like that?"

"Otto will live. And you've done everything you could." This was the only answer he could offer, Allina knew that. Karl pressed a kiss to her forehead, ran his hand in a soothing caress over her hair. "I have some good news for you, though. We just got word of Ursula and Rabbi Gutt-mann. Their families made it safely to Switzerland. My Aunt Adele says they're adjusting well."

"That's wonderful." Allina shifted again, trying to find a comfortable position. Sometimes it felt like the baby was kicking her spine. "*Ooof*. My back is killing me."

Karl's hands moved to the tender space above the base of her spine and began massaging it in slow circles, easing the pain.

"That's heaven," she murmured. "I didn't know I married a magician."
He certainly had the hands of one. "Have I told you how happy I am to
have you home, even if only for a week?"

"Hmmmm. There's the attitude I want to hear."

A soft flutter in her womb, and then a harder kick, made Allina go still.

Karl's fingers paused. "What is it?" he whispered.

She reached for his hand and pressed it to her stomach. They waited,
barely breathing. When the baby kicked again, he reared back and laughed.
"There he is."

She wriggled up, keeping both their hands pressed to her tummy. "Or
she."

"Or she," he agreed. Karl cupped hands around his mouth and pressed
them to her tummy. "Hello, little one. This is your father." He laughed
again and planted a loud, smacking kiss on her belly. "Do you see, my
heart? There's new life all around us today."

Allina pressed the emerald gown to her middle and twisted before the
mirror, examining her profile with a critical eye.

The dress was nearly as beautiful as the one she'd worn on her wedding
day. Its fabric was shot through with gold thread in an abstract pattern,
and the dress was cut beautifully with a deep neckline, shoulder-hugging
puffed sleeves, and an Empire waist that complimented her expanding
figure.

The gown was also a birthday gift from her husband—yet another in a
series of gifts he'd given her since their wedding. On the bed, still wrapped
in packing tissue, was a second gorgeous frock in indigo silk, along with
two sets of ballet slippers that matched the gowns.

"Let me spoil you a little," he'd coaxed before the modiste arrived. "It's
just a few dresses. We couldn't have the wedding you deserved."

She'd relented, in part because it pleased him, but also because she
needed the clothes. The rehabilitation program had taken its toll on her
work uniforms. Nearly everything she owned was spattered with finger
paint no amount of washing could erase, and she'd ruined several of the
items she'd gotten on loan from the other mothers. Thanks to her husband, a dozen sturdy aprons and six new outfits—most of them casual,

and each featuring clever designs that would take her through the balance of her pregnancy—were scheduled for delivery tomorrow.

Still frowning at her reflection, Allina heard the subtle snick of the front door as it opened. Her husband was home early.

Karl walked into the bedroom and joined her in front of the mirror. "Hello, beautiful," he said, tugging her gently back against his chest. Their eyes locked in the glass.

"I'm like a balloon."

He kissed her cheek. "Nonsense," Karl said, eyes crinkling at the corners. "You're lovely." His hands went to cup her belly. "How's your stomach today?"

"The same," she said. "When the nausea hits, there's nothing I can do but run for the bathroom. I can't believe I'm getting sick now." Her morning sickness hadn't started until the end of her fourth month. It was ridiculous.

"You're unique even in your pregnancy," he said, rubbing her tummy. "Why not try on one of your beautiful new dresses?" Karl planted a soft kiss on the side of her neck. "I'll help you." Keeping his eyes on hers in the glass, he undid the row of tiny buttons on the front of her shift. Then he cupped her breasts through her brassiere, circling his thumbs lightly over her nipples until she moaned.

"You're trying to distract me," she protested.

"A husband's privilege," he said with a last nip at her neck. But then he lent himself to the task, helping her out of her cotton dress and into the green velvet gown. The fabric was light and cool against her skin.

When Allina gazed into the mirror again, she was surprised. She looked . . . elegant. Sensual. Satisfied.

"You're a goddess," Karl said. "A modern-day Fricka."

"The goddess of marriage."

"And fertility," he added with a wolf's smile.

She leaned back against him with a sigh. "I feel pampered and beautiful, thanks to your extravagant gifts. But when will we find time to go to dinner or the theater?"

"Hmm, yes. About that . . ." The smile in the glass lost some of its heat. "We're going to the opera. The season at Bayreuth opens soon."

"The Wagner Festival?"

"Yes. It commences at the end of the month. I go each year. It's mandatory."

Allina's ears began to ring. She should have expected this. Everyone knew Adolf Hitler was a Wagner fanatic. She was the wife of a high-ranking SS officer. Of course she must go.

Karl massaged her shoulders as they stiffened.

"He'll be there, won't he?" she asked.

He nodded, kissed her cheek. "Yes. The Führer attends performances every day."

She was growing light-headed. "How long will we be at Bayreuth?"

"A week." He squeezed her shoulders gently. "I wouldn't take you if it was dangerous."

Of course not. He was protective to a fault. Still, a week in Adolf Hitler's presence would be torturous. Nerve-wracking.

Allina turned, and Karl's arms came around her. She pressed her cheek to his chest, inhaling his cool, clean scent. "If you tell me I asked for this, I'll hit you over the head with one of my new shoes."

Karl chuckled and pulled her closer. "Try not to worry. The *Reichsführer* has been singing your praises. As much as the Führer wants to meet you, he never discusses business or politics with women. All the ladies find him charming."

She snorted. "I'm sure."

He pressed his lips to her forehead. "All the wives go. You need more practice interacting with them."

"I know how to behave," Allina replied, shooting him a sour look. "How hard can it be to play a spoiled Reich wife? Pleasant, empty-headed, uninterested in politics. Hopelessly dull."

Karl threw his head back and laughed. "My heart, I don't expect miracles."

CHAPTER 29

Summer 1939
Sanspareil Rock Garden
Bayreuth, Germany

ALLINA

Allina gazed into the steel-gray eyes of Ilse Hess and prayed for her husband's swift return.

"I'm relieved to see you out and about, Frau von Strassberg," Ilse said.

Frau Hess was a hard woman, despite her round cheeks and overflowing bosom. Ilse and her husband, Rudolf, were confidants of Adolf Hitler. *They're his eyes and ears,* Karl warned early on, and so wielded a tremendous amount of power. The viper's words seemed kind enough, but her strident tone made Allina's stomach sink.

In the week she'd been at Bayreuth, dozens of SS officers and their scheming wives had swarmed to every cocktail party, dinner, and social event like flies on a carcass. Allina had come to the Sanspareil Rock Garden this morning for a respite from the farce. She'd settled on a bench in the corner of the garden, hoping for the chance to enjoy a peaceful hour among nature's wholesome creations.

No such luck. Ilse was every bit as calculating and cruel as Marga Himmler.

The older woman's brow furrowed when Allina didn't respond quickly enough. "Are you ill again? We were worried when you and your husband left dinner early last night. That simply isn't something one *does,* my dear, when one is seated next to the Führer."

Allina pulled herself together. "I'm truly sorry, Frau Hess. My stomach was plaguing me," she said. "And I'm afraid the heat may be too much this morning."

It was half past nine, but the air in the garden was steamy enough to make the sweat pool between her breasts and slide in warm trickles down her spine. Still, she'd prefer another ten degrees to ten more minutes in this creature's presence.

"Frau Hess," Karl called out, walking up to them. "What an unexpected pleasure. I was hunting down a cool drink for my bride." His eyes glittered with sympathy as he handed Allina a glass of cold water.

Downing the drink slowly, Allina kept her lashes half lowered to shutter her thoughts.

Ilse Hess presented her hand with a sniff. Karl bowed over it before bestowing a gallant kiss.

"I wanted to check on your wife, of course—and to confirm you'd both join us this evening at the reception at Villa Wahnfried. Frau Wagner is excited to host and expects the Führer to attend. I'd hate to have you spoil another audience with him."

"We wouldn't miss it," Karl said.

"Until tonight, then." Ilse gave a little finger wave and then returned to the group of simpering gossips in the corner of the courtyard.

At last, they were alone.

"Talk to me," he murmured.

"Frau Hess was baiting me," she whispered. The woman had ruled by intimidation all week. She'd been watching every move they made. "How can you stand it? So well-mannered on the surface, so . . . well-meaning."

"It's naïve to expect villains without grace," he murmured. "The most dangerous ones hide in plain sight. We both know how many monsters are on the loose." He took her hand. "Walk with me. There's something I want you to see."

They followed a winding path for perhaps a quarter mile. The walkway was bordered by tall beech trees that curved inward and blocked most of the sun's rays, offering shade and flooding the ground with golden-green light. It was easier to breathe here as the breeze cooled the moisture from her cheeks.

They crested the hill to find a curious, ornate building topped with a large glass dome. "This building guards a beautiful secret," he said as they ascended the steps.

In the middle of the space grew an old beech tree. Its upper branches nearly brushed the glass dome. Allina's eyes fluttered closed and she inhaled the cool scent of the forest. When she opened them again, the tenderness in her husband's expression stilled her.

"You're like this tree," he said. "Someone might look at it and think it's imprisoned in the structure. But this tree is the centerpiece, the heart of the building." He smiled. "Just as you're the center of my life now."

Allina wrapped her arms around her husband and pressed her face to his chest, listened to the steady thrum of his heart. "I love you."

"And I, you." Karl set his cheek on top of her head. "You'll find the strength to continue, no matter what happens, as this tree has for hundreds of years."

She pulled away and searched his face. "What do you mean?"

He captured the strand of hair that had escaped her chignon and tucked it behind her ear. "I want to grow old with you, until our teeth rattle around in our heads, but only a fool would fail to prepare for the worst."

Karl was too calm. He spoke these words as if he were ordering breakfast. "You're scaring me."

"Forgive me." He drew her hand to his heart. "Sir Nevile Henderson, the British ambassador, will be at Winifred Wagner's reception tonight. I didn't expect him at Bayreuth this year, but he's come to seek peace with the Führer. You must meet him."

"Why?"

"He needs to remember your face, my heart. And your name."

She stood quietly in his arms as the truth sank in. "I won't leave you."

"Hush." Karl gripped her shoulders. "You will, if it comes to that, and while I can ensure your safety, and the baby's."

No. Allina buried her face in his chest.

He murmured the next words in her ear, each one a soft and terrifying caress. "If Germany goes to war, we'll have to accelerate the work. Each plan we thwart, each person we save, is an act of treason. You told me that once. You accepted the risk. Now, you must accept that I have the right to protect you. Promise me you'll do as I ask."

Karl wasn't asking, of course; he was demanding. And while her husband's voice remained calm, there was desperation in the way he held her—in the tension in his body and the tight clasp of his hands. "I promise," she said. "I'll do as you say."

They left the garden hand in hand.

The rest of the day passed in a blur. Allina spent an unproductive half hour in their hotel room trying to nap, and then an hour pretending to read. When she began pacing the length of the room, Karl coaxed her into its decadent claw-foot tub. He washed her hair and sponged down her sticky, swollen limbs. His sensual attention helped Allina find release. When Karl brought her to bed, she managed a few hours of dreamless sleep before she woke to his kiss. She chose the indigo silk for tonight's festivities. Karl said it made her hair look like spun gold.

On their drive to Villa Wahnfried, Allina was completely refreshed, and certain she could carry off the rest of the evening. No, she wouldn't let anything shake her confidence—not the Führer, nor Sir Nevile, not even rumors of war.

When they entered Winifred Wagner's home and she came face-to-face with *Gruppenführer* Reinhardt Gud, Allina realized she was wrong.

His face was the same. The gray hair, the cunning silver eyes, the arrogant smile—they were all the same. He was shorter than she remembered, though, and seemed older, more than the intervening ten months should have made him. His shoulders drooped, and the elegant cut of his tuxedo couldn't hide its bagginess. He'd lost weight, then, and hadn't had time to take the suit to a tailor, not that the state of the man's clothing mattered. Nothing mattered, except that she keep hold of herself and not run, shrieking, from the entryway out onto the lawn.

Gud came to them as soon as he saw her. He hurried across the marble floor of the villa's reception hall to greet them as if doing so were the most normal thing in the world. "It's a pleasure to see you again, my dear." He bowed slightly and clicked his heels with precision, as an officer should. Only the curve of his mouth—that tight, knowing smirk—betrayed him.

A tremor went through her, quick as lightning, all the more brutal for its swiftness. A flash of him, of his body moving over hers in the back of his car and his rage-filled face, flew through her brain. She stepped back and bumped against Karl's broad chest at the precise moment his arm came around her shoulders to steady her. She'd forgotten he was there; for a moment, she had been that terrified girl back in Badensburg. Thank God. She could breathe again.

"Reinhardt." Karl's voice was loud and sharp. A deadly crack. He kept his arm around her shoulders and turned away, effectively blocking her body from Gud's view.

Gud was forced to retreat. "Karl," he said, backing up and to the side. His attention shifted, warily, to her husband's face. Gud's eyes were smaller for a moment and his nostrils quivered, in fear, perhaps, though that might be wishful thinking.

Then the moment was gone and he turned back to her. "You're beautiful, Allina. And blooming." Gud pinned her again with his gaze as it roamed the length of her pregnant body, his meaning clear: *I had you first.*

The sharp intake of Karl's breath made her go still. She looked at her husband, at his proud, beautiful profile, the nerve ticking in his jaw, the way he held his mouth with such precision. His face was pale against his black tuxedo jacket, and a fine sheen of perspiration appeared above his upper lip. The air around them was crackling with tension, sharp and bright enough that the whole room should have seen it, and thick with violence. Karl would kill him, right here, in the reception room of Winifred Wagner's home, if she didn't do something.

Allina wouldn't give Gud the dignity of words. Instead, she took her husband's hand and squeezed it, begging for silence while she stared the bastard down. She poured everything into the look: anger, loathing, disgust, pity, strength, and her victory over him. Gud's eyes went wide, as if he couldn't believe what he was seeing, so Allina jerked her chin higher. She wasn't a little girl anymore, nor innocent. He'd taken that from her. But she was no longer his victim. She wouldn't back down.

It was over in less than a minute.

Gud's face crumpled, slowly at first, as if it were imploding. First his jaw sagged, then a nerve began ticking below his right eye. He swallowed hard, throat muscles convulsing, and slowly curled and uncurled the hands at his sides. Finally, his gaze shifted to the cluster of people around them—men and women Allina hadn't noticed at first, but ones who'd moved in swiftly, sensing a drama about to unfold.

He dipped his head, and his eyes drifted to the floor.

Gud left without a word, after bowing one more time.

The group around them seemed to heave a collective sigh. Some seemed disappointed, like dogs who had appeared at the scent of blood and then been denied their dinner.

The release of tension left Allina shaky.

Tuxedoed waitstaff were offering hors d'oeuvres and champagne to a small gathering of perhaps fifty. Karl snagged two glasses from a passing waiter and handed her one as he downed the other in a single gulp. Her debonair husband licked his lips before taking the glass from her hand and drinking it as well.

"I'm going to kill him, eventually," he said in the same cool voice he'd used last night when making his dinner selection.

Allina dabbed the perspiration from his lip, managing to make a good job of it despite her shaking fingers. "He doesn't matter anymore," she murmured. This wasn't precisely true. Her unsteadiness was testament to that. But there'd be a time in the future when it *would* be true, and that was enough.

"You're magnificent," he whispered. He cupped her cheek, and his eyes zeroed in on her mouth. For a moment she thought he'd kiss her right here, in the middle of the reception.

A sharp voice rang out from across the room. "*Gruppenführer* von Strassberg!"

Winifred Wagner bustled over, dressed in a floor-length black silk dress that did an exceptional job of flattering her matronly figure. Frau Wagner was a handsome woman with a strong nose and chin and an equally bold personality. She always had a smile for everyone.

Her smile was tight with panic at the moment. "Please, save me," she said, once she'd reached them. "It seems the Führer won't be able to make my little gathering tonight, and I need to keep Sir Nevile occupied." She looked to Karl. "Let me introduce you. I'd be in your debt."

Without another word, she turned and walked across the room toward a man standing alone at the bay window, leaving Karl and Allina to follow.

Sir Nevile Henderson, the British ambassador to Germany, was a tall, gaunt gentleman with a distinguished profile that reminded Allina a little bit of a greyhound's. He had the saddest eyes she'd ever seen.

"I'm sorry, Sir Nevile," Frau Wagner said, once they'd joined the ambassador at the window. "I've heard the Führer is indisposed until after tonight's performance."

Henderson took Winifred's hand. "Frau Wagner, I believe you've done everything you can. I'm happy to enjoy your gracious hospitality." He dipped his head. "As well as the company of your guests."

Winifred nodded. "Then let me make my introductions. May I—"

A huge roar and boisterous cheers sounded outside, interrupting Frau Wagner's introduction. The noise, while startling, had become common this week. It meant the Führer's motorcade was making its way slowly through the crowds at Bayreuth.

Sir Nevile peered out the window for a few moments before turning back to Winifred. "Clearly, your Führer feels his presence does more good out there than in here. With me."

Frau Wagner's eyes widened. "I hope you still plan to seek him out after this evening's performance of *Das Rheingold*."

Sir Nevile bowed. "Of course."

Frau Wagner's smile became desperate. "Sir Nevile, may I introduce *Gruppenführer* Karl von Strassberg and his wife, Allina. Both are champions of our *Lebensborn* program."

Karl bowed. "It's an honor to meet you, sir."

"The honor is mine," he said in faintly accented German. Henderson's eyes twinkled when he turned to Allina. "Frau von Strassberg, you're in full bloom, and more beautiful than an English rose." Taking her hand, he pressed cool, dry lips to her knuckles.

Allina felt herself flush.

Sir Nevile shifted his attention to Karl. "I'm glad to speak to you tonight. Your *Reichsführer* has told me about the wonders of your *Lebensborn* homes. I understand each devotes considerable resources to mothers and their children, and that they assist thousands of women every year. I'd like to learn more, if you have the time."

"Of course," Karl said. "Although my wife is the expert, not me."

Henderson smiled at that—a genuine one that lit up his face. "I see. A woman of both brains and beauty. You're a lucky man."

"I am." Karl's arm came around her waist. "Sir Nevile, I wonder if we might also discuss a colleague of yours. A man by the name of Paul Kimball."

The change in the ambassador was so subtle Allina almost missed it. The man's eyes narrowed, and his chin tipped up a fraction. "Kimball? I know him well. He's devoted his life to assisting children. Orphans, in particular."

"So I've heard. We'd like to learn more about how Kimball runs his program. Perhaps you might arrange a visit for my wife," Karl added, pulling her closer. "She's always interested in learning new methods." He looked into Allina's eyes. "Aren't you, darling?"

The determination in Karl's gaze permitted only one answer. "Of course I am," she said.

Sir Nevile's eyes darkened. "I'm sure Frau von Strassberg would be welcome to visit any time. I'd be happy to help you make the connection, if need be."

Karl offered his hand. "Thank you, sir."

Sir Nevile took it, and they shook.

"How wonderful!" Winifred clapped her hands with glee. "You see? Germany and England aren't so different after all. Two countries passionately devoted to the well-being of children." She took the ambassador's elbow, claiming his attention again. "I see the Görings have come out to join my little party tonight. They're dying to spend some time with you. *Gruppenführer* von Strassberg, Frau von Strassberg, will you excuse us?"

Henderson bowed, and Winifred steered him away.

Allina sagged against her husband. "What just happened?" she whispered.

"A number of things," Karl said as he tugged her closer to the window. "Some spoken, some not, and at least one you won't be happy about."

For a moment they stood, hand in hand, and gazed out across the lawn. The sun was setting and it kissed each flower in the courtyard's manicured gardens with gold light.

"Who is Paul Kimball?" Allina asked, although her stomach knew the answer.

"A code," he murmured. "A way to get more children to England. And you, if necessary."

"I see."

He squeezed her hand. "I'll meet with the ambassador tomorrow before he leaves."

Allina stayed silent until she regained control over her voice. "The Führer is avoiding Sir Nevile."

"You picked up on that, did you?"

She decided humor was better than fear. "You shouldn't be surprised. Sir Nevile said I have both beauty and brains."

The look Karl gave her was searing. "I couldn't agree more."

"What are we going to do?" she whispered.

He brought her hand to his lips. "We're going to enjoy the opera tonight."

CHAPTER 30

Bayreuth

ALLINA

"Negotiations between Sir Nevile and the Führer have officially broken down," Karl said the next morning over breakfast. "Would you mind very much if we left a day early? We need to get as many children out of Germany as possible in the next few weeks."

This was devastating news, but the prospect of going home left Allina woozy with relief. "We could leave right now and I'd be the happiest woman in the world."

"No. Tomorrow is fine. There are plenty of details to be worked out first. Sir Nevile and I will meet this afternoon. While you rest."

Allina let her head loll back onto the cushion. "I suppose we're obligated to go to the opera again tonight?"

"And the artists' reception afterward at Villa Wahnfried, if you're not too tired," he said as they drove slowly onto the main road. "It should be an interesting party. Marta Fuchs is the only woman on the planet who can get away with insulting the Führer to his face."

Allina closed her eyes. "Wonderful."

She was grateful for the four hours of sleep she squeezed in at their hotel before the opera performance, because the artists' reception at Villa Wahnfried was a mad crush of people, cigarette smoke, and champagne.

The crowd didn't make Allina panic; at this point, she was beyond that particular emotion. But the energy in the house was frantic. People ate too much, laughed too hard. Everyone seemed to be on high alert.

Karl grabbed two glasses of champagne as soon as they entered the library. "For sustenance," he muttered, taking a gulp from one as he handed her the other. She sipped slowly, enjoying the sharp fizz against her tongue, and watched the room.

Marta Fuchs, the festival's soprano, was the center of attention tonight. She stood in the middle of the room with a crowd of admirers paying court around her. Frau Fuchs was a pretty woman—what many called "sporty," rather than beautiful—but her expressive eyes, pointed chin, and slim build made her perfect for the role of a Valkyrie warrior. The chain mail and winged headdress she wore onstage to play Wagner's Brünnhilde suited her.

Marta's gown choice for tonight's reception was surprising, but it suited her, too. She was dressed for her audience of admirers in a plain ivory satin sheath, matching gloves, and pearls at both ears and throat. Her light brown hair was in a loose chignon. These fashion choices were intelligent ones, and likely deliberate. Marta glowed in contrast to most of the other women in the room, who wore darker, fussier gowns and diamonds.

There was a noisy throng of people around the woman at the moment, five deep in some places, all seeking to pay homage.

"It must be exhausting," Allina murmured. "All that attention."

"Trust me," Karl said, as his arm came around her, "Marta Fuchs knows exactly what she's doing. This is sure to be her most convincing performance of the week."

He chucked his chin in Frau Wagner's direction as she made her way to the center of the horde. The two women linked arms.

Marta pressed hand to heart as her voice soared over the crowd. "Don't worry, my darlings, I spoke with the Führer just this afternoon. I shared how worried you all are. 'My Führer,' I said, 'we've seen the newspapers. The petrol stations sell no more than five liters at a time.' I told him rumors of war have been swirling at Bayreuth for days."

There was a hushed silence as her audience hung on every word.

"And what did the Führer say to that, dear Marta?" Winifred asked.

"He told me the rumors were nonsense, of course," Marta answered with an elegant wave of her hand. "Germany is simply converting its storage tanks to take synthetic fuel. The rationing will all be over in a few weeks."

Everyone in the room must have been holding their breath, for a roar of sighs erupted from the crowd.

"Believe this, my friends," Winifred Wagner promised with a broad smile, "for we've heard this from our Führer's precious lips. There will be no war."

"We're going to war," Karl said the next morning on their drive back to Munich.

Allina let her head fall back onto the seat cushion and closed her eyes. "And so the harder work begins."

He hit the steering wheel with enough force to make her jump. "I won't risk your life, or our child's."

"I don't plan on offering us up for slaughter." Allina was surprised at how calm she sounded. "I'm your partner in crime. You've said it yourself. Try not to let your emotions get the better of you."

Karl shook his head. "This isn't funny."

"We all need to keep our senses of humor. Including you, *Gruppenführer*."

That got a chuckle out of him. "God. I hated it when you called me that."

"That's why I did it."

Karl's hand went to her belly—as it did a dozen times a day, and more often at night while he slept. "I love you, my heart."

"And I, you." Allina brought her husband's hand to her lips, and when Karl's arm came around her, she moved closer and nestled into his embrace. She pressed her cheek to his chest, inhaled the cool, clean scent that belonged only to Karl, and listened to the steady beat of his heart.

PART 5

Basel

CHAPTER 31

Summer 1941
Sonnenblumen Haus
Starnberg

ALLINA

Katrine galloped into the kitchen with a squeal so loud it should have rattled every cup and saucer in the cupboard. Running to Allina, she buried her face in her mother's skirts.

"Mama!" The muffled cry was exuberant. Katrine clutched Allina's apron with grubby hands and pressed her sturdy little body close. The girl's mop of honey-colored hair trembled with excitement.

Laughing, Allina set down the apple she was peeling and hoisted up the giggling child. She set her daughter down on a clean corner of the worktable and took Katrine's face in her hands, examining every beloved detail. The little one's hair was a tangled mess and each pink cheek was streaked with dirt and freckled from the sun. Her dark blue eyes shone.

Allina's heart cramped with love. This child, named after Karl's grandmother, Ekaterina, brought the sunshine wherever she went. If the dried mud on her face and blue gingham dress were any indication, she'd been running amok in the garden.

"Where have you been, kitten? Where's Papa?"

With another giggle, the little girl pointed at the kitchen door.

As if on cue, Karl walked in, smiling and holding an armful of sunflowers. It was the largest, most beautiful bouquet she'd ever seen.

"Surprise!" Katrine yelled.

Allina held back tears of relief. In rolled-up shirtsleeves and with his hair devoid of pomade, Karl seemed ten years younger this morning. His hands and face were as streaked with dirt as his daughter's. Home for less than a day, he already looked more gentleman farmer than officer. It was nearly enough to make Allina forget about the damn war.

When Karl had arrived from Prague last night at sunset, he'd been exhausted, with sunken eyes and a face far too pale for summer. The bitter lines around his mouth had made Allina's stomach tumble, but instead of asking questions, she'd fed Karl while he gently reacquainted himself with his daughter. Allina had welcomed him into her body later, and his gentleness made her weep.

Afterward, Karl's dreams were violent enough to shake the bed. His moans had woken her three times. She'd ordered him out of the house after breakfast, hoping time outdoors with their daughter might revive him and help him to relax. The plan had worked.

"There's my husband," she said, letting her glance roam the length of his body. "You look yourself again."

"A husband bearing gifts." His grin widened and turned hungry. "Beautiful flowers for a beautiful wife." He strode to the table and kissed her soundly, sending the familiar rush of heat down her spine and all the way to the tips of her toes.

Katrine wouldn't have any of their nonsense. She bounced on the table until its legs squeaked against the tiles.

Karl's lips were warm and insistent, and Allina laughed against them before drawing reluctantly away. "Your daughter is accustomed to being the center of attention."

"I picked, Mama, I picked!" the little one shouted, proving the point. She made a mad grab for the bouquet, now slightly crushed between them.

Allina fussed over the sunflowers and pulled them neatly from Karl's arms. Each bloom was magnificent, with vibrant, lemon-colored petals and a tawny face that smelled of sunshine, the greenness of the field, and growing things. They'd sprouted up a foot in the last month, until they reached the windows on the first floor. The garden was as fully a part of the Sunflower House as the home's windows and walls and a constant reminder to Allina that there was still so much to hope for.

Karl leaned down to plant a kiss on his daughter's nose. "Our baby girl did an excellent job of picking them, didn't she?"

The little nose wrinkled in disgust. "Not a baby."

"No," Karl agreed gravely, brushing the dirt gently from his daughter's cheeks, "you're nearly grown, aren't you?" A flash of pain crossed his face, tightening his jaw, but it was gone so quickly Allina couldn't be certain she'd seen it.

She went to the sink to tend to the bouquet. Allina angled the thick, green shoots against the basin and filled the sink with a few inches of water to give the flowers a good soak.

Once that was done, she turned back to Karl, who was all smiles again. "She has your freckles, my heart. And your beautiful hair."

"That may be," she said, walking to the table, "but she has your every-thing else."

This was true. Hair and freckles aside, Katrine was wholly her father's—tall for her age and with Karl's proud cheekbones, deep blue eyes, and a pert nose that showed the promise of elegance. This similar-ity didn't end with her physical appearance. The child was as stubborn as a goat, and when she was angry or belligerent that soft, rounded jaw firmed to her father's marble one. Their daughter was so like Karl that Allina's breath sometimes caught in her throat. She found herself watch-ing Katrine, amazed by the way her gaze always seemed to take in every detail, and how it would turn inward when she was thinking hard, in an exact echo of her father's. Allina loved her daughter to distraction, and the weight of that love was a sweet, ever-present heat against her heart.

"Outside! Outside!" Katrine demanded. She bounced on the table again, making her impatience clear.

"Yes, my little kitten, we must go outside and play in the garden." Laughing, Karl plucked her wriggling body off the table and swung her overhead, prompting shrieks of terror-joy. Pulling his daughter into his arms, he held her close, raining kisses on her cheeks.

There. There it was again, that flash of pain across his proud features, although Allina wasn't sure of the reason. He was holding the child too tightly. She was straining away from him, trying to squirm out of his arms.

"Down, Papa!"

Karl complied with a self-conscious chuckle, and called out for her to stay close when she scampered into the dining room. He walked back to the table, wrapping arms around Allina's middle and molding his body to the curve of her back.

"We've made a mess of your newly polished kitchen," Karl said, pointing out the pattern of muddy footprints on the floor.

"Make all the messes you like." All Allina cared about was having him home. She'd seen her husband less than twenty days this year.

Karl kissed the sweet spot below her ear, raising goose bumps on her neck. He'd not shaved this morning, and the rasp of whiskers against her skin was as comforting as it was enticing.

"I wish I could give you more than three days," he murmured against her throat.

Allina pulled away and squared her shoulders, hoping to mask disappointment. "We'll make do. I don't have to work, thanks to Rilla. She'll handle the children until Friday."

Karl brought her hand to his mouth. She gripped his fingers and added, "And you'll tell me what's bothering you, won't you, sometime over these next three days." Her words were a statement, not a question. "You're torturing yourself. I can't stand it. I won't have you bearing your pain alone."

He closed his eyes but kept his lips pressed tightly to her palm. When their gazes met again, there was such loss in his that Allina's throat began to burn.

"I will, but not today. Let me enjoy a perfect day with my wife and daughter."

Afraid to say more, she nodded.

Karl's body jerked as he looked over her shoulder. His eyes popped wide.

"You're making strudel," he whispered reverently, gaze riveted on the apples, still half-peeled on the table. The pleasure on his face was intense, and his attention so rapt that Allina burst into laughter.

This man could make her find her humor, despite everything.

"It was meant to be a surprise," she said. "We harvested some of the early apples last week."

"You've been busy."

The pride in Karl's eyes made Allina flush. Running the Sunflower House while working at Hochland Home had been an adjustment. Nannies were in short supply, but Katrine seemed content enough accompanying her to work, despite Allina's misgivings. She kept her daughter close during the day—and away from the soulless schedules, thanks to her work on the third floor. Days off were precious, and spent with her daughter at home—cooking, gardening, and, sometimes, harvesting apples.

"Busy and grateful," Allina answered. "For our home. And for you, my love."

Hauling her against him, Karl gave her a last, hard kiss before he raced into the dining room with a whoop. A minute later, father and daughter galloped back into the kitchen.

"Oh yes," he yelled, lifting Katrine up onto his shoulders, "we will feast on Mama's strudel tonight." The kitchen door slammed with a sharp bang as the two people Allina loved most in the world ran into the yard.

The rest of the day was carefree. Karl seemed gratified to spend time with his daughter and managed to polish off most of the strudel. He roamed the small woods behind the house with Katrine until sunset, and spent hours making love to Allina after they put their daughter to bed.

The next day, Karl began fixing small items around the property, tackling each with a combination of efficiency and gusto. The wobbly boards over the back steps got sanded smooth and nailed down tight, the creaky root cellar door was oiled and reset, and a length of fence that had needed repair for more than a year was finally replaced.

Karl hummed while he worked, happy to do these minor projects. Allina watched him closely for a sign of the despair and bitterness he'd shown when he first arrived, but none appeared. Either her husband was better able to hide his emotions, or he'd come to a decision of some kind. Perhaps things weren't as dire as she'd thought.

But the coil of unease in Allina's belly told her otherwise.

She woke in the middle of the night to the light of the full moon streaming through the window and the comforting sounds of crickets and her husband's even breathing. Each inhale and exhale was deep and complete.

Allina wasn't fooled.

"You must tell me," she whispered, and reached for his hand. He gave no response except to wrap his large, warm palm around her smaller one.

Allina rolled onto her side to face him. In profile, Karl's face was a tight mask of pain. Wanting desperately to turn on the light, she hesitated. Some conversations were better had in the dark.

"I must find the strength to let you go," he said in a voice hoarse with grief. A lone tear slid down his cheek, silver in the moonlight.

Allina went still. *No, not yet. It's too soon.*

At the start of the war, he'd extracted a promise from her. She would take Katrine and flee Germany if it became too dangerous to remain. But as the months had passed, and as her life brimmed to overflowing with work and motherhood and worry for her husband, Allina forgot that pledge, conveniently stuffing it into a small, hopeful corner of her mind.

Now the time had come.

"Why?" she whispered, once she set panic aside. The single word was all Allina could manage. Her voice was shaking too much to say more.

Karl turned and settled into the pillow until they were nose to nose. He didn't answer at first, so Allina waited, breathing in the warm, yeasty scent of him while he ran fingers through her hair.

"I won't be able to protect you for much longer," he finally whispered. His eyes were black and hollow in the dim light.

Goose bumps raised on the backs of her arms. Allina looked over his shoulder and out the window to focus on the glowing moon. "Of course not. You're in Prague," she reasoned, with deliberate misunderstanding. "And the world is on fire. Still, I'm safer here than most other places."

On that point, she was right. When news of the air raids began circulating last summer, there were rumors, and then more than rumors, that many of the larger cities were constructing safety bunkers. Steinhöring was a quiet village with few resources. Like a faithful hound, *Schwester* Ziegler had sprung into action, enlisting the soldiers' help to reinforce the roof and create a shelter in the building's cavernous basement. Scores of schedules, protocols, and drills had ensued, increasing each time news reports came in of new attacks. Berlin. Heilbronn. Essen. Mannheim. Cologne. Bremen. Duisburg. And then last month, an attack on the ports at Wilhelmshaven in broad daylight . . .

A shudder ran through her. She'd never grow accustomed to it. Still, the odds were better here. The British had little interest in Hochland Home or Steinhöring.

"My reasoning has nothing to do with the war," Karl said, reading her mind. "Not directly."

What, then, had she missed? He was trying to ease some terrible blow by portioning out the truth in small bites, just as he'd done from the beginning. It was as maddening a character trait as it was endearing. Allina accepted her husband's need to protect her, yet she was blindsided. Had she grown soft because of her love for Karl von Strassberg?

"Why now?" When he didn't respond, she gripped his arm and shook it. "If you send us away, I must know. Why now?"

A long minute passed as he stared at her with a bleak smile. "You said it best, just weeks after we met, my heart," Karl said. He wrapped a tendril of her hair around his finger, tugging it gently before placing it with care onto the pillow. "The madness cannot end while he lives."

Allina's heart began thudding loudly in her ears. Perhaps it would stop altogether. Or maybe it wasn't that her heart would stop, but that time itself would cease to flow.

Time seemed to run backward as Allina relived the trajectory of their lives. She saw Karl on the night they'd met in the nursery, and his compassion for her tears. She relived the moment—the terror and the hope—on that cold winter afternoon when he'd met Otto and the other children, and then persuaded her to steal files for his secret project. She saw Karl on their wedding day, and on the morning after she'd given birth. Her logical, sophisticated husband had taken their baby into his arms, dropped into a chair, and quietly fallen apart.

Allina wished desperately they could slip back to any of those times, or to stroll again through the gardens at Bayreuth. Anything to pull him away from the precipice he seemed hell-bent on launching himself over. The resolve in his eyes told her there was nothing she could do to change his mind.

"Why must it be you?" she whispered as he gathered her in his arms.

For the next hour, and while Katrine slept blissfully unaware, Karl explained to Allina why it had to be him. He spoke about the conditions at Theresienstadt, about the hundreds who had died already and the thousands more who likely would, about the lice and the rats, and the men and women crammed ten to a room trying desperately to keep clean without soap or running water. He talked about Jockel, the newly appointed

Obergruppenführer, who'd sneered as he'd denied all attempts at securing extra food and blankets for the coming winter. Everyone at Theresienstadt was slowly starving. Last week, a brawl had broken out in the middle of the street. A dozen women had fought over potato peelings unearthed from the garbage pile.

"I looked into the faces of these women and realized any one of them could have been you," Karl murmured against her hair in a creaking voice that made her stomach twist. "Had my grandmother made a different choice, I might have been destined for Theresienstadt."

By the time he finished, Allina's throat burned with guilt. Here she was, tucked away in Hochland Home, turning a blind eye to what happened around her. While Karl had not offered to share the more brutal details of his work, she'd never pushed him. She hadn't wanted to know. How lonely her husband's existence must have been these past two years.

Allina reminded him of the children he'd smuggled out of the country, but he rejected that small comfort. Instead, he insisted on telling her about the hundreds he had allowed to die, and all those who would follow, at camps like Dachau and Buchenwald. And now, he and Markus were in charge of turning Theresienstadt over, into an internment camp. The horrors they'd seen were only the beginning. When they'd begun their work, Karl thought he could help, but the situation was beyond that now.

As devastating as those details were, the self-loathing in his voice was worse. Karl was wrecked with guilt. It was destroying him.

"Listen to me," Allina urged, cupping his face in her hands. "We could escape together. No, don't shake your head. We can leave, the three of us."

Karl turned away. "No."

She grabbed his arm, shook him roughly, as if the pressure of her hands could force some sense into him. "You've made arrangements for hundreds of others—"

"No, Allina."

"You've done enough," she pleaded. "More than most. There must be someone else—"

"Damn it, I said no!" He pulled away so abruptly that Allina tumbled onto the floor. By the time she'd scrambled to her feet, Karl was at the window, bracing himself against the ledge with arms that trembled. Head bowed, his breathing was rough and low, like a wounded dog's.

She walked up behind him, laid a hand on the center of his back. His nightshirt was soaked. There was more he hadn't told her, and, God help her, perhaps it was better not to know. But she couldn't leave him like this.

"Tell me."

Karl shook his head, hesitating. He only conceded after she begged, and then he spoke to the window and not her, in the high, broken voice of a much younger man.

"We were out on patrol in the neighborhoods last week," he said, "at the direction of *Obergruppenführer* Jockel. We'd clear out apartment buildings one day, then go back the next to make sure no one was missed."

Shaking, Allina rubbed his back, encouraging him to continue.

"One of my men found a little boy, tucked away in a cupboard," Karl said, looking down at his bare feet. "Hiding. He was Katrine's age, maybe a bit older. No more than three. And pale. Sickly. Jockel was with us when we found him. He looked the boy over with those cold, dead eyes of his and told me to take care of it."

No. The sour tang of copper rose at the back of her throat. She closed her eyes, trying to fend off the prickly dizziness.

"I pretended to misunderstand him," Karl said with a sharp laugh. "I picked up the boy and headed for the door, thinking I might sneak him to a family I'd met on the next street, or . . . I don't know. I don't know what I was thinking. There was nowhere to take him."

Karl turned to face her. His face was destroyed, eyes swollen with grief.

"Jockel called me back. I could see it in his eyes—the desire to test me. The need to make an example. He gave me his gun. Joked that mine was obviously not working properly."

"What did you do?" Allina whispered, although she already knew.

"I turned him toward the window," Karl said. He closed his eyes. "I told him to look outside, at the trees and the sky. I wanted the last thing he saw . . ."

Breaking down, Karl dropped to the floor. He curled into a ball and rocked, like a child or a madman. The force of his sobs seemed to shake the walls of their bedroom.

Allina remained frozen only inches from her husband, too sick with shock to offer comfort. She'd been a fool, naïve and willfully blind. Given all that had happened, everything she'd experienced, she should have known it would come to this. He'd warned her countless times in his own way, hinting at the horrors, giving everything but the words.

Karl von Strassberg's course had been set, much as Allina's had, years ago. All the wishing in the world wouldn't change things.

After a few seconds marked by his wrenching sobs, Karl held out a hand. Allina recoiled. It was instinct, and only a second's pause, but he caught it. She saw her horror reflected in the pain in his face.

Karl's smile was awful, a garish parody. "Yes," he choked out. "Exactly. You see it now, don't you? I've become what we hate." He held both hands out to her, palms facing upward, beseeching.

"How can I be your husband? How can I be a father to our child?"

Allina ran to Karl and embraced him. She wasn't strong enough to pull him off the ground. He refused to return to their bed. She remained on the floor with her arms and legs wrapped around her husband, as if doing so might keep him safe. They did not speak for the rest of the night, but Karl allowed Allina to hold him as he grieved for the life he'd taken, and for the man he'd become.

Morning came too soon. As the first feeble rays of heather light peeked through the curtains, they dragged themselves off the floor and into bed. Despite her exhaustion, Allina was unable to sleep. Grief was present in a bone-deep weariness and the burning heaviness in the center of her chest. She saw it in the dark bruises beneath her husband's eyes. His face was softer this morning, though, and more at peace, now that he'd bared his soul.

"There's nothing I can do to atone" were the first words he whispered when he turned to her.

Allina's heart was breaking. She had no reply to this, nothing that would mitigate his actions, and no way to convince him otherwise.

"Markus agrees with me," he said. "We must act now, before we fall completely out of favor." Karl explained that Jockel was convinced he and Markus had gone soft. Requests for food and blankets had tested the commander's patience. Even Karl's most recent actions had not suffi-ciently proved his loyalty. Jockel was watching every move.

"How will you do it?" Allina asked.

Karl shook his head. "That's not important. All that matters is your safety. If we fail, I must know you and our child will survive. Grant me that. Please."

He ran a hand very slowly down her side, from her shoulder to the curve of her hip. It was a tentative touch, a butterfly caress that made her shiver, but so measured and deliberate that Allina realized he was trying to memorize her.

The tears came then, and they rolled down her cheeks. There was nothing else to do but give her husband the gift of acceptance. "When?"

"Not long," he answered. "Six weeks on the outside. Likely less."

"Where will you send us?"

"To my aunt, in Switzerland." Those broad shoulders sagged. "I've already contacted Adele. Everything's arranged."

He told her, also, of one final goal: an attempt to smuggle another group of fifty Jewish children out of the country. If all went according to plan, they would be transported to Basel within days of Allina's arrival.

"Adele will need your help," he said. "She won't be able to manage without you."

Allina could tell from his wheedling that he meant to lighten their conversation. She gave in because it was what he needed, but Allina knew the truth. Her husband was trying to give her a purpose, and to share in it. It would be his parting gift.

Their third and last day was filled with simple pleasures, ones that slipped away as swiftly as the clouds that passed overhead. They spent most of it outdoors and shared a picnic lunch at the edge of the sunflower field, stemming back sadness for Katrine's sake. While his daughter napped, Karl explained the tasks Allina had to complete before her escape. Ever efficient, he'd drawn up a list. She was grateful for that; Allina found she couldn't concentrate on a thing he said, so intent she was on listening to the sound of his voice. He seemed to understand, but drilled the basics into her head nonetheless, repeating them at least a dozen times: *My office will make an emergency call about Adele's recent illness, with a request that you visit. Once Schwester Ziegler receives the call, you must arrange to be in Basel within forty-eight hours.* And the most crucial, albeit difficult directive: *Until then, you must go about your work as you normally do. No one can suspect.*

Late in the afternoon, after putting Katrine to bed, they spent their final minutes together strolling through the garden. Lacing his fingers with hers, Allina watched the sun set in a glorious burst of flame.

If only they could have another day. "Will I see you again, before?" she asked.

"Only if it's safe." He'd come to her if there was no possibility of repercussions afterward, Karl explained, and no obvious link between a visit and his mission. Every item of correspondence, every move he made, was now under Jockel's scrutiny. The commander might not be the smartest of men, but he had a rat's cunning nose.

"Our plan is dangerous, but there's a good chance we'll succeed." His lips were warm against her palm when he drew it to his mouth. "When we do, once things settle down, I'll send for you. Maybe then . . ." He shrugged and looked away.

Maybe then you'll be able to forgive yourself.

Allina pushed the thought aside, pushed everything aside except the need to hold him close before she let him go. She stood on tiptoe and pulled his face to hers, putting all her hope and terror into the hard kiss.

"I love you."

"I know," he said, and shook his head in wonder. He drew her into his arms, holding on so tightly her ribs creaked. Allina buried her nose in his shirt and filled her lungs with his scent.

"If I fail, tell her what you will about me," he choked out against her hair.

Allina clung to him and cried. The ache in her chest was so intense it felt as if she would fly apart, that only the pressure from his body kept her intact. She nodded when Karl whispered that he loved her and kissed her again. He wiped her tears and pushed her gently away before driving off into the night.

When Allina went back to work the next day, she escaped into the office, finding solace in paperwork and a welcome respite from the children. After a week of relative peace, however, she realized the truth behind her intense need for solitude. She was grieving alone, for her husband, all their lies and duplicity, and for every Hochland Home child she'd never be able to help. Worse, by separating herself from the children and Rilla, she was also pushing away any small moments of joy or friendship she'd found here.

From that moment on, Allina forced herself to take up her duties, to spend more time in the classroom and with her friend. She thought she masked her unease well, but Rilla seemed to pick up on it almost immediately. Her friend watched Allina closely, although she asked no questions. Still, when the awkward uncertainty swirled between them, Allina took her friend's hand and told another lie: "I'm only a little tired. Don't worry. I'm fine."

On her afternoons off, Allina kept busy with the tasks on Karl's instruction sheet. She sneaked out memorandums and work lists and photographs from Hochland Home, storing them in the wood box he'd given her, alongside the letters from her father that held the truth about her family. Karl had suggested she burn anything linking Allina von Strassberg to Allina Gottlieb or Allina Strauss, but she couldn't bear to do so. On this one request, she rebelled.

She packed a large suitcase, selecting clothes she could alter or layer for use across the seasons. She took a box of items Karl had set aside—heavy silver candlesticks and old gold coins and a good amount of his mother's jewelry—and drove to Munich to sell them at the list of shops he'd provided. As he'd directed, Allina divided up the reichsmarks into small packets, sewing several into the pockets of her coat, stuffing others into the lining of her purse, and mailing the bulk to his aunt Adele, nestled in wax paper at the bottom of a fruitcake tin.

Allina made an appointment at a beauty salon for mid-October, and one later in the month with her husband's solicitor, taking care to note the details of each in both the journal she maintained at Hochland Home and the personal diary she kept at home. She purchased tickets to a November performance of Strauss's *Friedenstag* at Munich's National Theater and affixed the tickets to the mirror above her dressing table. Allina knew she wouldn't make any of these events or appointments. That was the point. The events helped project a smoke screen of normalcy and forward thinking. If Karl failed and the SS came to the Sunflower House or Hochland Home to search for clues about her whereabouts, they'd find nothing incriminating. Instead, they'd see small bits of evidence that might be enough to give them pause. It could buy her an extra day or two, ones Adele might need to put an escape plan in place.

The only sources of joy during her first weeks of waiting were Katrine, and Karl's letters, which continued to arrive faithfully each afternoon. Allina would pull their daughter into her lap every night and read the letters aloud, since he always included a message for Katrine from her devoted papa. She'd pore over each letter well into the night for a hidden message, but never found anything that stood out. Karl's letters were loving and full of humor, childhood stories, and memories of their courtship. They were emotional and passionate, but nothing more than letters from a man who missed his family and wanted to remember better times.

So she waited.

By the beginning of the fourth week, the uncertainty began to frazzle her nerves. Allina woke each morning with a swirling emptiness in her stomach. Her first conscious thought was always: *Will the call come today?*

Her Hochland Home duties provided less and less contentment. She found herself snapping at the staff for no reason. Poor Wendeline dissolved in a puddle of tears one morning when Allina dumped a folded basket of laundry onto the floor, demanding that the simple, unassuming *Schwester* refold it.

Worse, Allina found it hard to continue the ruse with the children. As the days passed, she became increasingly short-tempered, and that irritation weighed on her conscience. They deserved better. Ever sensitive, the class responded with a series of small misbehaviors that escalated quickly. By the end of the month, her brood was an unwieldy circus of shouting, crying, and skinned knees and elbows.

Rilla picked up on her distress and, in her kind, typical way, took on extra shifts and wrangled paperwork off Allina's tottering pile. At first, she seemed gratified that Allina trusted her enough with the extra duties, but as Allina surrendered more without argument, Rilla began shooting long, assessing looks over the breakfast table.

"Are you pregnant?" Rilla asked one morning in the break room over tea and biscuits.

The shock made Allina drop her teacup.

"Wh-why would you say that?" she asked, and hurried to the sideboard to get a cloth to clean up the mess.

"You've seemed so far away for weeks," Rilla said. "I wondered."

Allina was certain she wasn't pregnant. Her courses had come a week ago. Still, Rilla didn't need to know that. She took her time to mop up the table before answering. It was the perfect explanation, so she let a tiny smile escape as she sat back down.

"It's too soon to know for sure."

Rilla chuckled and patted her hand.

By the next morning, word had gotten around. As it served her purpose, Allina nodded at the murmurs of congratulations from mothers and *Schwestern* alike. She even managed to laugh at Berta, who was recovering from the difficult delivery of her fourth child but managed a catty comment about the efficiency of Karl's pistol over breakfast.

Berta never missed a chance to go for the throat.

"Your husband's been busy," she said later that evening, over dinner. "I received a letter from my sweet Tedrick this afternoon. It sounds like *Gruppenführer* von Strassberg is out at all hours of the night in Prague." Arching one eyebrow, Berta slanted Allina a knowing, blue glance. "It's a wonder he has enough energy to perform his daytime duties."

A soft chorus of gasps rose from the table.

"Every officer must do his best to ensure the future of the Reich, of course, but your husband certainly seems ... *committed* to his nighttime activities," Berta added with a smirk. "I warned you, didn't I? He's grown tired of you, just as I predicted."

Rilla—sweet, loyal Rilla—jumped to her feet. "That's rich, coming from you. You've worked through half the regiment single-handedly."

Allina clamped a hand on her friend's arm, begging Rilla to sit down. The shocked titters at the table were the least of her concerns. If Karl's men were paying attention to his movements in Prague, then it's likely his superiors had noticed as well.

"You're awfully quiet, *Schwester* von Strassberg," Berta added, drawling out her last name in a lilting voice that made Allina go still. "Have you nothing to say? No, of course not." She slanted Allina a shrewd, assessing stare. "What secretive creatures you two have always been, slipping away into the gardens when he visits, even while on duty. We've all seen you whispering in the corners."

There were confused looks at the table now, and raised eyebrows.

Allina stood so swiftly the chair legs squeaked on the floor tiles. "We'll discuss this outside," she said, with a saccharine smile. "I'm sure our table mates have had enough of your nonsense." She walked for the door without a backward glance, relieved at the swift click-clack of Berta's heels behind her.

When Berta followed her into the hallway, Allina grabbed her arm, and advanced until they stood nose to nose, swiftly enough that the blonde hit the wall behind her and gasped.

"I've no intention of discussing my husband or my marriage with you," Allina snapped.

Berta's eyes went wide before she offered a cold, calculating smile—one that sent a shiver of dread down Allina's spine.

"There's been talk amongst the men," she hissed as the flush rose in her cheeks. "About what you two have been doing. The men talk to me, you see. They tell me everything. You're not who you say you are. I'm sure of it."

Had the men suspected Karl's clandestine activities? Or was it his bloodline, or hers, that was suddenly under suspicion? There were too many secrets to keep track of. Berta's piercing blue eyes pinned Allina, waiting for her to crack, and making it nearly impossible to breathe. But then Berta's eyelid twitched. The catty smile faltered. Berta was fishing—she had a knack for sensing weakness, then using innuendo to make her victims reveal more than they should.

"You know nothing about me, my husband, or our marriage," Allina answered, willing the quiver out of her voice. "But you and I—we both know what *you* are, don't we?"

Berta's head snapped back.

"I pity you, Berta," Allina said. "Your jealousy has been obvious for years. How lonely you must be."

Berta's eyes filled, but this was no time for sympathy—she recovered quickly, yanking her arm from Allina's tight grip.

"You're not who you say you are," she repeated in a trembling voice. "I'll prove it soon enough."

Berta broke away and hurried down the hall.

Allina exhaled a shuddering breath. Karl was risking so much to save the children at Theresienstadt. Berta was onto them both. If she was right, and his men suspected something, they were doomed. Time was running out, the walls were closing in, and Allina had no way to get a message to Karl without risking their safety. Despite her fear for her husband, Allina hoped his call would come sooner, rather than later.

CHAPTER 32

Autumn 1941

ALLINA

Rilla had never looked happier.

"He got down on one knee," she said, gray eyes sparkling. Pressing a palm over her heart, she reached for Alex's arm. A flush crept up the man's neck and flooded his face with color as he brought his fiancée's knuckles to his lips.

Every woman at the breakfast table, along with a dozen others who stood in a ring around them, dissolved in a chorus of coos and sighs.

It was as if the transformation from sweet girl to woman in full bloom had happened overnight. Allina reached across the table to pat her friend's hand. "I'm thrilled for you both!" she shouted, after the group erupted in conversation, squawking like so many geese. As the questions swirled around them—*Have you set a date? Will there be time for a honeymoon?* and most important, *What will you wear?*—Rilla smiled at Allina and mouthed, "I'll tell you everything later."

To the group, she held up a single hand. "We plan on a simple ceremony. There's no time for anything else. We'll go to the registrar's office on Saturday."

Another bright cloud of chatter erupted, but Rilla stopped all lines of questioning with an airy wave. "I don't give a fig about my dress. Besides,

Alex must return to Prague on Monday. We're lucky he could get three days' leave." She turned to Allina. "You'll come to the registrar's office, won't you? You'll stand up for us?"

Allina's throat tightened. "Of course I will."

"I wish Karl could be here," Rilla said, giving her hand a squeeze. "Alex told me he wasn't able to get away."

That bit of information was enough to make Allina start in her chair. When she turned her attention toward Alex, he wouldn't meet her eyes. Rilla's beloved became instantly enraptured with the face of his watch.

The rapid click-clack of *Schwester* Ziegler's heels against the floor tiles preceded the head nurse's arrival, as usual. When she broke through the crowd, her attention went straight to Allina. Her mouth was pinched in a sour pucker, and her eyes were sharp.

"We've just had a telephone call from Prague," she said. "I'm afraid I have a bit of concerning news from your husband."

The group inhaled a communal gasp. The head nurse raised her eyes heavenward and shooed them away with a muttered complaint about unnecessary drama. She sat down beside Allina.

"I'll come straight to the point," she said. "Your husband's aunt is ill, gravely so, I'm sorry to say. Some sort of lung ailment. The *Gruppenführer* asks that you attend her immediately."

In more than a month of wild imaginings, Allina had been certain she'd have to manufacture shock or concern. She'd practiced her response in the mirror. Yet here the moment was, and she had no need to pretend. Her heart was beating so hard she felt like it would leap from her chest.

"I see," Allina whispered.

"You've got excellent nursing instincts," Ziegler added. "I'm sure she'll be grateful to have you there."

The head nurse gave her the rest of the details in her usual no-nonsense manner. Allina was to travel to Basel by train as soon as she was able, preferably within a day. Adele's servant would meet her at the station in Basel. Allina could stay as long as was necessary, although the head nurse hoped two weeks would be sufficient.

"Rilla is capable of attending to your duties while you're away," she added. "Wendeline can help, and I'll have Marta pitch in, if necessary." She turned to Rilla and frowned. "That will cut your wedding festivities short. I'd hoped to give you Sunday as a free day. I'm afraid there's no alternative."

"It doesn't matter," Rilla said. She came around the table and gave Allina a sturdy hug, enveloping her in the scent of lavender shampoo. "Silly goose, don't you worry about a thing," she whispered into Allina's ear. "Alex and I will see you through."

"Very good," Ziegler said. "I'll leave Allina in your capable hands. Thanks to you both."

As soon as the head nurse left the room, Allina burst into tears.

"Oh no, no, no," Rilla insisted, pulling her back into a soft embrace. "You mustn't worry. Everything will be fine."

"I know it will," Allina whispered, lying to her friend another time. "But I'm sad I'll miss your wedding." When Rilla pulled a handkerchief from her pocket, Allina allowed her to wipe at her tears.

"You should leave tonight," Alex said. "You can catch the evening train at Karlsruhe. I'm happy to provide escort."

When Alexander's glance met hers, Allina saw compassion there, and sadness—and a flash of sharp intelligence that gave him away.

Rilla missed the look, so intent was she on lending Allina comfort. "You see?" she said, "How lucky is it that my Alex is here, today of all days, and free to take you to the station."

It became apparent immediately why Karl had advised her to pack beforehand. The rest of the day passed as the wind blows before a summer storm.

The house needed straightening, and cleaning settled her mind like nothing else. Once the housework was done, doubt crept in and Allina found herself second-guessing the plan. She checked and rechecked each item in her suitcase and fussed with the packets of reichsmarks she'd sewn into the lining of her purse and coat. Nearly an hour was wasted on the clues she'd planted in the house weeks before. The symphony tickets, her journal, even the appointment cards from the salon and solicitor were laid out for all to see. Were they too obvious? After shifting them from dressing table to hall table to the den and back again, Allina realized she had put them back in their original positions. Hang it all. What was done, was done. She took a half hour to bathe and dress before leading Katrine into the garden, where they spent a few precious minutes in the sun, cheeks pressed to the warm, fuzzy faces of the sunflowers. When might it be safe to return to the Sunflower House and the field Karl's grandmother had planted two generations ago?

Allina returned to Hochland Home at two o'clock with an hour to say good-bye. This was just as well because, despite her tiredness, she was jumpy as a cat. Katrine, who picked up on her frazzled nerves, was cranky and whining.

Rilla met them at the door to their classroom with her sunny smile.

"The children want to see you," she said. Rilla smiled and wrapped an arm around Allina's waist as she guided her into the room.

"Surprise!" the children yelled in unison. The little ones held up pieces of paper with brightly painted scenes in their hands. Wendeline beamed with pride from the back of the room.

"I told them you were going on a trip," Rilla said, plucking Katrine from her arms, "and that you were sad to leave Hochland Home for a few weeks. We painted happy pictures to cheer you up, didn't we, children?"

A chorus of cheers and sibilant *yeses* filled the room.

"Take your time," Rilla murmured, giving her a discreet nudge forward, "while I get us a cup of tea."

Allina was too tired to cry. The tears were there behind her eyes and at the back of her throat, but her body didn't have the energy to weep. Instead she picked her way among the desks, kneeling to speak with each child as they explained their handiwork. There were pictures of flower gardens and sunny skies, of dogs and cats and birds, of children playing and *Schwestern* tending, all painted in loud, happy colors. She praised each creation as chubby hands pressed them into her arms, and caressed pink cheeks and golden hair in silent good-byes.

Rilla came back into the room soon enough, with a now-giggling Katrine in her arms and a cup of prescription-strength tea.

"Sit down," she ordered. "Drink your tea while Wendeline gives the children their afternoon snack."

When Alex appeared in the doorway, Allina felt his presence as a physical jolt.

She couldn't speak. She just stood there, while her gaze took in Rilla, and then Alex, and, finally, the classroom.

Her time here was over. She'd wasted her last hour.

Allina reached into her purse for a parcel and handed it to Rilla. "I thought you might want to wear these," she whispered, as Rilla ripped away the paper wrapping, revealing the lace veil and gloves *Schwester* Ziegler had given Allina on her wedding day. When her friend's eyes overflowed with tears, she knew she'd made the right decision.

"They're perfect. I haven't had time to think about finding anything."

"I'm sorry I'll miss the wedding," Allina whispered. *I'm sorry for everything. For all the secrets and for not being a better friend, for abandoning the children, and for leaving you here, alone, to finish the work we began together.*

"You'll see each other again soon enough," Alex said, dashing over from the doorway. "We need to leave now, or you'll miss your train."

He clapped a hand on Allina's shoulder, making her jump again. "*Schwester* Ziegler had me load your suitcase into the car. It's time."

The ride to Karlsruhe, according to Alex, was a four-hour drive—hours which were oddly both the longest and shortest ones of her life. Alex seemed intent on giving her privacy; he neither attempted to trade pleasantries nor asked questions. The engine's purr soothed Katrine to sleep, leaving Allina alone with the contradictory jumble of her thoughts.

She'd come to Hochland Home a brutalized prisoner, then became both witness, and participant, to its horrors. Nevertheless, Allina had found satisfaction in the work and her ability to improve the lives of the children. She'd helped save dozens from extermination, thanks to the rehabilitation program. But there were hundreds, perhaps thousands more across Germany whom she would never have the chance to help. And what would become of those who'd improved, who thrived? They'd go on to lives in service to their Führer. Perhaps she was no better than the rest of the *Schwestern* at Hochland Home.

She'd found friendship and love here, but was leaving everything but her daughter behind, perhaps even her husband. Karl had gone to all lengths to protect her. Would he go to those same lengths to save himself?

Allina shivered. All thoughts down that particular road were hell-bent for bedlam.

Remember, her mind instructed as the car sped down the Reichsautobahn. *Remember how the birch and linden trees explode with color in autumn and how blue the sky is today. Remember the children. Remember what happened here . . .*

Allina jolted awake.

"You've been out for two hours," Alex said. "We're about forty minutes away."

It seemed impossible that she'd fallen asleep, but now that she was awake, Allina couldn't stand another minute of silence.

"What did he tell you?" she asked. "How much do you know?"

"As much, and as little, as you do," Alex answered with a grim twitch of the lips. "The less I know, the better. We each do our part, but alone."

So there was nothing Alex could tell her, no reassurances he could make. Karl would keep them all in the dark, for their sakes. It was maddening, what the man did to protect those he loved.

"Am I to believe that your three days' leave were coincidence?"

Alex threw back his head and laughed. "The paperwork came in two weeks ago. I requested leave to come to Rilla immediately, but your husband asked me to delay. He's the only man I'd do that for." He winked at her. "And that's a secret you and I will take to our graves. Rilla might kill me if she knew."

That he could joke about this was beyond absurd, but Allina found herself chuckling.

"It's going to hurt her the most if I don't return," she said, as laughter turned to tears. As all the secrets she'd kept had hurt her friend. Rilla had always been aware of more than she let on. And she'd always forgiven Allina for her lies of omission.

"My future wife is stronger than she seems." He took Allina's hand and squeezed it. "She loves you, but I think you know that. Don't think she'd accuse you so quickly, or forget your kindness. Neither will I."

The tears came in full force, and she let them roll down her cheeks. "You'll take care of her?"

"Always."

The rest of the drive was in a more comfortable silence. Once they arrived at the Karlsruhe Station, Alex handled her luggage and the tickets, leaving her to attend her daughter, who was still sleepy and, thankfully, docile.

His efficiency turned out to be necessary. As fog rolled into the station, a last-minute track change sent everyone scrambling. At last, Allina found herself in front of the right train with a scant five minutes to spare and the conductor urging everyone aboard.

"I must leave you now," Alex said, "after I fulfill one final instruction from your husband."

Before she could ask, Alex cupped her face and gave her a solemn kiss on the forehead.

When Alex pulled away, his cheeks were bright red. "He told me to do my best. I'm afraid it's all I can manage."

Allina choked out a teary laugh.

He got down on his knees to speak to her daughter. "Your papa told me to give you a kiss, as he couldn't be here to give you one himself," he said. When the little one nodded solemnly, he planted a soft one on her cheek.

"Please board!" the conductor yelled.

There was no more time for tears. Alex handed the conductor her suitcase and helped them up the stairs.

"Have faith!" Alex shouted as the train chugged away slowly. "God willing, you'll see him sooner rather than later."

Allina held her daughter close as they waved at Alex and watched him disappear into the fog.

CHAPTER 33

Binningen, Switzerland

ALLINA

Allina arrived at Adele's home at half past midnight, feeling bruised and so worn out she swayed on the steps.

When the door opened, she was shocked into silence.

Karl's beloved aunt was a far cry from the tower of strength she'd anticipated. Adele von Strassberg was the tiniest human being Allina had ever seen. The woman looked slight enough to blow away with the next stiff wind. Each facial feature was classic but also in miniature. She had Karl's aristocratic cheekbones, although the familial resemblance ended there. Adele's ivory skin was smooth for a woman in later years, and she had a sharp chin and auburn eyebrows that arched wickedly above amber eyes. With her head crowned in pin curls, and wrapped in a green satin dressing gown that pooled onto the floor, Adele seemed more forest fairy than human.

"Come in, my dear," Adele said as she waved her over the threshold. "You're worn through, and no wonder. Elias can bring in your bags," she added, gesturing to the dark-eyed, rangy young man who'd met Allina at the train station.

Adele ushered Allina down the hall. "Let's get you upstairs to your bedroom. You don't mind waiting until morning to see the house, do you?"

Adele pointed a slender finger at Katrine, who was deep asleep and flung over Allina's shoulder like a sack of flour. "With luck, this little one will allow you a few hours' rest. Can I bring you anything? Some toast and warm milk, perhaps?"

Gratitude and relief filled her, and Allina's legs nearly buckled. She declined the offer of food and followed the older woman upstairs, limbs growing heavier with each step. Her bedroom was done in massive amounts of ivory lace, but Allina was too bleary-eyed to take in most of the details. There was, however, a small trundle bed beside hers, for Katrine.

Adele pulled the toddler gently from Allina's arms and nudged her toward the bed.

"Sit down," she whispered.

Allina sank onto the plush mattress with a sigh. Her eyes fluttered closed as she surrendered to fatigue and the muffled sounds of Adele von Strassberg at work: the soft wisp of cloth against cloth as she slid Katrine under the covers, the purr of a suitcase zipper, and Adele's sweet humming.

Cool fingers cupped her cheek, nudging Allina toward consciousness.

"Let's get you comfortable," Adele murmured.

Allina let the older woman help her out of her clothes and into a nightgown, sinking into the gentle touch and the warm scents of vanilla and talcum powder. When Adele wished her good night and turned out the light, she managed a mumbled thank-you. Rolling to the center of the mattress, Allina pulled the comforter over her body and fell asleep.

She woke in the same position hours later, just after dawn and to the sound of her daughter's demanding little voice.

"Hungry, Mama."

Cracking an eye open, Allina saw two bright blue eyes peeking over the edge of the mattress.

"Hungry," the little one said again.

Allina's stomach gurgled in response.

Katrine giggled and pointed at Allina's belly.

Miracle of miracles, her daughter didn't seem concerned by their new surroundings.

As the sleep fog cleared, questions began circling in Allina's mind. *How long would they be here? When would the children arrive?* And more important: *How much did Adele know about Karl's plan?*

Heaving herself over the edge of the mattress, Allina nearly tumbled to the floor. Half of her body had fallen asleep. Groaning as the pinpricks spread through her legs, she rubbed at her feet to wake them.

"Mama, hungry," Katrine reminded helpfully.

"I'm hungry too, kitten." Allina pointed to their suitcase, lying open on the floor. "Pick out your clothes. We'll wash and change and see what Auntie Adele has for breakfast."

In twenty minutes, due in no small part to Katrine's eagerness, Allina managed to wash the necessary bits, dress them both, and tame her daughter's willful hair into braids. As they descended to the first floor, the yeasty scent of fresh-baked bread wafted up the stairs.

Katrine ran toward the blissful smell before Allina could stop her— and right into Adele, who was still in her dressing gown.

"Whom do we have here?" Adele called out, and picked up her great-niece. "Can this beauty be our Katrine?"

Suddenly shy, the little one giggled before burying her face in Adele's shoulder.

It was all so normal, so ordinary. Allina braced her hand on the wall for support. "I haven't thanked you," she said, throat tight with tears.

"Don't be ridiculous. You were dead on your feet last night." Adele said, eyebrows arching. "Besides, we're family." She set Katrine down and took the girl's hand, beckoning for Allina to follow. "We've much to discuss, but not in front of the child. Lisel has breakfast laid out. Let's get some food into you first. We'll talk after."

The three walked into the kitchen, where Adele introduced them to Lisel, a blond, round-cheeked young woman who served as her cook and personal assistant. The four ate family style on the butcher-block table, feasting on apple tart, sausage, cheese, and fresh-baked bread.

The food and Adele's easy familiarity tempered Allina's impatience to learn more about Karl's plan. By the end of the meal Katrine had settled in, and her happy chatter and giggles filled the room. She took a particular shine to Lisel, who answered a never-ending stream of questions about everything from the burnished copper pots that hung from the ceiling, to the birds chirruping in the tree outside the kitchen window, to the coil of blond braids wrapped around Lisel's head.

"It's no bother," Lisel said simply when Allina chided her daughter for asking so many questions. "I'm the eldest of nine. I've taken care of my brothers and sisters for as long as I can remember."

Twenty minutes were the outer reaches of her daughter's good behavior, after which Katrine hopped off her chair and proceeded to scramble around the kitchen table on all fours and bark like a puppy.

"Katrine," Lisel called out, cheeks dimpling, "would you like to go outside and see our garden? You can watch the birds take their morning bath if you're quiet."

The little blond head popped up. Quivering with excitement, she turned a begging gaze to Allina.

"Of course you can. Mind Lisel."

As soon as they were out the door, Adele took Allina's hand in a strong, bony grip. "Come. Let me show you the house," Adele said. "Then we'll have our chat."

When they entered Adele's parlor, Allina was dumbstruck. The room was— Frankly, she wasn't sure how she'd describe the room if asked. An antiques shop? A museum? A collector's lair? This parlor was nothing like the elegance and orderliness of the rest of the house. It was filled with ornate, obviously expensive furniture, but beyond that, every shelf and surface was crammed with silver tea sets and candlesticks, china and crystal, and enough artwork to make an antiques dealer claustrophobic.

"I receive all my guests here," Adele said with a grin. "What do you think of it?"

The truth hit in a flash. The room was crammed with enough precious objects that even repeat visitors wouldn't notice when a thing or two went missing.

"This is where you keep the pieces you sell," Allina said, "to pay for the children's transport out of Germany."

"Aren't you clever? Of course, the state of this room also helps maintain my reputation as a nutty old spinster," she said. "Karl was always partial to a pretty face, but I knew he'd marry a wife with brains as well. I take full credit for that."

The mention of his name was like an electric shock. Tears flooded Allina's vision.

Adele stood on tiptoe to pull her into a tight, surprisingly sturdy embrace. "I know, my dear," she whispered against her chest. "The waiting can be unbearable."

All her pain and fear—everything she'd held back for the last twenty-four hours, for the last month and more—poured out of Allina, rough and wild as an unchecked river, here in the parlor of a stranger who held her with the fierce protectiveness of a mother.

When the worst was over, Adele sat her down on a chaise longue. "Settle yourself," she commanded. "You can bear this. Karl tells me you're stronger than you know."

"But he's kept me in the dark." She gripped Adele's hand, begging. "Please, what did he tell you?"

"As little as he could get away with," Adele said drily. "That's how my nephew operates." Straightening her spine, she spoke in a clipped voice that brooked no argument.

"There will likely be resolution within a fortnight. We won't hear from him until the time is set. I know," she said, to Allina's moan of distress. "It will be hard to wait. But you'll get the sleep you need these next few days, as you're stuck tending to me on my deathbed." Adele snorted. "I shall make a miraculous recovery, of course. We'll plan some outings for you and the child toward the end of the week. You must show your face around town."

"Then what? What will happen after—?"

"We've prepared for any outcome," Adele interrupted in a less-sure voice, one that cracked and made Allina's stomach sink. She explained the necessity of faking Allina's return to Hochland Home, while she and Katrine remained here in hiding, or out of the country if it became prudent. Even if Karl succeeded—if Hitler was eliminated—the power structure in Germany would likely remain precarious for some time.

"He'll send for you and Katrine once it's safe," Adele said. "You must surrender to what will be. Trust him, my dear. All plans are in place. They have been for months."

"What will we do if he fails?" Allina whispered.

"We won't think about that now." Adele smoothed the hair back from Allina's face. "You must focus your mind on what you can do today. Otherwise you'll go mad."

The great monstrosity of a grandfather clock chimed nine o'clock. Its

ponderous *ding-dang-dongs* echoed throughout the parlor, as certain as
Adele's advice.

Once again, there was nothing to do but submit to the circumstances
of her life.

Allina took hold of herself, and shook her head to clear it. "You're
right. How can I help?"

Adele's amber gaze turned misty. "My nephew chose well. I'd love your
assistance with the children. Karl says you've a knack with them, and one
is in a sad state. She hasn't spoken since her arrival."

Another shock, and this one had her heart hammering in her chest.
"The children are here? Already?"

Adele's smile was proud. "Forty-six Jewish children arrived last week.
I housed more than a dozen for the first few days. It was as busy as a
train station," she said, rolling her amber eyes. "Thank God, Binningen is
a sleepy little village. We couldn't have managed sneaking them in and out
otherwise. All but two have settled into new homes."

The woman was a Valkyrie, disguised as an elf. "Where are they?"

"Come with me." Adele sprang up with the energy of someone twenty
years younger and walked to the far side of the room, which was dom-
inated by the ancient grandfather clock. Dropping to her knees, she
wedged a slender hand behind the clock's base. With a sharp click, the
clock unlatched from the wall, revealing a narrow doorway.

"My parlor holds more than one secret," Adele said with a wink. Behind the door was a staircase leading to the cellar. Hitching up the hem
of her robe, she bent to retrieve a flashlight from the top step. "I sing to
let them know it's safe," she said, switching on the light and handing it to
Allina. "Watch yourself. The stairs are steep."

They descended slowly to Adele's lilting, off-key version of "Here
Comes the Mouse." At the bottom of the staircase was a windowless, cavernous room bordered by a dozen cots. It was unfinished, with block walls
and a cement floor, but clean, and a row of hurricane lamps were set on
plain pine shelves affixed to the wall. They lent no warmth to the dampness, but gave off enough light to see by.

At the side of one of the cots stood a painfully thin girl of about nine
or ten, with a wan face and dark, mournful eyes. Dressed in a clean nightgown, she held hands with a smaller child who was lying on the cot and

staring blankly into space. The older girl smiled when she saw Adele; the younger remained unresponsive.

"Klára, this is my niece, Allina," Adele called out softly as they approached. "She's come to say hello. Perhaps she might even read to you and Sofie for a bit." Adele motioned toward a small stack of children's books on the shelf. "Would you like that?"

Klára nodded. The younger girl, Sofie, continued to stare at the wall.

"That's settled, then," Allina said, giving the girls a bright smile. "I adore books, and I'd love to read to you." She walked to the shelf and selected a volume of fairy tales by Hans Christian Andersen before perching on the bed next to the girls.

Adele grabbed the girls' meal tray, half eaten, and frowned. "Let's hope your reading helps these two work up their appetites. We must do better with lunch."

Allina stayed with the girls for the rest of the morning. Klára warmed to her quickly, enough that she forgot herself and leaned against her arm. Allina was careful not to touch Sofie for fear it might startle the child, but she included her in conversation, hoping the sound of her voice might help bring the girl back. It did not. Sofie remained as quiet as a ghost, and though her eyes seemed a bit more focused at times, they stayed on the wall.

The next five days were filled to the seams with activity. Allina spent mornings with her daughter and, thanks to Lisel's patient affection for the child, a good portion of each afternoon with Klára and Sofie. Sofie remained unresponsive, but Klára grew more animated as time passed. Her German was decent, and she was enamored of the stories. She asked questions about each and was comfortable enough on the second day to read aloud. Klára also revealed that she and her sister were alone in the world; they'd left Poland *after Mama and Papa disappeared two years ago.*

In the hours Allina wasn't occupied with the children, Adele lined up a list of chores to keep them both busy. The two women polished silver, aired out rooms, changed linens, and helped Lisel in the kitchen, often to the young woman's irritation. Allina called Hochland Home twice at

Adele's insistence, mostly to set the stage for the older woman's miraculous recovery. Rilla came on the line during the second call and regaled her with stories about the wedding. Allina's heart ached as she listened. She promised to return soon.

While amazed at Adele's stamina, Allina understood the frenzied activity was for both their sakes. Work meant less time to think, and fear for Karl was never far from her mind. It was only in the evenings, after putting the children to bed, that the two women spoke of him. Adele shared anecdotes of a boy's skinned knees and stubborn defiance. She cried when Allina told her about Karl's proposal and of the moment he met their newborn daughter. And the two wept together as Adele recalled her mother, Ekaterina—the country she left, the faith she had to abandon, and the secrets she'd kept, ones that had haunted her grandson and changed the course of all their lives.

The two women were careful to remain in this artificially constructed limbo. All stories of the past were welcome. Neither spoke about the future.

On Wednesday evening, a foster family came for Klára and Sofie—a young couple by the name of Bryner, who had a small farm outside Binningen but no children of their own. It was an uneasy parting for Allina. The hesitation in Klára's eyes made a lump form at the back of her throat.

"The Bryners are happy to have you stay with them," Adele said to Klára. Herr and Frau Bryner agreed with wide smiles.

Allina handed Klára the volume of fairy tales by Hans Christian Andersen. "A parting gift from me to you," Allina said. "You'll remember to read to Sofie each night, won't you?"

"Yes, ma'am." Klára clutched the book to her thin chest.

Then the miracle happened. A ghost of a smile played on Sofie's lips.

Allina sank to her knees and cupped Sofie's face in her hands. "You'd like that, would you?"

The little girl smiled again.

"My sister is getting better every day," Klára whispered. "She was just confused. And afraid. Last night, Sofie asked if we were dead."

A strained, painful silence filled the parlor as the four adults looked at each other, and then again at the children.

"Why would she think that, Klára?" Adele asked gently.

The little girl's ashy face paled further. "When we left Theresienstadt, they put us in a coffin. They told Sofie and me to be very quiet, or else we'd die for real. It was dark, and the ride here took forever, and we arrived in the middle of the night . . ." The girl shuddered before turning haunted eyes on Adele. "I'm ever so grateful to you, Frau von Strassberg, but the cellar is also very dark."

"You're not dead," Allina managed, though her throat was aching. She planted a soft kiss on Sofie's forehead. "You and Klára will have wonderful, long lives."

The two women kept smiles in place while the Bryners packed the girls into their car. They waved gaily as the family drove away. It was not until they returned to the parlor that Adele and Allina fell completely, hopelessly apart.

On Thursday morning at breakfast, Adele declared herself cured.

"Now that I'm recovering from my recent brush with death," she told Allina, flicking her fingers in the air, "it's time to show your face about town. You must do this in an ostentatious way. Have you brought a navy suit or dress, I hope?"

"Both," Allina replied.

"Choose whichever is most elegant," Adele ordered before Allina could ask why the color of her clothing should matter. "Dress your hair simply, in a chignon. Wear pearls if you have them. Put Katrine in her best clothes, too. I'll be up in twenty minutes."

Nonplussed, Allina did as she was told, and dressed in a fashionable navy suit. When Adele came into her room, the woman was holding the most astonishing hat Allina had ever seen. Done in glossy navy satin, the fussy confection was wide brimmed, plumed with navy and cream feathers, and trimmed with a dramatic polka-dotted veil.

"Pretty," Katrine cooed, chubby hands reaching for it.

"This hat," Adele said, holding it aloft as if it were a trophy and carefully out of the child's reach, "clearly belongs to the wife of an SS *Gruppenführer*. Everyone who sees this hat will remember you."

Allina's stomach twisted, for she guessed what instructions would come next.

"You must make your presence known today, and for the next several days," Adele continued as she pinned the hat to Allina's head at a daring angle. "People need to see you and hear you, so they will notice when you depart. Do you understand me?"

When Adele turned her toward the mirror, Allina nearly laughed. The hat was ridiculous, and not her style at all.

"Pretty Mama," Katrine said with a giggle.

"Rudeness doesn't come to you naturally," Adele continued. "If you cannot be a bitch, my dear, then maintain silence. And lift that chin of yours. There. Very good," Adele said when Allina complied. "You've no idea how arrogant a chin can make a woman." She painted Allina's lips a garish red before pulling the veil down over her face. "Don't worry. Elias will help you."

"Elias?" Allina asked faintly.

"He'll serve as your chauffeur. I've given him a list of cafés and shops," Adele said. "He will regale every shop owner with tales of your tender attention toward me and remind them you are the wife of my beloved nephew, *Gruppenführer* Karl von Strassberg."

"Wouldn't it be better if I kept a low profile, for your sake?" Allina asked hopefully.

Adele brushed a speck of lint off Allina's shoulder. "Absolutely not. Your presence about town will help maintain my reputation as a Nazi sympathizer."

At Allina's open-mouthed stare, Adele burst into laughter. "Surely, my nephew has schooled you in such tactics," she said. "The best subversives hide in plain sight."

Elias remained by their side all day, escorting them to a dozen cafés and shops in Binningen and Basel, and introducing her in the most obsequious fashion imaginable. She kept silent and unsmiling as Adele had suggested, although her daughter's sweet temperament won people over initially. As the day progressed, Allina grew accustomed to the fear and distaste in people's eyes, and how friendly smiles turned polite, then icy. Just as Adele had predicted, she overheard plenty of muttered comments about *that damn ridiculous hat.*

By the time they returned to the house, Katrine was peacefully asleep on her shoulder. Allina was exhausted, and perversely giddy.

A gray-faced Adele met them at the door.

"What is it?" Allina asked, panicked at the sheen of perspiration above the older woman's lip.

"Karl has moved up his timeline. A courier delivered this," Adele said. She handed over a slip of paper that read: 48, *my heart.*

"What does it mean?" Allina asked.

"The number 48 means we must fake your return to Hochland Home in the next forty-eight hours," Adele replied, "and make preparations to transport you out of the country if necessary." Frowning, she bit her lip. "As to 'my heart,' I can't be sure. He's broken with protocol."

"I know what that means," Allina said. She buried her nose in the sweetness of her daughter's hair and wept.

Adele decided it was best to wait until Saturday morning to enact their plan, which gave them an extra day to strategize. Lisel would serve as Allina's decoy, but the right outfit was essential, and they spent half of Friday debating how to dress her. Lisel was as slender as Allina but three inches shorter. In the end, they settled on Allina's navy dress, as it worked with minor alterations and coordinated with Adele's outrageous hat. Worn at the same jaunty angle, and with the veil pulled down, the hat would mask the differences in their features. Franka, Lisel's youngest sister, was Katrine's age, and would stand in for Allina's daughter.

Allina helped Lisel dress on Saturday morning and fashioned her hair into a low bun. She painted Lisel's mouth in the same bright red lipstick she'd worn on her trip into town. When she was done, the young woman appeared every inch a sophisticated lady and the wife of a *Gruppenführer.*

"Why are you doing this?" Allina asked. "You hardly know me, and it's an awful risk for you and your sister."

"I feed every child who comes through this house," Lisel said. "I know what your husband has done for them, what he's risking." She took Allina's hand. "Besides, there's very little threat to us. We'll change clothes on the train and get off at Mülheim. A car will be waiting with another set of fake papers to drive me farther up the line. Elias can pick us up at the Basel station this afternoon. We'll be home by dinner."

This may have been the truth, but Lisel was so tense her teeth chattered.

"Are you sure?" Allina whispered.

Adele came in, for once without knocking. "It's time. Elias is waiting in the car."

There was no chance for more than a hard hug, and no words that could adequately convey Allina's gratitude. Five minutes later, Lisel left Adele von Strassberg's home with a change of old clothes in a suitcase and Allina's papers in her purse.

Adele led Allina and Katrine into the cellar with a tray of cocoa and biscuits to sweeten their confinement. The space would be their home until they received further news. Katrine had an endless stream of questions, but they explained the situation to her as best they could.

Allina read to her from the library of children's books on the cellar shelves until she settled down. The little one fell asleep again within an hour, which left Allina alone with the tangled confusion of her thoughts. She feared for Lisel and was terrified for her husband. Despite all efforts to discipline her mind as Adele had suggested, panic hit at the oddest moments. It would not let her rest. Allina was sure all their careful planning was about to fall apart.

CHAPTER 34

Theresienstadt Camp

KARL

Karl always thought the prospect of his own death would terrify him. Months ago, when they'd first committed to their plan, he and Markus had pledged to help each other, to bolster each other's spirits until the last. There would be no begging for mercy, no weakness or capitulation. Instead, they'd meet their ends with bravado and good humor.

Now death was staring him in the face, but he found it didn't frighten him at all. No, death was a relief because Karl had failed. That failure was almost as bitter as the certainty he would never lay eyes on Allina and their daughter again.

From the look of the young men pacing the camp courtyard, this small group of soldiers was more agitated at the prospect of killing him than he was of dying.

Jockel was a cruel bastard. He'd handpicked men under Karl's and Markus's command for the task, choosing those who'd served under them longest, and the boys they knew best. A few were holding up well enough, presenting the stoic faces of soldiers preparing for duty. Most were pale and twitchy, shifting on their heels as they waited for the commander to arrive.

Ten men assigned to kill two traitors. It seemed like pretty good odds.

"Make sure to do a good job of it, Müller," Karl called out. He lifted his cuffed hands in a twisted salute. "Shoot straight, like I taught you."

Müller spun around and stared, swallowing hard. The boy's blue eyes—ones that had made all the Hochland Home girls swoon—brightened with tears.

"Christ. No need to torture him, Karl," Markus muttered.

"Silence!" The high, nasal voice of Commander Albrecht Jockel echoed against the courtyard walls as the man lumbered in like an ox. He stopped long enough to cuff Müller on the back of the head before turning to address the condemned.

"Markus Klemperer, Karl von Strassberg, you are accused of high treason against our Führer and the Fatherland . . ."

Karl tuned out the man's droning and focused on his breath, all thoughts turning inward. He'd made peace with God last night, but would not have the chance to do so with his wife. It was yet another regret in a long line of unforgivable acts when it came to Allina and Katrine. Guilt had kept him up all night, praying for their safety.

"Von Strassberg!"

Karl's head jerked up.

Jockel's face was a mottled red. The commander took a handkerchief out of his pocket and dabbed at the sheen of moisture under his bulbous, runny nose.

"Have you anything to say?" Jockel asked.

Snapping to attention, Karl clicked his heels without raising his arms. "I love my country. Everything I've done has been for Germany." He spat on the ground, an inch from the commander's boots. "I'll see you in hell, Jockel. Sooner rather than later, I'd wager."

Jockel slapped him across the face, nearly sending Karl to his knees. "Shut up!" The watery blue eyes bulged, and spittle foamed at the corners of his fleshy lips.

"What will you do if he doesn't, Jockel?" Markus drawled. "Will you kill us quicker? If so, by all means keep talking, Karl."

The courtyard descended into silence. It was then that a falcon swooped in, causing every soul inside to stop and gaze heavenward. The falcon screeched brightly as it flew in a low, wide circle above them. Its dun feathers sparkled against the deep blue of the autumn sky.

"Cover their eyes," Jockel ordered.

Müller came forward to tie a blindfold around Karl's head. The young man didn't speak, but Karl heard a strangled sob. Once he was done, Müller clapped a hand on Karl's shoulder.

The cloth was thick and the darkness complete. Karl wondered if the blindfold was for his sake, or for the men who would perform their duty this morning.

"Still there, Karl?" Markus joked. "It's dark in here."

"Until the end," Karl answered, grateful for his friend's voice. "See you on the other side."

"Ready . . ." Jockel called out.

I love you, Karl thought, holding Allina's face in his mind's eye, thinking of her moss-green eyes, her brilliant smile, her passion, her joy, her stubbornness, her anger—

"Aim . . ."

—Forgive me for failing, for the years we will not have, for every moment I will miss—

"Fire!"

Karl felt the bullets hit before he heard the roar of the pistols. The men shot true, for the pain was immediate and intense. Chest on fire, he dropped to the ground. An identical thud sounded as Markus fell beside him.

Then there was only the crunch of boots on gravel as the men marched out, leaving them alone in the courtyard. As the seconds passed, each one its own infinity, the falcon swooped in again, filling the courtyard with its joyous calls.

Seconds eased into minutes. Karl became aware of a thick, metallic tang filling his mouth, of how his heart was slowing, and the increased effort it took to breathe. A cool breeze washed over his body, and he shivered as the burning in his chest eased into a softer warmth. It was marvelous, how the pain slipped away. *Let the darkness come.* Let it take him like this, with Allina's lovely face still in his mind.

In an instant, he was dragged upward. Karl was startled to be gazing down at his own body; a body that was broken, yes, but peaceful and still, and cradled in a pool of blood.

A low murmur of voices rose. They were soft, and so numerous he couldn't make out what they were saying. As the voices grew louder, rushing over him with the roar of an ocean wave, they seemed to urge him higher.

Karl panicked and pulled away.

He needed to see his wife. His child.

The thought propelled him forward with a shot, through a buzzing tunnel of light and sound.

In the next instant, he saw her.

Allina was in a bed in a dimly lit room, cradling a sleeping Katrine in her lap. Enveloped in a golden halo of light, they looked healthy and beautiful and bursting with life. If only he could stay here. Karl would be content to watch them like this forever.

No. You cannot remain.

The voice was like a boom of thunder, clear and familiar. Karl turned to it.

His mother and father approached, holding hands as they walked slowly forward. They seemed impossibly young, even more vibrant than in his childhood memories. Arm outstretched in a graceful arc, his mother beckoned in the same way she used to when welcoming him home from school.

You can't stay here.

Finally understanding, the soul of the man who had been Karl von Strassberg let go and fell softly, gratefully, into the light.

CHAPTER 35

ALLINA

For five days, they lived in the dark.

The cellar was clean and had a working bathroom, and the hurricane lamps gave off enough dim light to read and eat by. Still, the absence of sunlight was disorienting and made them sleep more than usual and at odd hours. Despite her wristwatch, Allina struggled to tell between day and night. The meal trays Lisel brought to the basement became her main point of reference.

The change in Katrine broke Allina's heart as the days inched forward. "Go outside, Mama," was her initial, constant plea, but agitation turned somber the second day, and then sullen. By the end of their third day in the dark, the little one had shrunk into mournful silence.

Allina was anxious for Katrine, so she devised a schedule to create a sense of normalcy. After breakfast, they spent time drawing with wax crayons and playing quiet games. Afternoons were devoted to washing up and straightening the meager contents of the cellar. In the evenings, she read to her daughter and brushed and braided Katrine's thick, unruly hair.

The hardest hours for Allina were those spent alone while Katrine slept, because there was nothing to keep her anchored to the present. Instead, she found herself plagued by a hectic jumble of obsessive thoughts about Karl and their uncertain future. Adele insisted the lack of communication about his whereabouts was normal, but that didn't matter. Allina could barely breathe through her growing sense of panic.

On the first day of confinement, Lisel taught Katrine a game, one every child who passed through the house had learned. She called it "Mouse in the House."

"You must be as quiet as a baby mouse," she whispered in a singsong voice, "when Auntie Adele has guests in the house." Lifting a finger to her lips, Lisel twitched her nose, which produced a fit of giggles from her delighted audience.

"How quiet must you be?" she whispered.

"Baby mouse," Katrine answered in a very small voice.

"Very good. And when must you be quiet?" Lisel asked.

Her little nose scrunched up. "House?" she said.

Lifting Katrine onto her lap, Allina buried her lips in the soft mop of golden curls. "Don't worry, kitten. Mama will tell you when it's time to play mouse."

Adele received nine visitors in five days. None lasted more than twenty minutes, and the procedure was always the same. To announce a guest, Adele or Lisel would turn on the radio in the parlor before answering the door. This provided Allina with a thirty-second warning, and also masked minor noises that might come from the cellar. Once the guest was safely away, one of the women would turn off the radio to give the all-clear signal.

If a visitor came during the day, Allina would move her daughter to the cot farthest from the stairs. There, with her heart hammering in her throat, she and Katrine would play "Mouse in the House." Allina would cuddle her daughter and pat her bottom, coaxing her to sleep.

Evening callers were easier, since Katrine had always been a good sleeper. It was during those visits, with her daughter cocooned in blankets and dead to the world, when Allina gave in to curiosity. She'd creep to the top of the stairs to hear what bits of conversation she could make out over the music. The calls appeared to be social, mostly well-wishers who came to gossip and congratulate Adele on her speedy recovery. Allina was astonished at the cruel words that poured like poison from Adele von

Strassberg's mouth. The woman who'd helped save hundreds of children played the part of Nazi sympathizer with chilling accuracy.

Early on the morning of the sixth day, while Katrine was still sound asleep—about an hour before breakfast, if the faint aroma of bacon was any clue—the parlor radio came on.

Allina tiptoed quickly to the top of the stairs, sat down, and bent her head to the door. Adele was in conversation with a man who spoke in thickly accented Basel-German and with the clipped tone of a police officer. In contrast, Adele's imperious voice was brittle with fear, a warning that sent Allina's stomach tumbling. Horrified, she realized the officer was asking to speak with her.

"My niece is no longer in Basel, Officer Kupper," Adele said. "She tended me for two weeks but has returned home. It's been five, no, six days now."

The officer replied after a long pause. "My apologies, Frau von Strassberg. My commander received a telephone call from Munich this morning. He was sure we'd find your niece here."

"He's mistaken," Adele said loudly. "As I've already said, Allina has gone home. My driver saw her off at the train station."

"I've no reason to doubt you, ma'am," the officer said, "but Allina von Strassberg is not at Hochland Home, nor at her home in Starnberg. That's why I've come here to call on her."

"This is most distressing," Adele said, voice cracking. "If Allina has gone missing, we must do everything we can to find her and my grandniece. My nephew will be out of his mind with worry."

There was no immediate response from the officer. Allina heard only the first sweet, romantic strains of Strauss's "The Blue Danube." As the slow waltz began, the hairs raised on the back of her neck.

"As we have not been able to locate his wife, I must burden you with the difficult news I came to deliver today," Officer Kupper said in a softer voice. "I regret to report that your nephew, Karl von Strassberg, is dead."

There was a crash, the sound of china or crystal as it exploded on the floor, and then the high, keening cry of Adele's grief.

Allina remained on the steps, mute and motionless. She was aware of a loud buzzing in her ears but not of any answering pain in her body. Instead, there was stillness and shock, like the momentary panic after a deep cut to the arm—the instant before the agony hits, when one sees flesh flayed to the bone, but before the bleeding starts.

It was only after Adele switched off the radio and opened the cellar door that Allina began to howl.

She wasn't sure how long it took to return to her right mind. Allina became aware of Adele's tear-streaked cheeks and sweet-smelling embrace, then of a growing flurry of activity around her. Lisel grabbed a screaming Katrine and whisked her away, and Elias began appearing at odd intervals, each time with a different question for Adele to answer.

Eventually, Adele grabbed Allina and shook her hard enough to stop her crying.

"Now is the time for strength," Adele said, cupping her face. "Take hold of yourself."

Adele dragged her into the cellar bathroom, sat her down on the toilet, and proceeded to unpin and cut her hair. "You must leave Basel immediately," she said, as the long, golden locks rained down onto the cement floor. "Kupper told me Karl was executed by firing squad, but I received no notice from any of Karl's contacts. The chain is broken. That means we've lost a day, maybe two."

Allina's heart began to race.

"The SS has no jurisdiction here," Adele continued, "but they'll exert what pressure they can. The Basel police will return with more questions, perhaps even today. We'll be watched." She plucked at Allina's bangs and, with a satisfied grunt, drew her up to face the mirror.

Allina gazed at the stranger in the glass—a gaunt woman with chalky skin, swollen, red-rimmed eyes, and close-cropped hair that appeared a shade darker than usual.

"Where will we go?" she asked, touching the shorn ends. Her head felt light, as if it might float up to the ceiling.

"America," Adele answered. "It's safer for you there, with an ocean between us." Lips pursed, she narrowed her eyes, reconsidering Allina's hair. "The cut alters the shape of your face. The color is still too light, but there's no time to dye it. We need to get you on the road before the police return."

It was happening so fast. The room began to spin.

"You have ten minutes to pack your suitcase," Adele said, pushing her out of the bathroom. "I'll check on Elias."

Lisel was waiting just outside the door, hand in hand with a placid Katrine. The little one stared at her mother's face and shrieked in terror.

Her daughter's distress brought Allina fully into the present. Hoisting Katrine up on one hip, she pressed the child's chubby fingers to her short locks. "Don't be afraid, kitten," she crooned. "Mama has cut her hair, that's all."

After Katrine stopped crying, Lisel took her, leaving Allina with five minutes to pack. She dragged the suitcase from under her cot and pulled out a few items to lighten the load. Adele had warned against packing the wood box, but Allina refused that advice. It contained all she had left of her family, Karl, and her work at Hochland Home. She wrapped the box in newspaper and sandwiched it between heavier articles of clothing.

When Adele returned to the cellar, her face was a pale, grim mask of determination. She picked up Allina's suitcase and started up the stairs without a word.

It was time.

Unable to speak, Allina hugged Lisel, who began sobbing. Then she grabbed Katrine and followed Adele upstairs, where Elias was waiting in the kitchen.

Adele pressed a paper-wrapped parcel into his hands. "Food for the first part of your journey," she said, before turning her hard, amber gaze on Allina. "You've a long drive ahead. Trust Elias. He's done this many times. Now, hurry, both of you."

Allina followed them into the backyard, where a car stood idling. It was a crisp, blue-skyed autumn day, the sky so bright it hurt her eyes. Once the vehicle was loaded and Allina and Katrine were in their seats, Adele reached through the window to pull her into a fierce hug.

"Build a new life, far from here," she whispered. She kissed Allina on the cheek once, twice, then a third time. "Be happy, for Karl's sake. You're all I have left of him."

Elias drove away slowly, leaving Allina to watch this tiny warrior of a woman grow smaller in the side mirror. Adele von Strassberg smiled and waved and blew kisses at the car before she bent over at the waist and finally gave in to grief.

CHAPTER 36

Summer 2006
Englewood, New Jersey

KATRINE

"Elias drove without sleeping, straight through, for thirty hours," Mother says as we gaze out the window at the full moon, now high in the sky. "We stopped four times for supplies. Adele's contacts had food ready for us, different cars, and a new set of papers at each stop. God knows how many people your father paid off to ensure our safety."

And only God knows my mother's terror and bravery. Our lives feel like something out of a movie. Not for the first time today, I wish I could remember more—the joy and love and terror and pain, so I could be a better witness to my mother's life.

I reach for her hand. Even chilled, it's more comforting than I can explain.

"I didn't sleep a wink," she says before letting out a mammoth yawn. She doesn't protest when I suggest she lie down awhile, and lets me tuck her in with a knitted throw.

"We went south at first, toward Bern. That was the riskiest part, but it was easier to cross into France from there." Mother moves a finger through the air, tracing a path along the invisible map in front of her. "Then across France into Spain, and finally, Portugal. It took six weeks to secure passage from Lisbon, but Elias stayed on to look after us. He found an apartment,

and we posed as a family. He even hired an English tutor. Elias stayed until the end. He was the last face I saw when we left port."

"And then America. A new life." I'm here because of the help and sacrifice of dozens of people—my parents, Adele, Elias, Lisel, Alex, and many more whose names I will never know.

Mother nods. "Yes. And I came full circle, thanks to your father," she says, eyes soft with love. "The set of papers waiting for me in Lisbon were for a German woman named Allina Strauss. He remembered. First I was Allina Strauss, then Allina Gottlieb, then Allina von Strassberg, and, finally, I became Allina Strauss again. He gave me back my name."

We've cried so much today, but it seems there's no end to our tears. Here's a truth I hadn't anticipated, and maybe one more reason for all the years of secrets.

"I think it was a final message from him, Mama. He wanted you to leave all the pain behind."

"Maybe." She sniffs, fussing with a crumpled tissue to wipe our tears. "Adele and I traded letters at first, but she died in 1944. Heart attack. Lisel wrote in her stead to stay in touch, but I cut contact." Her lips tremble. "Ten years after the war ended, I received a letter from Rilla. I don't know how she found me. I never wrote back."

"Did you find out what happened to Karin, your friend from Badensburg?"

She shakes her head, lips tipped down in regret. "No. No, I never looked for her."

"You needed to leave the past in the past."

She nods, takes my hand. "Yes. That's exactly so."

There's another question I've wanted to ask for hours, one I've hesitated over, but the new ease between us gives me courage. "Mama, you never raised me in the Jewish faith. Is that why? You needed to leave the past in the past?"

We didn't attend religious services when I was growing up. Instead, every weekend was filled with activities—library and museum visits, English tutors, sports practice—always pushing forward toward my future. To the American Dream she'd worked so hard to give me.

"Partly." Her shoulders lift and she offers a lopsided smile. "God and I have always had a complicated relationship," she says, glancing down at our linked hands. "I was angry at him for a long time. Why would he allow such evil to thrive in the world?" She shakes her head, purses her lips as if trying to hold back the words.

I nod, waiting.

"After you went away to college, I tried. I attended Shabbat services for a short while, hoping to find a measure of peace. Hoping to find my mother again. But it only brought back the pain, and the memories. Of your father and the choices we made, all the children we couldn't save. So I stopped. I never went back."

My mother had buried that grief in her heart again, hidden it as surely as the box under the floorboards in her bedroom closet. She'd denied her faith and culture—alone with all those secrets and pain that festered over decades.

How tragically history has repeated itself in my family. How high a price they've paid.

"Perhaps you could try again, Mama," I say, cupping her cheek. "I could go with you. I want to." With the truth now linking us, it can't be too late. There are more stories to tell, and joy to be found.

"I'd like that." Her smile is genuine and soft, and a little sleepy. "Was I wrong, *Katchen*? Did I fail you in that way, too?"

"No, Mama." I kiss the forehead of this fierce, resilient woman who lost so much, yet gave me everything she could. "You were right. You did everything right."

EPILOGUE

Summer 2010
Englewood Cemetery
Englewood, New Jersey

KATRINE

The sun is warm on my face this morning, but the grass is blissful, damp and cool. It tickles my toes through low summer sandals as I take my favorite path to Mother's grave, wandering through rows of stately oak trees and past markers worn smooth from decades of rain and snow.

This cemetery is beautiful in summer, abloom with life along an expanse of land that's dedicated to remembering the dead. Each gravestone marks a family's love but tells little of its loss and struggle. God knows how many secrets have gone to these graves. I'm lucky my mother shared hers before she left this earth.

I had her with me three more years, and for that I am grateful.

My mother died on a brisk October morning. We'd spoken the night before and planned a day in the kitchen making meatballs and spaetzle. When there was no answer at the door, I thought she was in the garden and used my key. There was only stillness in the house, a queer emptiness that made me realize what had happened before I entered her bedroom.

Her eyes were closed and her face was peaceful. A soft smile graced her lips. I think my father must have come for her in her dreams.

I kneel at her grave, taking a moment to touch Adele's gold locket at my neck before tracing the engraved letters on my mother's headstone.

ALLINA STRAUSS

JULY 14, 1920–OCTOBER 7, 2009

BELOVED MOTHER AND WIFE

It's a simple marker for a woman who lived an extraordinary life. My cheeks are wet as I place the bouquet of sunflowers at the stone's base.

I made peace with my mother late in life, and it changed me in ways I'm still learning to understand. Secrets kept us apart for decades. Truth brought us back together in the space of a day. And the easy affection between us the last few years of her life was a gift I'd craved all of mine. We spent hours dancing to Mimi Thoma and Rudi Schuricke, and weekends in the kitchen with her aunt Claudia's favorite recipes. And she taught me German, slowly, patiently, so I could read my grandfather's words and the love letters my father sent almost seventy years ago.

At my gentle urging, we even attended Shabbat services now and again, to pray the way my grandmother and great-grandmother did. We were greeted with open arms each time, and my mother let me hold her hand and wipe her tears while she cried. She found friends there, too, ones who understood her journey better than I could. I'm so grateful for that. She blossomed like sunflowers do in springtime.

My mother was a Hochland Home nurse. She served at the heart of Heinrich Himmler's ruthless eugenics program even as she defied it, and managed to save dozens of children from medical experiments and extermination. Thousands of children were birthed in similar homes across Europe—all raised to believe they were members of a master race and then abandoned once the war was over.

For decades, the truth was veiled in secrecy. But there are whispers today from some of those children who are now my age and brave enough to tell their own stories. Tales of ostracization and shame, of depression, and the long, hard struggle to reconcile with the past.

Today, George and I will go to my mother's house and continue sifting through her things. We'll choose the items we want to keep and those we'll give away. I'll press my face to her clothes and remember. If I'm lucky, I'll catch one last lemony whiff of Jean Naté.

The girls are flying down next week to help us ready her house to sell. But first we'll be making some serious strudel. Strauss women are excellent bakers and I've finally mastered Mama's recipe.

When they ask about their grandparents, I'll retell every story. We'll shed tears over my mother's bravery and persistence, and how much she and Karl loved each other. The girls always marvel at the people their grandparents saved and the sacrifices made so I could have a chance at a decent life.

I've told my children everything—harsh and sweet, magnificent and painful, ugly and beautiful—because I'm done with secrets and the shadows they cast. Secrets can't exist in the light of truth, and while the truth can be painful to hear, its lasting gift is peace. I know this is true, because my mother taught it to me.

I place the smooth white stone I took from her garden onto her marker. Then I make the sign of the cross, kissing my fingertips at the end to send a prayer heavenward.

And walk home smiling.

AUTHOR'S NOTE

Why a novel about the SS *Lebensborn* program? The answer is simple: once I learned about facilities like Hochland Home, I couldn't get them out of my head.

Oddly enough, this novel didn't start out as a *Lebensborn* story. More than twenty years ago, I woke from a dream, went to my computer, and dashed out what became a draft of the first chapter. The final chapter came in a dream a week later, written in the same stream-of-consciousness mode. Both chapters involved a mother-daughter narrative and family secrets hidden in a box embossed with a swastika, but nothing more. Because I couldn't get those first pages out of my head, though, I decided to find the story and tell it.

I dug in and began researching. In the first week, I stumbled across a nonfiction book called *Master Race* by Catrine Clay and Michael Leapman. I was horrified and stunned—horrified at the perverse ruthlessness of Heinrich Himmler's eugenics program, and stunned more people didn't know about it. The information in that book haunted me. It would not let go.

Further investigation involved dozens of books, photos, and other resources from the U.S. Holocaust Memorial Museum in Washington,

D.C. Early on, I learned that in the final days of the war, Himmler ordered all records destroyed. The majority were—but enough remained to piece together the truth, although anecdotal stories contradict each other. To this day, some online sources maintain the homes were only for unwed mothers. Others claim women were stabled there and raped repeatedly.

After years of study, I understood the truth landed somewhere in the middle. While these homes began as havens for unwed mothers who gave their babies to "good Nazi families," there was something much more sinister afoot. Eager women willing to bear perfect Aryan infants for their Führer were referred by their doctors. Many applied, but acceptance was contingent on a woman's Aryan heritage, so as many as half were turned away. Those in the program produced multiple children, often with different fathers and in rapid succession. While Allina is an exception in this story, the women in these homes were very willing participants.

What transpired, then, to shatter Germany's conservative cultural norms? As early as 1935, youth movement leaders began promoting the institution of "biological marriage" to young women. They targeted the *Bund Deutscher Mädel (BDM)*, or League of German Girls, which was the female equivalent of the *Hitlerjugend* (Hitler Youth) for boys. Germany's population had been in decline for years and there was a surplus of women—a huge problem for Himmler, who needed to ensure the Thousand-Year Reich. Girls were reminded that while they weren't guaranteed husbands, as there weren't enough men to go around, they could do their duty and become mothers for their Führer. Sexual relations became sport, sport with a sacred purpose.

Reichsführer Himmler offered additional incentives in the 1930s to encourage German women to bear large broods of healthy children. Married couples received significant tax and financial benefits, and unmarried mothers were saluted by officers and members of youth organizations. By September 30, 1941, 4.7 million women had been decorated with the German Mother's Cross and belonged to what was colloquially called the *Kaninchenorden* or "Order of the Rabbit"—a tongue-in-cheek reference to a woman's ability to procreate quickly. Mothers with four or five children got a bronze cross, those with six or seven received the silver, and ones with eight or more were awarded gold.

It's estimated that as many as 25,000 children were born in *Lebens-*

born homes across Germany and in other countries, including Norway, Austria, France, and Denmark. The majority who survived were given to Nazi families to raise.

It's important to note that most *Lebensborn* children were unaware of the circumstances of their birth. But for those who were, for those labeled "children of shame" in their youth or who learned of their origins as adults, a disproportionate number suffered from mental health issues. Many personal stories have surfaced in the past decade. Some searched for their birth parents and were successful. Others never reunited with their mothers or siblings. I hope these children, who were born innocent into the world, found a measure of peace as adults.

And what of the mothers and nurses in *Lebensborn* homes, after the war? Many women were ostracized and labeled "town sluts"—that much is documented, although most mothers were dismissive of such judgment. Nurses and administrators faded into obscurity, but the interviews I found were unsettling. Medical professionals from the 1950s showed remorse for how the children were treated. Frau Hochreiter, who worked in the Child Welfare Center in Munich, expressed disgust in finding the Hochland Home children abandoned, hungry, and in dirty diapers at the end of the war, after Himmler ordered staff to leave. But by the 1970s, the answers changed. Some nurses refused interviews, others claimed they'd loved and nurtured the babies. Time shifted their perspective. No one wants to be a villain in their own story.

The Sunflower House is a work of fiction but based on historical facts that need little embellishment. I used any creative license sparingly, when necessary.

While the village of Badensburg is fictitious, it's similar to others of the time in the Rur Eifel region, which was a popular recreation destination in western Germany for the nearby regions of Cologne, Düsseldorf, Essen, and Bonn. As tourists could come and go with little suspicion, the town would have been an excellent location to coordinate opposition activities. Historically, a youth-based opposition movement in western Germany called the Edelweiss Pirates formed in the late 1930s, with groups in nearby Cologne (the Navajos) and Düsseldorf (Kittelbach Pirates).

Hochland Home was, indeed, the first *Lebensborn* home and opened in 1936. The home's physical layout is of my own creation, as I was unable to find a blueprint of the building. However, the facility's interior design, and the use of stolen furnishings from Germany's Jewish population is, sadly, true. Hochland Home's character training classes, intake procedures, nursing duties, schedules, and nutritional guidelines for both mothers and children are also documented—as are accounts of the children who suffered from neglect and failed to thrive.

Although most records were destroyed at the end of the war, those that survive paint a gruesome picture. Early memos reveal angry, unsatisfied adoptive parents. They expected *Edelprodukt*—top-quality goods—not sick and slow children. Some complained directly to Himmler. Others refused to pay funeral expenses for children who died after adoption. As a result, on Himmler's direct authority the *Lebensborn* organization permitted "the systematic elimination of all the abnormal children, who, according to the principles of selective eugenic reproduction, should never have been born." I'm very sorry to say that I found no information about rehabilitation programs of any sort; Allina and Karl's efforts are my own creation.

I made two choices regarding how women were addressed at Hochland Home. While the term *Fraulein* was typically used for unmarried women, by Himmler's decree, the term *Frau* became common in the 1930s to convey respect for unmarried mothers. As this might be confusing to the modern reader, I chose to refer to unmarried women as *Fraulein* in this book. In addition, the women at these homes often used aliases during their time there, but I thought that might be cumbersome as well, and chose to refer to them by their full names.

The excerpts from Adolf Hitler's 1939 address to the Reichstag and Himmler's October 1939 SS Order are direct translations from the originals. The *Lebensborn* Naming Ceremony—both the script used and physical description of the ceremony and decorations—are based on translations, accounts of actual ceremonies, and historical photos.

Many characters within this book, including Chief Medical Officer Engel, *Oberführer* Ebner, Heinrich and Marga Himmler, Ilse Hess, Sir Nevile Henderson, Winifred Wagner, and Marta Fuchs, among others, are historical figures. Karl, Allina, Katrine, and the mothers and nurses at Hochland Home are fictional and not based on particular historical figures. However, the inclusion of a failed plot to kill Adolf Hitler came from research about two assassination attempts—Operation Spark in 1941, and Operation Valkyrie in 1944.

In Allina and Karl, I also hoped to shed light on a story not often explored—that of Germans who were *Mischling*, with Jewish parents or grandparents who had to hide their identities and assimilate to save their lives. It's not generally known that as many as 150,000 men, including decorated veterans and high-ranking officers, were *Mischling*, nor that Hitler exempted those men as long as they denied their heritage. (It's also important to note that Karl's actions were very rare among SS officers, regardless of personal circumstance.) While Karl and Allina worked against the Reich at great peril, their positions protected them to an extent. As both witnesses and participants they became complicit and eventually were forced to make a choice. So this novel is as much about generational secrets, identity, and assimilation as it is about the *Lebensborn* program. My hope is that Allina's emotional journey with her daughter, Katrine, demonstrates that healing is possible when secrets are exposed to the light.

For readers interested in learning more about the *Lebensborn* program, Clay and Leapman's *Master Race* and Henry and Hillel's *Of Pure Blood* are excellent places to start. Those two books are also sources of information about the *Lebensborn* kidnappings. It's estimated that a quarter million children were kidnapped by the SS from German-occupied countries. While beyond the scope of this novel, stories of those children, many of whom were literally ripped from their parents' arms, are worthy of additional study.

Suggested resources on a variety of topics of this period are listed by category below. Some are out of print, but you may find them at your local library. If not, abebooks.com is a great site for reasonably priced second-hand and out-of-print books.

THE LEBENSBORN PROJECT/CHILDREN IN NAZI GERMANY

Children to a Degree: Growing Up Under the Third Reich, Horst Christian
Gold Is Where You Hide It, W. Stanley Moss
Hitler's Forgotten Children, Ingrid von Oelhaffen and Tim Tate

Into the Arms of Strangers: Stories of the Kindertransport, Mark
   Jonathan Harris and Deborah Oppenheimer
Master Race, Catrine Clay and Michael Leapman
Of Pure Blood (also published as *Children of the SS*), Mark Hillel
   and Clarissa Henry
Ten Thousand Children, Anne L. Fox and Eva Abraham-Podietz

WOMEN IN THE THIRD REICH

*Divided Lives: The Untold Stories of Jewish-Christian Women in
   Nazi Germany*, Cynthia Crane
Frauen: German Women Recall the Third Reich, Alison Owings
Mothers in the Fatherland: Women, the Family and Nazi Politics,
   Claudia Koonz
The Nazi Officer's Wife, Edith Hahn Beer

MEN OF JEWISH DESCENT IN THE GERMAN MILITARY

*Hitler's Jewish Soldiers: The Untold Story of Nazi Racial Laws and
   Men of Jewish Descent in the German Military*, Bryan Mark Rigg
Unlikely Warrior: A Jewish Soldier in Hitler's Army, Georg Rauch

GENERAL

Confront! Resistance in Nazi Germany, John J. Michalczyk
In Hitler's Germany, Bernt Engelmann
The Nazi Seizure of Power, William Sheridan Allen
The Order of the Death's Head, Heinz Höhne
The Rise and Fall of the Third Reich, William L. Shirer

WEBSITES

The U.S. Holocaust Memorial Museum in Washington D.C.
   (www.ushmm.org)
The Jewish Virtual Library (www.jewishvirtuallibrary.org)
Yad Vashem—The World Holocaust Remembrance Center
   (www.yadvashem.org)

ACKNOWLEDGMENTS

This novel was more than twenty years in the making, so there are many people to thank.

I'm forever indebted to Victress Literary and my rock star of an agent, Lizz Nagle, who believed in the power of this story and never gave up. When founding agent Shannon Orso passed in 2021, Lizz assumed an overwhelming responsibility. (You make Shan proud every day, Lizz.) Shannon was a junior agent at the Eric Ruben Agency before it closed, so a big thank-you to Eric for signing me initially.

I'm thrilled this novel found a home at St. Martin's Press and grateful to brilliant editor and amazing human Brigitte Dale, who fell in love with Allina's story and believed in my writing from the start. Brigitte steered me through the process with so much patience and kindness, and her thoughtful suggestions and questions, particularly about the characters of Karl, Rilla, and Berta, led to a much better book. Thank you, also, to Melissa Kravitz for input on German and Jewish culture. Lisa Davis had the thankless task of helping fix my comma issues (among many others). Her meticulous copy edits helped make this book the best it could possibly be. Finally, to the exceptional team at St. Martin's Press responsible for the production and marketing of this novel—thank you for your dedication in bringing Allina's story to readers.

I'm also grateful to dozens of friends, family, beta readers, and writing group partners who've asked about my research and manuscript over the years.

Elizabeth Almann read early chapters at a coffeehouse more than twenty years ago and told me to continue my research because I "had something interesting there," so I did. Years later and shortly before his death, Joseph Kosler reminded me the clock was ticking and to "finish that damn book," so I did. Special thanks to my mother and Claudia Cabrera, early beta readers who asked difficult questions in need of answering; my brother, Andre, and our Piasentini, Sorge, and Knepp cousins; the McHugh and Cabibo clans; and members of the Journey Within Church and the Inner Spiritual Center Organization. A huge shout-out goes to the R.M.A. Dynamic Duo, Lynn McHugh and Pat Sayers, for celebrating every milestone.

I'm also grateful for coworkers across three careers for their support— my DECA, ASU, and ADE friends, Verisk Analytics colleagues, and tribe at Imperfect Foods. And to Paul Kimball and Deb Meyer, both superb writers and editors, during my time at Verisk and after—please know that you helped me grow as a writer.

Two writing groups in the East Valley reviewed chapters and kept me going when I'd nearly lost faith, so this book wouldn't have happened without their input and friendship: Jackie McBride, Peggy Alfano, Mary Schenten, Christine Dixon, Barbara Duell, Angela Stephens, Bren Williams, Jill Sandstedt, Kacey Shea, Jennifer Valencia, Olivia Savage, Raxha Bhagdev, and Lisa Johnson LeCarre. To my fellow Victress Literary authors and team members, past and present—and Alisha West, Steph Scott, Jen Nielsen, Joshua Corneil, Robyn Dabney, Deena Remiel, Claire Bethke, Laura Reeves, Jennifer Della'Zanna, and Melissa Sutton Gaines in particular—your support means more than you know.

Finally, while Romance Writers of America is an organization for romance writers, the former Desert Rose chapter of RWA in Phoenix welcomed a historical fiction author who wanted to connect with others back in 2015. This was a game changer because I met my first agent at a conference they sponsored two years later. Thanks to those members for their kindness and continued interest, and for hosting events that taught me how to pitch my work.

ABOUT THE AUTHOR

ADRIANA ALLEGRI is a first-generation American whose parents lived in Europe before, during, and after World War II. She grew up on stories about how small acts of compassion saved lives. A former high school teacher and educational program administrator, Allegri also served as a writer/project manager for a leading data analytics company. After having spent fifteen years in the New York metro area, she is now happily relocated in Chandler, Arizona, with her two ornery rescue cats. *The Sunflower House* is her first novel.